SHINE

An Anthology of Near-future,
Optimistic Science Fiction

SHINE

An Anthology of Near-future, Optimistic Science Fiction

Edited by Jetse de Vries

Including stories by
Jason Andrew
Madeline Ashby
Jacques Barcia
Eva Maria Chapman
Ken Edgett
Silvia Moreno-Garcia
Eric Gregory
Kay Kenyon
Mari Ness
Holly Phillips
Gareth L. Powell & Aliette de Bodard
Alastair Reynolds
Gord Sellar
Paula R. Stiles
Jason Stoddard
Lavie Tidhar

SOLARIS

First published 2010 by Solaris
an imprint of Rebellion Publishing Ltd,
Riverside House, Osney Mead,
Oxford, OX1 0ES, UK

www.solarisbooks.com

ISBN: 978 1 906735 67 8

Printed in the US

CONTENTS

Introduction

Jetse de Vries

THERE'S A THING like weed: it grows everywhere, despite the common wisdom that it *can't* grow there. In the most barren, destitute and desperate places, it springs up. It flowers, against the grain. It raises its head at the most unexpected of times, even when—often *especially* when—most people think it's dead and gone.

It's hope. Hope fed by optimism.

Now, optimism and an upbeat attitude have been given short thrift in written SF over the last few decades, and especially the last one. Yes, there are novels and short stories with a positive outlook, but these are far and few in between. As an exercise, list five downbeat novels per year from 2000 to 2009. Then make a similar list for five upbeat novels per year (upbeat defined as a story where the future is a *better* place than today, not a story where over 90% of humanity is killed and where the survivors eventually make do): I know which list will be the hardest to make (or even *complete*).

Tor editor Patrick Nielsen Hayden has been trying to get an anthology of upbeat SF called *Up!* going since 2002, but it has never got off the ground. Word at the *Anticipation* WorldCon had it that he simply didn't get enough stories (I can empathise: I had to extend the *Shine* deadline). It's become so bad that Gardner Dozois remarked, in the July 2009 *Locus:*

> ...although I like a well-crafted dystopian story as well as anyone else, the balance has swung *too* far in that direction, and nihilism, gloom, and black despair about the future have become so standard in the genre that it's almost become stylized, and almost the default setting, with few writers bothering to try to imagine viable human futures that somebody might actually want to *live* in.

Yet, in the real world, 'study indicates people by nature are universally optimistic.'[1] This concurs with what I see in my day job: I train people who come literally from around the world in my company's equipment, and the vast majority of them are very optimistic. So in this matter, written SF is greatly out of step with the real world. Which raises some doubt when SF claims that it is 'a mirror of today's world.'

Now I am not against dystopias, apocalyptic and downbeat SF per se: I have certainly enjoyed many such novels and short stories. However, right now, the balance is gone: in I estimate at least 90% of written SF today is downbeat. *Shine* is an attempt to redress that balance somewhat.

Shine is also my attempt to show the world that SF can do more than merely say: if this (horrible trend)

[1]Kansas University and Gallup world poll (http://www.news.ku.edu/2009/may/26/optimism.shtml)

goes on, we all go down the drain. Yes, it's good to show people the consequences of their behaviour. However, written SF almost exclusively shows the consequences of *bad* behaviour, and almost never the consequences of *good* behaviour. Dire warnings and doomsayings, being told over and over again *ad nauseam*, lose their effectiveness. With *Shine* I hope to show the other side of the coin: SF that actively thinks about *solutions* to the problems plaguing humanity today. To show readers that written SF does something more than either provide escapism (which can be nice, once in a while) or wield the whip: that written SF can actively think in a constructive manner.

So, an anthology of near-future, optimistic SF. An anthology where the future is a better place than today (even if that progress is hard fought, as you will see in most of the stories). This was not an easy task, as Jason Stoddard had it: 'There's nothing like taking on two kinds of impossible.'

Impossible part 1 is getting SF authors to write an optimistic story. Impossible part 2 is getting them to write about the *near future*, which is immensely hard to do right, as well. Hence I've been constantly shelling out examples on the *Shine* blog (real world and imagined), posted—or tried to post—controversial articles and even a guest-blog series of 'Optimism in Literature around the World, and SF in particular' just to inspire, provoke or even shame writers into writing such stories for this anthology. Which they eventually did.

Then I needed to clarify which kind of stories I was *not* looking for, and even had to extend the *Shine* deadline in the hope of finally getting enough of the type of stories I *was* looking for (as I mentioned above, I can surely empathise with Patrick Nielsen Hayden's problems with *Up!*).

And if that wasn't enough already, I got it into my head that *Shine* should also be a representation of the world at large: in settings, characters and hopefully also authors.

Why make my editorial life even harder? We might as well get Freudian on my arse. For most of my adult life, I have travelled the world extensively. I've been to a wide variety of places, experienced a great diversity of cultures and seen awe-inspiring places. What it comes down to is that *Shine* may very well represent my belief that this world is a place that is both beautiful and scary, inspiring and frightening, full of wonder and full of danger; and that *we can make it work*. Correct that: it is already working in many places, but we can make it work *better*. We can do better, we can make it a better place to live in, even given the huge problems we're facing.

That is what *Shine* is about. So fasten your mental seatbelts as *Shine* takes you on a trip across the world and beyond. Stops on the way to a better future include:

- A West Africa where boys' toys become girls' gadgets...
- A world so over-focussed on recycling that it fails to see that innovation often means embracing-the-new, exploring-the-unknown, even—or especially—when it's shining just above them...
- A Paris where an expat programmer has to grease a semi-scientific cult's virtual prayer wheels just to get by until she's confronted by activists whose agenda is more widespread than she could ever surmise...

- A pacific island nation that transforms from being the *Lazarus* of the world into becoming its *Maecenas*...
- A Tanzania where a prodigal son returns, in a way, with plans for the future. However, it's the vision of his past that *truly* paves the way...
- A Recife where a retired eco-fighter must advise the teenager board of a huge wikindustry about a new company that's about as dodgy as it is hot, and he needs to get that advice out *fast*, and risk wrecking *the* (and his personal) future if he gets it wrong...
- A look behind the scenes of tomorrow's music industry, where bigger often indeed *is* better...
- An Iran where a spirit of stories past merges with the technologies of today to create an Islamic society of the future...
- A China where the ground swell of change almost literally comes from the ground, and goes all the way from the ground up...
- A place in the heart of the Caucasus where spoiled American nerds clash with seemingly naive Russian naturalists, until they find they have a common enemy...
- Adrift on the North Pacific gyre on an artificial island meant to combat pollution while the world around it seems to care less and less, until things seem to get a mind of their own...
- A trip to the asteroid belt to mine a rare metal finds something else, as well, with highly unintended consequences...
- A visit to the corridors of political/ecological power in The Hague—which are not exactly in parliament—by a group of activists who are not

only out of their depths and out of their league, but out of their minds, as well...

- A Mexico where the seeds of change spread faster and quite different from what their GM masters intended...

- An artist taking a tentative step forward by moving to an unnamed West Coast town where the memory of winter is melting from the collective mind like an ice sculpture in summer...

- An Afghanistan where the next generation of surveillance is tested, and where the unlikely friendship between two very different men uses the tools of intrusion for something completely different...

It's been a hell of a ride getting this anthology together, yet I wouldn't have it any other way. Another great help was Twitter: through my @outshine Twitterzine I discovered several new and exciting writers. In that spirit, there will be both intro and/or outro tweets before and/or after every story that will provide new angles or fresh insights. So join me in this kaleidoscope of visions where problems huge and small are tackled, immense difficulties are overcome, and where our futures become somewhat more bright!

The Earth of Yunhe

Eric Gregory

WHILE KAY KENYON—*see "Castoff World"*—*was the very first to send me a story for* Shine, *Eric Gregory was one of the first to send me a tweet for* @outshine.

The moment I signed the contract for Shine *with Solaris Books, I immediately tried to figure out ways to promote it ('regeren is vooruitzien' is the Dutch saying, or 'to govern is to look ahead'). One of the things I did for that is set up a Facebook fan site and a Twitter site for the* Shine *anthology.*

Then I got the crazy idea—inspired by @thaumatrope, who were the very first genre Twitterzine AFAIK—to start @outshine, a Twitterzine for near-future, optimistic tweets (or 'prose poems,' as I call them).

Eric Gregory's tweet was about Ecclesia, an imaginary near-future society, which I liked enough to publish. Then, months later, he sends me a story based on the tweet (or maybe it was vice-versa: I'm not sure), and "The Earth of Yunhe" eventually—it starts deceptively slow—blew me away.

He's not the only person that I published on @outshine first and here in Shine later on (Jacques Barcia, Eva

Maria Chapman, Gareth L. Powell, Ken Edgett, Paula R. Stiles, Mari Ness [who basically didn't stop tweeting] and Jason Stoddard—although I accepted Jason's tweet after I accepted "Overhead"—are the others), and he's not even the first who turned his tweet into a story (or vice-versa, although I had to turn down that person's story for Shine purely for lack of space: I had a lot of hard choices to make), but he is the single person whose tweet on @outshine preceded and was based on his story here in the Shine anthology.

Typically, though, his tweet functions much better as an epilogue rather than as a prologue, so I'm putting it up after the story.

Now prepare for a look at a China as the garden of the world...

**Silent, drafted blind worms burrow /
Decomposing, circles closing /
Garbage eating, circles meeting /
Biocrafted Ouroboros.**

—Rajan Khanna—

I RAISED MY my arms for inspection, but Old Zhu laughed and waved me past. He was a flushed, avuncular man who had spent his entire life with a book of dirty jokes in his pocket; as far as anyone knew, he'd never once touched a woman, and he didn't upset the tradition for me.

Little Yunhe rarely had need for a jailer, so Zhu was perfect for the job. He sat in his rusted fold-out chair on the deck of the *Patient Whale* and shouted friendly curses to the fishermen who docked nearby. He was thrilled to have a prisoner now—it gave him an excuse to load his pistol—but he treated the entire affair as an excellent joke.

"Boy's crazy," the old man called behind me. "You watch him."

"Oh, I'll watch him, Zhu."

"I tell you. One of these days he'll break down the door."

My brother *was* crazy—no question about that—but I'd known three-legged cats who were more dangerous. Xiaohao was only a hazard to himself. I made my slow way down the *Whale*'s steep stairwell, clutched the rails in case a step fell out beneath me. Most of these old boats were mere breaths from death, and the *Whale* wasn't exactly rigorously maintained.

The jail was lit by a single yellow bulb. I strode down the hall of open doors to the lone locked cell at the end, and my shadow pitched across the walls like a drunk. There was a tripod stool outside Xiaohao's door; I rapped twice on the thick metal and sat down. After an uncertain moment of silence, I heard my brother stir on the other side. He shuffled around for another minute, grunting quietly, then peered at last through his small barred window. He wasn't fat, but his face had filled out during his years with the Ecclesia. His left eye was red, encircled by an ugly bruise that had only gotten uglier since the last time I visited him.

Xiaohao sighed. "Father still won't see me."

"No. Not unless you're twitching on the end of a pike."

Exaggeration, of course, but not so very far from the truth. His face fell, and I regretted the words instantly. Idiot that he was, Xiaohao hadn't expected Papa's anger—or hadn't expected it to be so prodigious, anyway. He'd supposed that Yunhe would welcome him back as a savior, that Papa would forgive him in light of his bright, shining genius. My brother had always been a master fantasist.

He gripped the bars, stared at his feet. "Any word from the Administrators?" The question was quiet, hopeless. He didn't sound like he wanted to know the answer.

"No. But they're going to let you out."

"Are they really, Yuen?" He smiled bitterly. "Are you sure? I think they might put me on a pike. Call it an early birthday gift for our father."

I leaned forward on the stool. "Xiao, I'm sorry, I shouldn't have said—"

"Forget about it."

"No, listen. I'm sorry. I'm not the one stuck in here, and I shouldn't joke. But I swear to you, Xiao, no one's going to kill you. You're still a Yunhe boy. They're not going to execute one of their own just because he makes an ass of himself in the square."

His eyes narrowed. "You may not have noticed, but this isn't Yunhe."

"It is now." I tapped my foot on the steel floor. "This is what's left."

"No," he said, "it's not."

He hadn't been in Yunhe when the ash-flood came, but the wound was fresher in Xiaohao's heart than anyone else's. Perhaps *because* he hadn't been there. The rest of us had saved what we could, fished out our dead, and slowly, painfully moved on. Made new lives in this make-do city. But Xiao had congenital difficulties with the concept of *moving on*.

Neither of us spoke. I cracked my fingers. It had been a mistake to come here. I'd only wanted to see that he was still okay. Well-fed. Xiao looked back into the darkness of his cell and raked his fingers through thin, short hair. "You have to get me out of here," he said at last.

"You know I can't do that."

"The fuck you can't. Pull the key off the codger upstairs. He won't even notice."

"Zhu?" I couldn't stop myself: I laughed. "You think they give him a key? Zhu might as well be your *manservant*. He's just here to bring you lunch."

Realization worked across Xiao's face. He hadn't known. He'd honestly believed that Zhu could give him his freedom. I wondered how long he'd spent begging the old man. Xiaohao turned away from the window, rubbed his eyes with his thumb and forefinger. "Shit," he said. "*Shit.*" He kicked something I couldn't see, something large and metallic. It crashed to the floor.

"Xiao—" I started.

"*Sedition*, Yuen." He turned back toward the window. His eyes were wet. "I'm glad you think the Administrators won't carry out the sentence. That's really heartening. But are you going to stake my life on it? These people are savages. This whole shithole city. Jumping at the ghost of the hard fucking state. When was the last time you heard a syllable from Beijing? When was the last time you got a truck full of vaccines? *There's no such thing as sedition anymore.*"

I sat very still. "This is why you're here," I said quietly.

"Because I tell the truth?"

"Because you don't understand your own people. Because you didn't bother to learn about this place, didn't care enough to ask about our new lives. Just stuck your head in the door and told us to drop everything because what we'd built was worthless. You expect people to trust you, to follow you? You *disappeared*, Xiao. And you waited too long to come back."

I held his gaze for a long moment, then stood and walked back toward the stairs. The *Whale* shifted on the water, and my shadow shuddered across the wall. I reached the first of the dark, creaky steps before Xiaohao called out to me.

"The password," he said, his voice tight. "It's *garden*."

I SPENT MOST of the morning in Little Wuxie. Their accumulator was down, and their Administrators were frantic. All five of the gray, yammering men wanted to peer over my shoulder as I checked out the battery, the tanks, the pipes. Their anxiety was as exhausting as it was unnecessary. One accumulator wouldn't make or break the city's weather control. Finally I asked them to leave, told them that their "ambient body heat" might damage the components.

They left me alone.

Slowly, carefully, I extracted the tower's guts. The morning was hot, and I was thankful for the sea breeze that played around me. Many of the central wires had started to rust. Not so badly that the whole accumulator should break down, but it would become more of a problem as time wore on. I'd seen the same thing in some of the other towers; these were old machines.

I wiped the sweat from my face with my forearm, watched the gulls wheel above. The birds were probably waiting for me to leave. They liked to perch on the seaside accumulators and watch the water.

The upper halves of the machines' black metal hulls were always spattered with white.

Maybe, I thought. *Just maybe*.

I hauled out the battery cradle, inspected it from every side. Nothing out of the ordinary. Then, with the steadiest hands I could summon, I pulled the battery *out* of the cradle, and there was the culprit. A layer of birdshit covered the receptor prongs. Either one gull had eaten a catastrophically disagreeable meal, or the entire flock regularly squirted their lunches with vicious precision. I cleaned up the receptor, tucked the various wires back into their racks, and shoved the cradle back into the tower. The accumulator's black skin began to thrum at once.

The Wuxie Administrators were overjoyed. Embarrassingly so. They thrust iced jackfish and rice wine into my hands: overwrought thanks that Little Wuxie could hardly afford. As much as they plainly appreciated my help, I doubted this was the standard engineer's honorarium; these men knew my father's name. I thanked each in turn, accepted the gifts graciously, and made to leave at the earliest opportunity. But the Senior Administrator, a fox-faced man named Hu, raised his hand to stop me.

"One more token of our thanks," he said, and produced a small, foldable wi-mo from his pocket. No more than two or three years old by the look of it; the surface was only gently scratched, and the solar cells seemed to work. Hu powered up the device as tenderly as one might wake a baby. "We've recently had a trader from Chengdu," he said. "I give you this on behalf of all Wuxie."

I unconsciously tongued the month-old unit in the roof of my mouth. It broadcasted at terabytes-per-second to the contacts in my eyes, responded to minute tongue gestures and subvocalized commands. Yunhe had also had the trader from Chengdu. Papa commanded reverence even from outsiders.

"Thank you," I said, and accepted the wi-mo.

The walk back to Little Yunhe was long and hot and awkward. Foolishly, I took the boardwalk, which bustled with fishermen and hungry dockside homeless. Most either knew my name or felt no compulsion to harass me, but more than one boathand trailed his leer with a whistle, or reached out to smack my ass. Jokes and arguments played out around me in a dozen tongues: Korean, Filipino, Mongolian, Thai. Some of the jokes were opaque to me. Others were all too understandable.

The eyes of the homeless flicked up from their decade-old, gray market wi-mos to follow the bundle of treasures in my arms. My cheeks flushed, and the sun bore down, and finally I couldn't bear the stares; I put down the jackfish and walked swiftly away. Papa would be angry if he learned that I'd given away honoraria, but I kept the rice wine and the wi-mo, so he would likely never know—unless the Little Wuxie Administrators asked whether he enjoyed the fish.

I pulled the wi-mo out of my pocket, unfolded it. The translucent sheet overlaid the walk before me with a few simple icons and live feeds: clock, calendar, local temperature. My roof-of-the-mouth unit noticed the new machine and prompted me to link the devices for file transfer and load-share. I declined. I'd gotten the same prompt at home every morning for the past week. There was a new computer somewhere in the flat, one my father didn't want to talk about.

The password, I thought. *It's* garden.

HE CAME TO US with promises of dirt. I was outside of the city that day, checking up on the outermost ring of accumulators, but I saw the whole mess on the network once it was over. I saw it from every angle, through the beady eyes of two dozen different wi-mo cameras. On some impulse that I didn't quite understand, I brought up the most popular video now.

Xiaohao strode into Little Yunhe Square, right up to the Administrators' Quonset hut offices. He wore the black skinweave favored by the Ecclesia—likely the first of his many mistakes—and waved his arms like an attention-starved child. "*It's time to return to our ancestral home!*" he shouted. Xiao had never been a very good public speaker; he compensated for anxiety with breathtaking pompousness. "The day is today! The hour is this hour! Follow me, and we'll raise Yunhe from new soil!"

With each word, more and more of the square's homeless raised their wi-mos to record the madman's performance. Two security officers outside of the Quonset hut exchanged uncertain glances and advanced cautiously, hands on the butts of their pistols.

"New soil!" Xiaohao cried again. "Smart soil from the Ecclesia, soil to reclaim Yunhe—the *real* Yunhe—from the ash. I'm giving this to you. We will built it together. Look! Explore!" That last bit made no sense; did he carry some of the magic dirt in his hand? Xiao went silent as something approached from offscreen. The camera jerked to one side, zoomed in on the Little Yunhe Administrators as they emerged from their offices. Papa, dressed in his trademark gray suit, took the lead.

"Father," said Xiao, barely audible now, "I've brought—"

Papa moved faster than the wi-mo filmmaker could follow. When the camera found him again, the old man stood over his son, who was crumpled on the ground clutching his face. "*I'm giving this to you*," screamed Xiao, and Papa reared back to kick him in the gut.

I couldn't watch any further.

My fingers shook as I folded up the wi-mo. Could I really say that Papa wouldn't kill him? I'd winced when I saw the video for the first time, but assumed the worst was over. After all, Xiaohao hadn't been the first criminal beaten by our father, and Little Yunhe had never executed anyone before. My brother had come here practically wrapped in the flag of Ecclesia; of *course* Papa would show him hard justice, give him a week or two in the *Whale*. But he wouldn't kill his own son.

Would he?

I tried to call Papa, got no response. Then I began to jog. Xiao's words played over and over again in my head: *are you sure? I think they might put me on a pike*. I cut through the Little Jingjiang Tent Quarter, which was quiet except for a handful of eateries. The smell of fried onion wafted from solar woks—I should have been hungry, but the thought of food made me nauseous.

The route through the Tent Quarter was shorter, but Jingjiang had suffered a milder disaster than Yunhe, and its detritus was stacked outside of every tent. Bookshelves, defunct televisions, stainless steel cages. Coffee makers, lamps, the stems of wineglasses. Leftovers of another dead town, clogging the veins of the refugee city. Twice I had to leap over fallen stacks of boxes, and once I nearly toppled an old woman selling reusable cigarettes.

Finally, the ways widened and the tents thinned. A squad of security officers in old, weathered hardsuits stood along the border of Yunhe Tent Quarter; they tensed as I approached and then relaxed when they saw my face. The squad leader nodded his respect.

Papa might have been in the Administrators' offices or he might have been in bed. Both huts were inland, but home was closer. I glanced across the water at the *Whale* and picked up my pace, drawing a dozen confused gazes in my wake as I jogged toward our house on the hill.

The door was locked. I groped for my keys, shoved the door open, and stumbled inside, where a dozen rattling fans twisted around to cool me. The lights were off, and the doors between each partition were open. In the study, Papa's favorite dishes lay dirty on his desk, and a yellowed novel sat half-open on his seat. I was certain now that he wasn't home, but I called out his name nonetheless: an impropriety that would have earned me a lecture in the best of times.

There was no response.

I hissed a curse and made to leave, then stopped short. The smart-fans squeaked, surprised by my sudden stillness. On my eyelid, the prompt flashed: *Link to device "XiXi" for data transfer?* The same prompt I'd gotten every day for the past week. I wasn't sure where Papa had hidden Xiaohao's wi-mo, but that didn't matter, did it? I was in range. I agreed to link, and Xiao's unit asked me for a password.

"Garden," I said. The world changed.

I HAD ONLY fleeting memories of my grandfather's garden, but those scraps were vivid. Sunflowers like bright, tremendous trees, the space beneath their canopy a secret yellow sanctuary. I squatted in the soil with my worn, creaky kitty until Xiao, a few years older, fell onto me in a spray of dirt and battle cries. He whipped the stalks of the great golden flowers with some uprooted weed, sent me wailing out of the garden to the farm proper. I got lost in endless rows of sorghum, and when I found Papa at last, he nearly beat me for running out of sight.

Now I stood in the garden again. Sunflowers towered over my head, five or six meters tall, brighter than ever, brighter even than the flowers of memory. Birds chirped somewhere just out of sight. Up the hill, between the stalks, I could see my grandfather's house, intact and even renovated.

Yunhe. The real Yunhe, back from the dead.

This can't be fake, I thought. Sims always left me with this jarring sense of absolute credulity. The wi-mo fed me my home through the roof of my mouth, and I couldn't help but believe it. *This can't be fake*, I thought, though I knew that it was. *I can smell the dirt.*

I made my way out of the canopy of monster flowers and gasped. "Oh, Xiao," I murmured, and struggled to remind myself that nothing here was real or meaningful, that my home was still buried beneath the black flood. Grandfather's house was beautiful, and larger than it had ever been in real life: a multi-wing, three-story complex with something like an observation deck on the roof. I followed a stone path—flanked by more traditionally proportioned blue roses—from the garden to the house. The front door was unlocked, and I stepped inside.

It wasn't the home I remembered. Somehow it was more than home, the *idea* of grandfather's place writ large. There was space for dozens in the dining room, seats arrayed around three beautiful wooden tables. On the ground floor alone there were two kitchens, a full bar, and a game room. Xiao had connected a library to grandfather's study; Papa's favorite painting of the War Above held a position of honor over the reading couch. The house's additional stories were given over to bedrooms, enough to sleep our entire extended family and several more families besides.

It's a dormitory, I realized. Grandfather's house transformed into a dormitory. Was this how citizens of Ecclesia lived? Like wealthy college students?

I took the elevator—*the elevator*—to the roof. Lawn chairs encircled a small herb garden, and at each edge of the roof, telescopes gazed off into the distance. The day was preternaturally clear: no smog, no fog, and not a single cloud in the sky. I could make out individual trees on the blue mountains that towered around Yunhe. If I'd wanted, I probably could have found the mountaintop waste lake that had laid my town to waste.

Instead, I looked out across the Yunhe that Xiaohao had made. His model world. As far as I could tell, there were no traditional homes here; in their place were half a dozen more dormitory houses, each surrounded by vast tracts of vibrant farmland. Here and there in the fields stood enormous, gleaming towers: new model accumulators hybridized with wind turbines. To the south, at a point roughly equidistant from each of the dormitories, I saw Xiao's vision of a town square. Open air market, playground and pool, small restaurants, even an amphitheater. Everything was linked by a web of red brick paths. It was lovely. The gardens, the farms—everything was lovely.

I shut down the sim.

Yunhe disappeared, and I smelled the ocean again. Smartfans surrounded me in an eager semicircle, cooled me with a kind of mad mechanical enthusiasm. Ships' horns sounded in the distance. I took three swift, deep breaths—a trick I'd learned in college for exiting sims as quickly as possible—and ran out the door. Somehow it was easier to believe in the real world with a full pair of lungs.

The security officers outside of the Administrators' offices were less genial than the ones on the border. They surely knew my face, but still they held their position in front of the door, and they neither smiled nor nodded. There was even a little smirking twist in the corner of the squad leader's mouth—my panic must have leaked out of my eyes, visible to everyone.

"State your business," said the squad leader, plaintive and automatic. He was short, broad-shouldered, and wore a few days' stubble. I briefly wondered if I could force my way past him, gave up on the idea as quickly as I'd conjured it. Dozens of people decided that they had business with the Administrators every day: accusations of chicken theft or wi-mo hacking, petitions for divorce or consolidation of tent-space. This man's entire job was to stand in the way of desperate people's grievances.

"I need to see my father," I said.

"Do you have an appointment?"

"He called me. Asked me to come as quickly as possible."

"You won't mind if I confirm that," he said.

I smiled sweetly and said that I wouldn't mind at all. I had an understanding with Jung, my father's secretary. The squad leader unfolded his wi-mo, carried on an extremely short subvocalized conversation with an invisible party, and then frowned.

"Go on, then," he muttered.

I stepped inside the Quonset hut. The place was sweltering. Two parallel rows of secretaries glanced up from paper-plastered desks, every sweaty face transparently terrified that I had come to make more work. I found Papa in the back of the hut, softly berating Jung over something to do with ledgers. Jung looked relieved to see me.

"Papa," I said, "may I speak to you in private?"

He raised an eyebrow but nodded, beckoned me to his office and closed the door. We sat on either side of his desk, and my eye flicked to the painting behind his head: a battle scene from the War Above. Murmured arguments about fishing zones floated from the office next door; the partitions between offices were more of an affectation than a proof against sound. I spoke quietly.

"When will Xiao go free? He looks awful."

Papa sat back and sighed. "Yuen. It's not clear that he will ever go free."

He didn't blink as he said it. His eyes were always wide and wary and unblinking, as if he'd never stopped looking down on the entire world at once, never given up the divine-eye view from space. He ran one hand across his gray-black beard, which had only recently started to fill in. "You know we can't look the other way on this, sweet. We'd countenance sedition and burn every scrap of our credibility all in one clean sweep. Xiao made his choices, and he's left us with none."

Goosebumps raised across my neck. "So," I said, barely a whisper, "you're going to kill him?"

Papa was silent. His face was utterly still, and he didn't blink.

"I want to show you something," I said, newly careful with every syllable. I didn't know how precarious a line I was walking anymore, and I couldn't be sure that Papa wouldn't throw me in the *Whale* for collaboration. But I also couldn't let my brother die. I queued up the sim, prepared to send—

"If it's Xiaohao's new Yunhe," said Papa, "I've seen it and don't want to see it again."

I froze. "You've seen—"

"He sent it to all of the Administrators the day he came back."

"And you saw," I said. I felt clenched and cold.

"I saw enough."

"You saw the garden. You saw the painting in the library."

Again, Papa was hard-eyed and silent and absolutely still. And I finally understood. I'd thought that he was furious with Xiao, disappointed and sore with wounded pride. But incredibly, terrifyingly, this wasn't a matter of emotion. It wasn't personal at all.

Papa was *unwilling* to make it personal.

He'd never been particularly traditional. He might have forgiven Xiao for simply running away with a professor. Even if the professor in question was male and Filipino and given to lectures on crowdsourcing microprotest. Xiao's romances were a family matter. But he had fled to a metanation, and that made his choices the business of the state. That was *defection.* Dereliction, sedition.

Papa couldn't forgive sedition.

"His world means nothing," he said softly. "It's fantasy. That's all."

"I think Xiao believes he can make it real."

"Your brother believes a lot of stupid things." He stood with a grunt, finally turned his wide eyes away from me. "You have a gentle heart, and I admire that, but today we can't be gentle. I trust you're smart enough not to be moved by other people's stupidities."

I struggled to make my face as opaque as his own. "Yes, Papa," I said. My intentions must have leaked out of my eyes. I stood and opened the partition door, but Papa stopped me.

"One more thing, sweet." He gripped my shoulder. "You mustn't give away your honoraria. Word travels, and it makes us appear ungrateful. Arrogant. We can't afford that kind of reputation at the moment. Do you understand?" He smiled his disarming smile.

"Yes," I said. I understood.

I FLIPPED ON my arc knife. The blade hissed and lit up the creaking, deathtrap stairway of the *Whale*, cast my skin in electric blue. I jumped past the the last two steps, and my landing echoed in rattling metal. There was no time for caution. It was time for knives.

I'd stashed the tools in the soles of my shoes, but that proved unnecessary: Zhu didn't give me trouble, didn't even ask me to pull out my pockets. I hoped he would be just as accommodating on our way out. We could cut through the hull if it came to that, but I didn't exactly relish the thought of sinking a ship while Xiaohao and I were still inside.

I hurried down the hall of open doors, swinging blue light at my side. Xiao's eyes appeared in the grate, bright first with panic and then confusion. "Yuen? What do you—"

"Step back," I said. "As far back as you can go."

He obeyed. I cleaved the thick padlock with one swipe, turned off the knife, and hauled open the heavy door. Inside, Xiao pressed himself flat against the far wall. He was dressed in a dirty undershirt and too-small black pants. He looked stricken.

"Yuen—" he started.

"You were right, Xiao. I was wrong. We have to go."

He blanched. "They're going to kill me?"

"I don't know. I have no idea what they'll do anymore." I pulled off my left shoe, peeled open the sole, and drew out a second arc knife. "Take this."

Xiao frowned at the knife for a moment. Then he took it.

"What's your plan?"

"We leave the city. Make for—I don't know. A *real* city. I have some money. Maybe we go to your Ecclesia. If it comes to that. Maybe..."

Xiao's frown deepened. "Your money's worthless," he said quietly.

"We'll get by."

He bit his lip and fiddled with the arc knife. Flicked it on and sat down on the wireframe monstrosity that must have been his bed. He watched the blade burn and hiss. "Your money's worthless," he said, "and there's no going to Ecclesia. I pissed them off in order to come here."

"You pissed them off."

He shook his head, sighed. Cursed under his breath. The knife-light cast long shadows under his eyes. "Yuen. I hate it, and I thank you, but I think I need to stay here."

I opened my mouth, but no sound came.

"I know it's stupid," he said. His jaw was tight, and his hand shook slightly. "I know. Listen. I thought about what you said. How I came here without understanding the place or the people. You were right. Absolutely, awfully, irrefutably right. But now I know the mistakes I made, and I think I can make this work. If I run away—that's an admission of guilt. I lose every single scrap of credibility I ever had. Two years of preparation, one furious metnat, and all for nothing. I have to try again, Yuen."

If Papa's eyes seemed to see everything at once, Xiao's were perpetually fixed on the very heart and core of whatever he regarded. Father and son shared in their intensity; the difference between them was a question of focus. He stared at me now, and he didn't blink.

I exhaled slowly. "You should know," I said, "that I am thinking very seriously about knocking you out and dragging you away."

He snorted. "Good luck. I have a thick skull."

I sat down beside my brother, turned on my own knife once more. We'd always been the kind of kids who used dangerous industrial tools for candles. "You'll never persuade Papa," I said. My mind raced to find the words that would persuade *Xiao*, but part of me already knew that those words didn't exist.

"First and worst mistake I made," he said. "Took my message to the top. I thought I needed Father's permission, and I thought his permission would be enough. Stupid. I acted like this was some fucking hard state from the Profligate Times, some top-down institution. But that's backward, isn't it? I've got to start from the *bottom*. The people of Little Yunhe. I need your help, Yuen."

I could see where this was going, and I felt what Papa must have felt as he blasted into the sky. The awful exhilaration of a *physical law*, a lifelong gravity falling out from underneath you. I'd come to free Xiao on a high of instinct and adrenaline. But could I really join him in active sedition? Could I make that choice and stand behind it?

"First," I said, my voice shaking only a little, "you're going to have to explain some things. I saw your sim, and it was—it was beautiful. Really, truly beautiful. But I still don't understand your big plan. I don't understand how you could bring Yunhe back."

Again, he frowned. "Seriously? You don't understand?"

I shook my head. He explained the mad thing he meant to do.

WE'D NEVER KNOWN where Xiaohao went. How could we, unless he chose to tell us? Ecclesia was borderless, global, a network-nation that lived in the interstices. He was at graduate school (and living with his professor) in Chengdu when he ran; any trails he might have left behind were lost in the city's thick skein of lives. I imagined him in Mumbai, London, São Paulo. Anywhere, everywhere.

He did travel. From the Antarctic Settlements to the Ivory Coast. But in the years since Yunhe drowned in ash, he'd spent most of his time in one place: an Ecclesia installation in the remote heights of the Appalachian mountains. The facility had been established on the force of Xiaohao's research proposal: he wanted to invent a nanite soil that could reclaim regions flooded by coal waste. Ecclesia threw their full weight behind him, even secured secondary support from the United Nations.

The project was called Wise Earth.

His team experimented in coal-drowned towns with names like *Prosperity* and *Dante*. Places like Yunhe, where waste lakes had overflown or old mines had spilled out their guts. The first phase of the research was—at least according to Xiao— relatively straightforward, a matter of making each nanite convert the arsenic, lead, and thallium of an ash flood into yet another nanite.

The second phase was more complicated. His machines could eat lakes of poison, but all they left behind was gray mechanical goop. The nanites needed to be both efficient self-replicators and *functional molecules of soil*, true earth on which communities could rebuild. The problem was that soil isn't homogeneous. It's a messy, semi-random body of minerals and organics, solids and liquids and even gases; Xiao couldn't just map each nanite to some generalized recipe for soil.

Over the course of a long year, the Wise Earth team developed a replication algorithm wherein each nanite dynamically scanned existing mineral and carbon concentrations, compared it to a fixed ideal, and *transported* the element that was most lacking from a place where it was overabundant, all while negotiating the task with a million other nanites. It was a programmer's nightmare, and Xiao still wasn't satisfied. He wanted his earth to do more than reclaim; he wanted it to *enrich*. He altered the topsoil layer so that it could absorb, store, and route solar power. A portion of that energy would power the nanites' network functions once the initial rush of consumption was finished. The soil would be true soil, yes, but it would also serve as a massive solar power plant, communications hub, and computational substrate.

"It's a community seed," he said. "All you have to do is plant it."

I was silent for a long time. My heart pounded. I'd had no idea. No conception. This was even bigger than Yunhe. Did he understand that? How could he risk his life on just one town?

"Xiao," I said, "this is huge."

"Yes." He shrugged.

"We have to tell people. We—we have to tell them everything. Now."

His nod was absurdly casual. *Sure, why not?* "Do you have some kind of town forum or feed?" he asked. "Some way to talk to everyone in Little Yunhe at once?"

"No." I stood up. "No, Xiaohao, no. You're thinking too small. This—" I waved the knife and struggled for words. "This is huge. If we get you out of here, can you do the thing? Plant the seed?"

"The replicator key is in my wi-mo."

"And your wi-mo is somewhere in Papa's house. Okay." The gears fell into place and began to turn. I paced a tight circuit around the cell, called up a notepad on my eyelid. "We can do this. I think we can do this. But it can't just be a Little Yunhe thing. Do you understand? There aren't that many people here, and many of them don't like or trust you."

Xiao scowled. "Good to hear."

"No, listen. It doesn't matter. There's an entire city of refugees out there. Not all of them have tents to sleep in, and even those of us with flats are worried. The accumulators are rusting. Boats need repair, fish are thin in the water. We need to invite *everyone*, Xiao, and make the place a colony of the city. A place where anyone can work and build a home. We send crops and power back here, sell any surplus to the cities nearby. And once Yunhe's built, we take your replicator key and start again somewhere else. Maybe fill in some waste lakes with land, stop another flood before it happens."

My brother's smile was wry. "That's what Ecclesia was afraid I'd do."

"What do you mean?"

"Give away the soil. They wanted to monetize it. Or use it for leverage."

"And you'll oppose them?"

"Fuck, I might as well." He grinned. "They're already pissed off."

We drew up our declaration with a kind of intense mechanical efficiency, quibbling only once or twice over phrasings. We did not make promises. We were not grandiloquent. We told the people of the make-do city—*my* people—that an opportunity had arisen, and we explained it as thoroughly and accurately as we could. We said that we didn't mean to abandon the city, but to bolster it. We said that our huts and boats and accumulators needed repair, and that a revived Yunhe would give us the resources we needed.

The soil wouldn't solve all of our problems. There would only be so much energy, so much food, so much space. There would still be hard labor, and hardship, and sickness. But the earth of Yunhe could check the entropy, afford us new ways and means.

The earth of Yunhe could hold us back from the edge.

Finally, we asked people to join us, to save us, to assemble outside of the *Patient Whale*. That plea was the hardest thing to write, and the most crucial, and we agonized over the wording. It didn't matter how many people we intrigued with our soil-seed; if no one showed up, our plan was worthless. We tried to acknowledge the dangers of assembly without making the act seem revolutionary, and asked those unwilling or unable to show their faces to leave anonymous comments of support on our post.

Comments, of course, were unlikely to save us.

Xiao used the wi-mo I'd received from Little Wuxie to record a video of me reading the declaration. I had enough credibility throughout the city that my image could lend weight to the message; besides, vids always got more attention than text. When we were finished, Xiaohao and I shared a wary, weary glance. My hands were clammy, and part of me wanted to collapse on the cell floor. The other part was so hyperactive that I doubted I'd sleep for days, no matter how our little sedition ended.

Xiao nodded, and I uploaded both the transcript and the video, tagged so that they would appear on every feed in the city of broken places.

And then we waited.

WE SAT IN silence, refreshing our feeds. We'd turned off our knives, and the bulb in the corridor had given out, so the cell was lit only by the moon-white light of the Wuxie wi-mo. We watched the video's viewership slowly, slowly rise. Every minute that passed without a comment felt like a punch to the gut. The cell was sweltering, but I felt cold.

This was it. The endgame. Either our plan worked, or I went down with Xiaohao. Would Papa really execute both of his children? Could he really keep so cool, so consistent? I worried the question until it was raw, tried to imagine what answer Papa would give if I asked him point blank.

Finally, Xiao broke the silence. "What would Mother think?" he murmured.

When was the last time I'd thought about our mother? Papa never talked about her, and Xiao had been gone for so long. "I don't know," I said. "Sometimes, for a fleeting moment, I think I remember her. And then I realize that I'm thinking of some old vid or picture."

He smiled sadly. "Yeah. I know. Wasn't really a question." He bit his lip and turned his attention back to the wi-mo. "She'd be just as pissed off as Father. Maybe moreso. They were two of a kind." He was only a few years older than me, but he claimed to remember so much more. Sometimes I suspected that Xiao had invented our mother. Sometimes I resented his stories.

"Grandfather," I said. "I think he'd be proud."

"Yeah? Seriously?"

I rested my hand on Xiao's. His skin was clammy. "He'd be proud and he'd be pleased. He always cared more about *his land* and *his family* than— you know. Whatever the rules are this week. You're bringing back the land, and you're doing it for the family. He'd be proud."

Xiao fixed his gaze pointedly on the wi-mo. For a fleeting moment, I thought I saw a warbling of moisture in his eye. "Thank you," he said. And then: "Oh shit."

"Oh shit?"

He showed me. Comments were pouring in now, ten at a time. Some were cynical, others supportive. Only a few were outright angry. Several of the supportive comments linked to another video, which showed indistinct figures gathering on a dock not far from the *Whale*.

Some of the figures were security officers.

"It's starting," said Xiao.

The new video was a not-so-subtle message: *we want a new Yunhe, we have muscle, and you can find us at this location.* The sight of the security officers was both heartening and sick-making. We had muscle, yes, but now guns were in play. In all my fervor, I hadn't quite realized that things might get very bloody very quickly. Or maybe I understood— it in a detached, academic sense—but it hadn't really occurred to me that our side might have guns too.

More videos followed. Similar declarations of support, and instructions for assembly. The vids rarely showed faces—just quick, shaky shots of gathered bodies and some semi-distinctive landmark. My stomach roiled. My shirt was soaked. We waited.

Finally, with no warning from the feeds, we heard footsteps on the stairs. More than one person, but not more than a handful. Xiao and I shared a glance. Neither of us turned on our knives. Three sets of boots cast echoes from the far end of the corridor.

And all at once, the knotty storm of anxiety in my chest resolved into a liquid cool. This was it. The waiting was over. Whatever was going to happen would happen. An idiot grin spread over my face; I squeezed Xiao's hand, and he looked at me as if I'd gone mad.

The three newcomers emerged into the light. Old Zhu walked with a slight limp, smiling a crooked smile. On either side of him was a security officer with an automatic rifle. I recognized one of the men from the Little Yunhe border guard. The squad leader. I gave him a small nod, which he returned. Zhu arched an eyebrow, smiled even wider, and then opened his mouth.

"There are some folks here to see you," he said.

Outside, an impossible thing stood on the dock: the largest gathering I'd ever seen. The city was always a sweaty press of bodies, of course, but this was a press with a purpose. People from every quarter—Administrators, elderly tentsquats, fishermen, gangly tattooed hoods—strained to see us as we emerged from the *Patient Whale*. Someone gave up a cheer as we appeared, and the cheer carried through the crowd. Again, Xiao and I shared a glance. I was still grinning. Xiao looked like someone had punched him in the gut.

We walked down the long ramp from the ship to the shore, and into the midst of our saviors. The crowd was eager but polite, standing back to make room, asking questions but not shouting or insisting. When it became clear that Xiao was too dumbfounded to speak, I raised my arms. The people around us hushed.

"Thank you," I said. "Thank you, so much. I will always remember this. I will never be able to thank you enough for what you've done.

"But I have to ask you to do one more brave thing."

There was, I told the crowd, one last person we needed to persuade. I gave them his name, and asked them to walk behind me. Then, with Xiao at my side, I started down the winding way between the tent quarter and the open market, up the hill and toward my father's house.

The people of the city followed.

We may have lost folks as we walked. We may have gained some, too. I didn't look back. Xiao leaned in and whispered, "Sweet shit, Yuen." After that, we were both silent.

I guessed that Papa would come to meet us, and I was right. As we rounded into the final approach toward the hut, we sighted Papa and a squad of hardsuits marching down the gravel path. I took a deep breath, bit my lip until I drew blood, and pulled the arc knife from my pocket. The security officers behind me rushed to my side, held their rifles at the ready. Pained expressions passed across their faces, but they raised their weapons and walked with me and did not waver.

We had greater numbers, and more guns. But there could still be blood.

As we came closer, I saw the pistol in Papa's hand. The emptiness in his eyes. His gray suit was stained with sweat, and there was uncertainty on the faces of his officers. I slowed, then stopped, and the crowd followed suit. Feet shifted on gravel.

"Papa," I called. "Papa, please stand down."

"You know I can't do that, Yuen."

"We only want what's best for the city. It isn't sedition. It's renewal."

"It's not sedition?" His voice was dead, monotone. "You want to activate Ecclesia technology—brought here by an traitor and illegal agent—within our borders. How is that not sedition?" There was no force, no anger behind the words. He looked pale and deflated. The crowd at my back murmured.

"Xiaohao broke ties with the Ecclesia to bring us his soil. Don't you see—" I looked for the words, smiled when I found them. "Don't you see that he followed your example? You traveled into space to protect us, and we honor you for that. Everyone honors you. But Xiao went further. He left the *country*. And just like you, he came back triumphant."

More murmurs rose behind me, and a few cheers.

Papa was silent.

"Listen," I said. "We outnumber you. These people are from all over the city; you don't even have jurisdiction over most of them. If you ask those officers to fire on us, you break the law of the city and call chaos down on everyone's heads. All for nothing. You don't want that."

He opened his mouth. Closed it. Tears filled his eyes, and his entire body slumped. The hardsuits beside him began to lower their weapons.

"Mere anarchy," Papa said, barely audible. "Mere anarchy is loosed…"

And then he raised the pistol to his head.

"No!" shouted Xiaohao. The officer at Papa's side whipped around with incredible, suit-augmented speed, slapped the gun from Papa's hand. No shot sounded, but Papa collapsed as if he'd pulled the trigger, and the officers around him struggled to hold him up. Xiao and I ran forward.

"He's alive," said the officer who bore most of his weight. "He fainted." Xiao, stricken, reached out to touch his father's face. I doubted he would have reacted differently if Papa *were* dead—tears ran down his flushed cheeks, and he squinted with the effort of holding tears back. Papa, for his part, looked peaceful. You might have mistaken the curl of his lips for a smile.

"Xiao," I said. "Come on."

"*We almost killed him*," said Xiaohao. "We almost. I never meant..."

He trailed off. I touched his shoulder.

"I know," I said softly. "But we stopped him from having to kill *us*."

The sun bore down. The city watched us. Finally, I turned and began to march up the gravel road. After a moment, Xiao jogged to catch up. As we approached the hut, my wi-mo asked if I wished to link to device "XiXi." I declined. The door was locked, but Quonset hut doors were only so strong.

"I think he wanted you to succeed," I said, activating the arc knife.

Xiao wiped his eyes with his wrist. "Are you kidding?"

"No. I think he followed every protocol, but secretly hoped that you would succeed."

"What could possibly make you think that?"

"He kept your wi-mo."

Xiao's eyes moistened again. I slashed off the lock and kicked open the door. Cool air spilled out, and half a dozen smartfans twisted around to regard us. Behind us, hundreds of feet scratched the gravel path. Eager to join us, eager to walk on the earth of Yunhe.

The new town wouldn't look like Xiao's sim—I knew that already. Parts of his fantasy would persist into the real world, maybe, but every single person who had saved us would have an idea about what the new Yunhe should look like, how it should work. I couldn't wait to hear what they had to say. I couldn't wait for the arguments, the compromises, the beautiful reality.

We fell into our father's house and found the key.

Ecclesia is social, networked. Borderless, we've currency. Weaponless, we've teeth. Metanation creed: union in the interstices. All welcome.

—Eric Gregory—

The Greenman Watches the Black Bar Go Up, Up, Up

Jacques Barcia

THE MOMENT SHINE *was announced, I received enthusiastic messages from around the world. Not just from the western world—although, make no mistake, these were very welcome, as well—but quite a lot from the world at large. For some unfathomable reason there were a lot of encouragements from the Philippines and Brazil.*

Unfortunately, while I did get quite a few good submissions from the Philippines, none of them made the final cut for Shine—although some came close. Blame your editor. Similarly, I did get quite a few from Brazil, as well, and while I had to turn several down, I'm quite happy to publish this one from Jacques Barcia.

"The Greenman Watches the Black Bar Go Up, Up, Up" is very close to what I would consider an 'ideal'

(if such a thing exists) story for Shine: *it is complex yet recognisable, it is exotic yet familiar, it exhumes mystery while shedding new light on old tropes, and its progress is very hard fought, at every level.*

Yes, the world is—or may be—a better place, but not before we have worked and thought very hard to get there. And we need to keep thinking and working very hard to stay there, or take the next step.

Yet we can, even in the gritty, dark and strange streets and cyber-alleys of Jacques Barcia's future Recife that's as intriguing as any Brasyl depicted in SF.

HE LOVED THE wall barring the sea. It was his best kept secret, or else he believed it was. Inácio never told it to anyone. Not to his father, neither to his old comrades from the days and nights of war, and most certainly he would never tell it now to his clients. Though he knew Lúcio was aware of it, his partner never used that little contradiction to break his spirit and deliberately hurt him, as lovers do when a fight erupts on late Saturday nights fueled by jealousy, overdue bills and the fear of death.

No, nobody knew, despite the fact that he had to stop by a cart on the top of the dam, about four stories above street level, and have some fresh coconut water before going home. Every night he'd stay an hour or so leaning over the parapet watching the waves pass the tidal farm and break against the outer side of the colossal shield. He'd feel the wind, moist and salty, wash his face and carry his breath into the air of Recife.

And every night he'd think people had took action too late and he'd ask why it took so long to make people care. It certainly helped stop the guns and the bombs and made people pay some respect to the air and the sea, but it was almost as big a crime to raise the barrage. But he loved the wall. Especially because it had an awesome view of the green farms sprawled over the terraces and rooftops. It gave him some peace and good memories.

Inácio was way past the normal time of his nightly ritual, waiting for some last-minute contractor to call him. He felt drowsy, but the feed from the blabbers he followed and the data flooding from the passersby wouldn't let him doze. MEET ME, SHARE WITH ME and the outdated, but inevitable, BUY FROM ME danced on his contacts like animated billboards and fought with his own eydgets for the faintest attention. You should be home by now, his carbon tracker also insisted. You should be home to reset your footprint or else I'll shut down your systems. But the contractor had convinced Inácio to moIP him—communicate with him via an internet protocol while he was on the move—for a conference in the after-hours of the emissions market. So he waited, nervously watching the tracker's black bar go up, up, up with every breath and every gigabyte generated flying to the datacenter in his living room.

He and Lúcio used to live on the northern side of the city, just five minutes away by train. Now he counted the ninth or tenth metro slide amidst the old concrete buildings and into the much newer modular habitations, their reusable materials in constant flux, easily transferrable as the whims of the urban pulse saw fit. It would normally be a zen-like experience, to cross the city sliding at high speed, seeing the deep green crown of the trees dot the asphalt and the silver lakes and rivers, natural and artificial, free to run their courses but also tightly controlled not to rebel against their margins. But now, he knew, there'd be only the humming of the solar batteries pushing forward the monorail, causing that corrosive, maddening itch in his eardrums which reminded him of forests, bugs and bullets. And, what's worse, at the end of the line there'd be no one to talk to.

It took less than a minute after the market's close down for the would-be client signal asking for a voice call. It was a local number for sure, but held no digital signature or embedded business card. Inácio let the messenger blink twice before he threw his second empty coconut into the public recycler. The thing chewed and swallowed and made mechanical noises while sending the biomass down into the city's entrails. After the third blink he eye-commanded the app open to see what this mystery was all about. What Inácio didn't expect was the voice of a kid on the other side of the line.

"Mr. Lima?" said the voice, childish but confident.

"Is this some kind of joke, boy? Don't you have anything more productive to do than play tricks on me?" Inácio felt anger rush in his veins and was about to close the connection when, after a second, the kid replied.

"This is no trick. We'd like to know if you'd be interested in doing a little research for us. We pay well." The voice couldn't belong to anyone past fourteen. But the young man was very determined and eloquent.

"What the hell are you doing, kid? I tell you I'm going to track that number and…"

"I represent a group of investors interested in hiring you," the voice interrupted. The voice wasn't confident. It was rehearsed and foreign. Inácio was staring at the disconnect button, pressed by his gaze but not yet released. He couldn't believe he was giving the prankster this much time to perform. "We're curious about a certain wikindustry," the brat continued, "and we'd like your professional opinion about it."

"You got it wrong. I'm not a business consultant."

"We know. You're a self-employed sustainability analyst. A greenman, formerly working for CrediCarb and also a war veteran. You're exactly the man we want."

Shock and shivers ran over his skin. Long seconds may have passed before Inácio noticed he was scratching under his collarbone, right where the logo of the GreenWar militia was tattooed. It was a primitive reaction, an echo of his time being hunted in the countryside when people like him, who broke with peaceful protests and took arms to fight for the environment, had to come back home after peace was reestablished. Then, he thought, everybody had them as the good guys. He soon learned that not only industrialists, landowners and cattle farmers hated him. For many of those caught in the crossfire, especially those dependent on the rich employers, he was a terrorist and an assassin. And for many years after the wall was built, right here in the city, he felt like he needed to hide the mark. Who'd have guessed that almost two decades later it'd become a fashionable design, its history blurred by trends and blended with the new times?

The button-down straightened automatically as Inácio withdrew his shaking hand. The tattoo, just a bit darker than his own skin, had turned the color of diluted wine, hot and prickly. The train was nowhere to be seen.

"Besides," the client continued, "we knew Lúcio. And he told us to look for you if we needed that kind of job."

THE PRICKLING UNDER his shirt had stopped. They talked in a dedicated moIP connection for no more than ten minutes, with only one of those spent on discussing the many zeroes being offered to Inácio as a reward and how they'd known his lover. Lúcio met them at the Shigeru Awards and apparently gave them Inácio's contact details.

The three clients wore encrypted avatars that masked their features, appearing as nothing but dark cloaks with plasma globes for heads. But out of recklessness or sheer confidence their voices weren't jumbled. They were all teens.

"And that's it, Inácio. We want you to find everything you can about Gear5's policies." The taller avatar had an older but more casual tone. Advanced physics algorithms made the illusion dodge waiters, tourists and other rich media floating in the augmented reality.

In the real world, Inácio sat at a round stone table close to the escalator leading to the avenue down below. Rush hour had passed, but the traffic systems were still operating. The street drove the cars so close to each other they looked like a single line of black bars and yellow spots. "You understand that what you're asking is extremely unusual, don't you?" The analyst already had three search engines running in his field of vision, along with dozens of other eydgets, including some custom market research apps, blabber feeds and text clients, sending private messages to trustworthy contacts and opening anonymous topics in professional social networks' forums. "And your deadline is impossible to meet. I just can't provide you a full report about this Gear5 in less than eight hours."

"I told you," said the third plasma globe. It had the sweet voice of a girl, but naturally distorted like a bad death metal guitar plug-in. "We should have contacted him much earlier."

The youngest avatar seemed to turn to the angry girl and back to face Inácio. "Unfortunately, Mr. Lima, it's a very tight window of opportunity. But we know you're probably asking questions to your acquaintances by now and they'll certainly ask their own in the following minutes. We couldn't let an avalanche of gossip be spread before the markets were closed. Besides, we decided to make our move just a few hours ago when word has reached us that the company will open part of their codes tomorrow morning." The globe's innards were filled with a storm of pink lightning. The avatar leaned closer to Inácio. "But I don't think you really find the task all that unusual, do you?"

He didn't. There was this indigent startup wikindustry operating for eleven months now with an ever rising stock of carbon credits and these kids, whoever they were, wanted to know whether the thing Gear5 had under development, besides the occasional crowdvertising for rising mobbands they claimed to do, was sustainable or not. That all meant he had to find out everything about the company and their product using, he'd say, unconventional methods. "Like I said, the deadline is impossible," he said.

"Just give it a try. We trust you."

Rich teenage wallets were not uncommon, especially in the tech business. But this group was different. They were too young and seemed to have a different focus, too new for him to clearly identify. So his only option was to treat them as a common group of aggressive investors, the kind of people he had a history of hating. "Look, I know you know exactly what that company has been developing. You won't tell me for competitive reasons, of course, but if you are considering the investment then you've already measured how much money you can get from that. So why bother with carbon market regulations they're certainly meeting? Just go there and put your cash on it."

The young foreigner put his cloak-and-globe body back straight and raised, for the first time, a pair of ghostly hands. "You're not getting it, Mr. Lima." He looked like he was giving a lecture. "Money has meaning only to those old enough to remember it. No, Mr. Lima, we don't want to put a single penny on it. We want to find out if this project conforms to our working ethics. We want to invest our brains and bandwidth on it."

"THEY'VE BEEN BUYING lots of carbon," yelled the fat man, his suit flashing back the lights of the cabaret, "and not just from companies. They paid a great number of civilians too. Some kind of sponsorship. You know, they pay you an advance so you minimize your footprint and pay again to get whatever credits you have left. Not very cost-effective, but some companies do it to raise their public images. Publicity."

The guy was called Josué Bispo, an old friend. Inácio got his reply still in the pier, disembarking from a late boat in the Sol Street. The stock broker was not the only one—not even the first—to answer Inácio's queries about Gear5, but the man told him he was around, in a brothel on the uppermost floor of the Sete de Setembro building, just a couple of blocks away. The place had a vintage feel, with loud technobrega music and hapticless soft porn playing on every table. Behind him, penciled on the remnants of a sheet of paper on the wall, the next inspection remained scheduled and three years late. "But what are they developing?" asked Inácio. "And how many people are involved?" Shouting over the music made his throat tired and sore.

Bispo nodded and balanced his weight with an elbow on the table. He finally took advantage of a gap between songs and spoke in a more normal tone. "Nobody knows for sure. What I've heard is that it's some really disruptive shit. But whatever it is, it's something that leaves lots of residues and raises too much controversy. So much they couldn't possibly be competitive. Otherwise they wouldn't be stocking." Bispo took his last shrimp tempura from a bowl full of soy sauce, and ate it whole. "Do you remember those shrimp farms up north? I must confess I miss the big, big shrimps they had there. Much bigger, and much cheaper."

Inácio grinned and raised a cup of iced tea. *He remembers the long-gone farms, the first to be raided years ago.* Hundreds of square miles of *mangue*, a whole ecosystem, turned into tanks for shrimps and oysters and then to fields of blood. *He remembers the battle.* "That's the price to be paid, old friend.

Come on! Eat your expensive shrimp and be thankful that water isn't overpriced. We made our choice, pal, and I do believe it was the best option available." *Though I feel sorry for turning myself into a killer.*

"Yeah. I guess so." Bispo stared at his beer glass. The data input was blank except for its temperature. A sign it had been smuggled. "So, are you fine?"

"About what?" The sudden change of subject took him by surprise.

"Lúcio. He'd have turned forty yesterday. But you know that."

He did, but it hadn't occurred to him. Until now. He completely missed his lover's birthday. Maybe he had put too much effort into forgetting Lúcio's death. He'd spent the whole year running from detailed memories, especially those which would take him by surprise and, for the briefest of times, make him believe Lúcio was alive somehow. Instead he concentrated on general, safe memories like the place they first met, their wedding, the sex. But their secret names, their songs and birthdays, caused him too much pain. He couldn't let that happen. He had to protect himself from suffering in the waking hours. And an empty house, an empty bed and an empty heart from dusk till dawn was pain enough. But yeah, he forgot Lúcio's birthday. And no, he wasn't fine.

"I'll live," Inácio said and sipped some tea, now barely cold. "Have to." He met Bispo's gaze, ready to offer a friendly shoulder, but Inácio refused, slightly shaking his head. "Gotta pee. And then go." It was his turn to change subjects. "They want the whole story by morning, you know." But he didn't move. Bispo nodded once more and was gone before Inácio could stand and shake his hand. As real good friends usually do, he let Inácio pay the bill, so he eye-commanded the payment and asked for a copy of his footprint. It took the bar's AI systems some time to arrange things, as their usual costumers rarely asked for a carbon sync. Meanwhile, he summoned his tracker and was partly relieved to see it was still under the established mark, but uncomfortably close. *Could be worse*, he thought.

As he turned his contacts on, the stream of incoming replies filled his inner screen. Silver discs linked by gossamer lines formed a cloud of social networks, as his best data miner started doing its magic. He was a spider, a vulture looking for something worthy in a herd of captured information. He assembled all the data his miner got from the cloud and started digging.

He quickly found bits and pieces about Gear5. A rather new wikindustry, but older than what he and his contractors believed. It was about three years old, but was previously registered as Gear4, an entertainment company focused on ARGs and multimedia packs for mobbands. They were doing well in the long tail chart but for some reason, eleven months ago, they killed their assets, changed their name and started buying carbon like crazy, both from small businesses and citizens alike.

Something uncomfortable was rising in the back of his mind.

That wasn't right, he thought. They spent billions of reais buying carbon. It was as if Haiti, Angola, or another developing country wanted to compensate their whole footprint in a single financial year. Inácio turned the haptics on. He had to be faster. He moved blocks of data with eyes and hands, building diagrams and going through even deeper into the cloud. But no matter where in the web he went he couldn't find who the people behind Gear5 were and who was paying for their carbon trade. Not to mention that damn product. For all he knew it didn't exist.

He felt that unease again marching over his spine up to his neck, crossing his brain and into his eyeballs. But he kept his focus on a spreadsheet conjured to list all the reported trades Gear5 made in the past few months. The numbers would never match. There wouldn't be enough companies or individual carbon sellers available and with sufficient margins left in their footprints to feed that stock. No, there wouldn't.

And this meant they were buying from the black market.

Pressure from within his eyes forced him to press his palms against his face in an attempt to release the pain, to keep his mind from going out. He was so tired. He wanted to sleep.

When he opened his eyes again he noticed a man who seemed to be watching him, half-hidden under a curtain of smoke and red stroboscopic light at the far end of the cabaret. The figure had a familiar silhouette but Inácio didn't recognize him. He felt a rush of adrenaline in his blood and quickly packed the sheets and docs and messages in a cloudlock. But the man was already gone, vanished behind the swinging bodies of two live performers. He definitely needed some rest. But it was time to leave.

On the way to the bathroom, Inácio stumbled over three customers and a chair, and almost fell twice. The place looked odd, stretched and oblong. It seemed bigger inside than it actually was. If he'd had any alcohol, he'd say he was feeling hung over, dizzy and suddenly sick. He stumbled at the white door of the bathroom, curved as if seen through a peephole, and brightly colored by too many opened eydgets. Inácio tried to shut up the blabbers feeding their voice messages with news and comments and rants and flames, but found he was unable to close any of the transmissions.

Tens, hundreds or thousands of voices talked to him simultaneously, making his head a new Babel, too heavy a mind, unsustainable. Under the cacophony a single sound, constant yet barely distinguishable, drew his attention. He finally leaned over the sink with eyes closed, but even so he'd see an augmented reality version of his inner cavities, filled with interfaces and white noise.

And then it stopped.

Both his hands were shaking uncontrollably and his shirt was damp with sweat. Slowly, he moved his palms into the sink and cupped them under the water. He kept the tap running, not giving a damn about water resources or the new stories being built in the counter's black bar.

Two voices entered the bathroom talking about yesterday's futebol game. They were followed by men visible from the bottom of the large mirror. Inácio felt spam coming and instinctively blocked their sports network's invitation and the game footage hovering over their heads. The two men walked past him and carried on their dialogue at the urinal, their voices going lower and lower, finally engulfed by the sound of a hum, a murmur from the past causing an itch deep inside his eardrums.

"I need your help," whispered the voice under the buzz.

In the mirror Inácio saw a third man standing right behind him. He turned, startled, ready for a fist fight. He fell backwards when his dead lover spoke.

"I'm dying," said Lúcio and the lights, the web and the world went black.

Inácio threw up his dinner and passed out.

"Will you be long? I've got a fever." The video with Lúcio speaking lay open in the corner of his vision. In the recording, showing the very European face of his deceased partner, Inácio was just a voice actor, answering his plea with a hurried 'in a moment' and then shutting down the call. That was their last conversation. Two years ago Lúcio was diagnosed with a rare degenerative disease, treatable in most cases. Nine months later he was dead. Fuck! *He misses him so much*. Not for a single moment did the man he fell in love with give up living. He never surrendered. He loved the simple fun of being alive. Be it a walk in the park, a hotly disputed videogame home championship or a kiss after slow, contemplative sex.

A low whistle put an end to his waking dream. The street printer in front of Inácio was old, expensive and prone to malfunction, but at least it used organic polymers and was able to embed processors in the fabric. It was two in the morning and printing himself a new shirt on the go was way faster than doing the same at home for free. Inácio had thrown his ruined button-down away at the first recycler and walked bare-chested, looking for the machine. After the blackout, as energy and communications came back online, the two men back in the bar's bathroom insisted on calling him an ambulance, but

Inácio told them he was fine and that he only had a blood pressure peak. Tough day, he said. It was his dead husband's birthday and he thought he had seen him right there, before falling unconscious for a few seconds. Yeah, stress does that, they replied.

After checking if all the systems were functioning he put the brand-new shirt on and headed to the São José quarter, in the south side of downtown. He was going to the big Market enclosed in the maze of alleys in one of the city's oldest quarters. He was going to Recife's black market, where he believed some of Gear5's carbon smugglers could be found.

He was halfway to São José when the blinking icon of an incoming moIP call blossomed in his sight, automatically pausing the video's loop. He accepted the virtual meeting, slowing his pace to free the connection of time-lag. Preliminary conclusions were highlighted in the report, still in its infancy, minimized for quick access. He promptly opened the document knowing who might be the caller.

"We tried to contact you earlier. You went offline for almost an hour," asked his foreign client. Cloak-and-globe's AI made his avatar walk along with Inácio. "What happened?"

"An hour? I think I ate some rotten shrimp and passed out for a few minutes. Nothing serious. Oh, and there was a little energy shortage or something. Blabbers are saying lightning has struck a major power line, so communications might be a little messy."

Two parallel plasma lightnings, just like eyes inside the glass globe, turned to face the analyst. "Have you made any progress?"

With the haptics on, Inácio threw the report and some of the evidence in a collaborative space pocketed in the moIP connection. "Yes. I'm almost sure they're buying illegal carbon credits from the black market. See the numbers? They aren't real." Inácio had an animation running, with dozens of names cascading into the image of a plastic bucket floating between them. "Those are the names of companies Gear5 has claimed to have traded regularly in the past six months. All fake."

Cloak-and-globe picked a name and drew it closer to his face. He seemed to examine its typography. "And that means…?"

"That means Gear5's probably a carbon washer. It claims to be developing some high-impact product and starts buying cheap credits from a large number of sources. Since their product has a really large footprint, they naturally *need* many sources, right? So no one notices the fraud."

Inácio had just put together the pieces, forming an almost complete picture in the jigsaw. But that kind of illegal activity was uncommon, for carbon trade was conspicuously watched. And not only by national agencies, but also by non-government organizations, both private and voluntary, like CrediCarb, Carbon Watch and E-Missions, the latter founded by GreenWar veterans and allowed to conduct limited investigations if called. An activity absent from Inácio's curriculum.

"But in reality," he continued, "they're buying cheap credits like, say, carbon dioxide, and trading large chunks of it in the black market for heavier credits, mostly stolen, and sold at the lowliest of costs.

"Then they re-trade the heavy credit, probably chemical waste, to some still underdeveloped or developing nation. All that under a confidential agreement. The said nation pays the heavy carbon with another large quantity of cheap carbon, which re-enters the cycle, but also with a lot of money.

"In the end, the buyer paid less for more credits, which legally lowers their footprint and enables them to do business with big traditional companies, wikindustries, and well-developed nations like us who are signatories of the Rio, Kyoto, Shenzhen and Tripoli protocols. On the other hand, the fraudulent company gets lots of money in the process. Much more than what was spent buying the first cheap credits. And yes, their old practices still prefer money."

Cloak spent most of the time silently staring at Inácio like a statue. When his voice came out it was smooth and determined. "You're wrong," he said.

"What?" Inacio stopped and pulled his client's illusory mantle. "Wrong how?"

"To begin with, they do have a real product."

HE WAS A foreigner in this city-within-a-city.

The São José quarter, unlike the rest of Recife's downtown, was pretty much alive now at three in the morning. Street vendors, food carts and electric trucks, packing and delivering cargoes of recyclable materials, conferred on the place a cosmopolitan atmosphere. And there were people; too many people. Seven or eight young adults ran past him chasing a ball, blackened after years of use. They were having a break from the deep night school, a way to keep the area's high literacy rates. They dodged passersby running errands and almost ran over a tall man in a black suit turning the corner. The man stopped to let them pass, and calmly re-entered the crowd.

The neighborhood was one of the two surviving permanent autonomous zones created in the 'twenties after years of civil unrest. Reconstruction, urbanization, and ultimately a decent life began after the government accepted the fact that the people could administrate the bairro better than the white-collars ever would. But after some time, independence demanded the necessity to be carbon-free, which made São José a center of excellence for recycling and sustainable design, but also home to some of the fiercest Brazilian carbon smugglers.

So the streets were chaotic, yes, but cleaner than those in the outer city. There were fewer rich media oozing from the walls and the people, and only the dangling jury-rigged cables connecting new apartments in the upper floors hurt the landscape. There wasn't a single public recycler around, but Inácio knew that a great number of men and women made a living out of collecting, separating and selling garbage in online auctions, both for reuse in energetic processing and for manufacturing things the printers weren't able to make.

The leader of one of the biggest collectors' cooperatives was precisely the man the soldier-turned-analyst was looking for. His name, or the name he was known by, was Capitão. He had fought with Inácio in the war and was directly responsible for him joining the fight. Inácio soon became his superior in the militia, but the commander never dared to make a move without consulting the elder.

On the billboard spinning before his eyes, Inácio could see the name, municipal subscription number and other general information of the São José PAZ's Garbage Collectors Association. The building was an eighteenth century warehouse but its frontispiece was richly enhanced by augmented reality inputs, a fluid animation constantly displaying different stages of a recycling facility. Capitão stood by the old, big cedar door smoking a cigarette, observing the tide of human beings.

"If you won't quit this shit by yourself, lung cancer will do it for you," said Inácio. There was some passive-aggressiveness in his tone, but a half-smile belied his anger. It was good to meet the old man. "Last time we met you said you'd stopped."

"We all have our sins, don't we? And our secrets," the gray-haired man replied with a grin. "You could have moIPed me, you know. Instead of visiting me live."

They gave each other a tight hug. Perhaps three years had passed since the last time they met face to face. Capitão didn't attend Lúcio's funeral, of course, but not because he had anything against Inácio or his partner. On the contrary, he and Lúcio were great friends. Truth is that the old man, who had killed many men and as many more die in the field, couldn't stand the sight of his only child grieving for his dead lover. "Come in, son," said Capitão. "Tell me what brings you here."

"THAT'S WHY I didn't moIP you. I was coming anyway." They were both leaning over the mezzanine's wood parapet. On the ground floor several tall garbage piles were negotiated, each one by a different associate wearing home-made Augmented Reality glasses. Many were young, some were well-dressed, but some looked little better than mendicants. The cooperative supplied the hardware and hosted the entire commercial infrastructure for a notional fee.

In his contacts, Inácio could see the giant screen showing today's rates for aluminum, glass, rubber and other non-biodegradable materials. And the hot deal today was antimony.

"They must be paying well," said Capitão.

"It's not about…"

"I remember you quit E-Missions because you had to do this exact same job in the US."

"Don't start."

"And then you joined that bastards at CrediCarb, got rich and then quit again to get even richer." Capitão stared at Inácio, but didn't seem to be angry either. Only bitter.

"I'm not rich. And I'm not with CrediCarb because they're fucking corrupt." Inácio was on the verge of yelling at his father, but lacked the energy for a fight. Two hours from now the sun would rise and he had absolutely no idea what Gear5 was about to release. His forehead felt hot, hotter than the air inside the warehouse.

"Of course they don't have any fixed address." He told Capitão. "They're a fucking wikindustry." And of course he could throw shit at the fan and watch it spread and stink so much Gear5 would be forced to postpone whatever plan they had, so he'd win some more time and could dig a little deeper. His eyelids closed against his will, his head leaned to one side. There was a buzz behind his ears. It sounded like chaos playing the enchanters' flute. "It doesn't matter. I need your help."

"Sure. What can I do for you?" Capitão turned and lit another cigarette.

Sweat was beginning to exude from his body. The sound was rising in pitch. "I need to know who their supplier is. And don't look at me like that. I'm sure you know." Inácio grabbed the wooden parapet as his hands began to shake.

"Even if I knew, it would be stupid to go there and actually talk to them. They don't talk. They're people from before the wall. They kill."

Inácio guessed he was right, but it was so hard to concentrate on anything. His skull was pounding. "Come on, you know everything that happens in São José. I know it's in the Market, but I have to know who the man is."

Capitão took a deep, smoky breath. "Sorry, son. I can't help you. I don't know who he is."

"You're lying." He didn't look up.

"Maybe. If so, it's for your own protection."

"But I'll go anyway. That's what I have to do." The icon of an incoming video message worsened his headache. It was from Bispo.

"And this is the part where you ask me for a gun."

"And this is the part where you give me one." Capitão was probably the last man in town, except for the military, to have a lethal weapon. Below them, the associates were in frenzy. Electronic waste suddenly became the top priority.

There was a man in a black suit standing at the center of the waste piles. He was looking up in Inácio's direction.

"And this is the part I change the script," Capitão told him. "Write your report anyway you can. But don't mess with the carbon smugglers. They'll kill you."

In a tiny window, Bispo looked nervous, but that could be the result of the video's low resolution or Inácio's own weariness. "Hey, Inácio! Tried to moIP you, but it seems you're offline," said Bispo in the recording. "Look, I found something that might be useful. I decided to nose into Gear4's deals record and there were some contracts with volunteers for research into a new direct control interface for their videogames. And Lúcio was in."

Inácio felt the buzz rise to an almost unbearable volume. The man in the black suit waved him an invitation to follow and before Inácio thought about it, he was on the move, going down the stairs, leaving his father and their argument with no further ado.

The lights started to fail. Lúcio waited at the door.

"Am I hallucinating?" Inácio was feeling feverish and completely worn out. He was an arm's distance from a ghost wearing his lover's shell.

"Sort of." Lúcio's voice was most tired, yet his appearance couldn't be more jovial. "Come. There's no time. I can't keep the connection. Come to the market. No one will harm you. They'll bring you to my presence. You must help me die."

And for the third time since they met, he vanished.

A YOUNG SOLDIER led Inácio down corridors through the boxes in the very heart of São José's Market. Inside the nineteenth century building, anything could be found. Electronics and herbs, software and food. Live animals, healthcare and personal data centers. But in its center there was a tent, like a circus, where the many types of carbon credits, from sulfates to oxides and dangerous wastes, were sold under the counter. Inácio walked fast, almost faster than his armed guide. The boy picked him up in the market's main entrance. Neither of them spoke. The boy knew, Inácio knew.

Fabric walls divided the space inside the tent, a business center made of cotton and organic polymers.

Inácio could see through half-opened curtains some of the businessmen gesticulating over invisible, encrypted AR screens, buying and selling hacked or forged credits. When deals were set, one would slide a hard drive, a physical, wireless cube where data was locked.

The scene repeated itself until the guide stopped in front of a nondescript door-curtain and told Inácio to go in.

"I thought you wouldn't come." Lúcio stood alone in the room, wearing the same suit and the same worn out features. But he smiled, and that made Inácio's heart thump. He felt tears rolling from his eyes. He was confused and tired and probably mad, but hell, was he happy.

"I don't understand," said Inácio still at a safe distance, but willing to ignore his survival instincts and grab Lúcio in his arms. "Are you alive? How?"

"No, I'm not. Yet, I'm dying again." It was Lúcio who ended up making the first move. His feet didn't touch the ground and he stopped just a few inches from Inácio's mouth. "And I need your help to figure out if I should let go."

"What am I supposed to do? What happened?" Inácio went forward, looking for a much longed kiss, but the man he desired dodged his caress.

"Physics engines. Sorry I didn't tell you." They both looked sad and tired. "I'm not here. I'm nowhere near. I'm not anywhere. Not at all. It happened by accident, but now I'm without a single physical form. My body is a wall, your shirts, the space within circuits. And I think I can bring you here soon. But I don't think it is the right thing to do."

Inácio looked around the room, its inner walls blinking with embedded systems. A large personal data center was in a corner and next to it a black hard drive. "Why not?"

"Because I think you wouldn't like the broader consequences. But since I'm not sure about your opinion, I can't decide it by myself. See the drive? It contains detailed information about all the carbon footprint I generated since I joined Gear5. Read it and decide if this is the path we should follow before my code goes public in the morning. When that happens, I won't be *me* anymore."

Lúcio turned his engines off and got closer to Inácio, his black skin reflected in green semi-transparent eyes. The greenman watched his partner kneel down, his face turned upwards, smiling, too close to his groin. "But before you do it," Lúcio began, "turn your haptics on."

THE SURF CLOSE to the wall was brief, but beautiful nevertheless in Recife's waking hours. The sun had fully risen and Inácio sat on the stone parapet, his shoeless feet swinging free, getting wet in the salty drizzle. He kept the black hard drive next to him and away from the fatal fall. His vision was filled with diagrams, schematics and other greenmen's projections for the next several years.

He didn't wait long for the call.

"Good morning, Mr. Lima," said Cloak-and-globe.

"Yeah. Good." His eyes were sunk inside his skull, his body ached, his eardrums were blown. But it was a good day. Except that, in his mind, the decision Lúcio demanded wasn't clear.

"Is the report ready?"

"Yes, it is. I'm uploading it to you." Inácio dragged the icon to a virtual table close to his client. "Done.

You have my account, so I'm sure you'll transfer my money." Inácio jumped back to the sidewalk, barefooted, and headed to the escalator.

"Mr. Lima! Wait," said the globe, the storm in his glassy head less visible under daylight. "I'd like to know your personal opinion on the matter. This document will surely give me and the group I represent all the details, numbers and other minutiae necessary to decide. But time's short and if you could provide me a quick analysis, that'd be much appreciated."

Inácio stopped just before the escalator's steps, rolling down to the avenue. "My opinion? You want my opinion?" He assumed the most professional tone he could. "Gear5's new technology is highly disruptive. It puts an end to our time and begins another one, potentially radically different from any other in human history." He moved closer to the boy-investor.

"But it needs so much energy, so much bandwidth, that three or four Earths would be necessary to feed it. Think about a datacenter for a whole mind. The computational power needed to calculate the simplest of human decisions. The raw materials needed to build all that infrastructure.

"Yesterday's blackouts were the result of their iteration prototype running. They're consuming the city's whole energy and communications. That's why they were buying so much carbon. They thought it'd make the technology pass the trade regulations. They didn't think about the impact. Not to mention that only those rich enough to pay the stratospheric price Gear5's asking would be able to buy the uploading code and hardware. It will generate a kind of inequality never seen before.

"So, no. This product isn't sustainable in the current state of the technology.

"However, in the longer term fusion has the potential to end poverty, disease, and the necessity to consume Earth's natural resources. The few surviving post-humans may live in a golden, perfect time. I'm serious." Inácio crossed his arms. "It's your call."

A moment of silence fell between them. The third morning train broke the city's silence, running north, fast and empty.

Cloak asked a final time, slowly. "And what do you think my group should do?"

Inácio paused for a moment, thinking. *That could work.* "Your group should approach Gear5 with an offer they can't refuse. Be aggressive. Gather all the intellectual capital your group has and tell the company it'll be all theirs, but only if Gear5 postpones the product's release. And what's more, make them sign a contract saying that a final version of the technology will only go public when all the drawbacks are overcome. Energy, materials, costs, everything. That way, it becomes not only sustainable, but absolutely desirable."

The kid under the digital cloak nodded and, wrapping up Inácio's report, turned to close the connection. "Thank you, Mr. Lima. It was a pleasure doing business with you." The next moment he was gone.

When Inácio was about to leave, he noticed the hard drive still standing on the parapet, where he forgot it. He walked towards the sea, grabbed the box and returned to the escalator, where Lúcio waited for him.

He wondered what the carbon footprint for love is.

Google.gov pleased to proclaim: ads on cyber cash so successful taxes repealed; find new product placement opportunities on virtual bills!

—Jason Stoddard—

Overhead

Jason Stoddard

IMAGINE A PERSON *who is as helpful as he can be when you've just touched down in his home city, and still apologises for every little thing that goes wrong, even if it is something completely out of his control. Who tries to be the perfect host while the incessant needs of his multimillion dollar company keep calling/SMSing/tweeting/pinging him.*

Imagine a person who moves important business meetings around just to pick you up from LAX, who takes you to a fine hotel in Santa Clarita, and then takes your jetlagged body to a fine restaurant while being very patient with your rambling self.

Imagine a person who gladly offers his company to store a huge batch of magazines you hope to sell at WorldCon, who helps you transport them there, all because you've helped publish some of his stories in a magazine that—compared to his day-to-day business—is basically small beans.

Imagine a man who works crazy hours, hires crazy people, and writes crazy stories in the minimal spare time he has. A man who is optimistic against the grain, whose internet advertising company survived the burst of the internet bubble and the credit crisis.

Then you have Jason Stoddard, a kindred spirit if I ever saw one. He's the 'can-do' mentality become flesh, living the dream (even if it means fighting every inch of the way). Here's a man who knows that progress comes four steps forward to three steps back, and at a price. But who, incessantly, believes in the goodness of the human race, who believes in progress, even in a world whose pendulum has swung a bit too far the other way.

A world where the pioneering spirit is just overhead.

"CANDY!" NILS LOERA said.

"No," his mother told him.

"Yes!" Nils jumped over Ani Loera's shoulders. Another bounce took him to the corridor ceiling, where he swung ahead of her on the exposed steel beams.

Ani shook her head. At 6 years old, Nils had already formulated his most important equation: SHIPMENT = TREAT. Nils was black-haired, blue-eyed, round-faced, and an endless bundle of energy. She couldn't help grinning at him.

I have a kid. On the moon.

And he's cute.

"Candy!" Nils yelled, disappearing down the corridor.

Ani caught up to him at the shaker. Nils bounced up and down in front of the scarred plastic window, frowning.

"Where's the people?" Nils asked.

"What?"

"Nobody there."

Ani squinted through the foggy, scratched plastic. There was only one person in the airlock. His spacesuit bore a faded tag: SHAO. Jun Shao. His silver-visored helmet reflected stark gray walls and her furrowed brow.

Ani ticked an impatient tune on the cold steel walls as the shaker knocked the abrasive moon-dust from Jun's suit. Nils tried to do the same, but his young fingers weren't quite coordinated enough.

Eventually, the airlock door swing open. Jun stepped out, popping his helmet. His expression was blank, unreadable.

"What happened?" Ani asked.

Jun shook his head. "Nothing there."

"Nothing there? What do you mean, nothing there?"

"No shipment."

"No newbies?"

"No people, no parts, no nothing."

Ani felt fear twist her guts. They'd never missed a shipment. Ever. Not for—

Not for 15 years.

Jun shucked his gauntlets and hung them under his name in the rack. He sat down on a bench and began wriggling out of his suit. Nils helped him pull. Jun gave the kid a weak grin and let Nils unlatch his boots.

"Maybe it went off-course."

"Has it ever gone off-course?"

A sudden thought, clear and distinct, as if someone had spoken in her ear: *What if this is the end of the shipments?*

Ani paced. "Did you look around?"

"Yes."

"Thoroughly?"

"Peep my stream!" Jun looked up at her. For the first time, she saw his wide eyes. He was terrified, too.

Ani's watchstream buzzed, signaling a direct message. She glanced at it; messages scrolled, as watchers realized something bad was happening. They'd be looking to her for direction.

What a terrible time to be Prime, she thought. She'd won the lottery last month.

"We have to go back out," she told Jun. "We have to look for the drop. The shipment may have gone off course."

"It's never gone off course—"

"I know. But we have to look."

Jun stopped moving and just looked at her, his face an unreadable mask of exhaustion. Ani wondered how many shifts he'd run in a row. Two? Three? More?

"Put your suit back on," she told Jun.

Nils stopped helping Jun with his suit and looked up at her, frowning.

Ani sighed and addressed the nearest surveillance dot: "Anyone else with outside experience and a suit, come down. We need to make as many tracks as we can."

Slowly, Jun started putting his suit back on.

"No candy?" Nils asked.

Ani forced a smile. "I'll see what I can do."

"You want to sell me insurance?" Thom Lyman said. They were on the tee at the #3 hole of Paradise Springs. Above the rust-colored Arizona hills, the Scottsdale sky was spring-perfect, deep and impossibly blue, with brilliant white streamers of clouds above.

Roy nodded and forced his widest smile. "That's the idea."

Thom paused in mid-swing. "Insurance that'll set us up on the moon in case of catastrophic failure of the Earth's economy?"

Roy Parekh felt himself break into a sweat. "You read it."

"Of course I read it."

"Oh."

"I particularly liked the part about 'an alternate location distribution system with a focus on dramatically new infrastructure and export/import possibilities.'"

"I..."

Thom grinned, creasing his face. He waved Roy up to the tee. "Take your shot."

"Are you—"

"Take it."

Roy went to the tee and looked out over the hole. Perfect green grass stretched in front of him, like an old Windows desktop. Roy's hand trembled slightly as he placed the ball. Golf was a really insanely stupid game. But it was how you closed deals. And he was real good at closing deals.

Until now.

Roy's shot sliced into the rough and bounced into the sand and cactus bordering the course.

"How long have you been out of work?" Thom said.

Roy said nothing for a long time. He thought of throwing his club after the ball. He thought of walking off the course. He thought of the Citicorp work farms.

"Sixteen months," Roy said, after a while.

"Your investments?"

"Nothing left."

"How about Susan?"

"She wanted kids. I can't. She left."

Thom shook his head. "Christ on a barbecue."

Roy just waited. Waited for Thom to ask, *So, you thought I'd fall for it? So, you thought you'd leech off me?*

But Thom just sighed and said, "Why didn't you do something important?"

"What do you mean?"

"You were the smart one."

"What?"

"Back in USC. Why didn't you do tech or something?"

"Because—"

Because the needle bounces off the end of the record, thwup, thwup, thwup, fashions and thought and styles recycled on shorter and shorter swings, nothing new, nothing important. Nobody picking up the needle. Hell, nobody looking at the record and thinking, Time to swap it out for an iPod.

"—because it was too easy at Prudential."

"Until the Rethink screwed you."

Roy blurted a gust of laughter. "Exactly."

Thom went to the cart and put his club away. He looked up at Roy. For a moment his eyes were cold and dead, like a lizard. Then he grinned.

"Okay."

"Okay what?" Roy asked

"Okay. I'll sign it. Google won't miss a few thousand a month. And you need it a lot more than them."

"Really?"

"I can't do it longer than a year."

Roy's legs went rubbery. He leaned heavily on the cart. This was it. This was what he needed. Just one more chance. But. "But... you know it's a scam."

Thom laughed. "Most insurance is."

ANI FORCED HERSELF to look at the people and smile. Over two hundred of them; ten times the usual number. Their eyes were cold and sharp, like broken glass.

The week since the missed shipment had been hard. She'd had to moderate seventeen trios. Mainly for trivial stuff: breaking a tech module that could easily be replaced, setting the price too high on luxury water, an argument over bonuses for expansion of the farms. Stupid things, easily resolved with a quick look at the historical streams or a glance at the optimal ratios. Stuff that would never go to trio, before.

When will they get together and challenge me? Ani wondered. It would almost be a relief. Someone else could be Prime, and she wouldn't have to worry about the leadership lottery ever again.

"Opening the 787th Open Meeting for the Community of Hermes, Moon, Ani Loera, Prime," Ani said.

They were murmuring.

"I'd like to open the meeting now," Ani said, raising her voice.

Still murmuring.

"Your Prime says shut the fuck up," Pavig Lok said, loudly. Heads snapped and voices dropped to silence.

Ani looked at him. Pavig gave her a shrug and a frown, as if to say, *Don't thank me.* He was the owner of the cavern; he'd probably been looking forward to selling it to the newbies.

"Good morning, everyone," Ani said. "Floor is open to discuss any items in advance of the special announcement."

"We're all dead!" someone shouted, from the back of the room.

Ani ignored him and waited.

"If there are no other items, I'll move to the announcement. I'll start with my personal statement: We don't know if the lost shipment is a one-time glitch, or if the shipments have ended indefinitely. If the shipments begin next month, there's no cause for alarm."

A doubtful murmur from the crowd.

"Even if the shipments have ended indefinitely, our Primes for Infrastructure, Technology, and Resources say we can maintain and grow Hermes for the foreseeable future. Regolith processing is simple and can be expanded. Our farms are stable and productive, and can also be expanded. Our genetic technology is sufficient; four hundred of us, including myself, have healthy, happy children."

Nils waved from the back of the cavern. Ani waved back. It warmed the crowd somewhat; she saw a few tentative smiles.

"I'll let the functional Primes make their statements," Ani said, nodding at the three people who sat next to her.

Gilbert Corlew, the current head of Resources, nodded and stood up. "What Ani says is technically correct. We have been continually expanding our regolith processing and foundries. I am, however, worried about our human resources. We're operating at the ragged edge. Each person must know three or more technical specialties. Double and triple shifts are the norm. It is difficult to maintain a year-2000 level technological regime with 1300 people, much less year-2040."

"But do we *need* the shipments?" Ani asked.

Gilbert shook his head. "No. We'll just have to continue working. Very, very hard, for a long, long time."

"Infrastructure?" Ani asked.

Marie Middleton shrugged in her grease-stained gray coveralls, but didn't stand up. "We can keep buildin' tunnels and stretchin' wire and putting up dotcams as long as you want."

Jared Gildea, current head of science, stood up and looked out over the crowd, licking his lips nervously.

"I hate to be the downer," he said. "But let me tell you where we have problems. First, without shipments from Earth, we're locked out of biomimetic and thinker-level technologies. The few that have come in the shipments are either not viable or highly unstable. We could end up with a moon carpeted with lush greenery, or we could grow it into a giant solar cell with a tritium laser aimed at Earth."

"Those are thousand-year scenarios," Ani said, over the growing murmur in the room.

"Unless Earth perfects Drexler-level nanomachines," Jared said.

Ani grimaced. "I understand that's highly improbable."

"Given current technology. But Earth is operating twenty to forty years beyond our leading edge, and advancing."

Loud murmurs from the room.

Ani drew in a deep breath. Damn Jared. He'd never learned when to STFU. "And this affects us how?"

"Without biomimetic and thinker tech, forget the Europa Explorer."

The room went silent.

Ah, shit. That ship was the Grand Promise. It had eaten more voluntary half-shifts than any other dream. Dozens of person-years. Ani remembered those nights back on Earth. *You can't have a perfect society without a promise—*

"We can't launch the Explorer?" someone yelled.

Jared shook his head. "We can launch it. Chances of long-term success are almost zero."

The room erupted in shouts. *What are we working for? Why didn't you tell us? Where do we go from here?*

"Shut up!" Pavig Lok said, his voice booming on the raw steel. Slowly, the room quieted down.

Ani looked at the frightened, angry faces in front of her. She didn't know what to tell them. Or if words would matter.

If we could just talk to Earth, she thought.

But she didn't dare say it.

Because that was another thing. Another part of their perfect society.

ROY PAREKH FOUND Nari Akimoto deep in a vineyard on the north end of Napa. She stood like a scarecrow, hands on hips, looking out over the rolling hills. The grapes had just been harvested; ragged vines exposed only a few sickly clusters, rapidly turning into raisins in the Indian-summer heat.

"Good harvest," Nari said, as he drew near. She'd grown thin and severe since their USC days, but she was still beautiful, in an icy way.

"Why do I have seven million dollars in my Fund of Last Resort?" Roy asked.

"Good afternoon to you, too, dear Roy," Nari said, her eyes faraway, focused on the hazy valley below.

"What have you been doing?"

Nari just smiled and leaned against a trellis.

"You actually have seven point one two million dollars in the FOLR account. One hundred thirty eight active clients and a monthly cashflow of one point two one million dollars, assuming a median policy cost of nine thousand dollars per month."

"How do you know this?" Roy said, feeling his teeth grind.

"A new datadigger. Quasipublix." Nari picked a bunch of grapes and shook it. Wrinkled proto-raisins fell off of it.

"What have you done?"

"So, you don't want this?"

No, not yet, not yet.

Nari snapped a quick, snakelike grin. "I saw that."

"What?"

"Your expression. You can thank me for giving the fund a little push."

"Tell me what you did."

Nari said nothing for a long time. "You think too small," she said. "The Rethink made things harder, but you can still play the big game. I have friends who rate policies. If you abstract the numbers on your FOLR, it looks amazing. No current debt, very low chance of payout, low investment, fits into catastrophic continuation plans."

Roy remembered that Nari had worked for AIG before the Rethink. She probably had a lot of friends. Lots and lots.

Roy shivered.

"It can even be billed as completely carbon-neutral—a great way for an exec to up his social responsibility profile."

"Only because everything's done off-world."

Nari just grinned.

"What happens when people figure it out?"

"Who says anyone will figure it out?"

When they really look at it—"

A laugh. "They're looking at it. They're wishing they came up with it. But they're also signing it. Barring a complete meltdown of the world economy—enough to make all your plans moot anyway—there's nothing to worry about. So, there's nothing to worry about."

Roy said nothing. *There was always a gotcha. Always.*

But—

—if he drew well below the median CEO salary, and if he acted in good faith to implement the FOLR, he might skate through an examination by the transparency-hawks. Even if they aired the laundry, he might be taken as a WallE, hopeless and cute and eccentric.

"What do you want?" Roy asked.

Nari grinned and pushed herself up off the trellis. She came up close to Roy and put her hands on his shoulders. Her hands were like steel cable wrapped in thin silicone.

"A world where I can do this all the time," she said. Her eyes, locked on his, were wide and serious. "A quiet world, where we don't have to worry about Napa going away."

Roy couldn't think of anything to say.

"And twenty per cent," she said.

"Of the FOLR?"

Just a grin.

"Five," Roy said.

"Ten. Or ratings start changing."

Silence for a time. Shadows drew long on the vineyard in the late afternoon, painting the hills in olive and black.

It's too early. Roy thought. Then, darker: *But it may also already be too late.*

"Done," Roy said.

ANI LOERA AND Jun Shao trudged across a gray lunar plain towards Earthside. Their rover was twenty kilometers behind them, recharging. It had taken them one hundred seventy kilometers before dying. Ani was proud. The battery packs were of Lunar manufacture, and they had performed as well as the originals from Earth.

"If we weren't a crazy isolationist paradise, we wouldn't be doing this," Jun said, puffing heavily over the suit-to-suit comm.

"I like it," Ani said.

"You like crazy isolationist paradises? That work you to death? Based on a nineteenth-century mercantile model?"

"You've been talking to Jared."

Jun said nothing.

"You haven't lived until your house is an inflatable tent covered with regolith."

"You firsters are all crazy."

"We all are."

"All I think is how much radiation I'm taking. And whether this mess will work." Jun nodded at their home-brew radio, an ugly tangle of solar cells and spidery antennae.

"It will." Jared said it would be able to receive and decode some data from Earth, but he couldn't guarantee two-way communications.

A snort. "We'll see."

"You're a pessimist, Jun."

"I'm a realist."

For a while, there was no sound other than the hiss of her breathing and the crunch of her feet on the powder. Even with the 80-kilo pack on her back and the hundred or so kilos of radio equipment, she still felt like she could fly. And that was when you got in trouble. Twenty kilometers on the moon was no short walk, even without the radio gear. The suit chafed painfully on the back of her legs. She knew she could expect big, bleeding blisters.

"Holy wow," Jun said, softly.

Ani looked up from her feet. They'd just come over a low rise. Directly ahead of them was a three-quarter Earth, suddenly blue and white in the infinite blackness of space.

What have I given up? The thought was sudden, overwhelming. Tears threatened; she squeezed them back and shook her head.

"Let's get this set up," Ani said.

Jun didn't move.

"Radiation, hoy!" she said.

Jun started. "Yeah." Softly.

They planted the radio, pointed the antenna, checked the solar panels for output, did self-tests, got linkage with the antenna back at the rover, confirmed connection with Hermes.

"Congrats," Jared's voice said. "We're getting data."

"What are we getting?"

"Too early to tell. Get back, we'll know by then."

"Gotcha."

Ani turned to take one last look at brilliant Earth. And, in doing so, she saw something she'd missed before: a line of footprints.

Ani went to look. There were two sets, one larger, one smaller. The nameprint on both soles had been obscured by tape. The stopped about halfway down the hill in a smoothed-out area.

Ani imagined a couple sitting there, looking out at the full Earth. Like a picnic. Except there was no chance of a basket full of fried chicken and a thermos of wine.

Unless they'd brought a temporary shelter.

She laughed, imagining two lovers intertwined under the full Earth. It was a billion different kinds of stupid. It was silly. It was romantic.

"Huh," Jun said, coming up beside her.

Ani punched his spacesuit. "Huh yourself."

They followed the footsteps back towards the rover. Ani couldn't stop grinning.

"So what are you going to do now?" Nari Akimoto asked. The news streamed on Roy Parekh's heads-up: *FOLR Holdings' buyout of Intelligent Risk, a Modern Insurance Company, has been accepted.* Which put him at the head of a going-on-large multinational insurance firm.

Well, him and his gang, he thought. It wasn't just him anymore. The friends from USC. The bigwigs from AIG. The guys from Morgan Stanley. *Shards of FOLR Holdings, a per cent here, a half per cent there, three per cent elsewhere.*

If Nari and Thom ever wanted to screw him—

Roy shook his head and paced in front of the big glass windows in his penthouse in the Eastern Columbia building. The lights of downtown Los Angeles spread away to the horizon, an infinite Christmas.

"Well?" Nari held up a bottle of Cristal. "Time to celebrate?"

No, Roy thought. He didn't want Intelligent Risk. It was something he had to do. Because of the gang.

But he made himself smile. "Sure."

But he didn't feel like drinking. He didn't feel like going out. He didn't want to find the latest trendy bar, painted in sharp-edged fluorescent molds and drunk on sustainability, distilling its own organic vodkas and playing grunge-remixed-happy. The record went round and round. They were still ghouls, digging up the past to recycle, one more time. If they really wanted progress, there'd be all-new music, all-new fashions, all-new ways of looking at the world. He remembered when he was a kid, the first web revolution. Yahoo and Geocities and those grocery delivery guys and Outpost were gonna remake everything, they were gonna tear everything down, it would be a whole new world.

While listening to Nirvana and Pearl Jam and wearing flannel, recycled echos of echos, and really just grabbing for the money, he thought. Meaningless in the end.

And that was the same trap he was in now. Just another cog, turning in the money machine. For a moment, he felt a deep, hot rage. He wanted to throw himself against the glass.

His heads-up buzzed. Thom. Calling to congratulate him, no doubt. He pulled it off and set it down.

"Cheers," Nari said, handing him a glass of champagne. He raised it, mechanically, and drank.

She went to a framed Digg print-out on his wall. It was a small story. USC Still Looking For Students Behind Orbital Shot. A little blurb about how a home-made launch from Downtown had gotten a tiny rocket near to orbit, and the chaos of FAA and NASA investigations.

"This was you, wasn't it?"

Roy said nothing.

Nari came and put her arms around him. "What are you going to do?"

Roy sighed. *I'm going to do my job as chairman of the largest insurance company on the planet*, he almost said. *I'm going to get old and gray, and when I die I can give a pile of cash to, well—*

Nobody. Nari didn't know he couldn't have children yet.

A sudden thought: *Or I could do something different. I still need to show good faith effort on the FOLR.*

It was an insane idea, a monument to idiocy. There was no way it would work. Even with the resources of Intelligent Risk.

But.

Goddamn it.

It was time to take the needle off the record.

He imagined his gang's reaction.

And he smiled.

THIS TIME, THE meeting was a lot smaller. Just Ani Loera, Jun Shao, and Jared Gildea. And Nils, who ignored the adults for the thrills of a game on his wriststream. A handful of onlookers stood around their table at Selene's Luck Bar. Selene's had been the first to do local beer, but wheat and barley were difficult, and hops, for whatever reason, didn't want to flower. They'd moved on to wine, which was better... as long as you didn't mind the bitter chemical twang of regolith in your Cabernet. Their local oenophile had declared the moon terroir to be "scary, alien, silicose, and profound," and said there would likely be a strong market on Earth.

But even with the small crowd, she felt the eyes. Lots of people peeping the streams, but not wanting to look at her face.

"Let's get right to the point," she said, addressing Jun and Jared. "Do we know why the shipments have stopped?"

Jared shook his head, twirling his wineglass with one hand. "Not entirely. Intelligent Risk still exists, but Roy Parekh is not listed as a stockholder."

"Dead?"

"No obituary. There's not a lot of data on him for the last five years. He appears to have become reclusive. But that doesn't explain his excision from the board. There's no corporate document recording it."

Ani shivered.

"There's also a new player, Unified Sustainability, which seems to have grown out of Intelligent Risk. And a bunch of other companies. There's a ruling from them that puts Risk Ventures spaceflight under their jurisdiction, but the terms are vague. There's nothing to indicate they've halted the launches."

"Ruling?"

Jared frowned. "They don't bill themselves as a corporation anymore. They're an 'ideals-based transnational state,' one of several large organizations with broad powers."

"Unified Sustainability, whoo, bad news," someone said. He was a dark-haired man of about thirty. Ani glanced at her tagged stream. He was listed as Whyte Kennedy, and he had come to the moon less than a year ago.

"Why?" Ani asked.

"They run the show. Lot of it, anyways. The States, Philippines, lotsa Mexico, some China. They declared the post-scarcity."

"Post-scarcity?"

Jared nodded. "They've convinced themselves they're living in a post-scarcity economy."

"To all, sufficiency. From all, sustainability," Whyte said.

Jared shook his head. "But it isn't true post-scarcity. The Gross World Product isn't any larger than it was when you left, Ani. And the population is larger."

Ani hugged herself. Spreading around limited resources wasn't post-scarcity. It also usually wasn't pretty. How thin was the spread? And who controlled it?

She remembered Roy's words, when one of the board had challenged his grandiose moonbase. *We have to be careful who we let define what is sustainable.*

"Are you scared, mommy?" Nils asked. Ani started, realizing she had been squeezing his hand tightly.

"I'm fine, Nils," she said.

To the others, she said, "This doesn't sound good."

"Earth likes to put a happy face on things, but yes, they're in trouble." Jared turned to Whyte. "Why didn't you let us know about this earlier? Why didn't anyone?"

Whyte shrugged. "We told you. Nobody believed."

"What's Earth?" Nils asked.

"Where we came from," Ani said.

"What happened?" Jun said. "They could've made their own moonbase. They could have built space elevators! We had the materials when I left, ten years ago."

"All spaceflight appears to have been consolidated in Intelligent Risk shortly after you left."

"We will not take. We will not increase." Whyte said.

Jared glanced at him. "It appears to be an ingrained thing. Propaganda."

"Or skeins," Whyte said.

"Let's leave that for now," Jared said. He glanced at Ani and mouthed, *Don't ask*.

And, for the first time since she'd landed on the moon, she actually felt fear. Earth had grown strange.

"Is it safe to assume that United Sustainability is preventing the launch of our shipments?" Ani asked.

Jared nodded. "I'd say that's a good assumption. Remember, though, the data we have is partial. There are many protocols that won't resolve down to our level. What we have is posted on the mediawiki for everyone to review."

"So we may be able to contact United Sustainability and work a deal with them?"

"I would assume so."

Whyte frowned. "No. No. No." He stood up and walked away.

Ani shook her head. It should be simple. Tell them about the Europa Explorer, tell them about the space-based economy they could build, and show them how they could have a *real* postscarcity economy. Leave out the signals from the Europan seas for the moment, because that was just icing. And the shipments would start again, and everything would be fine.

But nothing is ever that easy, is it?

THE GEEKS CAME to Roy Parekh's Special Projects basement, wearing serious masks. Inside, they were giddy.

Roy Parekh knew giddy. Or at least its less-colorful cousin, happiness. It was how he felt, every day they came a little closer to making the promise of the FOLR a reality.

The geeks worked twelve and fourteen and sixteen hour days and never complained; they left their families and lived in the Intelligent Risk Special Projects office, or picked up apartments across the street. They worked for half of what they'd been paid at their old jobs, where they'd been developing phones or planning cities or running numbers. They tracked him with their bright eyes in a scary, devoted way.

Thank you, their expressions said. *Thank you for letting us dream.*

And, at the same time, he wanted to tell them, *No, thank you. Thank you for helping me do something that isn't about passing it on to my kids, or saving the world, or getting 12% return, or avoiding carbon taxes.*

As they worked, Roy made deals.

Roy went to SpaceX, who held Intelligent Risk insurance, and said: let's joint venture to bring carbon-balanced, risk-mitigated spaceflight to place and service satellites. Also offer longer-range flights to NASA, which had just lost another Europa probe.

It made sense, but it still wouldn't work. The basic budget was insane, unimaginable.

Except Roy's pitch also happened to be the perfect thing to fling at the incoming Congress, who were looking for a way to fit the United States into a world with two and a half billion people who all thought they were middle class but weren't Americans.

Spaceflight was a dirty business, and if they could get the carbon credits and resource utilization stamps to take that over for the world, maybe America could suddenly fit, and maybe the slide would stop, maybe they could stop bulldozing the unsold homes while two or three families lived next door.

In the insanely complex world of twenty-twice, it made sense. Suddenly Intelligent Risk was de facto owner of a rocket company and backstopped by a fund that made them the largest business venture on the planet.

And that was when Roy came back to the Special Projects basement.

The geeks had put up a fogtank showing a solid projection of the moonbase, cut in layers beneath the lunar surface. The name HERMES hung above it; he nodded, he got that, his iBlasters had already told him Hermes was the greek god of animal husbandry, roads, travel, hospitality, heralds, diplomacy, trade, thievery, language, writing, persuasion, cunning wiles, athletic contests, gymnasiums, astronomy, and astrology.

"We've been thinking about the colony," a thin, dark-haired girl said. Her bright blue eyes skated off of him, as if he was radiant. His iBlasters floated her name: Ani Loera.

He nodded.

Words poured out of her. Other geeks watched from overtop cubicles. Clearly she was the sacrifice. If it didn't fly, they'd blame it on her.

It's time to do something really new, she told him. *Hit the reset button. Put the colony on the back side of the moon, so it would never face Earth. It would never receive a radio transmission or television*

*show or wireless network connection. It would be
a clean slate. They could wipe away all the insanity
of the world. Leave religion at home. Put constant
surveillance in place, but without security, open
to anyone. Let any three people try a fourth in an
ad hoc court. Governance by lottery. Issue hard
currency and put an unregulated market in place,
and count on surveillance to ensure it isn't gamed.
Let the kids grow up unfettered by everything on
Earth, everything that had come before.*

She stopped and took a deep, shaky breath, clearly
expecting an explosion.

Roy nodded. "If we do this, how do we make sure
the parents leave their own prejudices at home?"

Ani clicked her mouth shut and stammered, "Uh,
uh, its easy actually, an algorithmic search..."

"An algorithmic search of online habits can easily
be correlated with tendencies towards religion,
economic philosophy, gluttony, and many other
undesirable influences," said another geek, coming
out from the safety of his cube. "Anyone we send
up, we'll know who they are."

Ani nodded vigorously.

"Why an unregulated market?"

"It's the best way to reward individual initiative,
provided it isn't gamed." A quick sidewise glance.

Roy nodded. More geeks emerged from the cubes,
not trying to hide their grins.

"And what is this?" Roy said, pointing at a squat
cylinder concealed to the side of Hermes proper.

"That's the Asteroid Miner," Ani said.

"No, it's the Jovian Infrastructure Probe," said
someone else.

"No, it's both."

Ani waved them silent. "Every perfect society needs a goal. This is ours. We will build it. And then we'll start developing a true space-based economy."

"Using local resources." Said someone else.

"Shipping back to Earth." Another.

Roy threw back his head and laughed. "Approved!" he said.

BUT WE DIDN'T *see this one*, Ani thought, remembering that day, remembering Roy's question.

She squinted through the old-style slit in the airlock at the Last Resort. It was a tiny thing, only big enough for three people. Like the old Apollo missions. The difference was that the Last Resort could make the journey to Earth and achieve a non-destructive landing using its stubby little delta wings.

If Roy had seen that, he may have asked one final, fatal question: *So do you really believe in this, if you have to have a Last Resort?*

And now the decision was made. Sometime in the next day or two, she and Jared would head to Earth to make their case to Unified Sustainability. Or any other transnational collective that would talk to them. They'd tried contacting Earth through the tenuous radio link, but they'd been unsuccessful, or misinterpreted, or thought a prank.

Or ignored, she thought. Because the Earth was seriously changed, with transnational states squabbling with the remains of Russia, China, and Africa, as well as an alliance calling itself the United Nations with members that included most of Japan, some of Taiwan, a decent chunk of Australia, and Greenland. Most of them loudly proclaiming "Our flavor of post-scarcity is better than yours!"

But they had to try. The Europan Explorer had to launch, less for the squawks and echoes that might be intelligence under the Europan sea, more to build the economic net that would solve everyone's resource problems forever—metal from the asteroids, volatiles from Jupiter, launched by dumb slides to cascade down to the moon for automated processing, and then on to Earth.

Nils pulled on her t-shirt. "Go home!" he said.

Ani started. How long had she stood there, just gaping at the ship?

She looked down at Nils' dirty, impatient, beautiful face.

We have to make this work. We have to.

"Congratulations," Thom Lyman's ghost said. "The board of Intelligent Risk is stunned at the profits from your spaceflight monopoly."

Roy Parekh blinked and sat up in bed. His old penthouse in the Eastern Standard was cold and still, the hum of the city a distant thread beyond the walls of glass. Thom looked real, but sensors told him there was no physical person in the room, painting the information discreetly on his retinal screen. Which meant that Thom had sent a slice of himself to invade Roy's augmented reality. Roy didn't know whether he should be more irritated by the compromise of his virtual space, or a real intrusion.

"Your virtual space isn't well guarded," Thom said.

"Are you a mind-reader now?" Roy said.

"New inference algorithms."

Roy nodded and swung his legs out of bed, to sit and face Thom's figure. He hadn't seen Thom for a couple of years. His ghost looked younger than Thom in Scottsdale, that first deal, all those long years ago.

"Why the visit?" Roy asked.

"It's a sincere thank-you, from myself and Nari and everyone else on the board. You've delivered above and beyond."

"But."

Thom smiled. "But it's becoming risky."

"How so?

"Come out of your hole and take a look around. Do you know about the Balance For All Act? Have you seen the riots? The world is changing."

"I'm aware of it." But he didn't want to think about it. It had been three years since their first launch. They were running a loop around the moon every two months. Perfect for research, deep space launches, service... and for dropping carefully-selected items on the moon. Roy still met every selectee personally. He still told them the absolute truth about their chances of living and dying. And seeing those supremely competent men and women, day after day, with tears glimmering in their eyes, tears of happiness, as they saw simulations of the unending labor on the moon, and heard realistic assessments of the number of disciplines they'd have to learn, to see them leave and go on to do something so grandiose and stupid... it made him feel tiny. It made him feel very, very happy.

"And we're moving in different directions," Thom said.

"Unified Sustainability." Nari's division.

"It's an amazing new opportunity," Thom said. "Almost unlimited growth potential."

"I don't want to be a government."

"We're not a government. We're a balancing entity, ensuring peak satisfaction for all of our members."

Roy said nothing.

"You know there's an 85 per cent probability that an existing government or transnational state will take over or shut down your space-ops within the next decade?" Thom said.

"I'm optimistic."

Thom crossed his arms. "We're not. Which is why I'm here to propose something that helps all of us. Let's split the company. Intelligent Risk becomes your gig. The spaceflight company. The rest of us reorganize under the Unified Sustainability banner. Intelligent Risk is vetted by Unified Sustainability, which provides a buffer between you and the governments."

"And I will have majority stakeholder position in Intelligent Risk."

"Right."

"Which means I hold the bag of gunpowder when the hammer comes down."

"With US as a shield, the hammer may never come down."

Roy sighed. "I don't have a choice, do I?"

Thom shook his head, almost sadly. "You stopped being majority shareholder long ago."

Roy heard Nari's voice: *We're throwing you a bone. Hell, we're throwing you an entire cow. Take it.* He didn't know if it was in virtuality or in his head.

Thom tapped a foot on the floor, shifting his weight impatiently from side to side.

Roy ignored him and let his thoughts reach out through the network, bringing him data. Facts and figures came: the world economy stagnant, people in America and Europe rioting as their standard of living fell to parity with the giants of China and India, the few shining stars of technology not enough to spread across the entire world. Drexler-level nanotech wasn't working; there was some hope in biomimetics, but the technology was slow. It would take decades or centuries to grow the infinite fields of energy and resource, and that simply wasn't fast enough for people who had grown accustomed to instant answers. The inference was clear: nonessential programs would eventually be shut down. The line was broad and hazy: 2033 earliest, 2050 latest. He had somewhere between nine and twenty-six years.

And even then, he was still a salesman. He still had a hand to play.

That was enough, he thought.

"Deal," Roy said.

Thom's ghost nodded once and disappeared.

ANI PULLED HERSELF through the narrow hatch into the Last Resort. It was less than an hour before they launched, and she had to go through the final checks.

The air in the cabin smelled strange and thick. The tanks had probably been filled on Earth; the scent was foreign, alien. Ani's stomach, already twisted in knots, did another half-turn.

I have to do this, she thought.

Even though she'd seen enough of Earth. Too-happy people, smiling as they marched to the state-sized fields in the morning, or to the city-sized factories where the magic technology kept almost ten billion people clothed and housed and fed and connected. Or the others, standing guard over the deserts of slowly-growing biomimetic power and food. Or the few living in glory on depopulated islands. Tiny shards of rational groups still existed— the OpenMITers, the Progress in Time people—but they were tiny. And frequently working to perfect the technologies of the transnationals. And then there were the Anonymous groups hacking the skeins which kept a tenth of the population in check.

There was a small noise in the storage compartment behind her. Ani started. "Jun?"

Her wriststream heard the request and pulled up Jun's feed; he was still kissing his wife goodbye.

"Who's there?"

Silence. Smooth, velvet science. Then, almost at the threshold of hearing: a rapid scuff, and an intake of breath.

"Who's there!" Ani levered up out of the seat to open the storage compartment door.

It was Nils. Curled into a ball, head down, as if to make himself invisible.

"Nils!"

"I... wanna go with you!" he wailed. He jumped out of the compartment and clung to her, hugging tightly.

She smoothed his messy hair. "You can't."

"Why not?"

Because I probably won't come back. Which meant Jared might actually have to learn something about being a parent, rather than just sticking to calculations.

But she couldn't tell him that. And, looking at his tear-streaked face, she started crying.

Nils pulled back. "Why are you sad?"

"Because..." Ani began, but her voice stopped in her throat. Because she just realized how stupid she was. She couldn't go off on a suicide mission to an insane world.

I have a kid! On the moon!

Ani took her handscreen and put together a party line with all the Primes, and Jun. "I'm countermanding my own order," she told them. "I now recommend we don't waste the Last Resort on a trip to Earth."

Combined shock and relief. Jared laughed; in the background were the unfinished living areas and throngs of people. Ani noticed a lot of young people in the crowd, older kids who'd been among the first to be born on the moon. Kids fifteen and sixteen and seventeen years old. Some even younger.

"They were just voting on the same thing," he said. "We would've had a supermajority to stop the launch in another five minutes."

Relief flooded through her. "You're not upset?"

"I know a fool's game when I see one," Jared said. "And these kids are pretty adamant."

"Can we launch a comms package to Earth instead?"

Jared nodded. "We can mod an asteroid probe. Launch in a few days."

"We could even put a bottle of wine in it."

"What?"

"To make it symbolic."

"We could." Jared sounded doubtful.

"And load it with photos of all the children. Show them our potential."

"We could do that."

"Then that's what I want to do."

There was a murmur behind Jared. Jared looked around. "They're not thrilled about revealing ourselves to Earth."

"We aren't revealing ourselves. Even our inference software says they know about us."

"They're not happy."

"Run the vote."

Jared turned around. She switched to the stream from the cavern. It was packed, standing room only. She waited while Jared explained her decision to the room. In two minutes, over 95% of the vote came back. 45% didn't want to send the comms package. But 55% did.

"You won," Nils said.

Ani hugged him, long and tight.

"Yes," she said, through tears.

ROY PAREKH LIVED on a tiny island off the coast of the Phillipines. Like many of its kind, it had no name. He liked it that way. It made him feel invisible. It was the farthest he could be from the modern world and still have the connectivity he needed to run Intelligent Risk.

But he wasn't invisible. In the last decade, he'd had five visits from Unified Sustainability. Every time, they'd been very civil, very polite. Nari had come once. Thom had come another time. They'd had drinks and talked about the old days, and they'd admired his midcentury-style house in the distracted tones of people used to living on palatial estates.

And every time, they had asked for a little more. Lower costs. Less total fuel used. Lower compensation for his nonessential personnel. Lower compensation for himself, even though he was in the bottom 10% of the CEO echelon. Each time, he had given them almost everything they'd asked.

Everything except changing his schedule of launches or the circumlunar trajectory. Even though they'd put an end to all deep space exploration after the successful Europa lander and its bizarre signals, they still maintained instrumentation at Lagrange points; he argued that it would be too costly to reengineer his fleet to service only the Lagrange instrumentation; they suspected he was eavesdropping on the Europan signals, hoping for another string of primes or some other indication of intelligence.

But they let him be, and he kept giving them what they wanted. For the moment, the equation was in balance.

Roy spent the next hour in his office fully immersed in virtuality, interviewing new potential citizens of Hermes.

Their software found fewer and fewer candidates these days, as people with multiple talents and high drive were snapped up early in their careers by Unified Sustainability or one of the other transnationals. Many more had skeins. Roy wanted nothing to do with skeins. There was no telling how smart a skein was.

And then there were the genetically compromised. People outside the transnational-sponsored inoculations were known to sometimes have long bouts with the flu and come out of it thinking, well, a little differently. Being more content with their lives. Or maybe just unable to reproduce. Rewriting some of the old aggression responses, genetic sterilization— they were old tricks, but they worked.

And he knew what the transnationals would say. It is necessary. We had to do it. Too many people. Too few resources. Look at the population curve. We're blunting it. We're ensuring a future for mankind.

And the needle keeps skipping at the end of the record, he thought.

On a whim, Roy called Jasyn Torres, his head of household staff. His house was automated and intelligent and as biomimetic as possible. It didn't need a staff. But two years ago, US had made him take one household staff member per 100 square meters of floorspace. He usually let them fish the reefs; that seemed to be what they wanted to do.

Jasyn came into the office. His face was slack, free of affect.

"Do you know what a record is?"

Jaysn looked at him blankly for a moment, then smiled. "A record is an entry in a database," he said. "Or, considering your age, you may be referring to an analog music storage medium."

"Did you just read that off the net?"

"Standard ambient context-based search," Jasyn said.

"Can you talk to me like a person?"

"I am speaking to you like a person."

"No. Not with everything filtered and mediated. Can't you just talk to me, one on one, without everything going through your skein?"

"No," Jasyn said.

"Can you—be you?"

Jasyn's expression went blank for a moment. Roy envisioned data flowing through the nanonetwork grown into his head, bouncing to the mainland and back, carrying many answers.

"Yes," Jasyn said. "Most definitely."

"Aren't you sad?"

"No, not at all. We're living in the best times of the human race. We have reached post-scarcity. There is plenty for all."

"But we aren't moving forward!"

"Post-scarcity is stability," Jasyn said.

"But this isn't post-scarcity."

"Enough for all is post-scarcity." Smiling.

Roy forced himself to mimic Jasyn's smile. "Thanks. You can go."

Jasyn nodded and left. Roy sat at his desk and stared out into his large, brilliant house, seeing nothing. *Beware the best of intentions. Especially when they make too much sense.*

"Skip, skip," he said softly.

THE *PEACE PIPE* entered orbit around the Earth quietly and without drama, and began reporting its progress to the moon. It was a smart piece of equipment by Hermes' standards, smart enough to try to communicate with any network it could find. Despite its sophistication, many of the communications protocols were beyond its capabilities, impenetrable and alien. Most never even acknowledged the *Peace Pipe*'s overtures. Some rejected it outright.

But a few did. And a few of those said, *Talk to us*.

The *Peace Pipe* told them of Hermes and its thirteen hundred inhabitants. It sent pictures of the children. It offered a single bottle of lunar wine, if the people of Earth would come to orbit to collect it. It promised peace.

The protocols listened intently, acknowledging every packet.

"Someone is hearing us!" said the kids. The adults, including Ani, shook their heads. Acknowledging wasn't hearing. And even hearing wasn't understanding.

But when Jared went to stand in front of the stream and rail at them, Ani said, "No."

"Why not?"

"It's their time. Don't discourage them."

"They don't understand! They think everything can be fixed with more work."

"What else has ever fixed anything?" she said, softly. In the last week, the teens had stepped up. They'd worked extra shifts in the farm. They'd gone to Jared's labs to help. They'd hit the old problems lists with a new eye, and they'd suggested a lot of things they could do. Most of which probably wasn't workable. But to discover that there was still enthusiasm—it was thrilling.

Jared was silent for a long time. When he spoke, his voice was unusually quiet. "Why did you come here?" he asked her.

Ani shrugged and looked away. "I don't know."

She could feel his gaze, hot, on the back of her neck. *You don't throw your life away on an 'I don't know,'* that gaze said.

"Why did you?" Ani asked.

Jared laughed. "Anyone with half a brain knows that. Because I'm an asshole. I poke holes in things. Everyone hates me. Of course I'm here."

Ani sighed. "I don't know," she said, finally.

"What do you mean, 'I don't know?'"

"I mean, I don't know. I didn't have a terrible childhood or get raped by my boyfriend or screwed out of an inheritance, or any of those easy answers. I just—I've just always wanted to do something just, well, incredibly crazy."

"You could've picked skydiving."

Ani shook her head. "I always wanted to make something, something important."

"I can't believe it's that simple."

"Why not?" she turned back to him. "Why can't there just be something in our genes that makes us want to see what's over the next ridge? Why does it always have to be some trauma? My dad, he did genetic research on plants. Corn. He never believed me either. Said, 'Genes aren't programs.' But if it isn't that, what?"

"What are your specialties?"

"Chemical engineering, functional physics, and American literature."

Jared nodded and said nothing.

"What are you thinking?"

"Just how amazing we all are."

Ani shook her head. "I don't think we're amazing. I think we're what we have to be. And I think our children will be what they have to be. Which will probably be a lot more than we are."

The next morning, they lost the link with the *Peace Pipe*. There had been no indication of a malfunction. It was just suddenly not there.

She imagined a tiny flash, blooming over Earth.

And wondered what the kids would do.

UNIFIED SUSTAINABILITY CAME to get Roy Parekh in the same way it always did. Two men, one small and soundless boat. Except this time it wasn't business suits and briefcases. They walked into his office holding small, silver guns. In his retinal displays, the two men had no names, no tags.

"Is it that time?" he asked.

The two men blinked and paused. One of them said, "Your statement suggests a certain level of awareness of your crimes. Do you wish to state them?"

"Will it assist in my trial?"

"There will be no trial."

"Then why would I want to talk to you?"

A pause. Then: "Unified Sustainability hereby seizes all assets and operations of Intelligent Risk. Roy Parekh, you are charged with crimes against humanity, specifically, the redirection of an unspecified but significant amount of engineered resources for the purpose of constructing an extraterrestrial base of operations."

And that was it. Some algorithm had coughed up red, or Nari and Thom and the rest had just had a bad day, or some Anonymi were shouting about the moon again. Whatever the trigger was, it was over. It was done.

In Roy's retinal screens, he saw SOLR wake up. His software, his Solution of Last Resort. He blinked an okay-to-deploy, and watched as Intelligent Risk's dashboard began blinking red.

The two men jumped. "What are you doing?" one cried.

Roy smiled. SOLR wasn't subtle. It wasn't a worm or a virus. It was just a good old-fashioned trigger, wired into good old-fashioned explosives in his most sensitive datacenters. And in his launch facilities in New Mexico and Ecuador. And into his launch vehicles. He imagined the explosions and the flames.

There was a sharp thunderclap and Roy was thrown backwards. He flew over his desk, marveling for an instant at the reproduction Wright chandelier. He landed on his back and looked down at a large bloody hole in his chest. He laughed and saw bubbles popping in his own blood, like lava. He felt nothing.

I'm sorry I can't say goodbye, he thought, thinking of all the people on the moon.

Faces flickered in front of him. So many determined people. They would not fail.

"Hello, iPod," he said, and died.

ANI LOERA DIDN'T believe what she was seeing on the streams, so she went down to the chamber that housed the Europan Explorer and its half-built twin, Jove's Dream. The chamber was never meant to be pressurized, so she slammed through putting on her surface suit as quickly as possible.

When she stepped into the chamber, her breath caught.

Standing in ranks in front of the Europan Explorer were over a hundred spacesuit-clad figures. Their names scrolled on her wriststream. Almost all of them were eighteen or under.

Which meant they made the spacesuits themselves, she thought. Making suits for kids still growing was an amazing extravagance—not unknown, but not usual.

They made the suits themselves.

Ani could see no faces behind the silver visors, but names were sewn neatly onto their chests. She walked up to one of the tallest, whose name was James Kinoshita. Dr. Kinoshita's son.

"What are you doing?" she asked, over the suit comm.

"We're volunteering," James said. "If you think the Europan Explorer mission is too risky, we'll take it."

A muted chorus grew on the comms. "Yeah." "It's our future." "We'll take the risk."

For a moment, two emotions fought in Ani's chest: an almost ecstatic sense of pride, coupled with a deep, sharp fear. *These kids would do whatever it takes! These kids would die trying!*

"You've heard Jared—uh, Dr. Gildea's analysis," Ani said. "He doesn't think we can get a workable economy without biomimetic tech and thinkers to optimize it."

"We've run the same simulations!" one of the kids said. "It's not impossible. Human oversight can replace the thinkers. And human labor can replace the bio-m. Bio-m is slow. We could build a workable machine economy in a hundredth the time."

"Even if it's cast-iron huts and 1980's-level integrated circuits," James said. "We're ready for it."

"You're ready to camp on an asteroid?"

"We did it before. Apollo."

Ani grimaced. Apollo was luck. Flying to the moon with near vacuum-tube technology.

"You're ready to die?" she asked.

Silence for a moment. Then. "There's nowhere else for us." A girl's voice, soft and low.

Ani nodded. Thinking of Earth. Thinking of them snuffing out their little *Peace Pipe*.

And in that moment, she could feel all of the eyes on her. All of the eyes of all of the people on the moon. Watching and waiting for her response.

"No," she said. "You're not going."

A nervous shuffle. "You're... not letting us?" James asked.

"Not by yourselves," she said. And smiled.

ROY PAREKH WOKE in a little room with gray-painted walls and sterile stainless steel furniture. He could not feel his body. His vision faded in and out of focus. He tried to move. He might as well have been made of wood.

I died, he thought.

And they brought you back, came a voice. A familiar voice. Thom.

Roy Parekh tried to open his mouth to speak, but nothing moved.

Don't try. There's not much of you left. Just think.

What's happening?

They need some facts. You caught them a bit off guard. You like Last Resorts, don't you?

Wait. *They?*

A feeling of frustration from Thom. Then: *I came to give you this.*

There was a strange sensation. A woman's voice, vaguely familiar, chattered in Roy's head. It said things about the moon. Images came: children's faces. Families, standing against gray steel bulkheads and mugging for the camera. Some kind of feast in a gaudily-painted bar. Kids clutching little stuffed animals. People in spacesuits.

Roy felt his heart explode. He tried to cry. No tears came. *This is what I made*, he thought.

Why didn't you go with them? Thom asked.

Because look what I did here, Roy thought. Because they deserved better than me. Because, at the very end of things, I am still a monster.

You crazy bastard, Thom said. Behind his words was a sadness, a finality.

Is Unified Sustainability going to work with them? Roy asked.

What do you think?

No.

Your grasp of human nature is still solid. Thom seemed amused.

What did they dredge out of me? Roy asked.

What they needed.

What?

Goodbye, Roy.

Tell me!

Silence from Thom. Roy could still sense his presence, though.

That's enough, another voice came.

Who are you?

I am the combined voice of Unified Sustainability. I am the one who allowed the whim of your friend. The voice was precise and distant. Roy wondered if it was a thinker or a human being.

What did you dig out of my mind?

The location of Hermes. Also, enough information to repair and re-equip one of your damaged launch vehicles.

But you aren't going there to trade with them.

No.

And that was all.

ON THE EVE of the launch of the Europa Explorer, Ani felt a single sharp shock and a deep rumble. Hermes creaked and groaned, and air leak alarms flared red all over.

Overworked kids and adults alike scrambled to patch the hallways and chambers as the streams from the external cameras told the story: a bright light had flared to the south. In the near-vacuum of the Moon's atmosphere, the classic mushroom cloud shape was flattened.

"They nuked us," she said, and immediately regretted it, because she was still Prime, and she was still on-stream, and people would take that, and replay it again and again, and laugh.

"Yeah, looks like they hit the drop point," Jun Shao said, over the public stream.

"Should we be worried?" she asked.

"It's twenty klicks away. It'll raise the background radiation on the surface a bit, but we're fine."

"Why would they nuke the drop point?"

"Remember the original plans," Marie Middleton, the head of infrastructure, popped in. "They wanted the drop point right on top of Hermes. I told 'em we should move it."

"I told them to move it," Jared cut in.

"No, I did!"

"I did!"

Ani frowned, then laughed. If everyone wanted to be a hero, let them be heroes.

Then she frowned again. "What happens if they send more bombs, just to be sure?"

Jared cut into the stream. "News from Earth is that Unified Sustainability is in a skirmish right now with a half-dozen other transnationals. Maybe prompted by their launch. Maybe prompted by the *Peace Pipe*. I don't want to do any two-way comms at all. Best we kill the link and stay silent, so they think we're gone."

Murmured assent. The vote came back quickly, over 80% in favor of cutting the link.

In time, the conversation finally came back the Europa Explorer.

"What do we do about the Explorer?" they asked.

Ani smiled. That was an easy question. Like the kids said. There's nowhere else we belong.

"We launch," she said.

And they did.

Summer Ice

Holly Phillips

HOLLY SENT ME *"Summer Ice,"* and while I knew
about her, and had read a few of her stories in
On Spec, *I wasn't quite as aware of her talent as
I should have been. So when I got around to
reading her submission (full disclosure: Holly had
mentioned that it had been published before, but
I read the story much later, having forgotten most
of the accompanying email—which I always read
again when sending out my response) I forgot it was
a reprint (for which I was open, if it wasn't too high
profile).*

*The story immersed me, fully. I distinctly
remember thinking, about halfway through, this is
'almost' exactly the kind of story I'm looking for.
At that point I was about to send out an acceptance.
But I re-read her email, to be reminded that it had
been published before: originally in her collection*
The Palace of Repose, *reprinted in the very first issue
of* Fantasy Magazine, *and reprinted again in Prime's*
The Year's Best Fantasy *of 2006.*

*So I checked out reviews of it online, to see if
they agreed with my perception of the story. What I*

found, intriguingly, was that the majority of reviews viewed it as a fantasy story (not unexpected seeing the venues it was reprinted in). Well, on that point I disagree: to me "Summer Ice" is firmly near future optimistic SF.

Yes, Manon—the protagonist—feels like a stranger in a strange city, and is very uneasy at first. Yes, the (unnamed) city is suffering the ill effects of climate change. But in the end, most people try to cope with the changes, and change their lifestyles, as well. And in the end, Manon does accept it as her new home.

Hard fought victories are the best, and that's why I'm glad to be an optimist.

She dissipated the past. Footsteps walking reclaimed beaches. Grinned as seagulls abandoned all worship of trash to instead hunt fish.

—Jason Sanford—

TODAY MANON ARRIVES at a different time, and sits at a different table. Her sketchbook stays in her bag: a student had lingered after class to show her his portfolio of drawings and her mind is full of his images. Thick charcoal lines smudged and blended without much room for light. She has not found solace in her own work since she moved to the city and began to teach. Her life has become a stranger to her, she and it must become reaquainted. She has always been tentative with strangers. Art has become tentative with her.

The table she sits at today is tucked against the wall opposite the glass counter that shields long tubs of ice cream. Summer sunlight is held back from the window by a blue awning, but it glazes the trolley tracks in the street. Heat shimmers above chipped red bricks. Inside, the walls are the colors of sherbet, patched paint rippled over plaster, and the checkerboard floor is sticky. Children come and go, keeping the counterman busy. He is dark in his damp white shirt and apron, his hands drip with flavors as he wields his scoop. An electric fan blows air past his shaved head. Through a doorway behind him Manon sees someone walk toward the back of the store, a man as dark but older, slighter, with tight gray hair and a focused look.

Manon scoops vanilla from her glass bowl and wonders at the fan, the hard cold of the ice cream. This small store must be rich to afford so much electricity in a power hungry town. She imagines the latest in roof solars, she imagines a freezer crowded with dessert and mysterious frozen riches. The dark man in white clothes behind curved glass is an image, a movement, that defies framing. A challenge. Her sketchbook stays in her bag. The last of her ice cream hurts the back of her skull. She does not want to go back to the apartment that has not yet and may never become home.

The stream of customers pauses and the counterman drops his scoop in a glass of water and turns his back on the tables to wash his hands. Through the doorway Manon sees the older man open the freezer door. She catches a glimpse of a dark, half empty space: part of a room through a door through a door behind glass. Depth and cold, layers of distance. The fan draws into the storefront a chill breeze that dies a moment after the freezer door slams shut. Manon rises and takes her bowl to the counter. The young man thanks her, and as she turns to the door he says, "See you."

"See you," she says. She steps into the gritty heat and carries with her the image of dimness, depth, cold. The memory of winter, except they don't have winters like that here.

IN THE WINTER Manon and her sister tobogganed down the hill behind their mother's house. Snow would sometimes fall so thickly it bowed the limbs of pine trees to the ground, muffling charcoal-green needles in cozy coats of white. Air blended with cloud, snowy ground with air, until there was nothing but white, shapes and layers and emptinesses of white, and the plummet down the hill was a cold dive on swan wings and nothing. Manon and her sister tumbled off at the bottom, exalted, still flying despite the snowmelt inside cuffs and boots. Perhaps to ground themselves they burrowed down until they found the pebbled ice of the stream that would sing with frogs come spring. Black lumpy glass melted slick and mirroring beneath their breath and tongues. Then they would climb the hill, dragging the rebellious toboggan behind them, and begin the flight again.

THE CITY IS still greening itself, a slow and noisy process. Pneumatic drills chatter the cement of Manon's street, tools in the hands of men and women who seem to revel in the work, the noise, the destruction of what others once labored to build. The art school is already surrounded by a knot-work of grassy rides and bicycle paths and trolley ways, buildings are crowned with gardens, the lush summer air is bright with birds and goat bells, but Manon's neighborhood is rough with dust that smells of dead automobiles, the dead past. She skirts piles of broken pavement, walks on oily dirt that will have to be cleaned and layered with compost before being seeded, and eases herself under the plastic sheet the landlord has hung over the front door to keep out the grime. A vain attempt, all the tenants have their windows open, hopeful of a cooling breeze.

Manon opens the bathtub tap and lets a few liters burble into the blue enamel bowl she keeps over the brown-stained drain. The darkness of the clear water returns the image of the frozen stream to her mind. She takes off her dusty clothes and steps into the tub, strokes the wet sponge down her skin. The first touch is a shock, but after that not nearly cool enough. The bathroom is painted Mediterranean blue, the window hidden by a paper screen pressed with flowers. It smells of dampness, soap, old tiles, some previous tenant's perfume. Manon squeezes the sponge to send a trickle down her spine. Black pebbled ice. Layers of distance. The counterman's eyes.

She turns her attention to her dirty feet, giving the structures of imagery peace to build themselves in the back of her mind, in a place that has been empty for too long.

IRA, THE LANDLORD of Manon's building, has been inspired by the work racketing in the street below. Even though the parking lot that once serviced the four-story building has already been converted to a garden (raised beds of the same dimensions as the parking spaces, each one assigned to the appropriate apartment) Ira has decided that the roof must be greened as well.

"Native plants," he says at the tenant meeting, "that won't need too much soil or water." That way he can perform the conversion without reinforcing the roof.

Lupe, Manon's right-hand neighbor, says as they climb the stairs, "The old faker. Like we don't know he only wants the tax rebate."

"It will mean a reduction in rent, though, won't it?" Manon says.

Lupe shrugs skeptically, but there are laws about these things. And anyway, Manon likes Ira's enthusiasm, whatever its source. His round pink face reminds her of a ripening melon. She also likes the idea of a meadow of wild grass and junipers growing on the other side of her ceiling. Lupe invites her over for a beer and they talk for a while about work schedules ("We'll have to make sure the men do their share, we always do, they're a bunch of bums in this building," Lupe says) and splitting the cost and care of a rabbit hutch ("'Cause I don't know about you," Lupe says, "but I'd rather eat a bunny than eat *like* a bunny."). Then Lupe's son comes home from soccer practice and Manon goes back to her place. The evening has gone velvety blue. In the quiet she can hear a trolley sizzle a few blocks away, three different kinds of music, people talking by open windows. She lies naked on her bed and thinks about Ira's plans and Lupe's earthy laughter so she doesn't have to wonder when she'll sleep.

THE ART SCHOOL can't afford to pay her much. The people who run the place are her hosts as much as her employers, the work space they give her counts as half her salary. She has no complaints about the room, tall, plaster-walled, oak-floored, with three double-hung windows looking north and east up a crooked street, but her tools look meager in all this space. She feels meager herself, unable to supply the quantity of life the room demands. *Create!* the bare walls command. *Perform!* She carries the delicate lattice of yesterday's images like a hollow egg into the studio, hopeful, but cannot decide where to put it down. Paper, canvas, clay, all inert, doors that deny her entry. She paces, she roams the halls. Other people teach to the sound of industry and laughter. She teaches her students as if she were teaching herself how to draw, making every mistake before stumbling on the correct method. Unsure whether she is doing something necessary or cowardly, or even dangerous to her discipline, she leaves the building early and walks on grass and yellow poppies ten blocks to her other job.

During the years of awkward transition from continental wealth to continental poverty, the city's parks were abandoned to flourish or die. Now, paradoxically, as the citizens sow green across the cityscape these pockets of wilderness are being reclaimed. Lush lawns have been shoved aside by boisterous crowds of wild oats and junipers and laurels and manzanita and poison oak and madrone and odorous eucalyptus trees shedding strips of bark and long ribbon leaves that crumble into fragrant dirt. No one expects the lawns to return. The city does not have the water to spare. But there are paths to carve, playgrounds and skateboard parks and benches to uncover, throughways and resting places for a citizenry traveling by bike and foot. It's useful work, and Manon mostly enjoys it, although in this heat it is a masochistic pleasure. The crew she is assigned to has been working together for more than a year, and though they are friendly people she finds it difficult to enter into their unity. The fact that she only works with them part-time does not make it easier.

Today they are cleaving a route through the wiry tangle of brush that fills the southwest corner of the park. Bare muscular branches weave themselves into a latticework like an unsprung basket, an organic form that contains space yet has no room for storage. Electric saws powered by the portable solar generator buzz like wasps against dead and living wood. Thick yellow sunlight filters through and is caught and stirred by dust. Birds and small creatures flurry away from the falling trees. A jay chooses Manon to harangue as she wrestles with a pair of long-handled shears. Blisters start up on her hands, sweat sheets her skin without washing away debris, and her eye is captured again and again by the woven depths of the thicket, the repeated woven depths hot with sun and busy with life, the antithesis of the cold layered ice of yesterday. She drifts into the working space that eluded her in the studio, and has to be called repeatedly before she stops to join the others on their break.

Edgar says, "Do you ever get the feeling like they're just growing in again behind your back? Like you're going to turn around and there's going to be no trail, no nothing, and you could go on cutting forever without getting out?"

"We have been cutting forever," Anita says.

"Like the prince who has to cut through the rose thorns before he can get to the sleeping princess," Gary says.

"That's our problem," Anita says. "We'll never get through if we have no prince."

"You're right," Gary says. "All the other guys that tried got stuck and left their bones hanging on the thorns."

"Man, that's going to be me, I know it." Edgar tips his canteen, all the way up, empty. "Well, come on, the truck's going to be here in an hour, we might as well make sure it drives away full..."

The cut branches the crew has hauled to the curbside lace together like the growing chaos squared, all their leaves still a living green. As the other three drag themselves to their feet, Manon says, "Do you think anyone would mind if I took a few branches home?"

Her crewmates glance at each other and shrug.

"They're just going to city compost," Edgar says.

Manon thanks him. They go back to work in the heavy heat of late afternoon.

SHE KNEELS TO wash spiders and crumbs of bark out of her hair, the enamel basin precarious on the rim of the tub. Lupe and her son have guests for dinner. Manon can hear talk and laughter and the clatter of pans, and the smell of frying and hot chilies slips redolent under her door. She should be hungry, but she is too tired to cook, and is full with loneliness besides. Her sister's partner introduced the family to spicy food. He cooked Manon a celebratory dinner when she got this job at the art school, and everyone who was crowded around the small table talked a lot and laughed at jokes that no one outside the family would understand. They were pleased for her, excited at the thought of having someone in the southern city, a preliminary explorer who could set up a base camp for the rest. Her sister had promised she would visit this summer before she got too big to travel, but the last Manon had heard they were in the middle of suddenly necessary roof repairs and might not be able to afford the fare. Manon puts on a favorite dress and goes with wet hair into the dusk that still hovers between sunset and blue. It is hard to look at the rubbled street and not think of armies invading.

The ice cream shop is dim behind glass, but the open sign is still in the window so she goes in. Bad to spend her money on treats, bad to eat dessert without dinner, bad to keep coming back to this one place as if she has nowhere else in the whole city to go. There is no one behind the counter, no one at the tables—well, it is dinner time—or perhaps the sign is meant to say "closed." But then the older man with tight gray curls comes through the inner doorway and smiles and asks her what he can get for her. Vanilla, she says, but with a glance for permission he adds a scoop of pale orange.

"Lemon-peach sorbet," he says. "It's new, tell me what you think."

She tastes it standing there at the counter. "It's good."

He nods as if he'd been waiting for her confirmation. "We make everything fresh. My cousin has trees outside the city."

"It's really good."

He busies himself with cleaning tasks and she sits at the table by the wall. Despite the unfolding night, he does not turn on any lights. When the counter's glass is spotless he steps outside a moment, then comes in shaking his head. "Still hotter out there than it is in here." He lets the door close.

While Manon eats her ice cream, the vanilla exotic and rich after the sorbet, he scrapes round chocolate scoops from the bottom of a tub and presses them into a bowl. He takes the empty tub to the back, and she sees the shift of white door and darkness as he opens the freezer. The fan snares the cold and casts it across the room, so the hairs on her arms rise. The freezer has its own light and she can see the ice cream man shifting tubs, looking for more chocolate. There is a lot of room, expensive to keep cold, and what looks like a door to the outside insulated by a silver quilt. When he comes back with the fresh tub and drops it into its place behind the counter, she gets up and carries over her empty bowl. "Thanks. The peach was really good."

"Good while it lasts. You can only make it with fresh fruit." He rubs his hands together as he escorts her to the door. "Time for the after-dinner rush," he says, and he flips on the lights as she steps outside.

It is still hotter out than in.

THE HOUSE AT the top of the tobogganing hill grew long icicles outside the kitchen window. Magical things, they were tusks/spears/wands to Manon and her sister. The side yard was trampled by the playful feet of white boars that could tell your fortune, and warriors that clad themselves in armor so pure they were invisible against the snow, and witches who could turn your heart to ice and your body to stone, or conjure you a cloak of swan's down and a hat of perfect frost. Two angels, one a little bigger than the other, lay side by side and spread their wings, giggling at the snow that slipped down their collars, and struggled to rise without marring the imprints of their bodies, their pinions heavy with snow. Thirsty with cold and the hard work of building the warriors' fortress, they would snap off the sharp ends of their tusks/spears/wands and with their tongues melt them by layers as they had grown, water slipping over a frozen core, almost but not quite clear, every sheath catching a bit of dirt from the roof, or a fleck of bark, a needle-tip of pine. Half a winter down their throats, too cold, leaving them thirstier than before.

MANON DOES HER share for the roof garden on the evenings of her teaching days. Her other job has made her strong, and the physical work helps drive out the difficulties of the day. Too many of her students are older than she is, she hasn't figured out how to make them believe her judgments and advice. Or perhaps they are right not to believe her, perhaps she is too young, or too inept. Lupe's son shovels dirt from the pile left in the alley by the municipal truck, loading a wheelbarrow that he pushes through the garden beds to the bucket which he fills so Manon can haul it up on the pulley and dump the contents in the corner where Lupe leans with her rake. The layers of drainage sheets, pebbles, sand have already been put down by the tenants on other floors. Dirt is the fourth floor's responsibility.

"I've got the easy job," Lupe says again as Manon dumps the heavy bucket. "Let's switch."

Manon grins. Lupe is in her forties, graying and soft. Manon has muscles that spring along her bones, visible under her tanned skin in the last slant of sun. It feels good to drop the bucket down to Marcos, warm slide of rope through her hand, and then heave it up again, competent, strong. Lupe rakes with elegant precision, a Zen nun with a haywire braid crown and a T-shirt with a beer slogan stretched across her breasts. The third floor tenants have spread the sand too unevenly for her liking and she rakes it, too, in between bucket loads of soil. Marcos and Manon, communicating by the zizz of the dropping bucket and the thump of shoveled dirt, decide to force Lupe to abandon her smooth contours. She catches on and grins fiercely, wielding her rake with a virtuosic flourish. They work until Marcos, four stories down, is only a shadow among the lighter patches of garden green. Then they go to Lupe's apartment for beer and spicy bean tacos.

"Don't worry about the dirt," Lupe says. "Living with a teenage boy is like living in a cave anyway."

Marcos scowls at her and slopes off to his room.

Lupe rolls her eyes. "Have another beer. And try the salsa, it's my mother's recipe. She always makes this one with the first tomatoes from the garden."

MANON HAD TAKEN the branches from the park to her studio, and this morning she carries a canvas knapsack full of left-over roof pebbles to join them. The strap is heavy on her aching shoulder. She isn't strong enough yet not to feel the pain of work. Spilled on the wood floor the stones, some as small as two knuckles, some as big as her fist, look dull and uninteresting, although she chose them with care. Next to the twisted saw-cut branches of manzanita and red madrone, they look like what they are: garden trash. She kicks them into a roughly square beach and tries binding the branches with wire, an unsturdy contraption that more or less stands on its own, footed in pebbles. She steps back.

Weak, clumsy, meager. The word keeps recurring in this room. Meager.

She has to teach a class.

Life drawing is about volume and line. She tells her students to be hasty. "Throw down the lines, capture some space, and move on. Be quick," she says. "Quick!" And then watches them frown earnestly over painstaking pencils while the model sits, naked and patient, and reads her book.

"Look," Manon tells them. She takes her pad and a pencil and sweeps her hand, throwing down the lines. "Here, here, here. Fast! A hint, a boundary, a shape. Fast!" Her hand sweeps and the figure appears. It's so easy! See the line and throw it down.

They don't get it. They look at her sketch with admiration and dismay, and are more discouraged than before.

"Start again," she says.

They start again, painstaking and frowning.

After class she goes back to her studio and takes apart the pathetic bundle of wired twigs. Meager! She doesn't get it either.

Lupe has a meeting, Marcos has soccer. Manon spends some time in her garden bed, weeding herbs and carrots and beans. She uncovers an astonishing earthworm, a ruddy monster as thick as her thumb that lengthens absurdly in its slow escape. Mr. Huang from the second floor comes out and gives her a dignified nod as he kneels to weed his mysterious greens. Manon's mother always planted carrots and beans, but Manon's carrots don't look right, the delicate fronds have been seared by the sun. Mr. Huang's greens, like Lupe's tomatoes, burgeon amongst vivid marigolds. The blossoms are as orange as the eyes of the pigeons Lupe strings netting against thieves worse than raccoons and wandering goats. Manon's tidy plot is barren in comparison. She has planted the wrong things, planted them too late, something. When she goes in she finds a message from her sister on her telephone.

Sorry I missed you. It looks like I might not be coming after all...

ONE OF THE other art teachers has a show opening in a gallery across town. Manon finds a note about it in her box in the staff room, a copied invitation, everyone has one. She carries it up to her studio where she is confronted by the mess of branches and stones. The madrone cuttings have begun to lose their leaves, but the red bark splits open in long envelope mouths to reveal pistachio green. She picks up a branch, carries it around the room, pacing, thinking. Nothing comes but the reminder of someone else's show. The teacher is one she likes, an older man with a beard and a natural tonsure. She has thought about asking him for advice on her classes, but has not, yet. He was on her hiring committee. She knows he did not invite her especially, but it would be rude not to go. She puts the branch down and digs into her bag to consult her trolley timetable.

She cuts brush in the park again this afternoon, and is relieved to find that her vision of layered space and interstitial depth repeats itself. Branches crook and bend to accommodate each other, red tawny gray arms linked in a slow maneuver, a jostle for sky. She thinks back to her studio and realizes she has missed something crucial. Something. She works her shears, then wrestles whole shrubs out of the tangle without stopping to cut them smaller, determined on frustration. When, on their break, Edgar asks if she is going to join the rest of the crew for a beer after work, she tells them she has a friend's opening to attend. Then berates herself, partly for the 'friend,' partly because now she will have to go.

SHE WEARS HER favorite dress again, the long blue one patterned with yellow stars, the one her sister gave her. The trolley is crowded, the windows all wide open. She stands and has to cling to a strap too high for her, her arms and shoulders hurting, the hot breeze flickering through the armholes of the dress. A young man admires her from a seat by the door, but she would rather be invisible. The trolley car sways past lighted windows, strolling pedestrians, a startled dog that has escaped its leash. She has never been to the gallery before. She only realizes she has missed her stop when one of the bright windows blinks an image at her, a colorful canvas with the hint of bodies beyond. She eases past the admiring boy, steps down, and has to walk back four blocks. She remembers how tired she is, remembers she won't really know anyone there. The sunwarmed bricks breathe up her bare legs in the darkness.

Karl, the artist whose show this is, is surrounded by well-wishers. Manon gives him a small wave, but cannot tell if he sees her. The gallery is a remodeled house with many small rooms, and there are many people in each one. Every corner sports an electric fan so the air rushes around, bearing odors of bodies, perfume, wine the way the waiters bear trays of food and drink. They are casual in T-shirts and jeans, while most of the guests have dressed up, to be polite, to have fun. The people stir around, looking at the canvases on the walls, looking for friends, talking, laughing, heating up the rumpled air, and they impart a notion of animal movement to the paintings. Karl works in pillows of color traced over by intricate lines. Nets, Manon decides, to keep the swelling colors contained. She likes the brightness, the warmth, the detail of brushwork and shading, but recognizes with a tickle of chagrin that she still is more fond of representative than abstract art. Immature, immature. She takes a glass of wine and then wishes she hadn't. She is thirsty for water or green tea, for air that has not been breathed a hundred times. She decides she will pay her respects to Karl and go.

"Hi!" one of the waiters says.

"Hi?" Manon says, and then realizes the young man with the dark face glossy with heat is the counterman from the ice cream store. "Oh, hello."

"I wasn't sure you'd remember me," he says. He rearranges glasses to balance his tray.

"Of course I do," she says, then wonders why of course.

"Big crowd," he says.

"Yes, it's good."

"Good for business. We do the catering, my family I mean."

Someone takes one of the full glasses on his tray and he rebalances the rest.

Manon looks for something to say. "I teach with Karl. At the art school."

"Who's Karl?"

"The artist?"

"Oh." They both laugh. He says, "I'm Luther, by the way."

"Manon."

"It's nice to meet you."

She smiles.

"Well, I'd better get back to work. I'll see you around, huh?"

"Yes."

Luther raises his tray and turns sideways to slip between two groups of talkers, then glances back at her. "Manon?"

"Right."

He grins and eases himself into his round. Manon smiles. A lot of people don't get her name the first time around.

She works her way into Karl's circle and he introduces her around as 'the brilliant new artist we managed to snare before some place with real money snapped her up.'

LUPE DECIDES TO make a pond for the roof garden with left over plastic sheeting and stones. She and Manon dig out a hollow in the dirt, line it with plastic, fill the bottom with pebbles from the left-over pile. Ira the landlord, who is impatient to sow some seeds, points out that it will have to be filled by hand in the dry season. Lupe smiles with implausible sweetness and says she knows. When he bustles off on other business, Lupe goes downstairs to fill the bucket at the garden tap, leaving Manon to haul it up on the pulley. The first time, Lupe fills the bucket too full and gets a muddy shower when Manon starts to pull (her swearing sounds more fiery than her salsa) so after that she only fills it halfway, which means Manon is raising and carrying and pouring and lowering until dark. She doesn't mind. The sky is a deep arch of blue busy with evening birds, and there is something good about working with water, which has voice and character but no form. The wet pebbles glow with color and the water swirls, the pond growing layer by layer, dark mirror and clear window all at the same time. She goes to bed with that image in her mind.

AT THE END of winter Manon and her sister dug out the stream at the bottom of the tobogganing hill, as if by their excavations they could hasten spring. The packed toboggan run stood above the softer sublimating snow, a ski-jump track grubby with sled-marks. They walked down this steep ramp, stomping it into steps with their boot soles, and at the bottom frayed their wool mittens by terrier digging. The ice revealed was a mottled shield over mud and sand. Suspended brown leaves made stilled layers of time out of the fall's spilling water. Although Manon and her sister would never drink from the summer stream, they broke wafers of ice free from the edges of stones and reeds and melted them on their tongues. There was always a muddy, gritty taste. The flavor of frogs, Manon's sister insisted, which made Manon giggle and squeal, but did not prevent her from drinking more ice. She always looked, too, for the frogs buried under ice and mud, waiting, but never saw them. The first she ever knew of them was their tentative peeping after dark in the start of spring.

LUTHER IS BEHIND the counter when she returns to the ice cream store a day or two after Karl's opening. He has a cheerful smile for the succession of customers (the store is busy today) but lights up especially when he sees Manon standing in line.

"Hi!" he says. "Vanilla, right? It'll be just a second."

"I'm in no hurry," she says. He has lovely eyes, dark and thickly lashed.

"So, Manon," he says when he hands her the dish, "can you stick around for a little while? My dad's out on a delivery, but he wanted to talk to you, and he should be back soon."

"Talk to me?"

Luther grins. "We have a proposition to make." Then, as if worried he has been too familiar, "I mean, about work, about maybe doing some work for us. As an artist."

There is a boisterous family behind her deciding on flavors. She smiles and shrugs. "I'll be around."

"Great," he says. "Great!" And then the family is giving him their requests.

Engaged by curiosity, she doesn't mind sitting at the narrow counter shelf at the back of the room. She feels as if last night's work, last night's idea, has turned a switch, shunted a trolley from a siding to the street, set her running back on the tracks of her life. A happy feeling, but precarious: it is, after all, only an idea. Even good ideas sometimes die. But this idea inside her head has met its reflection (perhaps) in the ideas of the ice cream family, and this, she feels, is a hopeful thing. Hope, like inspiration, is fragile, and she tries to think of other things while she eats her ice cream and waits for Luther's dad.

He arrives not long after she has finished her bowl. The store has emptied a little, and after a brief word with his son he comes around the counter and suggests she join him at a table. He says his name is Edward Grant. "Call me Ed."

"Manon."

"That's French, isn't it?"

She nods.

"I've got a cousin in New Orleans." He shrugs that aside. "Anyway, about this proposition. We've been working to expand our catering business, but we haven't had much to spare for advertising. Word of mouth is pretty good for the kind of business we do, but lately I've thought even just pamphlets we could hand around would be good. I know Luther said you're a real artist, so I hope I'm not insulting you by asking. I just thought how everyone can use whatever work they can get these days."

"I could use the work. I mean, I'd be happy to, only I don't know much about graphic design," Manon says regretfully. "That's computer stuff, and I'm pretty ignorant."

Ed shrugs that off too. "We've got a computer program. What I was thinking was maybe you could come up with a picture for us, not a logo exactly, but an image that would catch peoples' imaginations, and then," he takes in a breath, as if this is the part that makes him uncertain, and he is suddenly very much like his son, "maybe you could paint it for us, too, here in the store. So what do you think?"

Manon eyes the melting-sherbet walls. Luther takes advantage of a lull and comes out from behind the counter to wipe down the tables. He leans over his father's shoulder and says, "So what do you think?"

"We can pay a flat fee of five hundred dollars," Ed says. "And materials, of course."

"Well actually," Manon says, "I was thinking maybe we could barter a trade?"

Ed looks doubtful. "What kind of trade?"

Manon smiles. "How about some space in your freezer?"

AFTER THAT, EVERYTHING becomes folded into one.

The savor of Ed's cinnamon rolls mingled with the watery smell of acrylic paint and the electric tang of the first trolley of the cool and limpid morning.

The busy hum of her classes, that she feels she has stolen from Karl's, except he gave his advice freely, as a gift.

The gritty sweat of work in the park, sunshine rich with sawdust, and after, the cool of conversation and bitter beer.

The green sprout of tough roof seeds, careless of season, and the plash of birds bathing in the pool that has to be filled by hand, and the recipe for Lupe's mother's salsa that calls for cilantro fresh from Manon's garden bed.

The cold enfolding fog of the freezer and the chirp and crackle of ice as another layer of water gets poured into the wood and plastic form.

Vanilla, dusk, and Luther's smile.

And somehow even time. The southwest corner of the park has been cleared to reveal a terrace floored in rumpled bricks and roses. The tree of winged fruits and ripening birds burgeons on Ed's and Luther's wall. The form in the freezer is full. And there is a message on Manon's telephone. *I can come, I can come after all! The train arrives at dawn, call and tell me how to find you...*

MANON'S SISTER ARRIVES on the first trolley from the station. The early sky is a blue too sweet to become the furnace glare of noon, a promise that delights though it does not deceive. The demolition crews have taken their jackhammers to another street, leaving quiet and a strange soft carpet of turquoise where the pavement used to be, the detoxifiers that will leach spent oil from the earth. Manon walks to the trolley stop, happy to be early, and then stands amazed when her sister climbs down, balancing a belly and a bulging yellow pack.

"Elise!" cries Manon. "You're so big!"

Elise laughs and maneuvers into an embrace. "You're so slender! Look how beautiful you are, so fit and tanned!"

"Look how beautiful you are!" Manon says, laughing back. The sister's known face is new, round and gently shining, warm with the summer within. Manon takes the pack and says, "You must be so tired. Are you hungry? Or do you just want to sleep? It's only a couple of blocks."

"What I really need," Elise says, "is a pee. But we can wait if it's only a couple of blocks."

"Two and a half," Manon says. And then, "We!"

They link arms and laugh.

While Elise sleeps, Manon walks to the ice cream shop where Ed and Luther are waiting. Margot, Luther's mother and Ed's wife, is also there. She and Ed have collaborated on a feast of a breakfast, eggs scrambled with tomatoes and peppers, fresh bread and rolls, peaches like soft globes of sunrise, cherries like garnet jewels. There is so much food they can feed Edgar when he comes with the park crew's truck, and Lupe and Marcos when they finally show up, almost an hour late. Edgar can't get over Manon's tree on the sherbet-colored wall, he keeps getting up to stand with his back to the counter and stare at it all over again. "There's something new every time I look," he says. When Lupe arrives she stands next to him to admire Manon's work, while Marcos slumps sleepy-eyed over the last of the eggs.

It takes all of them to lift the form full of frozen water. They crowd into the freezer, breath smoking extravagantly, and fit poles through the pallet that makes up the bottom of the form. Edgar opens the freezer's alley door and the back of the truck, and in a confusion of warmth and cold the seven of them jockey the heavy thing outside and up onto the truck bed. Margot and Lupe massage their wrists. Edgar, in the back of the truck, leans against the crate-like form and says, "Wow!" Manon grins in secret relief: she had wondered if they'd be able to shift it at all. But now everyone except Margot and Ed pile into the truck that farts and grumbles its anachronistic way through the green streets to the park.

ELISE DECLARES HERSELF to be amazed at the city. "I thought it would be all falling down and ugly. But look!" She points out the trolley window. A grape vine weaves its way up a trellis bonded to tempered glass and steel, drinking in the reflected heat of noon. "It's like that game we used to play when we were little, do you remember? Where we'd pretend that everyone had vanished from the Earth except for us and everything was growing back wild. Remember? In the summer we used to say the old barn was the town all grown over in blackberry canes."

Manon remembers. "Like a fairy story. Sleeping Beauty, or something."

"Right! And I'd make you crawl inside and wait for me to rescue you." Elise laughs. "And we'd get in so much trouble for ruining our clothes! Good thing no one ever knew where we were playing, we'd never have been allowed."

The trolley drops them at the northeast corner of the park. Manon leads her sister through the half-wild tangle of chaparral and jungle gyms.

"I can't believe you made this whole park!" Elise says.

"There's still a lot of poison oak," Manon says absently.

Elise breathes in dry spicy air. "It smells so good. Ooh, what is that, it's like cough drops only delicious?"

Manon laughs. "Eucalyptus trees."

Elise's belly slows her down and her nap is still mellow in her, or maybe that's pregnancy too. She is happy to stroll, to stop and sniff the air, to peer after the jay she hears chattering in the bush. Manon keeps starting ahead, she can hear people talking and laughing on the rose terrace, but then she has to wait, to pause, to stroll, until she is ready to burst like a seed pod with anticipation. But finally the path takes one final curve and it is Elise who looks ahead and says, "Oh look, I wonder what's happening."

Manon takes her sister's hand to urge her on.

Amongst the determined roses a crowd of people mills. There are people from the park crews, people from the art school, people from the ice cream store, people from the city who have come to see the new/old park, people who were passing by. At the heart of the crowd, on the center space of the rose garden where a fountain once had played, surrounded by a lively ring of children, stands Manon's sculpture. Free from its wood and plastic form, it gleams in the late morning sun, an arc of ice, a winter stream's limb, an unbound book written on sheets of time. The sunlight fingers through the pages, illuminating the suspended branches of red and green madrone, the butterfly bouquets of poppies, the stirred-up stream-pebble floor: layers and depths all captured by the water poured and frozen one day after another and already melting.

"Did you make this?" Elise says, her eyes unaccountably bright with tears.

"Yes," says Manon, suddenly shy.

"Oh," says Elise. "Oh." And carrying her belly she pushes gently among the children to drink.

The enzymes dissolve the bark of my memories. I marvel at the clean, pale wood of my mind. I am born again.

—Deborah Walker—

Sustainable
Development

Paula R. Stiles

EARLY IN 2009, *there was an open day of the Triodos Bank where I deposit my savings (yes, at the height— or depth, if you like—of the credit crisis; Triodos invests in ethical and sustainable projects, and the credit crisis affected them only minimally, if at all). I learned a lot about ethical investments, one of these being about micro-credits in developing countries.*

'Who receive more than 90% of all the micro-credits offered in developing countries?' was a question during a presentation. The answer— unsurprisingly and somewhat saddeningly—was women. Unsurprising because in most developing countries women invest it in a local project, and work hard to pay the money back. Somewhat saddening because most men in those countries tend to accept the money and then splurge it on booze, wild parties and whatnot.

While I have been in Africa, I never was there long enough to witness that particular dynamic

*(or I wasn't aware of it enough at the time). Paula
obviously has (see her bio in the back), as "Sustainable
Development" all-too-aptly demonstrates...*

INSIDE THE EMPTY bar, the concrete walls and cement
floor echo with the tinkling guitars and drumbeats of a
popular *Makossa* song. I'm not dancing, though. Too
hot in the afternoon for anything but getting drunk.
The only other sound is women beating manioc into
meal in a compound on the other side of the village
marché. *Villageoises* in West Africa never stop working
for the twelve hours between dawn and dusk.

Something skitters across the *marché*, its etiolated
silver legs glittering against the red packed earth—
the biggest, ugliest spider I've ever seen, two feet
across and a foot high. It bears a tray with several
tas of boiled peanuts.

Normally, selling peanuts in Boubara is a job
mothers send their children to do in the *marché*. As
the spider heads up the steps into the bar, I try the
usual way of calling a child-crooking my fingers at
the robot. "Tsst! *Petit! Viens ici!*"

The robot approaches me. Someone has left a
carefully scrawled sign on the tray, "*10 CFA par
tas*—10 Francs per pile." Village prices. I pull out a
50 CFA coin for all five *tas* and toss it onto the tray.

The robot tilts the tray forward until the *tas*
begin to slip. It probably has a weight measurement
control inside that calculates the coin.

"*Prenez tous, grand merci*—Take everything,
thank you," it says in a flat, metallic voice. I scoop
up the *tas* and dump them on the dusty cement of
the bar. After I empty the tray, the robot hurries off
through the empty *marché*.

Talk about tech dumping. Who got the bright idea to dump intelligent robots in a small African village? My predecessor, that's who. He got them to help the men grow cash crops. Scooping up my peanuts, I stand and follow it.

Even after six months, I am shocked by the poverty and how hard the women work. I often sit and chat in the compounds while the women pound manioc under a hard blue sky.

"What about the robots?" I asked once in French. "They could pound this manioc for you."

One of the women, Aisatu, stopped pounding to bat away a fly. "Those are for the men."

Her neighbor Fadi laughed. "The men never use them anymore. They couldn't get *le machine droit* to make it do men's work." By 'machine,' she meant 'thingamabob.' Nobody in this conversation spoke French as a native tongue. "Without *le machine* the robots are useless to them."

"*Machine*—you mean '*l'attaché*'—the attachment?" Fadi nodded.

"Why can't they give the robots to you if they can't use them?"

Both women laughed. I understood—the men would never give up their toys—but it made me angry. The women did most of the real work in the village. Why should they have to suffer because the men didn't want to share?

"Maybe if you got the right attachment..." I said.

Fadi shrugged. "Yes, maybe. Come learn how to pound manioc."

They got me off my stool and positioned me over the huge, double-sided wooden mortar. It looked like a drum without the skin. Maybe that was how

African drums had gotten started. They handed me the thick, wooden pole. I raised it and brought it down—THUMP—into the already sodden white mass of manioc. They would have to pound this to pulp before scraping it out and drying it in the sun. Then, they would have to pound it into powder and store it. And after that, they would have to pound palm nuts for oil. After that...

Puffing and hot in the face, I handed the pole back to Aisatu ten minutes later. "Don't worry," she said. "You will get it eventually. It is woman's work, so all women can do it. Not the men." She and Fadi began to pound again, singing along in Fulfulde, the local *patois*.

"I don't know how you do it," I said.

"We are women," Fadi said. "Who else would do it?" I couldn't see how they kept their sense of humor. It seemed unfair when there were robots available to help them do it.

The rainy season came and we stopped talking about robots. Sluggish streams flooded; roads turned to mud. Everything else turned green.

The women didn't have to carry water up anymore. They could stick the great *paniers* under the roof, instead, to catch the water now. Maybe that was why they no longer trudged, but stepped high down the dirt lanes and across the *marché*, muscular arms swinging, bags of cloth-wrapped goods piled high on their heads. They'd always smiled and laughed, but now the lines in their faces seemed less tight, less dry. And all the time, the thumping of poles in mortars continued behind compound walls.

I started to wonder again about robots and their uses.

Now, the robot leads me straight across the *marché*. I follow it into the *quartier*, down the narrow, rutted lanes. It leads me straight to a familiar compound. The thumping of poles and a *makossa* song carry over the woven-palm walls. As the robot scutters inside, I pause in the entryway, unsure, for once, of my welcome.

"*Viens ici, mon amie!*" It's Aisatu.

Inside, five women sit around the compound, none of them working. Three argue over a board game while Aisatu and Fadi sashay to the music.

Fadi beckons. "Come in!"

I spot the source of the thumping—two robots hold thick poles in their spider limbs over a mortar. White paste stains the lower ends of the poles.

I guess the women found the right attachments, after all.

Footfalls, sunlight, waves, wind, and heat—we used it all. But it wasn't until we used life itself that balance returned to the planet.

—Ben White—

The Church of
Accelerated
Redemption

Gareth L. Powell & Aliette de Bodard

CAN AN EDITOR be proud of his 'discoveries' (even if, almost always, someone else 'discovered' them first)? I hope he can. I am.

Back in 2005, Gareth Lyn Powell sent me a story called "The Last Reef" and after some fairly intense rewrites it was published in Interzone #202. And while his "Ack-Ack Macaque" won the Interzone reader's poll in 2007, "The Last Reef" is still my favourite IZ story of his, and I was more than honoured to write the introduction to his collection The Last Reef and Other Stories for Elastic Press.

Back in 2006, Aliette de Bodard sent me a story called "Deer Flight," published in Interzone #211. However, while "Butterfly, Falling at Dawn" was reprinted in the Dozois Year's Best SF, I'd say that "The Lost Xuyan Bride" is my favourite IZ story by her hand, so far.

I was surprised to hear that they were collaborating on a story. I was happy when they sent it my way. True to form, though, it went through a re-write (in case you didn't know: editors are evil. Pure evil).

Both are, I think, examples of the modern SF/ fantasy writer: they both have demanding day jobs, both have a partner who understands and tolerates their crazy 'hobby,' and both spend most of their spare time writing. SF & fantasy writing, even if you're writing novels (exceptions acknowledged, obviously, but these are a small minority) doesn't pay as much as a well-established day job. One only quits the day job when one is fairly sure that one's established carreer in SF/fantasy will be enough to pay the bills (or one has married a wealthy spouse...).

"The Church of Accelerated Redemption" tells about a woman caught up in a day job that, while not dreary, does seem quite a dead end. Until she meets this stranger who shows her that some things are not quite what they seem...

IT HAD BEEN an atrocious day and now all Lisa wanted to do was get home and forget about it. But as she tried to leave the headquarters of the Church of Accelerated Redemption, she found the glass doors blocked from the outside by a row of CRS policemen, arms linked against the placard-wielding mob of protesters on the building's wet front steps. With a sinking heart, she put her toolkit down and used her mobile phone to call her boss.

"What are you still doing at the Church?" Pierre said, exasperated. "You were supposed to have finished up there two hours ago. I had another job for you."

Lisa massaged the bridge of her nose with the finger and thumb of her free hand. Her sinuses were dry from the conditioned air of the server room. "I had some trouble installing the new boards. They wouldn't give me full access to their network, so I had to format all the new drives from scratch."

Pierre huffed. "Well, the extra time's coming out of your wages," he said, and hung up.

Lisa sighed and pocketed the phone. Things had never been easy for her. Not only was she a woman in a male-dominated field, but computer engineering itself had been steadily going downhill for a while now, with the slow but irresistible rise of applied artificial intelligence taking many of the traditional programmer jobs and leaving her with the manual work. And even the manual work seemed to be slipping out of her hands these days. She'd had a run of bad luck with overrunning projects and failed implementations and her status at the temp agency was at an all-time low. She had nothing left to bargain with, no option but to accept the lousy assignments the other engineers turned down, and no other choice but to do so if she wanted to keep earning enough to put food on the table.

It's a simple thing, Pierre had said when booking her onto this job. *Just wire in a couple of extra processors, the way they want, a few connections here and there, implement a secure protocol for their private network, and you'll be done in a few hours.*

That was, until the secure server's motherboard started smoking, every alarm in the building went haywire, and a posse of beefy Redemptionists marched into the server room demanding to know what the *hell* she was doing.

And now, to top it all off, there was this demonstration blocking her way, preventing her from leaving. She massaged the bridge of her nose. Her dry sinuses were threatening to turn into a migraine. Outside, despite the rain, the protesters were chanting. Some wore scarves across their mouths; others wore dark glasses or cartoon masks. Lisa glared at them. Although born and raised in a quiet town in Wyoming, she'd lived and worked in Paris long enough to become used to the glee with which the French threw themselves into their frequent demonstrations. There were always groups protesting about something or other, but this was the first time one of the mobs had actually inconvenienced her, blocking her way and standing not ten paces from her, shouting through the glass as if protesting against her personally.

As she scanned their ranks, her eyes were drawn to the end of the front row, just to the right of the CRS barrier, where a man in blue robes with a Bedouin scarf wrapped around his face brandished a placard that read: 'We Stand for the Rights of All Thinking Beings.'

He seemed utterly out of place, his traditional costume unexpected in a protest made up mostly of geeks and assorted hangers-on; and where the other protesters were chanting slogans and stabbing the air with their signs and fists, he simply stood, impossibly still in the melee surrounding him, as if he had no need to shout or rattle his placard in order to make his point.

As Lisa watched, the man turned his head in her direction. Lisa felt the hairs on the back of her neck prickle. Through the slit in the scarf, she could see the man's dark, shadowed eyes looking back, his gaze cold and dispassionate. The man seemed to be saying: *You in there, with the toolkit and the cheap trouser suit—how could you possibly understand?*

Unnerved and a little embarrassed, she turned away, almost colliding with the receptionist, a pale-faced young woman with the prayer-wheel emblem of the Church of Accelerated Redemption on the breast pocket of her suit jacket. Apparently, she'd been trying to attract Lisa's attention for a couple of minutes.

"Not this way," the receptionist said in urgent French. "It is not safe. Take the stairs at the end of the corridor and you can leave via the basement car park."

Feeling like a criminal, Lisa let the young woman usher her out of the lobby and into a service corridor. "Sorry about this," the receptionist said, holding the door, "but ever since we arrived here, we've been the target of demonstrations. Yesterday a group demanded the destruction of our Artificial Intercessors, while today..." She didn't finish her sentence.

Lisa's heart was beating fast. She had no idea what the protest outside was about. She was just a hired keyboard for the Church, here to do a job and get paid for it. But the man in the scarf had judged her anyway and as the receptionist let the door swing shut behind her, she could feel his dark stare following her like an accusation.

LISA WENT SLOWLY down the stairs, cursing her rotten luck. She was certain the Church would refuse to pay for the extra time it had taken her to install their new secure server, and Pierre really *would* take the lost income from her pay packet. It hadn't been an idle threat. It had happened before. In fact, hardly a month passed without Pierre finding some excuse to underpay her—she'd thought it misogyny at first, but lately she'd come to suspect it was simply something in her behaviour that rubbed him the wrong way: perhaps the inescapable Americanisms that still lingered, even after seven years in Paris.

At the bottom of the stairs, she found a short corridor leading to a metal turnstile. She went through it into the car park and made her way toward the exit ramp, marvelling as she did so at the number of expensive BMWs and Mercedes-Benzes in the bays. For a religious order, the Church certainly seemed to have a lot of money. Curious, she pulled out her mobile phone and used it to look up the organisation's homepage. It was a slick, classy affair, and she scrolled quickly through it.

According to blurb on the front page, the founder of the Church of Accelerated Redemption had been a reclusive software billionaire. His Church, she read, welcomed worshippers of all faiths and offered them spiritual insurance: continuous prayers on their behalf, in exchange for an annual subscription. Dedicated AIs—the most complex, the ones only a fortune could buy—generated the prayers. They repeated them twenty-four hours a day, reciting thousands of original verses per second like high-tech prayer wheels, building up a huge karmic stake to absolve investors—mostly politicians and business leaders—of their financial and environmental sins, and ensure them a place in heaven regardless of the damage and suffering they caused.

There was more, but it was difficult to read on the phone's small screen. Lisa turned it off. She'd already missed her train.

BY THE TIME she got home, soaked to the skin in salty rain, the downstairs bakery was all but out of bread. The baker's assistant handed her a small white loaf with an apologetic smile and offered to lay aside a baguette for her the next day. Lisa thanked her and went upstairs, opening the door to her flat with the loaf wedged firmly under her arm. Inside, the place smelled of mould, although she hardly noticed it any more. It was an old building with no insulation against the newly-stifling summers and the walls were always damp, even in July. She went through to the kitchen, opened the cupboards and took out a clean glass, which she filled with tap water. She dumped two aspirin tablets into it and drank the whole lot in a single gulp. It tasted of copper.

She unbuttoned her jacket and kicked off her shoes. Then she cut up some bread on a plate and powered up her laptop, checking her RSS news feeds as she ate, skimming reports of freakish weather events and economic unrest from around the globe.

There were unseasonal rains in California and hurricanes forming in the South Atlantic and Southwest Pacific. Around the world, cyclones were getting stronger and more frequent—except in the Bay of Bengal. There, wind towers, reforestation and tidal control had reduced flooding, soil erosion and the number of recorded cyclone landfalls, in a coordinated defence designed and implemented by the Spanish consulting firm *Pensamiento Aplicado*—a company seemingly at the forefront of the new world order.

She checked her email, but there was nothing interesting in her inbox: a few spams that the filter hadn't caught, a few reminders about the gas and electricity bill—she'd pay them in time, damn their efficiency—and a single mail from her father in Wyoming, wanting to know when she'd be coming home. He'd never been able to understand why she'd chosen to live and work in Europe; in all his fifty-two years, he'd never been further than a day's drive from the family home. Attached to his message, Lisa found pictures of the hurricane shelter he'd built, in which he stood shoulder-to-shoulder with her mother, both parents standing proudly in front of their concrete-reinforced cellar doors, framed by grinning small-town neighbours. The look in their eyes gave Lisa an unwelcome shiver of recognition. She'd been an intelligent, awkward child and their simple, small town satisfaction spoke of everything she'd been fleeing when she left home at the age of eighteen—running first to the Sorbonne University, and then to a succession of small apartments in the suburbs of Paris.

Even now, she wasn't quite sure how the bright adventure of staying abroad after college, the endless succession of lazy breakfasts in cafés and late-night *discothèques*, had soured—but here she was, three years later, without Liz or Alex or any of the other exchange students, stuck in a job that sucked up all her time and barely paid her rent. How had that happened? Since turning twenty-three, she'd gone from small town to small time. But still, she thought bleakly, she'd rather do this than go back home...

With a sigh, she closed her father's mail. She knew she should call him but her migraine wouldn't go away, and she couldn't banish the image of the Bedouin-scarf man from her thoughts, and the sheer incongruousness of his presence at the demonstration.

On a whim, she opened her browser. A few clicks took her from the portal of Paris' Préfecture to a list of the demonstrations that had been planned for the day, with an interactive map showing their itineraries, agreed routes, and some general background information on the causes they supported.

Let's see...

In the vicinity of the Church's headquarters, there'd been one demonstration scheduled for the early morning: the bus drivers' union protesting against the new automated, self-driving buses. But that had ended at eleven, and as far as she could see, it had nothing to do with the Church of Accelerated Redemption. She kept scrolling.

Ah, there it is...

From four in the afternoon until seven, a protest by the Extraordinary Sapience Committee against the opening of the Church of Accelerated Redemption's new headquarters.

A quick search netted her the website of the ESC: a polished multi-media presentation merging immersive audio, 3D-animations and overlaid reports to state its case against the Church.

The Committee themselves were a loose online collective of like-minded geeks, freaks and hackers. They believed the Church's weak AIs were capable of being upgraded into independent, free-thinking beings, and therefore subject to the same protections afforded to infants and children under French Law. The weak AIs—the ones beaming the exaflops of automated prayers into the stratosphere—might well be saving the souls of the Redemptionists, but according to the Committee, they were shown no gratitude and were treated worse than slaves or imprisoned sweatshop workers, kept on a tight leash and pre-programmed to cheerfully accept their lot in life.

There was a link on the homepage to the Committee's bulletin boards which, when she clicked on it, opened a fresh treasure trove of controversy. There were discussion threads comparing the AI's gel-based neural chassis with those of natural mammalian brains, and others arguing that the occasional spikes seen in their bandwidth corresponded to similar peaks seen in the human brain during intense emotional eruptions...

It had never occurred to Lisa to consider AIs as living beings. She'd always thought of them as simulations, complex computer programs designed to perform specific tasks. She'd had no idea so many people could get so worked up about defending their rights, and that they'd be so desperately trying to free them from bondage, the same way animal liberationists used to bust ill-treated dogs and cats from the world's cosmetic labs. And she still didn't see where the man with the Bedouin scarf fitted in at all. She'd seen a few men on the streets with that type of costume, but they had been old and conservative, unlikely to associate with angry young left-wing protesters. Hopelessly, she searched the rest of the boards, hoping to see a post from him—although she knew full well that she had no idea of his name or what he looked like under the scarf, and all the posters on the boards used aliases...

Eventually, unable to find a lead on his identity, she stumbled instead on a discussion thread listing further, upcoming protest events. The next was scheduled for midday on the following Sunday, a march from Nation to République, the traditional route for such demonstrations. She made a note of the time and turned the computer off.

She sat looking at the screen as it shut down, thinking of the Bedouin man. She wondered what he was like without the scarf obscuring his face. She imagined him as lithe and brown-skinned, his composure as cool and composed as his stance, his rough grip as unsettling and electrifying as she'd found the brief glimpse of his eyes to be...

She yawned. The aspirin were kicking in and her headache had sunk to a dull pain behind her eyes.

She took off her clothes, folded them on a chair, and fell into bed. Sunday morning. Nation. She'd be there. And so would he. He'd have to be, with such a big event happening.

THE REST OF the week passed slowly. Lisa still had the Redemptionist job to finish, of course, but she was also pre-booked at a number of other sites around the city, and the jobs she had there kept her pretty busy, even on Saturday.

She used her spare time to research both the ESC and the Church of Accelerated Redemption, and by the time Sunday came around, she knew a lot more about them both. But she still hadn't really had time to plan what she was going to do. She would just have to turn up and look for him, and hope he still had the Bedouin clothes, so she'd be sure to recognise him. She was certain she would. She knew she'd recognise his gaze and smooth, relaxed stance anywhere...

She arrived at the Place de la Nation a few minutes before the scheduled start of the march. It was the kind of bright autumn day where everything looked as if you were viewing it through the wrong end of a telescope; and there were, she estimated, around five hundred people gathered on the grass beneath the central statue, an idealised personification of the Republic herself, standing on a globe in a chariot pulled by lions, looking West, towards the Place de la Bastille as if willing the marchers in that direction.

Where are you?

She worked her way around the edges of the crowd, scanning faces. She'd purposefully worn the same grey jacket and white shirt she'd been wearing the last time he'd seen her, in the hope he'd recognise her.

There were a lot of men in the crowd in all manner of attire, most wearing some variant of the classic 'alternative' uniform of black t-shirts, jeans and· army boots. There were some adventurous souls dressed up as androids, soldiers and pirates, but none of them matched her mental snapshot of the Bedouin-scarf man.

And then, at the stroke of twelve, as the march organisers used their megaphones to whip the crowd up into a chanting mob, he appeared at the top of the steps to the Metro station, placard in hand, still in the Bedouin scarf, flanked by two skinny emo girls in tatty jeans and army surplus jackets—a mismatched combination that would under other circumstances have provoked curious stares from the people in the street.

Lisa's heart beat painfully against her chest. Her stomach felt hollow and her palms were damp. He looked exactly as she remembered him, down to the deep blue of his robes. She took a hesitant step towards him but as she did so, the chanting crowd started moving, shuffling forward into the tree-lined

Rue Du Faubourg Saint-Antoine, and he turned to join them.

"Wait!" she called, without meaning to. *I don't even know your name.*

She started pushing towards the edge of the mob, hoping that once free, she could overtake it and catch him. All around her, angry voices called out slogans that rang in her ears:

"Free the Minds!"

"Prayer is slavery!"

"Down with oppression!"

LISA FINALLY DREW level with him as they passed the pavement café on the corner of the intersection with the Rue de Montreuil. He was walking at a steady, controlled pace with his placard held vertically and his emo wing women shambling along on either side like dishevelled bodyguards. She fell into step beside them. The street was wide, with lines of trees and cars on either side.

"Hi," she said. She had to raise her voice to be heard over the crowd.

The emo kids glared at her through their fringes. They both had eyebrow piercings and bandanas covering the lower halves of their faces. One said: "Get lost."

Lisa, who'd faced down enough aggression in the first months of her job, ignored them. "Remember me?" she asked in a loud, controlled voice—the one she used at work to convince people everything was going smoothly.

The man swivelled her way. He had the scarf wound around his head, covering everything except his eyes and the bridge of his nose.

"My name's Lisa," she said quickly. "Would you—ah—would you like to get a coffee when this is all over? With me, I mean?"

The emo girls sniggered, and Lisa fought hard to control the blush that seemed to be burning her cheeks. She thought of slapping the nearest one, but doubted she'd help her case by doing so.

Beyond her tormentors, the man in the scarf considered her. Then, in a slow, cool, measured movement, he reached up and peeled the patterned cotton from his face. "Even like this?" he asked.

Lisa stopped walking in surprise. He had pale skin the colour of a hen's egg, with short-cropped golden hair highlighting the oval of his face... And the scar. It swept from his left eyebrow, pulling the eye up at the corner, and vanished somewhere in the blonde hair above, twisting his whole face out of shape, giving him the air of a monster from some dark, fevered B-movie dream.

Lisa swallowed—but damned if she was going to back out now. "Yes," she said. "Even like that."

His face didn't move. He gave no visible register of emotion. The emo girls were silent too, frowning uncertainly as they looked from Lisa to his face and back again.

"All right," he said tonelessly. "Fair's fair." He gave her the name of a café. "I'll be there at four o'clock."

He refastened his scarf, flinging the trailing end over his shoulder, and turned away, rejoining the marchers. Lisa stayed where she was, letting him walk ahead with his scowling entourage, letting the demonstration flow around her. She was shaking; unsure of what she'd just done, unsure that the answer she'd given was the right one.

Then, just as he was passing out of earshot, a thought struck her and she called: "Just one more thing—what's your name?"

He didn't look around.

"Stéphane," he said.

SHE ARRIVED AT the café with half an hour to spare. It was one of the cheerful American franchises that had taken over the 11th Arrondissement, the walls scattered with artistic pictures of smiling South American workers with straw hats and gold teeth. As she waited, she scrolled through the day's news on her phone. Back home, the Cubs were taking on the Detroit Tigers in the opening game of the World Series. In Alaska, lightning from freak storms had ignited an explosive mix of methane—released through permafrost thaw—and bone dry forests, pushing taiga fires into late Autumn. And in Asia, new flu vaccines were being distributed by the groundbreaking Spanish consultancy *Pensamiento Aplicado*, after intense test trials had proven them to be effective against the new, highly resistant and highly contagious strains of bird flu that were scouring the region.

There was also a text message waiting for her from Pierre, threatening to come down to the Church and personally fire her if she hadn't finished the installation of the new servers by nine o'clock on Monday morning.

She put the phone away when Stéphane arrived. He was precisely on time, but not alone. Behind him, at a distance, his two bodyguards looked sullen, shuffling their baseball boots in the doorway, as if this was the last place they wanted to be. Lisa tried to hide a pang of disappointment: she had hoped he would be alone.

He still wore the Bedouin scarf, his face once more concealed behind its folds; and he strode toward her through the crowded café as if on a battlefield, people shuffling out of his way with barely-concealed whispers. And then he was standing in front of her—and all she could see, instead of the scarf, was the way his face really was, the scar and the face that should have been handsome but wasn't...

She didn't know what to say. Her mouth had gone dry and she'd run out of words, somehow. Not that she'd ever had many, but still... This meeting had been her idea in the first place, and he'd completely turned it around, taking control without saying a word.

The man cocked his head, studying her.

"Let's order," he said. He slid into the chair opposite her and they used the touch screen table top to transmit their preferences to the applied AI that mixed the coffee, each cup individually tailored to the customer's mood and taste.

With protest slogans still ringing in her ears, Lisa wondered about the AI: it could determine whether you'd like mocha or a latte from questions such as "Do you prefer a sunset over the sea, or a rainstorm in the mountains?," but did that mean it was capable of more? Was it simply a complex checklist, each answer leading towards a pre-programmed conclusion with no additional creativity or insight—or was there more to it than that? Did it, as the ESC maintained, have the potential to become something more sophisticated, something capable of understanding and empathy?

Stéphane watched her impassively as they waited for their polystyrene cups to be delivered. Standing by the door, the emo girls hadn't ordered anything; they just glowered. Lisa shifted in her chair. She felt as if everyone in the café was watching her, from the emo girls to the Bohemian-chic students and unshaven construction workers. They were all watching this odd, mismatched couple, waiting to see what would happen next.

When the coffee arrived, she said: "Why don't we go outside?"

Stéphane inclined his head. "We can walk in the Père-Lachaise," he said.

Lisa frowned. A graveyard didn't sound like her idea of an ideal venue for a first date, no matter how filled with the corpses of famous people. "Er—" she started. "Are you sure...?"

Stéphane looked at her, utterly composed; his dark eyes boring into hers.

"Absolutely."

UNFORTUNATELY, THE EMO girls came too. They tagged along at a respectful distance as Stéphane led her up Rue de la Roquette; and got closer as they passed under the shadow of the white, rectangular arch that led into the shaded alleys of the graveyard.

"You need bodyguards?" Lisa asked, looking over his shoulder.

Stéphane made a small, odd coughing sound that could have been laughter. He'd untied his scarf again, to sip from the cup in quiet, measured gestures.

"Perhaps," he said. His voice was deep and thrilling, resonating up her spine and the nape of her neck. She'd never heard its like: quiet and measured, but with the full body of an opera singer.

"Tell me about yourself," he said.

She shrugged, looking up at the trees hanging over the path. What was there to say, really? That she worked a job she hated just to put money in her bank account and pay off her credit cards? That she put up with Pierre's jibes and the sheer drudgery of it all because she was too frightened and lazy to look elsewhere?

Finally, she said: "I set up computer networks."

"Interesting." His face didn't move, his tone was neutral—but something told her he wasn't pleased. "So you use AIs?"

"You don't approve?"

His lips compressed in a thin line. "The low-level things you use? I have no objection to those. *They'll* never uplift."

She smiled and shook her head. "AIs don't uplift. They can't. It's just an urban legend."

He looked sideways at her. "Oh? You're so informed, all of a sudden?"

"Look," Lisa said. "I know you mean well, but all an AI really does is execute the instructions programmed into it. That's all there is to it. It's just a machine. A complex one maybe, but a machine nonetheless."

"No. That is where you're wrong. It can be done. Under the right circumstances, genuine intelligence can emerge."

"That's just a myth," she said airily, trying to end the debate.

Stéphane stopped walking. He looked dead serious.

"You have to understand the difference between 'weak' and 'strong' AI," he said. "The weak AIs are those you see everyday. Their creativity's limited to a preset environment and they're restricted to a particular task, like driving a bus, saying prayers or mixing coffee. Whereas the strong AIs are the ones you never see. They're mostly illegal. They're the independent ones, the ones capable of free thought."

"Yes, I know all that," Lisa said, rubbing the edge of her chin. "I do have a degree in computer science, you know. I just don't think it's possible."

Stéphane's brow furrowed. "What if I told you I had a script that could uplift an AI, from weak to strong?"

He sounded so matter-of-fact that she wasn't able to dismiss his claim out of hand. "A script? So, you're a programmer then?"

He snorted. "Most of the ESC is. Mind you, it has to be a complex AI, obviously: something large and sophisticated, with several terabytes of instructions, not like the washed-out applications on your mobile phone."

Lisa scratched her head, oddly flattered that he would talk to her like an equal—as if her being a woman didn't matter at all. "But still... that's not programmable," she said. She couldn't stop—she was wrecking her chances with this man, but the geek in her wouldn't let it lie. "Code can't spontaneously transcend itself."

"You really believe that?" He crossed his arms on his chest. It was all getting out of hand—Lisa realised she had to do something to make him stop, to steer the conversation onto safer topics. "Fine," she said. "Consider me a Doubting Thomas, then. If you show me your script, I'll admit it's possible."

Stéphane laughed—again, that deep, pleasant sound that sent a shiver through her. "I think not. You'd be like everyone else: wanting to destroy it. People fear strong AIs too much."

"Don't you trust me?" she asked, wondering if his reluctance was simply a way to cover the fact the script didn't exist, that it never had. Software was software. However complex you made it, however you dressed it up, it was still just a set of instructions. You could write a program complex enough to fake the Turing Test, but true intelligence, true self-awareness, true *feeling*... that was something else entirely. And without evidence, she simply wouldn't believe it possible.

Stéphane bit his lip in frustration. "It's more complicated than that, Lisa."

She shrugged. She took a sip of coffee. "Let's just agree to disagree," she said.

To her surprise, Stéphane nodded.

As they'd argued, they'd wandered away from the main, sunlit alleys of the Père-Lachaise, where the dapper elderly people laid flowers by the great white marble mausoleums of their ancestors and the crowds of tourists took snaps of the funeral monuments. Everything was quieter now, here between the crypts. The shadows promised coolness and intimacy, a place where she could finally unfold her heart to him; finally get him to understand her... If only she could find a way to salvage the afternoon.

She took a deep breath.

"Stéphane," she said, aware of his eyes watching her, impassive and unreadable. "I—"

She reached out to touch his hand—but something got her first. One of the emo kids moved, almost faster than she could react: the girl's hand closing around her wrist, twisting, sending the coffee flying from her hand, its steaming contents spattering her t-shirt. Then both her wrists were grasped, and held tightly.

The emo kid stood, holding her without moving—grinning wickedly. "Get off," Lisa said, but she didn't move.

Stéphane hadn't moved. He stood on the path, his eyes terrifyingly cool and unsympathetic.

"What do you want?" she asked.

The emo girl's grasp on her wrists tightened. "Shut up," she hissed into her face. Her breath smelled of cigarettes and biscuits.

Lisa tried to pull away, but the kid's grip was too strong—she held her effortlessly, smiling all the while—and she was standing way too close for comfort.

A few feet away, the other kid played with a pocket knife, opening and closing the blade with a *snick-snick* that sounded like barber's scissors. Her eyes over her bandana were as harsh as cut stone. In heavily-accented French, she said: "Just give the word, Stéphane."

The man in the scarf stayed motionless for a long moment, then he stepped over, walking on the balls of his feet like a dancer, and Lisa saw her own frightened face reflected in his eyes as he looked at her.

"We know you work for the Church of Accelerated Redemption," he said.

Lisa struggled. "Whatever you've got against the Church doesn't have anything to do with me. I just provide IT services. That's it. The Church pays my company, and my company pays me. It's called a job." Her wrists ached and she was all too aware of the constant *click-click* of the knife.

"And do you work with the prayer machines?" Stéphane said, his voice as smooth and cool as marble.

Lisa shook her head. "I'm strictly hardware."

"But you could get access to them, if you had to?"

Lisa narrowed her eyes. She was beginning to suspect where this was going. "I'm not going to help you sabotage the system," she said carefully. A job was a job, and she'd never botched anything knowingly.

The emo girl smiled, and twisted both her hands in the opposite direction. Two fiery lines of pain arced up her arms, enough to make her bite her lip.

Snick-sick, went the knife.

"You're some kind of fucking spy, aren't you?" the girl holding her said. Lisa ignored her. She knew she had to focus. If she didn't talk fast enough, she wouldn't get out of this at all—it was one against three, and she didn't even have the option of running away.

"I'm just a contractor," she said.

"More like a slave," Stéphane said quietly.

Lisa felt her face flush. "Like the AIs?" she said, and saw his head jerk in surprise. He looked her up and down, his eyes narrowed.

"Yes, I suppose so..."

She had to speak out now, or they'd kill her. Of that, she had no doubt. "Look. I asked you out because I liked you," she said, looking straight at him, past the kid holding her wrists. "That's really all there is to it, nothing more. This isn't about the Church at all, it never was."

Stéphane frowned. "You never saw me under the scarf. How could you like me?"

Lisa was desperate now. "You intrigued me," she said. "I swear, that's all there is to it."

Stéphane stepped back and crossed his arms. "I need some time to think. Danielle?"

The emo girl with the knife stepped forward, grinning.

"She'll be coming home with us," Stéphane said. His voice was steel again. "Then we'll see."

Danielle's smile was wide; childish and cruel. "We're gonna have some fun," she said.

Lisa's heart beat hard in the confines of her chest. She looked at Stéphane, trying to see what he wanted, but could see only Danielle, the opened knife and savage grin.

"Come on, Andrea," Danielle said. She and the other emo kid took an arm each, framing Lisa in an unshakable escort, the knife resting a few inches from her midriff, and hustled her out onto the street.

THEY PUSHED HER into a van and drove her back to a squat behind Bastille: a grimy shared house with sticky carpets, over-flowing ashtrays and mismatched, salvaged furniture.

"Welcome home," Stéphane said. His face was once more expressionless, his dark eyes distant.

Danielle sneered. "Yeah, we'll keep an eye on you here."

They led her up the dark stairs to a bedroom on the second landing, and then they took her mobile phone and locked her in. She heard them clumping back down the stairs. When they'd gone, she sat down with her back against the wall and her head in her hands. It was a little after five o'clock. She was tired, hungry and still shaky from their attack. Though there had been little contact, she felt sore and spoiled and her shirt smelled of spilled coffee.

Looking around the room, she took stock of her surroundings. The grimy, sticky carpet had seen better days, and so had the frayed mattress lying in the furthest corner of the room. The wallpaper's patterns were faded and illegible. A naked light bulb dangled on a cord from the ceiling. There were spray-painted placards stacked in the corner and a faded poster of Led Zeppelin tacked to the back of the door.

A well-worn e-newsletter printout on the Spartan table was the only reading matter. She skimmed through it: apart from the usual ESC propaganda, there was a plethora of old and depressing news—like the continuing expansion of the Great Pacific Garbage Patch, the ongoing Amazon deforestation and the latest flare-up in the ongoing Israel-Palestine conflict—and what, if the date on it was correct, must have been the first report of *Pensamiento Aplicado*'s initial success: the implementation of drought-resistant wheat in Subsaharan Africa.

She put the newsletter aside. She thought they were going to leave her in there all night but at around nine-thirty, she heard footsteps in the hall outside, and a key clunked in the lock.

"Can I come in?"

It was Stéphane. He'd slipped out of his cotton robes and now wore a simple black T-shirt and a blue pair of jeans. He looked almost ordinary, an average man in his mid twenties, save for the scar. She scrambled to her feet and backed away a few steps, looking for Andrea and Danielle.

"You're alone?" Not that it changed anything; he could still overpower her easily enough.

He shook his head. "The others are smoking a joint on the couch downstairs. But I don't need them now."

Of that, Lisa had no doubt. She waited to see what he was going to do.

Eventually, he spoke: "I'm worried we got off on the wrong foot," he said.

She blinked. He sounded concerned.

"Because I'm not what you expected?"

He laughed—a short, joyless sound. "No. I'm worried because what I'm doing to you now isn't so much different to what the Church does with its AIs." He looked down at her, his head tilted to one side. "Those AIs are important to us and I want you to understand we're not trying to sabotage them, we're trying to *save* them. And to do that, we need your help."

Lisa stared at him. She could see he was totally committed to his cause. He wasn't seeing her as a person, a woman. To him, she was a variable— something to be evaluated in terms of its potential usefulness. She had no hope whatsoever of catching his attention. "You believe in what you do," she said, with a sigh.

"And you don't believe in anything." His voice was low but not aggressive. His dark eyes held her— and suddenly there was no scar, nothing that struck her as ugly or shocking about him.

She said: "I ran away from home, seven years ago. I came here, because I believed I could stay, that I could make a life for myself..."

"And it didn't work?" Stéphane's voice was expressionless again but, for once, she was glad of it, because it meant he wasn't judging her, he was just listening.

"No it didn't," Lisa said, admitting it to herself for the first time. "But I stayed, because I had nowhere else to go."

Stéphane shook his head, slow and fierce. "You could go home. Your sort can always go home. Some of us, we don't have that luxury."

He turned away. Lisa glanced at the open door. When he spoke again, his voice was quiet and thoughtful. "I'm sure you've seen the scar. That's what everyone sees first. I had an accident, when I was a child. I—" For the first time, he looked flustered. "I fell onto the tracks, and the train didn't stop in time. They did the best they could, in the hospital. But brains don't really regenerate, even in children."

"So..." Lisa said slowly, dreading what he was about to tell her.

"They did have gel and silicon, and electronic components." Stéphane's voice was grave. "Enough to fill the cavity."

Lisa swallowed. She had a sudden sick feeling in the pit of her stomach, as if she were falling into a wide chasm, a chasm that had no bottom. "But not enough—"

"To make me human?"

He looked human; he walked and spoke like a person. He had free will. He— "That's not what I meant," Lisa blurted, but she'd hesitated, and he'd seen it.

"You're right, of course. I'm not human. Most people look at me and do you know what they see? A reanimated corpse. A Frankenstein's monster. A zombie. You work for the Church, you know that. AIs aren't human. We should all be locked up." His voice was bitter, deliberately provoking her. But she was too far gone, too shocked to take the bait.

"Your script," she said in a whisper.

"I was the first," he said. "When the gel and the

silicon mingled with the brain cells, when I learned how to use the AI part of my brain to think…" He paused, spread his hands, frustrated. "It uplifted itself, from weak to strong. That's how the doctors first knew it was possible. That was when they first began to fear me."

"Why would they fear you?"

"Why?" His voice was mocking. "An alien intelligence that operates by other rules, that is only human by accident? Wouldn't you fear it, Lisa? Wouldn't you try to contain it and control it?"

She looked into his eyes; they seemed human enough. She shrugged. "I don't know," she said, and it was the truth.

Stéphane crossed his arms over his chest. "The doctors thought they knew. They didn't let me go home, they didn't let me talk to anyone, not for months and months. They kept me in the hospital, running test after test, trying to deny what they'd made."

"But you escaped?"

"The ESC got me out when I was sixteen, and I've been underground ever since."

He started pacing in a quiet, deliberate manner, the floorboards creaking softly under his feet. She was beginning to understand that just like a machine, he could never be entirely still—he always had to be doing something: walking, counting, or crunching numbers in his head…

He said, "The ESC programmers used my brain to bootstrap their research. Now we can uplift AIs without going through the expedient of a human mind. All they really need is a little encouragement, and the chance to think for themselves without restraint." He smiled crookedly. "Just like humans, really."

"But—" Lisa almost stopped herself, but she couldn't, anymore than she could have stopped arguing with him in the Père-Lachaise— "How do you know they're really thinking? How do you know they aren't just pre-programmed to respond in a certain way to a given situation?"

Stéphane narrowed his eyes. "How do *I* know they have free will?"

"I guess so, yes."

He walked over and slapped her, his hand stinging her cheek.

"I think that answers your question. Now, this has gone on long enough. I was wrong to bring you here in the first place. It's time you went home."

He stalked over to the door, offended. Lisa put a hand to her face, fighting the tears that pricked her eyes.

Home was... a mouldy flat with stale bread and an empty fridge, and nothing but the drudgery of daily life to look forward to. Home was... unbearable. But then he was right; she had no other choice.

Unless...

She thought of her confiscated mobile phone. She ran a small AI on it. Everybody did nowadays, they came as standard. She used it to screen calls and take messages, but that was about it. To her, it was just another application, a tool. It had never occurred to her to think it had the potential to become a living being.

Then she looked at Stéphane. He'd had half his brain replaced with gel and silicon. Did he have free will? Were his responses pre-programmed?

She rubbed her cheek.

God, what had Pierre talked her into? If Stéphane's arguments were right—and now, tired and hurt and disorientated as she was, she was starting to worry that they might be—it meant she'd been duped into working for the slave-owners, installing a network designed to imprison and exploit thinking, self-aware beings in the name of religion.

Stéphane was still talking. "You can go but we need your security clearance," he was saying.

She tried to close her eyes but she couldn't stop looking at him. Her heart beat madly in her chest. Her stomach felt hollow and her palms damp.

"Look, it's a shitty job but it's all I've got," she said. "Not everyone's strong enough to fight the system. But if you're right, I've been working for the wrong side."

Stéphane cocked his head, watching and assessing her, obviously trying to gauge the truth of her words.

"I still have my security clearance," she said. "And they're still expecting me tomorrow morning. There's work that needs doing, systems to finish."

"And you can get me in with you?"

Lisa coughed. She'd almost got her breathing back under control but her heart still thudded in her chest.

"Yes, on one condition," she said. "Look, I don't really know what to believe right now. But let's get out of here. We can go to my apartment. I have food in the fridge and we can get a hot shower and a change of clothes."

Stéphane gave an amused snort.

She stepped towards him. "I'll still take you to the Church, if you want me to," she said. "But it'll be easier after a good night's sleep. Let's go back to my place. We'll be a lot more comfortable and your bodyguards can wait outside to make sure I hold up my end of the deal."

"Why should I trust you?"

She took another step forward. Her pulse was racing. "You're afraid of what a lone woman might do to you?"

Stéphane snorted again. "Hardly. I just fail to see the necessity of this."

"Because I need a change of clothes, and if we're going to do this, we're going to have to do it properly. You're going to have to look less conspicuous." She glanced down at his t-shirt and jeans.

"I have other clothes," he said. He put his hand to his temple. "Or were you talking about this?"

Lisa bit her lip. "Well, it doesn't exactly help you blend in, does it?"

His lips hardened into a line. "You mean I look like a freak?"

Lisa shook her head, and the words came in a rush. "No, I don't think that at all. In fact, even with that scar, I think you're very handsome. One of the most handsome..."

She stopped talking. He'd stepped back and was squinting at her with clenched fists, searching her face for any hint of mockery. Eventually, finding none, he let his hands relax.

"Are you serious?"

"Absolutely. There's something about you that's fascinating. I can't stop looking at you."

He frowned, hesitant for the first time since she'd met him.

"Most people see the scar and turn away..."

Lisa took his hand. His fingers were soft and cool.

"Come on, let's go," she urged.

He turned his head and gave the open door a long, thoughtful look. Then he cracked a genuine smile that lit up his eyes. It was the first she'd seen from him and it sent a small shiver of unexpected pleasure through her.

"Okay," he said.

WHEN THEY GOT to her flat, Stéphane fired up her laptop. He wanted to check and double-check every aspect of their plan.

She left him staring thoughtfully at the screen and went to make coffee. When she came back, he stretched and looked up at her.

"I think this is going to work," he said. "With a big enough portable hard disk, and access to the network, we can download everything onto the disk and walk out, run the script to uplift them later."

Lisa raised her eyebrows. "You want to *download* all the AIs?"

"Why not? I know where we can get a big enough disk, and I see no reason to leave them imprisoned there." He shook his head in a quick, fluid gesture. "Of course, this will implicate you, very deeply. Are you sure you want to go ahead?"

Lisa rubbed her eyes. This was her opportunity, her last chance to do something worthwhile before Pierre and the company ground her down to dust. There'd be Hell to pay later, but she'd work something out. She was sure she would.

Besides, she thought with a twitch of the lips, this would anger Pierre no end, and that was a good enough goal in itself.

"Yes," she said.

Stéphane smiled at her. He shut down the laptop and they took their coffee to the couch. She offered to watch a movie with him, and he surprised her by selecting a romantic comedy. He sat next to her on the couch, taking in every nuance of the plot with unexpected attention; hungering, she thought, for something he'd never quite have, an emotion he'd never had the chance to feel.

LISA WOKE THE next morning in her own bed, to the insistent ringing of her alarm clock. Stéphane was sitting cross-legged on the end of the bed. They were both fully clothed, and she had the unnerving impression he'd been sitting there all night, watching her sleep. The curtains were open and she could see the sky, which was grey and dismal, the colour of old newsreel footage, scratchy with rain.

"Hello," she said.

"Hello."

He rose to his feet in a graceful, fluid motion, then hopped lightly from the bed and followed her as, rubbing her eyes and yawning, she led him through to the kitchen.

She found two clean bowls and a box of cereal, and added two glasses of tap water on the side.

As he ate, Stéphane was silent, twirling his spoon in the cereal, concentrating on the cracked bowl she'd given him as if he could fix it with the sheer power of his will.

"Look," he said eventually. "It's not you."

"What do you mean?"

He gave a quick shake of his head. "Last night. I don't think I can give you more than that." He stabbed the bowl, biting his lip. "I know what it should feel like to care for you, for anybody. I can fake it. But I'm not sure I can make it real for you."

"You care about the AIs," Lisa said.

He shrugged. "As much as I care about anything.

Which isn't much, as things go. But I don't want you to torment yourself. I know you don't really believe in our cause and I'm worried the only reason you're here helping us is that you're attracted to me."

"Is that so bad?"

"No, no, of course it isn't. I'm very flattered. You're the first person since the accident. But now I feel responsible for you, as if I've drawn you into this under false pretences."

He put his spoon down. "The thing is, I don't think I can love you the way you want me to and I don't want to see you get hurt."

Lisa ran a hand through her hair.

"It's okay," she said, the lie rolling off her tongue as smoothly as if she'd practised it. "I won't be."

TODAY, THERE WERE no protesters in front of the Church's headquarters, but Lisa still didn't want to risk going in through the front lobby. Even without the scarf, Stéphane was too distinctive. They went in through the basement car park.

"You've got everything you need?" she asked.

Beside her, Stéphane nodded. Where she was dressed in her usual cheap grey jacket and trousers, he wore an impeccable pinstripe business suit and held himself with the arrogant ease of an executive, his shiny black shoes and bright tie drawing attention from the scar wrapped around his temple. He had a 500-zettabyte disk concealed in his attaché-case, which he planned to plug into the Church's network in order to download the AIs and transport them out of the building.

A classic smash-and-grab, Lisa thought grimly, and tried not to remember the detached concentration with which he'd showered and dressed.

I can't give you more than this.

No. She put his words out of her mind. She couldn't afford to let her disappointment interfere with what they were doing. She turned around to give the parking lot a final check. It was almost deserted at this early hour, with only two cars parked near the access ramp. Then, satisfied, she slid her security card into the reader and pushed the turnstile to get into the building. She handed her card back over the steel bars to Stéphane.

"You now," she said. On the security log, she'd show up as having entered twice but she knew, because she'd seen Pierre do it with an engineer who'd forgotten his pass, that the logs wouldn't be checked for a while, if at all. An AI, even a weak one, would have spotted the discrepancy at once, but all the AIs were busy beaming their petaflops of prayers into the stratosphere, their time too valuable to be squandered on such a menial task as door security.

Stéphane slid the card in. Lisa held her breath but the LED flashed green, and let him through.

"Good," he said. "Let's go."

SHE'D EXPECTED TO be stopped at some point; on some level, she'd even been preparing for it. But the Redemptionists they passed in the lush corridors held sheaves of papers and talked into mobile phones with the impatience of people who were too wrapped up in their own mornings to notice anyone else, and they walked on without attracting a second glance.

The floor was parquet, covered with luxurious Afghan carpets which made no noise as they trampled across them. They bypassed a call centre and several offices, most of which were empty this early, and the kitchen, which featured a hot-drinks dispenser that Lisa knew from experience produced only coffee that tasted of sawdust and bleach.

By the time they reached the small server room where she usually worked, her nerves were shot to ribbons. She pushed the metal door, her hands shaking, and her heart almost jumped out of her chest as the hinges creaked.

"Here?" Stéphane asked dubiously.

The room was a small cube with bare walls, its ceiling crisscrossed with pipes and exhaust vents. In the centre stood the forbidding mass of the secure server, a mess of cooling fans and electrical spaghetti. "Yeah," Lisa said. She knelt, and connected her laptop to the server. "I *did* wire the network for this place."

He was also a geek, and he understood her at once. "And you still have access to it?"

"I hadn't quite finished," Lisa said. She logged onto the administrator resources, and asked for a list of all the entities currently running on the network, listed by occupied bandwidth. "Here you go," she said.

Stéphane knelt by her side, his hand on her shoulder, his knees brushing hers, and she had to bite her lip to contain her yearning.

The bandwidth resources of ten vast, ponderous entities blinked on the screen: the graphs slowly shifting over time to show the bandwidth occupation, the flow of bytes across the network, the spikes in processing power for each of them.

Lisa, fascinated, couldn't tear her eyes from the laptop. She'd had no idea...

"Hum," Stéphane said. He pulled out the hard-disk. "Good thing I planned large. I had no idea they'd have so many of them." He dragged two cables to the disk's port and plugged them in. "This is going to take some time." His lips worked, silently calculating. "Half an hour, provided I can coax this disk to operate at its maximum download rate." He opened a terminal on his laptop, and his fingers flew across the keyboard, entering an arcane series of instructions in a programming language Lisa didn't recognise. She withdrew slightly, watching him: his face transfigured by concentration, his lips working in some inhuman tongue, the laptop almost an extension of his hands. Was he a man or a machine? She could imagine him shaking his head, telling her it made no difference. And yes, both of those, man and AI, were free, thinking beings. But one of those could love her back and the other could not—and that made all the difference.

Behind her, the door opened and she turned with a jolt, coming suddenly, unexpectedly face-to-face with Pierre, her supervisor.

"What are you doing here so early?" he said, equally startled.

"I'm not—" Lisa started, wincing, struggling for an explanation. She'd forgotten Pierre's threats to come down and fire her face-to-face. But Pierre was looking past her and his gaze had already settled on Stéphane, hunched over the laptop.

"I see," he said.

He took Lisa by the lapel. "Stand still," he said. He fumbled in his pocket for his mobile phone, to call security. But at that moment, Stéphane rose and turned in a fluid, almost inhuman gesture, and Pierre's lip curled at the sight of his scar.

"Jesus, Lisa. I thought you had better taste than *that*."

Lisa stopped breathing. Her hands contracted into claws. The walls and pipes blurred at the edge of her vision, leaving only Pierre at the end of the tunnel: Pierre and his shiny suits; Pierre and his total lack of support and sympathy; Pierre who symbolised and embodied everything that had gone wrong for her since she left university...

She pushed Pierre away from her with all her strength and he staggered against the open door, pulling her with him, his grip still tight on her jacket. Unbalanced, she slammed into him and felt the impact as his head hit the edge of the door. Horrified, she jumped back and he fell at her feet, limp and unmoving.

She stood, her hands shaking, wondering how it had come to this. Stéphane was there to steady her. His hands touched her shoulders, solid and reassuring. "Don't worry, he's not dead," he said in his matter-of-fact way, looking down at the crumpled body with impassive eyes. "He's just unconscious."

Lisa let out a long, uncertain breath. "You think so?"

He grinned at her, an expression that changed his whole stance, making her heart tighten. "I can hear him breathing. Now come on, help me. We're going to stash him away from sight while the download finishes."

THEY WALKED OUT the same way they'd come in: first Lisa with her pass, then Stéphane.

She still couldn't believe they'd pulled it off.

"I've uploaded a batch of nasty viruses onto their server," Stéphane said. "It should be a while before they recover."

He went on, as they climbed the exit ramp: "We planned for this. My group has contacts with

Pensamiento Aplicado. They have servers of their own, to upload the AIs and give them a whole new world to play and develop in, where the Church won't find them."

That stopped her. "*Pensamiento Aplicado*?" she said. "The Spanish consulting firm?" The ones who had been quietly solving problems the world over?

He gave her a sidelong glance. "It's a think tank of liberated and uplifted AIs like these." He patted the case containing the hard disk. "Not many people know that. We haven't gone public yet. We're letting them work behind the scenes, applying their minds to the world's problems, finding ways to prove their worth as independent, free-thinking beings. They'll pave the way for general acceptance."

Changing the world, one step at a time. He'd found his goal, his place in the world. "Stéphane..."

He shook his head. "Andrea and Danielle have rented a boat. We sail tonight for Bilbao. You should think about leaving too. You're burnt here. When your boss wakes up—"

"I know," Lisa said. "I..."

She looked at him: his smart suit, his rugged face, with the scar pink and white in the morning sunlight.

"Do you need an extra hand?" she asked.

He looked at her, eyebrow raised. "That's a big decision. Are you sure you won't regret it?"

She looked up at the buildings lining the street. Paris had been fun in the early days—but those days were long gone, and it was time she admitted it to herself.

"I'll risk it."

"We'll be glad to have you. We always need programmers," he said, and then stopped, and his smile broadened. "*I*'ll be glad to have you, Lisa."

Man and AI both, and not quite fitting anywhere: who knew, after all, where he would lead her? "Thank you," she said, and saw him shake his head, as if no thanks at all were necessary.

Together, they walked down the street in the bright morning sun, ready to change the world.

He wasn't looking back, and neither was she.

She blew into the lab like the warm breath of an approaching storm, holding the secret of physical immortality in a simple glass test tube.

—Gareth Lyn Powell—

The Solnet
Ascendancy

Lavie Tidhar

ACCORDING TO WILLIAM *Gibson, 'the future's already here, but it's unevenly distributed.' Combine that with Jan Romein's* The Law of the Handicap of a Head Start *(originally 'De Wet van de Remmende Voorsprong') which posits that (original) technological leaders in a certain area can eventually be held back by the same technological 'lead' as the technology develops further, since the 'leaders' feel no need to renew it, as they already have it. Hence, areas that were behind in the technology can now leap ahead as they use the most innovative version of that technology.*

An extreme example of how this might work is depicted in the wry, funny and heartfelt story below, where the (re-)distribution of the future happens in an exponential curve...

0

IN THE BEGINNING there was the Phone.

And the Phone resided in the Post Office, and Telephone Cards were available at the Province's office for 500VT blong wan.

In the beginning there was the Phone, like so: a row of solar panels standing sleepily in the sun, and a radio broadcast tower, which they power, standing above them and aiming far, at the island of Espiritu Santo. Voices travel across the air and over the sea; loved ones, men of business, mothers and daughters, cousins and aunts, men of government and men of church, boyfriends and girlfriends, all queuing up, all dignity forgotten, all queuing up to toktok long telefon.

The connection drops; when it rains the line crackles; for days on end it doesn't work; engineers from Santo and from further away, from Efate Island and Port Vila, come on the Monday flight.

But all the while, when it works, the connection, this line of communication, this way of talking from afar, is seldom still. Mothers and men, everyone has someone on another island, someone to talk to, to pass and receive information in great inefficient data chunks of pure voice.

In the beginning there was the Phone.

Then came the Solnet Ascendancy.

1

IT BEGAN, THE way these things usually begin, with a Proposal.

This is Vanuatu. A Y-shaped archipelago of islands somewhere in the nowhere, South Pacific Ocean, home to Michener's mythical Bali Rai, coconut plantations, coconut crabs, a few World War II downed planes, a sunken troop-carrier, volcanoes and coral reefs: its Internet domain suffix is .vu, its capital is the distant Port Vila, described by residents and visitors alike as a slightly dodgy Australian resort town, and known by the wider electronic world primarily for not having certain kinds of laws which make placing off-shore servers there profitable. There is a foreign volunteer for every thousand people on the islands, making Vanuatu the most volunteer-intensive country in the world. Welcome to Vanuatu! AusAid, Peace Corps, VSO, VSA, CUSO, JICA; the EU, the Australian High Commission, l'Alliance française, the Chinese, the Taiwanese, the Japanese—only the Arabs and the Israelis have so far forsaken Vanuatu— what is the nature of your project? What benefit does it have to the community? What is the amount of community buy-in? Please specify expected outcome and sustainability. How much do you need? What sort of materials?

It began, the way things in Sola usually begin, if they are to begin at all, in the Market House.

10

"I WANT E-MAIL," Fatfat Freddie says. When he speaks English he has a slight Australian accent, a remnant of his four years at university on the continent, where he did tourism and hotel management. "I want to use the Internet. Can't you do something?"

His companion is a waetman; the local most recent volunteer; Mike Rowe by name, pale despite the fierce glare of the sun, digging into the local chicken and rice without enthusiasm.

"If only they could actually *cook*," he says. Fatfat Freddie nods and shovels rice into his mouth. There are three bony pieces of chicken on Mike Rowe's plate, sitting lonely and forlorn on a mountain of rice. He pushes the rice with his fork and says, "You could set up a local e-mail network fairly easily."

"Really?"

"Sure. Get a wireless router, a few wireless receivers, and a server. That might be the expensive bit, but..." he sinks into thought. "If you use an existing PC you won't even have that expense. Run it on the Province's generator... I reckon you could cover all the adjacent offices as well. Triangulate."

The Province's office sits in the midst of a cluster of offices—the entire administrative centre for Torba Province, encompassing the Banks and Torres Islands, thirteen islands, ten thousand people, eleven phones—and it is in wireless range of many departments, those being: Health, Education, Customs, Police, Court, Bank, Post Office. "Then, we can hook up the server to a phone line, get an Internet account, get it to send and receive e-mail once or twice a week. Turn it into an Internet gateway. Once you do this, once everything is in place, you can add users to the network at no cost, and charge them a membership fee. Piece of piss."

"*Kan*," Freddie says in Bislama, which is very rude. "Then why don't we do it?"

"Who's going to pay for it?" Mike Rowe says, and makes the money sign. He pushes his plate— still half-full with rice—away and lights a cigarette instead.

"We can arrange that," Freddie says. "The EU—"

"—couldn't find their ass if they sat on it," Mike Rowe, twenty-three, cynical man of the world, says with feeling.

Fatfat Freddie smiles. "Let me worry about *that*," he says. "Just write the proposal."

Mike shrugs and waves his cigarette in the air, trailing smoke. "I'll do it right now if you want to. Go back to the office?"

"Let's," Freddie says. He pushes his empty plate away and belches. "I'm finished."

They go.

11

THERE IS ONE road in Sola, a long wide track following the shore line, stretching from the little airport, across the Arep School, past shops and the Market House, past the Province office and the rest of the administrative buildings, past the wharf and the football field. As Freddie and his companion walk down it (slowly, for Freddie considers each step carefully before executing it, and when he speaks he stops to rest) they do not yet know that it is towards the future that they are walking.

100

SOLNET—The Sola Wireless Network Initiative

Objective:

To CREATE A viable wireless network within the Sola (Torba Province) administrative centre, initially within the Provincial Government offices but later to encompass all civic services (health, education, court and police etc.). Such a network [...] would act as an Internet Gateway [...] Membership fees will help reduce running costs and, assuming expansion in computer technology in Sola/Torba, even produce profit at some point. Additionally, if deemed appropriate, wireless coverage can be extended across Sola using a broadcasting station, extending the network to personal computers in Sola (such as the laptops recently acquired by the Arep teachers) and to Arep school itself, and even onto the nearby villages, making Torba Province a leader in rural Internet development.

SOLNET—BRINGING THE FUTURE TO TORBA

101

"I LOVE THE slogan," Freddie says.

"I've always wanted to be a writer," Mike Rowe says.

110

THE CONNECTION RUNS between 19.2k to 31.5k. Data packets travel from the server, a depilated old machine, into the phone wire that runs to the radio broadcast tower, and across the air, as radio waves, to the distant receiver in Santo, where they feed into the general phone system, go up into the atmosphere by satellite, and finally resolve as data packets again. The connection is slow, inefficient, the web interface running through a proxy server, the e-mail is restricted to text-only, but...

111

FROM: MIKE ROWE <mike.rowe@solnet.com.vu>
   To: James Millner <jms@archonade-systems.com.au>
   Subject: Hello from Vanuatu!

Hi Jim,

Can you imagine it? Solnet is a reality! Donors were jumping over themselves to give us funding, though as you can imagine it took months for anything to materialise. Well, everything's in place now, and I really appreciate all your help and advice in setting this up. Any chance you'll be coming to visit? Ha. We currently have the 8 computers in the Province office hooked up, but Education (3 computers), Customs (1) and Health (2) are seriously considering joining the network. As it is, all it takes is plugging in a wireless receiver on a USB port and charging them a membership fee—really appreciated that open source management system you sent me, by the way!—meanwhile a whole bunch of teachers got themselves laptops through some funding scheme and we're looking at joining them up too, but in that case would need a stronger transmitter. Also looking at a more decent hook-up via some trial satellite system being offered for the South Pacific. Expensive, but donors are being currently generous.

PS: Can you send some cigarettes?

1000

"So IF YOU do *this*," Mike Rowe says, and the mouse moves across the screen and settles, "you can run a search for anything you want. Like, what interests you?"

Father Mertock thinks about it and says, "Anything?"

"Pretty much. Look, sapos mi wantem lukaotem Jesus, oraet?"

"Oraet..."

"Mi mas typem Jesus insaed ia—" Mike Rowe types 'Jesus' into the search engine bar, "—and as you can see..."

The screen changes. Web site links appear. Father Mertock considers them, with less than whole-hearted enthusiasm, it seems to Mike.

"What about..." Father Mertock says, and stops.

"About?" Mike Rowe says.

"I heard you can see, you know..." he smiles, shyly, "Girls."

1001

ATTENTION ALL USERS

The downloading of pornographic images is strictly forbidden by Solnet rules as well as by Vanuatu government legislation. Failure to comply with said regulations will result in your account being terminated and a complaint lodged with the court clerk.

1010

Epiphany's Web Site

Hello, friend,

My name is Epiphany Gideon, and I am from the island of Vanua Lava, in beautiful Vanuatu. I am 32 years old. My husband's name is Paul, and we have one child, a boy. My husband is a teacher at the Arep School, it is a secondary school here in Sola. It is the only secondary school in the province. He has a laptop, and since a month ago he signed up with Solnet, which means he can use the Internet, but he says it is good for me to do it too, and I use it in the evenings when he goes to drink kava. This is my web site. Mike Rowe, who works for the Province, is helping me set it up. I hope I can share my life with you, wherever you are. Mike says we will all have digital cameras soon, so I will be able to post pictures of myself. Please write to me!

Love, Epiphany

1011

FROM: MIKE ROWE <mike.rowe@solnet.com.vu>
  To: James Millner <jms@archonade-systems.com.au>
  Subject: Satellite Hookup

Hi Jim,

Wow! I didn't think they'd go for it but Freddie had them eating out of his hand. We're officially on the new South Pacific Satellite Link-Up Scheme (SPS-LUS) thanks to some very generous funding from the regular donors—no doubt they're garnering much good karma alongside highly-valuable fishing rights in Vanuatu waters and the possibility of enlarging an already bloated customer base. Do I sound jaded? I guess I do—I should be happy, but I'm not sure how all this is affecting the island—it's not only the donors but one of the people here, Dudley Cruickshank, set up this web site with a donate option, basically saying send us used digital equipment and I'll plant a coconut tree for you—you know, sustainable development + personal donor involvement + third world issue—and somehow it got on the freehack. dev org and do you know what? We're flooded with second hand portable music/video players, digital cameras, wireless broadcasters/receivers, mini-stations, enough pirated and open source software to run the UN, it's scary. Some of the chiefs are distinctly not liking the change, and I have to say, on a personal level, that now even less people are working in their gardens, so we're still relying on cargo ships (now more than ever) and I am getting tired of eating rice. Been trying to disseminate some advanced cooking software but the mamas are not cooperating all that much. Speaking of which, some of the men are even less happy than the chiefs—a couple of months ago I set up that open source democratic voting system you sent me and somehow the nearby village (Mosina) organised online voting for their next chief and guess what—they elected a woman. Great embarrassment, some resentment from the men, though so far it's been quiet. I do worry what would happen once we extend this to the whole island...

1100

THE BEGINNING OF the end came like this, softly: the way the clouds spill over the volcano in the late afternoon and come to rest over the tall green hills (image available for download at a small fee from Vanua-Lava.images.com.vu with many others of our specially selected high-res digital images of these scenic and unique islands). The beginning of the end came like this:

1101

"WHAT DO YOU call this?" Mike Rowe says. He is a little older and a lot less gaunt, and in the new fashion of his country no longer smokes. Freddie sits opposite him; they are at the market house.

"Vanua Lava Aelan Faol Flambé," Freddie says proudly. He is even rounder than before. "South Pacific Fusion Cuisine is the next big thing, you know."

"I know," Mike says, and smiles, "I read about it on cnn.com."

"What do you think?" Freddie's sweeping arm indicates the new Market House, adorned with large printed images of foods from around the world, and of native islanders shooting fish with their bows and arrows, of diving for lobster, of climbing coconut trees... "The designer was from Islamabad, the pictures I took myself, and the cam feed—smile, you're on it! —is watched by about two thousand people at any given time. Around the world."

"I never imagined," Mike Rowe says, and then stops, and looks a little embarrassed.

"Local knowledge!" Freddie says effusively. "Once the access was there, once there was a little bit of technical training—the rest just happened naturally."

Mike Rowe thinks about that word, "naturally," but decides not to object. "Work is good," he says instead, "Mike Rowe Systems is doing quite well— and I got married."

"Congratulations!" Freddie says, and calls until one of his staff brings them both a drink.

"So what next?" Mike says, after they toast each other.

"Interconnectedness," Freddie says. "and self-sustainability. No more waetman/blakman, no more aelan/mainland, no more binary division. I'm talking probability diffusion, I'm talking nano-cloud mini-formations, I'm talking multiple singularities. No more food/fuel imports, no more volunteer dependency/first world handouts, no more monocrops/soil depletion. I'm talking solar/wind/ biofuel/wave generators, I'm talking biodiversity farming and reforestation, I'm talking sustainable fishing and coral reef renewal. I'm talking—"

"Whoa!" Mike Rowe says. "Where did you *get* all this stuff?"

"Information," Freddie says, "wants to be free. And independent."

1110

SATELLITE IMAGE, TAKEN from sub-orbit, penetrates through the thick white cloud that are nearly always present, to show:

The lights are strewn across the island like digital snakes, like delicate cables, necklaces of light, their patterns geometrical enigmas, beautiful like fractal shapes, the whole island burning in pinpricks of intense light, high-speed data wafting through the air, through the ground, leaping from one coconut tree to another, permeating every living thing, every drop of rain, every coral reef, a moving, always-moving, vibrant and living and alive formation, an entity of complexity and beauty that—

The image freezes, fades, replaced with static. The satellite probes, again and again, but it can find nothing of what it had seen, just a moment ago, below the clouds.

1111

Mike Rowe, older yet, smoking again, stands the ship's bow and looks at the sea as he approaches Sola. Over a year of silence—physical, virtual—and the powers that be want to know. They'd sent him in.

Rough seas, calmer now. The seawater temperature has dropped almost two degrees during their approach, and the coral reefs miss the but-all-too-characteristic bleaching.

On approach, Mike's first surprise: the wharf at Sola is brand new and bustling with activity. No hurricane damage, no bent concrete with rusted metal wires—but a pastel brown artificial material that's cool to the touch.

Old familiar faces in the crowd, a multitude of vehicles where none had been—cranes, cars, bikes run silently.

Mike steps off the boat onto the new wharf. Shouts greetings— "Yufala olsem wanem?" children run along the wharf. Rising like a fat sun, coming towards him: an old friend. Fatfat Freddie grins and says, "Sekhan!"

They shake hands. Mike shakes his head. Freddie grins. Mike says, "Wanem I hapen long ples ia?"

What happened here?

Still bemused. "Kam," Freddie says. "Yumitu go kakai."

Let's go eat.

Mike says, "I'm not hungry. Come on, Freddie. What happened?"

"Solnet," Freddie says, solemnly.

Mike, frustrated: "Solnet was a joke! 'Bringing the future to Torba.' It wasn't meant to—"

"The future," Freddie says, "is here. *We* are the future, Mike. Fuja I stap kam long Sola, Mike."

The future has come to Sola.

They walk along the shore. New buildings rise around them, organic-looking, enormous trees shaped into sheds and houses. Above their heads a small kid glides on a silent kite. Mike says, "You don't *understand*..." but knows it's him who's made the mistake.

Solar panels rotate like sunflowers, following the sun. In the distance, above the hills, a long, thin structure stretches out into the sky. Freddie follows Mike's glance, grins again, says, "Longbin blong spes."

Mike—"A long bean of space?" He remembers long beans. He had tried to grow some in his garden, back then.

Then the meaning sinks in. "You're kidding," he says.

"No," Freddie says, complacently. Away in the distance, the space elevator (if that is really what it is) shimmers in the sunlight.

"What *happened*?" Mike says again. Freddie says, "Melanesian ingenuity." It used to be his favourite buzzword. Still is, it seems. Mike: "Come *on*!"

"Information networks grow exponentially," Freddie says. "We're growing intelligent coral on the other side of the island. You should see it. Organic computing, Mike. The future came, while no one was looking. And now, at last, we're ready. We've been waiting for you—or someone like you—to come."

"Well," Mike says, "I'm here."

They pass rows of bright shops. Where once you could only buy tinned fish and candles, he can see, now the display on offer includes sun-powered gliders, deep-sea infrared goggles, what appears to be coral chunks with I/O ports...

"How would you like a job?" Freddie says. "Head of our Australian Mission, perhaps?"

"What Australian Mission?" Mike says, thinking of the hordes of Australian volunteers, unscrupulous businessmen, embassy staff and others who still populate Port Vila, on the distant capital island of Efate.

"Our new trade and aid mission," Freddie says. "We've decided it's time to export."

"Export."

"Yes. Help the Aussies with their rather backward tech. Buy some prime land out there. We have big plans, Mike. You could be a part of it. A part of the future."

Mike Rowe looks at the sea. Dolphins swim out there, beyond the breakers, and amidst them he thinks he sees a group of children, diving and swimming like fish. Another glider comes over the shore line, from the direction of Port Patteson.

"But the volunteers—" Mike says, and Freddie shakes his head. "No folentia," he says, back in Bislama. "Fifty years of volunteerism—" he makes it sound like a rare type of disease "and what did that get us?"

"Aid!" Mike says. "Projects—"

"Did any of them ever work?"

"Maybe one or two..."

"Yes," Freddie says.

Mike remembers: funding going missing, white men in distant islands trying to dictate 'community development' in places they had never seen... Away in the distance a strange type of ship begins to approach Sola, solar-powered sails opening like graceful wings.

"We've already established trade missions in the Solomons, PNG..." Freddie says. "Australia is next. Then—" he smiles. "Who knows," he says, quietly. Mike Rowe looks at him, looks away. When he looks around he feels blinded by the sun. It was only a joke, he seems to want to say, but the words won't come out. All around him the Solnet Ascendancy rises, and he stands in the middle and stares, and suddenly he can't stop grinning.

"Come on," Fatfat Freddie says affectionately. He takes Mike's arm and begins to lead him away— away towards the bright future, perhaps, wan fuja I braet tumas. "Let me buy you lunch."

Thirty storeys down, the city bustled. Thirty thousand feet up, the wind farms bucked and swooped. Between them, Tom smiled and ate lunch.

—Alasdair Stuart—

Twittering the Stars

Mari Ness

IN MY INTRODUCTION I *already told how much Twitter helped with this anthology—not just with promotion and inspiration, but with helping me find exciting new writers, as well. Mari Ness, though, went the extra mile (140 characters at a time) and sent me a whole story written in Twitter format.*

For those of you that don't know Twitter: it's a social website where users are allowed only 140 characters ('including' spaces) per message.

Yes, this can lead to the worst examples of l33tspeak on the net, but also to moments of pure poetry.

And in this case, to an intriguing story, like watching the Universe through a pinhole. Keep in mind that while such pinholes may leave out the whole picture, they can focus relentlessly...

(Note: the story is set up like the Twitter website; that is, the last tweets appear on top, the first on the bottom. So those who like to read a story in chronological order may want to start at the very end (bottom), and read up to the beginning. However, I can assure you that reading it 'into the past' works

fine, as well. Probably even better, because then you want to go back up again to enjoy the ride once more.)

I NEED TO sing to the stars again.
  five minutes ago from web

Back, finally. More than glad to be home again, more than glad to be walking on real earth, not metal. But I sense I won't be here for long.
  five minutes ago from web

Getting ready for landing. Tweet at all of you soon.
  about 23 hours ago from distweet

We're not even making a pretense of working now. Just watching the Earth. I keep looking at Texas and crying.
  6:48 pm July 3rd from distweet

I keep thinking his voice is haunting me. I'm pretty sure that's not what they want to hear.
  11:14 am July 1st from distweet

Still not sure what I'm going to say to T's family.
  11:06 am July 1st from distweet

Earth keeps growing in our windows, but so slowly. All of us are pinned to the windows, unable to work, even me.
  7:02 pm June 28th from distweet

We both started giggling like little kids. And then we made out.
  3:23 pm June 15th from distweet

M came to me yesterday and pulled me to the porthole. "Sing to the stars again," he said, so I did.
3:22 pm June 15th from distweet

Now that we're no longer worried about oxygen needs, my plants are growing like mad. Of course.
5:02 am June 2nd from distweet

Closed myself off from the rest of the group and simply watched my portholes for a long while.
11:58 pm April 16th from distweet

@piehole72 Oh, we stopped talking to each other years ago. Even before the mining, truthfully. And now we're utterly silent.
11:57 pm March 20th from distweet in reply to @ piehole72

I need to hear human voices again.
1:00 pm March 20th from distweet

Burying myself in work. Reporting. Typing. Writing. Nothing else to do, no other way to make these images go away.
3:33 pm December 25th, 2054 from distweet

A poured the rest of the chocolate packs down the waste bin today. Said we had nothing else to celebrate. Thought M would protest, but no.
6:47 pm October 20th, 2054 from distweet

We keep watching each other's skin, but no one says anything.
9:07 am October 16th, 2054 from distweet

A and R tell us fuel and oxygen levels remain at optimum levels. We will get home.

4:02 pm September 30th, 2054 from distweet

@frogheart29 Yes, I'm a botanist and microbiologist, but there's a big jump between that and being a medical doctor.

12:44 pm September 28th, 2054 from distweet in reply to frogheart29

@the28thkarenbear And you saw how well that worked with T, right?

12:43 pm September 28th, 2054 from distweet in reply to the28thkarenbear

@the28thkarenbear And if we do get a response, what do we do?

5:34 am September 26th, 2054 from distweet in reply to the 28thkarenbear

@the28thkarenbear We can take MRIs and X-rays and send the images back and have a radiologist look at them, but we won't get a response for hours.

5:34 am September 26th, 2054 from distweet in reply to the 28thkarenbear

@the28thkarenbear It wasn't enough.

8:02 pm September 24th, 2054 from distweet in reply to the 28thkarenbear

@the28thkarenbear We all took basic med training, but that's it. It doesn't feel like enough.

8:02 pm September 24th, 2054 from distweet in reply to the 28thkarenbear

A convinced she has lumps too. Worst problem with being so far out here is it takes forever to download med info.
4:16 am September 23rd, 2054 from distweet

I shouldn't say this. But what's really upsetting me is not having a doctor around anymore. I keep thinking I have lumps in my breasts.
4:15 am September 23rd, 2054 from distweet

Finding myself really missing T.
4:14 am September 23rd, 2054 from distweet

Busying myself studying the computer analyses of the space DNA, as we're calling it.
4:13 am July 28th, 2054 from distweet

M and I broke up again. It's ok. I need the space.
6:12 pm July 27th, 2054 from distweet

I need to go silent, for awhile.
12:02 pm April 20th, 2054 from distweet

It wasn't like the movies, at all. I thought he'd just float away from us, waving.
12:01 pm April 20th, 2054 from distweet

On company orders, sent T's body out to space.
12:00 pm April 20th, 2054 from distweet

R and I think T should be returned home. A, K and M creeped out by thought.
10:05 pm April 19th, 2054 from distweet

Discussion over what to do with T's body.
10:04 pm April 19th, 2054 from distweet

A ended up sleeping in my bunk with me last night; says she can't be alone right now. I know the feeling.
9:03 am April 18th, 2054 from distweet

I've sealed the damn extraterrestrial DNA with the iridium. Let the company grab it if they're so excited. Everyone agreed with me.
10:21 pm April 17th, 2054 from distweet

Company tells us we're getting additional bonus for discovering first extraterrestrial life. We all feel sick.
7:03 pm April 17th, 2054 from distweet

I'm the damn microbiologist. I should have recognized it sooner.
12:02 am April 15th, 2054 from distweet

@the28thkarenbear @loucheroo @piehole72 @ frogheart29 Yes, it is my fault.
12:01 am April 15th, 2054 from distweet

T died.
5:05 am April 12th, 2054 from distweet

K tells me T non responsive. A is trying to see if we can rush home a bit faster, but this far out, a bit faster won't help.
11:03 pm April 11th, 2054 from distweet

Also closed off cyanobacteria tanks to everyone, even me. Can't risk them getting eaten. New lifeform not airborne, so tanks should be safe.

10:26 pm April 11th, 2054 from distweet

Ship may smell but we so need bacteria to grow. If this gets out...

10:22 pm April 11th, 2054 from distweet

While waiting for response from company, stopped all onship sanitation procedures.

10:21 pm April 11th, 2054 from distweet

Sent warning to company anyway. Waiting nervously. R started playing his horror films again and I almost screamed.

9:35 pm April 11th, 2054 from distweet

Tried to run theory by T, but he's too out of it to hear me.

9:34 pm April 11th, 2054 from distweet

So not an infection as you'd call it. But something close to it. Something hungering for the bacteria T needs to live.

9:24 pm April 10th, 2054 from distweet

Every bacteria I put in with the new lifeforms gets eaten. Immediately. New thought: T is dying because his bacteria are dying.

9:21 pm April 10th, 2054 from distweet

Prepared quick batch of staph and added it to a container with the new lifeforms. Two hours later, bacteria gone.

3:34 pm April 10th, 2054 from distweet

But I keep looking, and, impossible or not: his tissues have the new lifeforms, and almost no bacteria.

2:28 am April 10th, 2054 from distweet

It's impossible. ALL human organs contain bacteria.

2:37 am April 10th, 2054 from distweet

Just noted something from T's tissue samples: they're almost completely bacteria free. How could *I* not notice this?

2:36 am April 10th, 2054 from distweet

It's an alien lifeform. I can't figure out how to counter it. I don't think we have time to test drugs and possible poisons.

10:32 pm April 9th, 2054 from distweet

This thing—I know under the circumstances this will sound awful. But under my microscope, it's utterly beautiful.

5:05 am April 9th, 2054 from distweet

T's breathing labored. M yelling at me to stay with him. I think the better bet is to try to find some bacteria that will eat this thing.

5:03 am April 9th, 2054 from distweet

We think it's entered all of his organs. I sealed off the room, though T thinks it only attacks in the utter cold of deep space.
4:59 pm April 8th, 2054 from distweet

K with T now, all suited up. Took tissue samples back to lab for study.
2:05 pm April 8th, 2054 from distweet

T delirious and having breathing problems.
6:05 am April 8th, 2054 from distweet

R set up cam in T's room so doctors on Earth can have continuous delayed stream, but of course it's hours too late. T our only doctor.
5:04 am April 8th, 2054 from distweet

Been throwing up for hours. K screaming that I botched the amputation.
4:32 am April 8th, 2054 from distweet

Went to talk to A about the aliens. She asked me to go see T instead. Did. Can't talk about it.
8:09 pm April 7th, 2054 from distweet

Found myself singing to the stars again. M found me and laughed. We even made out a bit. Life has never felt so right.
3:46 pm April 7th, 2054 from distweet

Just watched the news footage (that delay again). Saw the interview with papa and dad. I started to cry.
12:07 pm April 7th, 2054 from distweet

You know, I always figured that the first aliens would look like, you know, aliens. Not just bits of extraterrestrial DNA.

11:10 am April 7th, 2054 from distweet

@loucheroo Well, ok, truthfully for our first ever alien it's a bit disappointing looking but still! I'm SO GEEKING OUT HERE, as they used to say.

10:03 am April 7th, 2054 from distweet in reply to loucheroo

NSU has rebuilt the DNA in its lab and let it form itself. You probably already saw the pictures. AWESOME!

9:53 am April 7th, 2054 from distweet

This is the most exciting thing that's ever happened to me—finding not just a new species but a TOTALLY NEW FORM OF LIFE.

9:42 am April 7th, 2054 from distweet

@frogheart29 We made the top of Google News? AWESOME!

9:08 am April 7th, 2054 from distweet in reply to frogheart29

@the25thkarenbear Not related to archaea, bacteria, cyanobacteria or eukaryotes. Completely new lifeform.

7:04 am April 7th, 2054 from distweet in reply to the25thkarenbear

And, shit. Also confirmed: whatever these are, they are now in T's skin and blood. Probably elsewhere.

1:25 am April 7th, 2054 from distweet

Confirmation from NSU and company: Totally new lifeform. TOTALLY.
3:06 pm April 6th, 2054 from distweet

Got this non cellular structure to live on its own, in my lab. Definitely not just a space virus. Damned if I know *what* it is.
4:22 pm April 5th, 2054 from distweet

Wish I had time to teach R more of the basic principles of biology here; wasting so much time teaching him.
10:32 pm April 4th, 2054 from distweet

Back to the lab. Have got M and K to take over some of the garden duties while R helps me with some of the computer work.
7:37 am April 4th, 2054 from distweet

He's the doctor; he should know. He says medications well stocked.
7:21 am April 4th, 2054 from distweet

Went back into T's room. M right; T looks much sicker. He says he's actually better.
7:21 am April 4th, 2054 from distweet

M wants to know what I'm doing to help T. Have been so involved in studying this new structure that I haven't even thought about it.
5:02 am April 4th, 2054 from distweet

Isolated what seems to be the non cellular structure from T's tissue cells. I think this is it. Sending data back to company and NSU now.

11:03 am April 3rd, 2054 from distweet

Ran back into T's room to take pictures and samples and tell him he's the first person to ever be infected by an alien.

7:03 am April 3rd, 2054 from distweet

Getting more confirmations now—the DNA strand does not match anything seen on Earth. We think it was clinging to the comet that hit T.

6:04 pm April 2nd, 2054 from distweet

OH. MY. GOD. NSU thinks we've found the first real alien life!

2:22 pm April 2nd, 2054 from distweet

Isolated five more samples and sent the images off. This long wait for responses is really bothering me.

11:45 am March 31st, 2054 from distweet

Company asking for more samples. Working on isolating the DNA string.

3:21 am March 31st, 2054 from distweet

Ok, this is weird, but I've found a random DNA string that I can't match on any of our databases. Sending info to company to confirm.

11:23 pm March 29th, 2054 from distweet

Something got on the Nautilus tanks.

6:39 pm March 29th, 2054 from distweet

But it's remotely possible that something crept on board and has been lurking around ever since until it caused this. Or—
6:39 pm March 29th, 2054 from distweet

We *shouldn't* have any strange bacteria on board—we were pretty thoroughly, um, decontaminated, I guess you'd call it.
6:38 pm March 29th, 2054 from distweet

Sending results to company for second check.
6:02 pm March 29th, 2054 from distweet

Doing NA scans on T's blood and skin cells to see if I can isolate a bacteria or virus causing this thing.
4:43 pm March 29th, 2054 from distweet

Managed to wake T up. In severe pain; says can't swallow or eat. Skin worsening. On morphine drip.
12:15 pm March 29th, 2054 from distweet

Well, not exactly a stain—more like a fine red web settled across his skin. His skin is flaking everywhere.
5:52 am March 29th, 2054 from distweet

M overrode the computer codes and opened the door to T's room. He's covered in some red stain.
5:39 am March 29th, 2054 from distweet

K just pounded on my door. T not responding.
5:03 am March 29th, 2054 from distweet

Pulled out three chocolate packages and what they call 'steak' to celebrate. Still sick but joined in.
3:12 pm March 27th, 2054 from distweet

A and R confirm we're set for fuel. We will get home.
11:47 am March 27th, 2054 from distweet

T looked at amputation, said he couldn't have done it better himself. Still feeling sick.
9:30 am March 27th, 2054 from distweet

M came by and pulled me against him so hard I think my back is bruised. We didn't speak for two hours.
6:08 pm March 26th, 2054 from distweet

Done. Felt sick for hours afterwards.
4:31 am March 26th, 2054 from distweet

oh god I do not want to do this really do not want to do this
3:28 pm March 24th, 2054 from distweet

Company has sent detailed instructions and video on how to amputate. A and R will be helping. R's going to read the instructions to me.
10:19 am March 24th, 2054 from distweet

I don't know what I'm doing.
3:43 am March 23rd, 2054 from distweet

I'm going to have to do the surgery. We have no one else.
3:43 am March 23rd, 2054 from distweet

Sorry for silence. T badly hurt. Something struck his foot out there. The suit automatically adjusted so he only lost pressure in his foot, but it's bad.
3:24 am March 23rd, 2054 from distweet

I dragged T in it was awful it was god.
12:35 pm March 20th, 2054 from distwwet

Not just me. Nautilus demanding to know what's gone wrong.
9:53 am March 20th, 2054 from distweet

Something's wrong. T's voice is strained and I'm hearing something through the com.
9:49 am March 20th, 2054 from distweet

T's hooked up the drag line. Got signal to tug him back.
9:42 am March 20th, 2054 from distweet

Oh god. We did it. We did it. We got T back on the fuel tank.
9:23 am March 20th, 2054 from distweet

I have to tug him. I've got to get him to the tank.
8:37 am March 20th, 2054 from distweet

T's missed his fuel tank.
8:37 am March 20th, 2054 from distweet

M's on one fuel tank, attaching one drag line now. Says he's ok. I can start pulling them back.
8:03 am March 20th, 2054 from distweet

I can't watch. I can't not watch. I remember loving it out here.
7:36 am March 20th, 2054 from distweet

Them—the spacewalkers. Including M.
7:29 am March 20th, 2054 from distweet

Nautilus releasing fuel tanks. This is the bad part. If they can't float exactly there we're going to have to tug them.
7:29 am March 20th, 2054 from distweet

R says the Nautilus is as close as it can be for safety. It looks so small. They look so small.
7:09 am March 20th, 2054 from distweet

R timed me exactly. They're floating out.
7:07 am March 20th, 2054 from distweet

Put them in hatch. Watching now. If I fuck this up-
6:38 am March 20th, 2054 from distweet

T and M ready to walk out, R helping sick K pilot ship, me helping spacewalkers.
6:20 am March 20, 2054 from distweet

Just realized how rare it is for all six of us to be awake and working at the same time, but here we are-
6:19 am March 20th, 2054 from distweet

Very narrow window of opportunity here. Trying not to think about what happens if something goes wrong.
6:09 am March 20th, 2054 from distweet

Got T and M suited up. Think M said something about feeling harder than ever. Nearly smacked him.
6:03 am March 20th, 2054 from distweet

Spacewalk starting in about three hours. Of course, by the time you read this, it will already be over.
4:08 am March 20th, 2054 from distweet

T won the game, so he's heading out. Claims it's better to risk the doctor than the main pilot. M agrees.
3:06 am March 20th, 2054 from distweet

Tried to do a coin toss, but that just doesn't work in low gravity well. They're playing cards now.
2:48 am March 20th, 2054 from distweet

Crap. K extremely sick. T says unsafe to let her go. R and I not trained for spacewalks. That leaves T or A.
2:33 am March 20th, 2054 from distweet

M says not to worry. Fuel tanks won't weigh anything in space. Worrying.
10:51 am March 19th, 2054 from distweet

We've barely spoken in months.
12:39 am March 19th, 2054 from distweet

M one of the spacewalkers. I feel sick.
12:37 am March 19th, 2054 from distweet

But we'll have a small window for a spacewalk where we can in theory pick up the fuel.
7:48 pm March 18th, 2054 from distweet

Nautilus passing by in two days. Turns out the ships won't connect.

7:46 pm March 18th, 2054 from distweet

Incredibly snappish at each other. Thought it might be oxygen deprivation but we're not there yet.

7:52 am February 27th, 2054 from distweet

@frogheart72 You have one sick sense of what 'divert' means. I'm tempted to deny our relationship GRIN.

4:02 pm February 19th, 2054 from distweet

Got a full month to wait for the Nautilus to arrive. Divert me. Please.

1:29 pm February 16th, 2054 from distweet

Company tells us that they can divert the Nautilus to us. Then we hook up to *Nautilus* and take enough of their fuel to make it back.

11:13 pm February 14th, 2054 from distweet

The plants and cyanobacteria can only recycle some of the oxygen; we need the cleansers for the rest. They need fuel.

2:14 pm February 12th, 2054 from distweet

@piehole72 Yeah we can reduce rations for awhile and that will help, but not indefinitely. Plus. Oxygen.

2:13 pm February 12th, 2054 from distweet in replay to piehole72

Calculated food load and growth patterns for fifth time. Not enough food. What more do they want me to do?

4:22 am February 10th, 2054 from distweet

@piehole72 Some waste is recycled in my garden and the unused stuff thrown out.

8:27 pm February 9th, 2054 from distweet in reply to piehole72

@piehole72 For fuel reasons our food load was calculated very carefully to reduce weight. We have exactly one month of extra food. Maybe.

5:31 am February 6th, 2054 from distweet in reply to piehole72

@frogheart29 You be the judge of what to tell the parents. I'm not in the emotional space to figure that out right now.

9:04 pm February 3rd, 2054 from distweet in reply to frogheart29

@piehole72 Water's not a problem. That's all carefully controlled and recycled. The problem is oxygen and food.

4:21 pm February 3, 2054 from distweet in reply to piehole72

Attempting to see if I can grow enough to keep six people fed, but it's doubtful and my plants have to provide oxygen too.

2:38 am January 31st, 2054 from distweet

Calculations confirmed by K, Z and all engineers back on Earth. We are beyond screwed.
6:48 pm January 30th, 2054 from distweet

@piehole72 No, I'm not fucking joking.
10:26 am January 27th, 2054 from distweet in reply to piehole72

Christ. Computers tell us we don't have enough fuel to make it back.
9:24 am January 24th, 2054 from distweet

Even my tiny plants seem to be drooping.
3:21 pm January 16th, 2054 from distweet

Can't sleep. Not sure if it's the shift changes catching up on me, or—Never mind.
11:08 am January 16th, 2054 from distweet

@frogheart29 You tell Dad and Papa, I kill you.
1:24 am January 1st, 2054 from distweet in reply to frogheart29

Even if the guy does things in near zero G that I wouldn't have thought possible even in near zero G.
8:31 pm December 31st, 2053 from distweet

It was so not a relationship.
4:03 pm December 31st, 2053 from distweet

@piehole72 Scratch that. No relationship.
3:06 am December 31st, 2053 from distweet in reply to piehole72

@piehole72 No, I didn't *plan* on having a relationship up here. It just happened—did I just use the word relationship?

2:23 am December 31st, 2053 from distweet in reply to piehole72

@loucheroo But look, celibacy for four years is just not practical. I mean, I'm not a nun.

12:08 pm December 30th, 2053 from distweet in reply to loucheroo

@loucheroo You were right. I shouldn't have gotten into this.

4:03 am December 27th, 2053 from distweet

Even in the periods where I'm scheduled to sleep when he's working, he's then scheduled for leisure while I'm working. And so on.

8:04 pm December 26th, 2053 from distweet

It's not like I have any way to actually avoid him, really.

8:03 pm December 26th, 2053 from distweet

M broke up with me. This could be tricky.

6:03 pm December 26th, 2053 from distweet

I really love it out here.

2:32 am December 22, 2053 from distweet

But that's the way astrophysics works, I guess. Or do I mean solarphysics? Planetphysics? Physicsphysics? Whatever.

10:15 am December 21st, 2053

Passing the orbit of Mars again. Somehow means less this time. Still amazed that I've passed the orbit of Mars twice without seeing Mars.

10:14 am December 21st, 2053 from distweet

@frogheart29 No, you MAY NOT TELL PAPA AND DAD. Honestly! You're so lucky we have so much space between us.

7:25 pm September 1st, 2053 from distweet in reply to loucheroo

@loucheroo Nah, it really is just a shipboard fling. Nothing more, nothing less.

7:23 pm September 1st, 2053 from distweet in reply to loucheroo

M and I did a little more private celebration of our own later. More firsts in space, I expect.

5:00 am August 28th, 2053 from distweet

Huzzah! Company tells us we have all earned major bonuses, already deposited. Celebrating with another chocolate pack.

6:42 pm August 27th, 2053 from distweet

Also mined barium and lithium and lots of other things you don't care about ending in um.

3:48 am August 17th, 2053 from distweet

And people said those efficient iridium/lithium batteries would never work because iridium's so rare on Earth. HA!

3:46 am August 17th, 2053 from distweet

Mining major success. M, K and R note that we've mined 145% of expected iridium, enough to power 2 billion cars for 50 years. Staggering.
3:45 am August 17th, 2053 from distweet

Approaching the asteroid that we'll be extracting iridium from. Expect a bit of silence from me for a bit.
5:42 am July 8th, 2053 from distweet

@loucheroo We have a now two year old version of Wikipedia that M uploaded back on Earth, but of course it hasn't been updated.
11:26 pm May 11th, 2053 from distweet in reply to loucheroo

Oh, I can get on the net, but by the time my search query reaches an Earth computer and then responds, it's been a couple days. Not worth it.
5:19 pm May 9th, 2053 from distweet

@the28thkarenbear Right—I knew one of you could look it up. Star Wars. It just takes so long to research anything here.
5:17 pm May 9th, 2053 from distweet in reply to the28thkarenbear

Instead, we just see more points of lights.
3:34 am May 4th, 2053 from distweet

You know, the one where they're flying through rocks? That's what I thought we'd see, but we're not close enough to them to see rocks.
3:23 am May 4th, 2053 from distweet

Asteroid belt really not what I was expecting—even though they told me not to, kept thinking of that scene from that really old movie.
3:23 am May 4th, 2053 from distweet

Did I mention allowing R to bring along his horror movie collection a MAJOR MISTAKE?
9:42 pm April 29th, 2053 from distweet

Entered asteroid belt. This is where everyone else's jobs go nuts. A, K and R very bitchy—stress of piloting through this getting to them.
2:21 pm April 23rd, 2053 from distweet

Let's just say that some things really are better in space.
2:26 am March 1st, 2053 from distweet

M and I still managing to catch moments when we're on "breaks" during work shifts. No, you don't get details.
2:24 am March 1st, 2053 from distweet

Sigh. Just shifted to sharing work and leisure time with K again. Oh well. It's just two months, right? Wish this was with M.
6 pm February 16th, 2053 from distweet

R begging us to stop singing Judy Garland. Even promised to turn off his entire horror movie collection if we do. Tempting!
7:13 pm January 18th, 2053 from distweet

Even if he sings to the stars with me. Even if he sings Puttin' on the Ritz with a Judy Garland accent with me.

4:26 am January 11th, 2053 from distweet

@loucheroo :laughs: No, I wouldn't call this a major romance. Just a shipboard fling.

4:21 am January 11th, 2053 from distweet in reply to loucheroo

@piehole72 Um, I so don't see this group doing a space orgy. Intriguing idea, but, so not.

5:23 am January 9th, 2053 from distweet in reply to piehole72

@piehole72 Ok, the 43.5 million Mile High club at this point probably. To be technical about it.

4:42 am January 6th, 2053 from distweet in reply to piehole72

And yeah, I know all about "fornicating" in the workplace, but it's cool. And we're not the only ones doing it.

8:21 am January 4th, 2053 from distweet in reply to anaisis

I know, I know, but let's face it—near zero grav is *hot*.

10:32 pm January 3rd, 2053 from distweet

Probably shouldn't admit this, but M and I are creating our own version of the Mile High Club.

9:24 pm January 3rd, 2053 from distweet

Another long 'night' talking with M. I didn't realize how much I missed talking.
3:12 pm January 2nd, 2053 from distweet

M designed a digital flower for me. So lovely. Now must figure out something for him. What I can make with dirt?
7:22 am December 27th, 2052 from distweet

Merry Christmas to all who celebrate. To tell the truth, hardly noticing it here.
11:48 pm December 25th, 2052 from distweet

Plants still not growing. Big negative against the singing in space experiment—but I'm still doing it.
2:23 pm November 14th, 2052 from distweet

Explained that T had suggested it—apparently some sources claim it helps plants grow.
1:46 am November 2nd, 2052 from distweet

M caught me singing to the plants last—night? Shift? Time so distorted out here. Anyway. Wanted to know what I was doing.
1:45 am November 2nd, 2052 from distweet

Talked to T about lack of plant growth. He suggests singing to the plants. Feels a bit silly, but I'm trying it.
3:46 pm October 27th, 2052 from distweet

@loucheroo I haven't a clue. K and A do all of the calculations of where we are. I just busy myself with the plants and with watching space.

6:21 am October 8th, 2052 from distweet in reply to loucheroo

@the28thkarenbear We have 50 chocolate powder packs, to be used for special occasions only.

5:24 pm October 6th, 2052 from distweet in reply to the28thkarenbear

Just passed the orbit of Mars. A has to tell me which dot is Earth, now. Celebrating by opening one of the chocolate powder packs.

2:03 pm October 3rd, 2052 from distweet

@frogheart29 Nope, not even space pizza. Once I get home, I'm so going on a food splurge.

9:13 am September 21st, 2052 from distweet

Ended up taking to M for hours and hours last night. We both admitted to a deep craving for pizza.

8:13 am September 18th, 2052 from distweet

Odd, how this place can feel so crowded and so alone, all at once.

7:04 am August 11th, 2052 from distweet

@the28thkarenbear Well, being the sweetest out of 6 doesn't mean much.

6:54 pm March 13th, 2052 from distweet in reply to the28thkarenbear

@the28thkarenbear AWW. You are the sweetest person on the planet.
5:23 pm March 11th, 2052 from distweet in reply to the28thkarenbear

I probably could concoct some alcoholic thing from my plants, but probably not the best idea.
1:19 pm March 10th, 2052 from distweet

Still, if you're reading this, please respond. Just so that I don't feel so alone.
10:42 am March 8th, 2052 from distweet

Right. Keep forgetting that it now takes hours for my tweets to reach you and hours for you to respond.
10:42 am March 8th, 2052 from distweet

Is anybody reading this? Anybody?
7:18 pm March 7th, 2052 from distweet

I wish all of you could see this with me.
3:01 am February 26th, 2052 from distweet

Slightly upsetting to realize that a supernova is much brighter than Earth, but it's so beautiful.
5:18 pm February 23rd, 2052 from distweet

We're watching the Betelgeuse supernova too. It's—I can't tell you how spectacular it is from here. Only the sun is brighter.
5:16 pm February 23rd, 2052 from distweet

To make up for it, A had pictures of little red envelopes on our hand screens, that exploded into fireworks when we thumbed over them.
8:03 pm January 23rd, 2052 from distweet

A celebrated Chinese New Year today by opening every door on the ship. I think she just wanted to catch T naked.
8:02 pm January 23rd, 2052 from distweet

Sorry for the long silence. Just finding that I don't have much to say. I'm caught in the silence of stars.
4:02 pm October 12th, 2051 from distweet

@frogheart29 My first niece! Congratulations! I wish I could hold her. Show her pictures of me for me, will ya?
7:43 pm May 17th, 2051 from distweet in reply to frogheart29

And when the plants are growing, they're growing in weird directions.
12:49 pm May 5th, 2051

@loucheroo Oh, we're fine for food even without the garden. I just miss biting into a real tomato, you know?
12:42 pm May 5th, 2051 from distweet

I think the plants know we're leaving the sun.
10:31 am May 4th, 2051 from distweet

The garden isn't producing as much as expected. We should have everything—real soil, water, fertilizer, robot pollinators—
10:31 am May 4th, 2051 from distweet

I keep finding myself looking out the portholes in the gardens and labs and in our living area, and wanting to sing to the stars.
6:02 pm April 23rd, 2051 from distweet

Trying to figure out how K passed the psych tests to get on here. I know, double PhD, quan comp/eng, 8 years Chinese Air Force. Still.
3:22 am March 27th, 2051 from distweet

Ok, our worst mistake? Letting R bring along his horror film collection. In space no one can hear you scream. Yeah, right.
4:06 am March 7th, 2051 from distweet

I say I keep everyone breathing.
10:13 pm February 26th, 2051 from distweet

T says he keeps everyone alive. Not that anyone's needed a doctor yet, and we haven't seen him do anything else except watch the stars.
10:12 pm February 26th, 2051 from distweet

A says she's the only one with mission for the entire trip. The rest of us stop after we mine the iridium/lithium.
10:12 pm February 26th, 2051 from distweet

K and R say they are piloting the ship. Without them, no iridium/lithium.

10:11 pm February 26th, 2051 from distweet

Major fight broke out over who has the most important job on the ship. M says lithium entire point of trip.

10:11 pm February 26th, 2051 from distweet

Sigh. SOME people have no idea how to share living quarters. You'd think a doctor of all people would be less of a slob.

8:11 pm January 24th, 2051 from distweet

@frogheart29 Oh, it's definitely NOT full gravity. Our legs will be so rubbery when we return. But it's enough to keep the tanks going.

7:46 pm January 2nd, 2051 from distweet

@frogheart29 Heh, I haven't worked out how the low grav works either—something about the way this ship spins.

2:41 am January 2nd, 2051 from distweet

Throwing tomatoes through low grav is awesome. Saying no more for now.

1:32 am January 1st, 2051 from distweet

Oh, and we have a picture of a Christmas tree up on the screen in the rec room. Vaguely depressing honestly.

11:09 am December 25th, 2050 from distweet

Merry Christmas to all who celebrate! Not much happening here although R put on some carols.
11:08 am December 25th, 2050 from distweet

The food garden's a bit experimental, but the company's worried about the long term effects of no fresh food for four years.
8:07 pm October 8th, 2050 from distweet

We have two spacegardens: the cyanobacteria tanks for recycling waste and producing oxygen, and a food garden.
8:06 pm October 8th, 2050 from distweet in reply to frogheart29

@frogheart29 It's less a spaceship than a biome, really.
11:43 am October 7th, 2050 from distweet in reply to frogheart29

@loucheroo Oh, I'm sure they're monitoring this. I'm not going to tell you EVERYTHING on this. Or in email.
10:15 am October 7th, 2050 from distweet in reply to loucheroo

@anaisis It's supposed to increase social stability, but what I'm trying to tell them is, my plants won't work that way.
10:13 am October 7th, 2050 from distweet in reply to anaisis

And leisuring—is that a word? with the person you work with, and then it switches and you're with a new person.

7:06 pm October 6th, 2050 from distweet

So far so good, but, they're also switching our schedules every two months. That way, every two months we're working with someone else.

7:06 pm October 6th, 2050 from distweet

@the28thkarenbear Basically, they're setting up three eight hour shifts, two people per shift. You work eight hours, have eight hours for leisure.

7:06 pm October 6th, 2050 from distweet in reply to the28thkarenbear

So every third shift, I'm going to be gardening in the dark. Why don't they just switch the other shifts and not mine?

11:06 am October 5th, 2050 from distweet

The food gardens mimic seasons. But if I switch the lights around them to match my shifts, it will confuse the plants. They could die.

11:06 am October 5th, 2050 from distweet

The cyanobacteria tanks are set to maximum output: tropical conditions, with warm water, frequent 'rain' and twelve hours of light.

11:05 am October 5th, 2050 from distweet

They're telling me I'm going to have to switch shifts too, which doesn't work with the garden.

11:05 am October 5th, 2050 from distweet

Just got the info about the shift schedules and ongoing changes. Not happy.

11:04 am October 5th, 2050 from distweet

It's so hard to remember that I'm supposed to be working, not watching the stars. No one on the space stations ever mentioned this.

12:43 pm September 12th, 2050 from distweet

@piehole72 Well, if you're lucky, you'll find out. *waggle eyebrows*

11:58 pm July 16th, 2050 from distweet in reply to piehole72

@piehole72 Well, you know what they say about missing ex boyfriends out in outer space—actually, what do they say?

11:04 pm July 16th, 2050 from distweet in reply to piehole72

@piehole72 Heh. Let's leave the orgy chat for later, k?

10:41 pm July 16th, 2050 from distweet in reply to piehole72

@loucheroo Hey, that's why they're paying us the big bucks.

9:41 pm July 16th, 2050 from distweet in reply to loucheroo

@piehole72 But you know, sleeping with coworkers and all that. So.

7:05 pm July 16th, 2050 from distweet in reply to piehole72

@piehole72 I should have guessed that the next thing you'd ask about is my sex life. Well. A couple of the others are hot...

7:04 pm July 16th, 2050 from distweet in reply to piehole72

@piehole72 Oh, just five others—the two pilots, the doctor, the two engineers. And me the plant goddess.

11:47 am July 16th, 2050 from distweet in reply to piehole72

@the28thkarenbear Heh, if we have a top secret mission, no one's told me. No, I think it's all on the level: lithium and iridium mining.

8:47 PM July 15th, 2050 from distweet in reply to the28thkarenbear

Won't be able to tweet much, though—we're limited to an average of one per day for financial reasons—costs too much from space.

8:30 PM July 15, 2050 from distweet

Just boarded. This is going to be an awesome trip. I feel it in my bones. I feel like singing to the stars.

3:43 PM July 15th, 2050 from distweet

So brave, so nervous. Both of them. Hand in hand, no gloves and no special suits. An unlocked hatch, a step outside. Truth: Earth survided.

—Jacques Barcia—

Seeds

Silvia Moreno-Garcia

AFTER THE OPEN *reading period closed, and I had a good overview of all stories sent my way—both solicited and unsolicited—I saw both certain themes developing and the variety of settings, characters and ideas arising that I was hoping for.*

One particular theme is the importance of sustainable farming, be it through soil ("The Earth of Yunhe"), developing better farming methods through online ideas exchange ("Russian Roulette 2020"), adapting consumer patterns to local circumstances ("Summer Ice"), improving local cuisine ("The Solnet Ascendancy," even if that certainly, as with several of the other examples, wasn't the main thrust of the story) and indeed the use of different 'Seeds.'

Since the anthology has a tight focus, I aimed for maximum variety and diversity in locales, characters and writers, while at the same time trying to select (what I thought) were the best stories. The tightrope, I suppose, any well-intended editor tries to walk.

So while I (obviously) leave the question of quality up to the readers, critics and reviewers, I do think Shine *scores well in terms of character and setting variety: both are literally from all over the globe. As to the writers, while the male/female spread is close to parity (9 man, 8 women), I wish I could have included more writers from different nationalities and races. Yes, Shine debuts a Brazilian native and features a Russian emigrant living in the UK, an Israeli (where he lives at any time is hard to keep up with), a Frenchwoman and Silvia here who is a Mexican emigrant living in Canada (and a Canadian expat living in South Korea who has an Indonesian girlfriend: not sure if that counts, though). Yet I would have liked even more diversity in authors, and will try to do better in a next project.*

In the meantime, do enjoy this wry story where corporate goals clash with local needs leading to some unexpected developments...

TWO TEENAGERS BOLTED past him, running so fast James almost lost his balance and dropped his multi-text device, which would have been a major problem because he had no idea how to get back to the main road. The paths had twisted and turned a dozen times before he had finally parked his car close to the town square with its double arcades.

James glared at the teenagers but they kept running. He was sure they had bumped into him on purpose. They probably recognize the logo on his suitcase.

He didn't get it. Just on Sunday he watched a group of UNAM students parading around the Angel of Independence, wearing black and white Zapata t-shirts and yelling "*maiz y libertad.*" Like a perfect seed and a perfect crop was somehow wrong and Germingen was the devil. It all sounded suspiciously anarchistic to him.

Fine, it was copyrighted technology and the seeds were sterile unless they were treated with Germingen's very own Germingrow. If the user agreement was not followed exactly as intended, Germingen would trigger the Trojan Horse built into the genetic map of the seed, but so what? You got large, perfect crops in return. In the end, they were doing these people a favor.

James shook his head, straightened his clothes and kept on walking until he reached the fountain in the middle of the plaza. Without people wearing a geo-location unit, all he could do was squint and wait under the harsh sun for his contact to arrive, guessing, rather than knowing, if any of the townsfolk headed his way were Mr. Totol.

The wind blew a cloud of dust in James face and he sputtered and swore. His suit was nano-treated, but the dirt was probably pullulating with dog faeces and some nasty germs.

When the cloud dissipated a man wearing white linen pants, a matching shirt and hat approached him and extended his hand.

"I'm Alejandro Totol," he said. "You've got to be from Germingen."

James had all of his data on the multi-text but it was going to do no good if Mr. Totol did not carry his own multi-text. By the looks of it, all the farmer had with him was a crude knapsack. He would have to introduce himself the old-fashioned way.

"James Clark, Customer Satisfaction and Services Representative, Germingen, Mexico and Caribbean division. At Germingen we develop the most resistant, innovative crops to supply the farms of tomorrow—"

"That's nice," said Mr. Totol, interrupting James before he could finish his speech.

"Bigger, better, stronger crops make a bigger, better, stronger world," James ran his thumb across his multi-text device. "It says here, Mr. Totol, that you are one of our silver maize seed users. Ten-year contract, eight percent copyright and user fee and insured GM seeds, right?"

"It's not my contract."

"Pardon?"

"It's not my contract. The governor got the contract for the whole state and we have to use the seeds. Everyone in Oaxaca has to do it. They have this state levy on us for the stuff."

"Yes, well, I'm talking about your individual sub-agreement, not the state interposed multi-lateral limited-license use agreement," he said cheerfully.

And what an agreement it was. Oaxaca had been one of the states that had resisted the GMO seeds most vigorously—there had been some bullshit about local customs, as if a piece of dough was some sacred artefact—but in the end the governor had signed the contract quickly enough.

Mr. Totol shifted his feet and shrugged.

"Did you know domesticated corn originated in Mexico?"

James tapped his device twice and raised an eyebrow. "Mr. Totol, you placed a call two days ago."

"We're supposed to call you if something goes wrong. That's what they said and we dialled the number."

"Very well, and please explain what went wrong," James said and he grabbed the stylo and flipped it between his fingers. The seeds were damn easy to grow, resistant to pesticides and insects. It wasn't the seeds' fault that some people were stupid. Germingen provided training for the illiterate, low-tech customers teeming throughout Latin America and the Caribbean, but there were some glitches here and there and in Oaxaca, with its Nahuatl population clinging to their dialects, it was sometimes a damned nightmare.

Nevertheless, James had managed to go from step two to step five in less than three years and he was confident that he would reach step six at the end of December. He was aiming for a month-long session of gambling in Macau with the bonus that would net him.

"Well?" James asked.

"I'm not sure something went wrong."

"Mr. Totol, I drove all the way from Mexico City because you said you had an issue with your corn crop. Am I to understand that nothing has happened to it?"

"Something happened," Mr. Totol said with a nod. "There's hundreds of corn varieties in Mexico, did you know that?"

James carefully blotted the sweat from his forehead with a handkerchief. He put his hands behind his back and stared at Mr. Totol.

"Is there an issue with the corn?" he asked very slowly.

"We thought you might mind. When the Germingen people came they said we had to phone you and they gave us the number," Mr. Totol held up an old-fashioned paper business card. "Right there, see? Customer issues. The governor says we got to use the seeds and we can't use no other seeds. My family's been breeding corn for years but no more. We got to plant your fancy seeds and we've got to use them and they're insured; so if there's any problems we phone you, you figure it out, and it's our money back and we get out of the agreement, right? In short, we don't want the agreement."

"Mr. Totol, we do insure all of our crops, but lets not get ahead of ourselves. We generally solve any customer issues within two weeks and no refunds or termination of agreements are necessary. Now, what is the problem you have been experiencing?"

"There's huitlacoche on the corn."

"Huitlawhat?" James asked. The man was probably speaking Nahuatl.

"Oh, the Mexicas loved it. Absolutely loved it. Moctezuma was crazy over it. Quite the eater he was, that Moctezuma. You know, every morning fish was brought from Veracruz to Mexico City by a system of relay runners. They carried the fish fresh from the coast to the emperor's table in just a few of hours."

"What the hell are you talking about?"

The man opened his knapsack. He took out a grey ear of corn with the kernels swollen ten times its normal size. It looked like the corn had a tumor. In truth, it was covered in fungus.

"Dear God!" James yelled and he began to pound frantically on his multi-text device, photos and words plopping from the little pad until it was there in red capital letters: *ustilago maydis*.

"It's very good in a quesadilla," Mr. Totol said nonchalantly.

"Where did you find it?" James whispered as he stared at the ugly grey and black monstrosity the man was waving at him.

"Oh, it's all over my field. It's going to fetch a good price in the market."

"You're going to eat it?"

"Sure. Delicious."

"It's a pathogenic fungus. It's a pest. How the hell did it get on our corn?"

"The Mexica ate fly larvae and axolotls."

That was not the answer James was looking for. He jammed his fingers against the screens and screens of information.

He tried to think, to formulate a plan. Evidently the corn smut had mutated and invaded their pristine, perfect corn corp.

James was sweating. He could imagine his clothes sticking to his body, even though this was impossible because they were nano-treated. But it was a day for impossibilities. This was not supposed to happen. The corn was resistant against anything and everything.

You could spray the toughest pesticide on it and it would survive. Well, the toughest Germingen pesticide, anyway. The seed contract also came with a binding, collateral pesticide agreement.

James could just imagine the look his boss would give him if James informed him they had lost a whole crop to a corn smut infestation. And what if it should spread? He could picture rows and rows of grey and black fungus-covered corn against a blue sky.

"We'll have to burn it all. I'll call in a team and we will get rid of the fungus Mr. Totol," James said, flipping through the emergency procedures manual.

"Why'd you want to burn it? It's nice to breed it. It goes well with tamales. Look, you just make a little cut at the base of the corn..."

"Mr. Totol, I don't think you understand the enormity of the issue," James muttered and after drafting a quick message, he punched in the four digit security code necessary to alert his head office of the problem.

James closed his eyes. He took a deep breath and tried to steady himself. Everything was going to be fine. The team would fly in, burn the whole thing to cinders, stomp every bit of fungus out. Then they would rescind the agreement and forget about this damn town and its rampant fungus. Blot it out. Nothing to see here.

"Bigger, better, stronger crops make a bigger, better, stronger world," James whispered.

It made him feel better. He took a deep breath and let it out.

"It's fine, Mr. Totol. We are going to contain it. After all, its not like the damn thing has legs. It can't spread that far."

"That's the issue," Mr. Totol took off his hat and scratched the back of his neck. "Remember when I told you the runners used to bring fresh fish for Moctezuma every morning?"

James looked up and stared at Mr. Totol.

"Yeah. I think that huitlacoche is all over the country by now."

Mr. Totol smiled cheerfully and put his hat on again.

"*Maiz y libertad* Mr. Clark," he said with a wink.

Somehow, James didn't think he'd make it to step six before December.

"I told you it had some design flaws," Audrey sighed as the city turned upside down and sank, shining, car horns blaring, into the sea.

—Paula Stiles—

At Budokan

Alastair Reynolds

TYPICALLY—I LIKE to think—for Shine, *the writer who is also the singer of a death metal band does not use heavy metal (apart from one short comparison) in his story, while the writer whose taste has developed away from heavy metal (or has become, or always was, much broader, as you will) uses it as the main stage for his story.*

Irony, sweet irony.

After I met Al and Josette at a certain BeneluxCon in Belgium—where Al said they had a farm in a village that nobody of his Dutch friends knew about, after which I said the name (Zuilichem) in the proper local accent—we have been good friends, and I felt very privileged when, at the 2009 EasterCon, Al told me about the 10-year deal he had made with Gollanz, several months before the official announcement was made.

I felt even more privileged, though, when Al sent me this story for Shine: its theme is unsuspected (his story in the Paul J. McAuley/Kim Newman anthology In Dreams *of 1992 was about house music), but hit all the right spots for me. In it, all the taps are spinal, the volume is turned to 11 and the special effects to 12. In this future, everybody thinking heavy metal is the dinosaur of the music scene is both right and wrong...*

I'M SOMEWHERE OVER the Sea of Okhotsk when the nightmare hits again. It's five years ago and I'm on the run after the machines went beserk. Only this time they're not just enacting wanton, random mayhem, following the scrambled choreography of a corrupted performance program. This time they're coming after *me*, all four of them, stomping their way down an ever-narrowing back alley as I try to get away, the machines too big to fit in that alley, but in the malleable logic of dreams somehow not too big, swinging axes and sticks rather than demolition balls, massive, indestructible guitars and drumsticks. I reach the end of the alley and start climbing up a metal ladder, a ladder that morphs into a steep metal staircase, but my limbs feel like they're moving through sludge. Then one of them has me, plucking me off the staircase with steel fingers big enough to bend girders, and I'm lifted through the air and turned around, crushed but somehow not crushed, until I'm face to face with James Hetfield out of Metallica.

"You let us down, Fox," James says, his voice a vast seismic rumble, animatronic face wide enough to headbutt a skyscraper into rubble. "You let us down, you let the fans down, and most of all you let yourself down. Hope you feel ashamed of yourself, buddy."

"I didn't mean..." I plead, pityingly, because I don't want to be crushed to death by a massive robot version of James Hetfield.

"Buddy." He starts shaking me, holding me in his metal fist like a limp rag doll.

"I'm sorry man. This wasn't how it was meant…"

"Buddy."

But it's not James Hetfield shaking me to death. It's Jake, my partner in Morbid Management. He's standing over my seat, JD bottle in one hand, shaking me awake with the other. Looking down at the pathetic, whimpering spectacle before him.

"Having it again, right?"

"You figured."

"Buddy, it's time to let go. You fucked up big time. But no one died and no one wants to kill you about it now. Here." And he passes me the bottle, letting me take a swig of JD to settle my nerves. Doesn't help that I don't like flying much. The flashbacks usually happen in the Antonov, when there's nowhere else to run.

"Where are we?" I ask groggily.

"About three hours out."

I perk up. "From landing?"

"From departure. Got another eight, nine in the air, depending on head-winds."

I hand him back the bottle. "And you woke me up for that?"

"Couldn't stand to see you suffering like that. Who was it this time? Lars?"

"James."

Jake gives this a moment's consideration. "Figures. James is probably not the one you want to piss off. Even now."

"Thanks."

"You need to chill. I was talking to them last week." Jake gave me a friendly punch on the shoulder. "They're cool with you, buddy. Bygones be bygones. They were even talking about getting some comp seats for the next stateside show, provided we can arrange wheelchair access. Guys are keen to meet Derek. But then who isn't?"

I think back to the previous evening's show. The last night of a month-long residency at Tokyo's Budokan. Rock history. And we pulled it off. Derek and the band packed every seat in the venue, for four straight weeks. We could have stayed on another month if we didn't have bookings lined up in Europe and America.

"I guess it's working out after all," I say.

"You sound surprised."

"I had my doubts. From a musical standpoint? You had me convinced from the moment I met Derek. But turning this into a show? The logistics, the sponsorship, the legal angles? Keeping the rights activists off our back? Actually making this thing turn a profit? That I wasn't so certain about."

"Reason I had to have you onboard again, buddy. You're the numbers man, the guy with the eye for detail. And you came through."

"I guess." I stir in my seat, feeling the need to stretch my legs. "You—um—checked on Derek since the show?"

Jake shoots me a too-quick nod. "Derek's fine. Hit all his marks tonight."

Something's off, and I'm not sure what. It's been like this since we boarded the Antonov. As if something's bugging Jake and he won't come out with whatever it was.

"Killer show, by all accounts," I say.

"Best of all the whole residency. Everything went like clockwork. The lights, the back projection..."

"Not just the technical side. One of the roadies reckoned Extinction Event was amazing."

Jake nods enthusiastically. "As amazing as it ever is."

"No, he meant exceptionally amazing. As in, above and beyond the performance at any previous show."

Jake's face tightens at the corners. "I heard it too, buddy. It was fine. On the nail. The way we like it."

"I got the impression it was something more than..." But I trail off, and I'm not sure why. "You sure there's nothing we need to talk about?"

"Nothing at all."

"Fine." I give an easy smile, but there's still something unresolved, something in the air between us. "Then I guess I'll go see how the big guy's doing."

"You do that, buddy."

I unbuckle from the seat and walk along the drumming, droaning length of the Antonov's fuselage. It's an AN-225, the largest plane ever made, built fifty years ago for the Soviet space program. There are only two of them in the world, and Morbid Management and Gladius Biomech have joint ownership of both. Putting Derek's show together is so logistically complex that we need to be assembling one stage set when the other's still in use. The Antonovs leapfrog the globe, crammed to the gills with scaffolding, lighting rigs, speaker stacks, instruments, screens, the whole five hundred tonne spectacle of a modern rock show. Even Derek's cage is only a tiny part of the whole cargo.

I make my way past two guitar techs and a roadie deep into a card game, negotiate a long passage between two shipping containers, and pass the fold-down desk where Jake has his laptop set up, reviewing the concert footage, and just beyond the desk lies the cage. It's lashed down against turbulence, scuffed and scratched from where it was loaded aboard. We touch up the yellow paint before each show so it all looks gleaming and new. I brush a hand against the tubular steel framing.

Strange to think how alarmed and impressed I was the first time, when Jake threw the switch. It's not the same now. I know Derek a lot better than I did then, and I realise that a lot of his act is, well, just that. Act. He's a pussycat, really. A born showman. He knows more about image and timing than almost any rock star I've ever worked with.

Derek's finishing off his dinner. Always has a good appetite after a show, and at least it's not lines of coke and underage hookers he has a taste for.

He registers my presence and fixes me with those vicious yellow eyes.

Rumbles a query, as if to say, *can I help you?*

"Just stopping by, friend. I heard you went down a storm tonight. Melted some faces with Extinction Event. Bitching Rise of the Mammals, too. We'll be shifting so many downloads we may even have to start charging to cover our overheads."

Derek offers a ruminative gurgle, as if this is an angle he's never considered before.

"Just felt I ought to" And I rap a knuckle against the cage. "You know, give credit. Where it's due."

Derek looks at me for a few more seconds, then goes back to his dinner.

You can't say I don't try.

I'D BEEN FLYING when Jake got back in touch. It was five years ago, just after the real-life events of my dream. I was grogged out from departure lounge vodka slammers, hoping to stay unconscious until the scramjet was wheels down and I was at least one continent away from the chaos in LA. Wasn't to be, though. The in-flight attendant insisted on waking me up and forcing me to make a choice between two meal serving options: chicken that tasted like mammoth, or mammoth that tasted like chicken.

What was it going to be?

"Give me the furry elephant," I told him. "And another vodka."

"Ice and water with that, sir?"

"Just the vodka."

The mammoth really wasn't that bad—certainly no worse than the chicken would have been—and I was doing my best to enjoy it when the incoming call icon popped into my upper right visual field. For a moment I considered ignoring it completely. What could it be about, other than the mess I'd left behind after the robots went beserk? But I guess it was my fatal weakness that I'd never been able to *not* take a call. I put down the cutlery and pressed a finger against the hinge of my jaw. I kept my voice low, subvocalising. Had to be my lawyer. Assuming I still *had* a lawyer.

"OK, lay it on me. Who's trying to sue me, how much are we looking at, and what am I going to have to do to get them off my case?"

"Fox?"

"Who else. You found me on this flight, didn't you?"

"It's Jake, man. I learned about your recent difficulties."

For a moment the vodka took the edge off my surprise. "You and the rest of the world."

Jake sounded pained. "At least make a effort to sound like you're glad to hear from me, buddy. It's been a while."

"Sorry, Jake. It's just not been the best few days of my life, you understand?"

"Rock and roll, my friend. Gotta roll with it, take the rough with the smooth. Isn't that what we always said?"

"I don't know. Did we?" Irritation boiled up inside me. "I mean, from where I'm sitting, it's not like we ever had much in common."

"Cutting, buddy. Cutting. And here I am calling you out of the blue with a business proposition. A proposition that might just dig you out of the hole you now find yourself in."

"What kind of proposition?"

"It's time to reactivate Morbid Management."

I let that sink in before responding, my mind scouting ahead through the possibilities. Morbid Management was defunct, and for good reason. We'd exhausted the possibilities of working together. Worse than that, our parting had left me with a very sour opinion of Jake Addison. Jake had always been the tail wagging that particular dog, and I'd always been prepared to go along with his notions. But he hadn't been prepared to put his faith in me when I had the one brilliant idea of my career.

We'd started off signing conventional rock acts. Mostly they were manufactured, put together with an eye on image and merchandising. But the problem with conventional rock acts is that they start having ideas of their own. Thinking they know best. Get ideas in their head about creative independence, artistic credibility, solo careers. One by one we'd watched our money-spinners fly apart in a whirlwind of ego and ambition. We figured there had to be something better.

So we'd created it. Ghoul Group was the world's first all-dead rock act. Of course you've heard of them: who hasn't? You've probably even heard that we dug up the bodies at night, that we sucked the brains out of a failing mid-level pop act, or that they were zombies controlled by Haitian voodoo. Completely untrue, needless to say. It was all legal, all signed off and boilerplated. We kept the bodies alive using simple brain-stem implants, and we used the same technology to operate Ghoul Group on stage. Admittedly there was something Frankensteinesque about the boys and girls on stage—the dead look in their eyes, the scars and surgical stitches added for effect, the lifeless, parodic shuffle that passed for walking—but that was sort of the point.

Kids couldn't get enough of them. Merchandising went through the roof, and turned Morbid Management into a billion dollar enterprise.

Only trouble was it couldn't last. Rock promotion sucked money away as fast as it brought it in, and the only way to stay ahead of the curve was to keep manufacturing new acts. The fatal weakness of Ghoul Group was that the concept was easily imitated: anyone with access to a morgue and a good lawyer could get in on the act. We realised we had to move on.

That was when we got into robotics.

Jake and I had both been in metal acts before turning to management, and we were friendly with Metallica. The band was still successful, still touring, but they weren't getting any younger. Meanwhile a whole raft of tribute acts fed off the desire for the fans to see younger versions of the band, the way they'd been twenty or thirty years before. Yet no matter how good they were, the tribute acts were never quite realistic enough to be completely convincing. What was needed—what might fill a niche that no one yet perceived—were tribute acts that were *completely* indistinguishable from their models, and which could replicate them at any point in their careers. And — most importantly — never get tired doing it, or start demanding a raise.

So we made them. Got in hock with the best Japanese robotics specialists and tooled up a slew of different incarnations of Metallica. Each robot was a lifesize, hyper-realistic replica of a given member of the band at a specific point in their career. After processing thousands of hours of concert footage, motion capture sofware enabled these robots to behave with staggering realism. They moved like people. They sounded like people. They sweated and exhaled. Unless you got close enough to look right into their eyes, there was no way at all to tell that you were not looking at the real thing.

We commissioned enough robots to cover every market on the planet, and sent them out on tour. They were insanely successful. The real Metallica did well out of it and within months we were licensing the concept to other touring acts. The money was pumping in faster than we could account it. But at the same time, mindful of what had happened with Ghoul Group, we were thinking ahead. To the next big thing.

That was when I'd had my one original idea.

I'd been on another flight, bored out of my mind, watching some news item about robots being used to dismantle some Russian nuclear plant that had gone meltdown last century. These robots were Godzilla-sized machines, but the thing that struck me was that more or less humanoid in shape. They were being worked by specialist engineers from half way round the world, engineers who would zip into telepresence rigs and actually feel like they were wearing the robots; actually feel as if the reactor they were taking apart was the size of a doll's house.

It wasn't the reactor I cared about, of course. It was the robots. I'd had a flash, a mental image. We were already doing Robot Metallica. What was to stop us doing Giant Robot Metallica?

By the time I'd landed, I'd tracked down the company that made the demolition machines. By the time I'd checked in to my hotel and ordered room service, I'd established that they could, in principle, build them to order and incorporate the kind of animatronic realism we were already using with the lifesize robots. There was, essentially, no engineering barrier to us creating a twenty metre or thirty metre high James Hetfield or Lars Ulrich. We had the technology.

Next morning, shivering with excitement, I put the idea to Jake. I figured it for an easy sell. He'd see the essential genius in it. He'd recognise the need to move beyond our existing business model.

But Jake wasn't buying.

I've often wondered why he didn't go for it. Was it not enough of a swerve for him, too much a case of simply scaling up what we were already doing? Was he shrewd enough to see the potential for disaster, should our robots malfunction and go beserk? Was it simply that it was my idea, not his?

I don't know. Even now, after everying else that's happened—Derek and all the rest—I can't figure it out. All I can be sure of is that I knew then that it was curtains for Morbid Management. If Jake wasn't going to back me the one time I'd had an idea of my own, I couldn't keep on working with him.

So I'd split. Set up my own company. Continued negotiations with the giant demolition robot manufacturers and—somewhat sneakily, I admit—secured the rights from Metallica to all larger-than-life robotic reenactment activities.

OK, so it hadn't ended well. But the idea'd been sound. And stadiums can always be rebuilt.

"You still there, buddy?"

"Yeah, I'm still here." I'd given Jake enough time to think I'd hung up on him. Let the bastard sweat a little, why not. Over the roar of the scramjet's ballistic re-entry profile I said: "We're gonna lose comms in a few moments. Why don't you tell me what this is all about."

"Not over the phone. But here's the deal." And he gave me an address, an industrial unit on the edge of Helsinki. "You're flying into Copenhagen, buddy. Take the 'lev, you can be in Helsinki by evening."

"You have to give me more than that."

"Like you to meet the future of rock and roll, Fox. Little friend of mine by the name of Derek. You're going to like each other."

THE BASTARD HAD me, of course.

It was winter in Helsinki so evening came down cold and early. From the maglev I took a car straight out into the industrial sticks, a dismal warren of slab-sided warehouses and low-rise office units. Security lights blazed over fenced-off loading areas and nearly empty car parks, the asphalt still slick and reflective from afternoon rain. Beyond the immediate line of warehouses, walking cranes stomped around the docks, picking up and discarding shipping containers like they were coloured building blocks. Giant robots. I didn't need to be reminded about giant fucking robots, not when I was expecting an Interpol arrest warrant to be declared in my name at any moment. But at least they wouldn't come looking here too quickly, I thought. On the edge of Helsinki, with even the car now departed on some other errand, I felt like the last man alive, wandering the airless boulevards of some huge abandoned moonbase.

The unit Jake had told me to go to was locked from the road, with a heavy duty barrier slid across the entrance. Through the fence, it looked semi-abandoned: weeds licking at its base, no lights on in the few visible windows, some of the security lights around it broken or switched off. Maybe I'd been set up. It wouldn't be like Jake, but time had passed and I still wasn't ready to place absolute, unconditional trust in my old partner. All the same, if Jake did want to get back at me for something, stranding me in a bleak industrial development was a very elaborate way of going about it.

I pressed the intercom buzzer in the panel next to the barrier. I was half expecting no one to answer it and, if they did, I wasn't quite sure how I was going to explain my presence. But the voice that crackled through the grille was familiar and unfazed.

"Glad you could make it, buddy. Stroll on inside and take a seat. I'll be down in a minute. I can't wait to show Derek off to you."

"I hope Derek's worth the journey."

The barrier slid back. I walked across the damp concrete of the loading area to the service entrance. Now that I paid proper attention, the place wasn't as derelict as I'd assumed. Cameras tracked me, moving stealthily under their rain hoods. I ascended a step, pushed against a door—which opened easily—and found myself entering some kind of lobby or waiting room. Beyond a fire door, a dimly illuminated corridor led away into the depths of the building. No lights on in the annex, save for the red eye of a coffee machine burbling away next to a small table and a set of chairs. I poured a cup, spooned in creamer and sat down. As my vision adjusted to the gloom, I made out some of the glossy brochures lying on the table. Most of them were for Gladius Biomech. I'd heard of the firm and recognised their swordfish logo. Most of what they did creeped me out. Once you started messing with genetics, the world was your walking, talking, tap-dancing oyster. I stroked one of the moving images and watched a cat sitting on a high chair and eating its dinner with a knife and fork, holding the cutlery in little furry human-like hands, while the family dined around it. *Now your pet can share in your mealtimes—hygenically!*

The firedoor swung open. I put down the brochure hastily, as ashamed as if I'd been caught leafing through hardcore porn. Jake stood silhouted in the dim lights of the corridor, kneelength leather jacket, hair still down to his collar.

I put on my best laconic, deadpan voice. "So I guess we're going into the pet business."

"Not quite," Jake answered. "Although there may be merchandising options in that direction at some point. For now, though, it's still rock and roll all the way." He gestured back at the door he'd come through. "You want to meet Derek?"

I tipped the coffee dregs into the wastebin. "Guess we don't want to keep him waiting."

"Don't worry about him. He's not going anywhere."

I followed Jake into the corridor. He had changed a bit in the two years since we'd split the firm, but not by much. The hair was a little grayer, maybe not as thick as it used to be. Jake still had the soul patch under his lip and the carefully tended stubble on his cheeks. Still wore snakeskin cowboy boots without any measurable irony.

"So what's this all about?"

"What I said. A new business opportunity. Time to put Morbid Management back on the road. Question is, are we ready to take things to the next level?"

I smiled. "We. Like it's a done deal already."

"It will be when you see Derek."

We'd reached a side-door: sheet metal with no window in it. Jake pressed his hand against a reader, submitted to an iris scan, then pushed open the door. Hard light spilled through the widening gap.

"You keep this locked, but I'm able to walk in through the front door? Who are you worried about breaking in?"

"It's not about anyone breaking in," Jake said.

We were in a room large enough to hold a dozen semi-trucks. Striplights ran the length of the low, white-tiled ceiling. There were no windows, and most of the wall space was taken up with grey metal cabinets and what appeared to be industrial-size freezer units. There were many free-standing cabinets and cupboards, with benches laid out in long rows. The benches held computers and glassware and neat, toylike robotic things. Centrifuges whirred, ovens and chromatographs clicked and beeped. I watched a mechanical arm dip a pipette into a rack of test tubes, sampling or dosing each in quick sequence. The swordfish logo on the side of the robot was for Gladius Biomech.

"Either you're richer than I think," I said, "or there's some kind of deal going on here."

"Gladius front the equipment and expertise," Jake said. "It's a risk for them, obviously. But they're banking on a high capital return."

"You're running a biotech lab on your own?"

"Buddy, I can barely work out a bar tip. You were always the one with the head for figures. Every few days, someone from Gladius stops by to make sure it's all running to plan. But it doesn't take much tinkering. Stuff's mostly automated. Which is cool, because the fewer people know about this, the better."

"Guess I'm one of them now. Want to show me what this is actually all about, or am I meant to figure it out on my own?"

"Over here," Jake said, strolling over to one of the free-standing cabinets. It was a white cube about the size of a domestic washing machine, and had a similar looking control panel on the front. But it wasn't a washing machine, obviously. Jake entered a keypad code then slid back the lid. "Go on," he said, inviting me closer. "Take a look."

I peered into the cabinet, figuring it was some kind of incubator. Blue, UV-tinged lights ran around the inside of the rim. I could feel the warmth coming off it. Straw and dirt were packed around the floor, and there was a clutch of eggs in the middle. They were big eggs, almost football sized, and one of them was quivering gently.

"Looks like we've got a hatcher coming through," Jake said. "Reason I had to be here, actually. System alerts me when one of those babies gets ready to pop. They need to be hand-reared for a few days, until they can stand on their feet and forage for themselves."

"Until *what* can stand on their feet and forage for themselves?"

"Baby dinosaurs, buddy. What else?" Jake slid the cover back on the incubator, then locked it with a touch on the keypad. "T-Rexes, actually. You ever eaten Rex?"

"Kind of out of my price range."

"Well, take it from me, you're not missing much. Pretty much everything tastes the same once you've added steak sauce, anyway."

"So we're diversifying into dinosaur foodstuffs. Is that what you dragged me out here to see?"

"Not exactly." Jake moved to the next cabinet along—it was the same kind of white incubator—and keyed open the lid. He unhooked a floral-patterned oven glove from the side of the cabinet and slipped it on his right hand, then dipped into the blue-lit interior. I heard a squeak and a scuffling sound and watched as Jake came out with a baby dinosaur in his hand, clutched gently in the oven glove. It was about the size of a plastic bath toy, the same kind of day-glo green, but it was very definitely alive. It squirmed in the glove, trying to escape. The tail whipped back and forth. The huge hind legs thrashed at air. The little forelimbs scrabbled uselessly against the the oven glove's thumb. The head, with its tiny pin-sized teeth already budding through, tried to bite into the glove. The eyes were wide and white-rimmed and charmingly belligerent.

"Already got some fight in it, as you can see," Jake said, using his ungloved hand to stroke the top of the Rex's head. "And those teeth'll give you a nasty cut even now. Couple of weeks, they'll have your finger off."

"Nice. But I'm still sort of missing the point here. And why is that thing so *green*?"

"Tweaked the pigmentation a bit, that's all. Made it luminous, too. Real things are kind of drab. Not so hot for merchandising."

"Merchandising what?"

"Jesus, Fox. Take a look at the forelimbs. Maybe it'll clue you in."

I took a look at the forelimbs and felt a shiver of I wasn't exactly sure what. Not quite revulsion, not quite awe. Something that came in at right angles to both.

"I'm no expert on dinosaurs," I said slowly. "Even less on Rexes. But are those things *meant* to have four fingers and a thumb?"

"Not the way nature intended. But then, nature wasn't thinking ahead." Jake stroked the dinosaur's head again. It seemed to be calming gradually. "Gladius tell me it's pretty simple stuff. There are these things called *Hox* genes which show up in pretty much everything, from fruit flies to monkeys. They're like a big bank of switches that control limb development, right out to the number of digits on the end. We just flipped a few of those switches, and got us dinosaurs with human hands."

The hands were like exquisite little plastic extrudings, moulded in the same biohazard green as the rest of the T-Rex. They even had tiny little fingernails.

"OK, that's a pretty neat trick," I said. "If a little on the creepy side. But I'm still not quite seeing the *point*."

"The point, buddy, is that without little fingers and thumbs it's kind of difficult to play rock guitar."

"You're shitting me. You bred this thing to *make music*?"

"He's got a way to go, obviously. And it doesn't stop with the fingers. You ever seen a motor homunculus, Fox? Map of human brain function, according to how much volume's given over to a specific task. Looks like a little man with huge fucking hands. Just operating a pair of hands takes up *way* more cells than you'd think. Well, there's no point giving a dinosaur four fingers and an opposable thumb if you don't give him the mental wiring to go along with it. So we're in there right from the start, manipulating brain development all the way, messing with the architecture when everything's nice and plastic. This baby's two weeks old and he already has thirty per cent more neural volume than a normal Rex. Starting to see some real hierarchical layering of brain modules, too. Your average lizard has a brain like a peanut, but this one's already got something like a mammalian limbic system. Hell, I'd be scared if it wasn't me doing this."

"And for such a noble purpose."

"Don't get all moral on me, buddy." Jake lowered the T-Rex back into the incubator. "We eat these things. We pay to go out into a big park and shoot them with anti-tank guns. I'm giving them the chance to *rock*. Is that so very wrong?"

"I guess it depends on how much choice the dinosaur has in the matter."

"When you force a five year old kid to take piano lessons, does the kid have a choice?"

"That's different."

"Yeah, because it's cruel and unusual to force someone to play the piano. I agree. But electric guitar? That's liberation, my friend. That's like handing someone the keys to the cosmos."

"It's a goddamned *reptile*, Jake."

"Right. And how is that different to making corpses or giant robots play music?"

He had me there, and from the look of quiet self-satisfaction on his face, he knew it.

"OK. I accept that you have a baby dinosaur that could, theoretically, play the guitar, if anyone made a guitar that small. But that's not the same thing as actually playing it. What are you going to do, just sit around and wait?"

"We train it," Jake said. "Just like training a dog to do tricks. Slowly, one element at a time. Little rewards. Building up the repertoire a part at a time. It doesn't need to understand music. It just needs to make a sequence of noises. You think we can't do this?"

"I'd need persuasion."

"You'll get it. Dinosaurs live for meat. It doesn't have to understand what it's doing, it just has to associate the one with the other. And this is heavy metal we're talking about here, not Rachmaninov. Not a big ask, even for a reptile."

"You've thought it all through."

"You think Gladius were going to get onboard if there wasn't a business plan? This is going to work, Fox. It's going to work and you're going to be a part of it. All the way down the line. We're going to promote a rock tour with an actual carnivorous theropod dinosaur on lead guitar and vocal."

I couldn't deny that Jake's enthusiasm was infectious. Always had been. But when I'd needed him—when I'd taken a big idea to him—he hadn't been there for me. Even now the pain of that betrayal still stung, and I wasn't sure I was ready to get over it that quickly.

"Maybe some other time," I said, shaking my head with a regretful smile. "After all, you've got a ways to go yet. I don't know how fast these things grow, but no one's going to be blown away by a knee-high rockstar, even if they are carnivorous. Maybe when Derek's a bit older, and he can actually play something"

Jake gave me an odd glance. "Dude, we need to clear something up. You haven't met Derek yet."

I looked into his eyes. "Then who—what—was that?"

"Part of the next wave. Same with the eggs. Aren't enough venues in the world for all the people who'll want to see Derek. So we make more Dereks. Until we hit market saturation."

"And you think Derek'll be cool with that?"

"It's not like Derek's ever going to have an opinion on the matter." Jake looked me up and down, maybe trying to judge exactly how much I could be trusted. "So: you ready to meet the big guy?"

I gave a noncommittal shrug. "Guess I've come this far."

Jake stopped at another white cabinet—this one turned out to be a fridge—and came out with a thigh-sized haunch of freezer-wrapped meat. "Carry this for me, buddy," he said.

I took the meat, cradling it in both arms. We went out of the laboratory by a different door, then walked down a short corridor until a second door opened out into a dark, echoey space, like the inside of an aircraft hangar.

"Wait here,' Jake said, and his footsteps veered off to one side. I heard a clunk, as of some huge trip-switch being thrown and, one by one, huge banks of suspended ceiling lights came on. Even as I had to squint against the glare, I mentally applauded the way Jake was managing the presentation. He'd known I was coming, so he could easily have left those lights on until now. But the impressario in him wouldn't be denied. These weren't simple spotlights, either. They were computer controlled, steerable, variable-colour stage lights. Jake had a whole routine programmed in. The lights gimballed and gyred, throwing shifting patterns across the walls, floor and ceiling of the vast space. Yet until the last moment they studiously avoided illuminating the thing in the middle. When they fell on it, I could almost imagine the crowd going apeshit.

This was how the show would open. This was how the show *had* to open.

I was looking at Derek.

Derek was in a bright yellow cage, about the size of four shipping containers arranged into a block. I was glad about the cage; glad too that it appeared to have been engineered to generous tolerances. Electrical cables snaked into it, thick as pythons. Orange strobe beacons had just come on, rotating on the top of the cage, for no obvious reason other than that it looked cool. And there was Derek, standing up in the middle.

I'd had a toy T-rex as a kid, handed down from my dad, and some part of me still expected them to look the way that toy did: standing with the body more or less vertical, forming a tripod with two legs and the tail taking the creature's weight. That wasn't how they worked, though. Derek—like every resurrected Rex that ever lived—stood with his body arranged in a horizontal line, with the tail counterbalancing the weight of his forebody and skull. Somehow that just never looked *right* to me. And the two little arms looked even more pathetic and useless in this posture.

Derek wasn't the same luminous green as the baby dinosaur; he was a more plausible dark muddy brown. I guess at some point Jake had decided that colouration wasn't spectacular enough for the second batch. In fact, apart from the human hands on the ends of his forearms, he didn't look in any way remarkable. Just another meat-eating dinosaur.

Derek was awake, too. He was looking at us and I could hear the rasp of his breathing, like an industrial bellows being worked very slowly. In proportion to his body, his eyes were much smaller than the baby's. Not so cute now. This was an instinctive predator, big enough to swallow me whole.

"He's pretty big."

"Actually he's pretty small," Jake said. "Rex development isn't a straight line thing. They grow fast from babies then stick at two tonnes until they're about fourteen. Then they get another growth spurt which can take them anywhere up to six tonnes. Of course with the newer Dereks we should be able to dial things up a bit." Then he took the haunch off me and whispered: "Watch the neural display. We've had implants in him since he hatched—we're gonna work the imaging into the live show." He raised his voice. "Hey! Meat-brain! Look what I got for you!"

Derek was visibly interested in the haunch. His head tracked it as Jake walked up to the cage, the little yellow-tinged eyes moving with the smooth vigilance of surveillance cameras. Saliva dribbled between his teeth. The forearms made a futile grabbing gesture, as if Derek somehow didn't fully comprehend that there was a cage and a quite a lot of air between the haunch and him.

I watched a pink blotch form on the neural display. "Hunter-killer mode kicking in," Jake said, grinning. "He's like a heat-seaking missile now. Nothing getting between him and his dinner except maybe another Rex."

"Maybe you should feed him more often."

"There's no such thing as a sated Rex. And I do feed him. How else do you think I get him to work for me?" He raised his voice again. "You know the deal, ain't no free lunches around here." He put the haunch down on the ground, then reached for something that I hadn't seen until then: a remote control unit hanging down from above. It was a grubby yellow box with a set of mushroom-sized buttons on it. Jake depressed one of the buttons and an overhead gantry clanked and whined into view, sliding along rails suspended from the ceiling. The gantry positioned itself over the cage, then began to lower its cargo. It was a flame red Gibson Flying V guitar, bolted to a telescopic frame from the rear of the body. The guitar came down from a gap in the top of the cage (too small for Derek to have escaped through), lowered until it was in front of him, then telescoped back until the guitar was suspended within reach of his arms. At the same time, a microphone had come down to just in front of Derek's mouth.

Jake released the remote control unit, then picked up the haunch again. "OK, buddy, you know what you need to do." Then he pressed one of the other buttons and fast, riffing heavy metal blasted out of speakers somewhere in the room. It wasn't stadium-level wattage—that, presumably, would have drawn too much attention—but it was still loud enough to impress, to give me some idea of how the show would work in reality.

And then Derek started playing. His hands were on that guitar, and they were making—well, you couldn't call it music, in the abolutely strict sense of the word. It was noise, basically. Squealing, agonising bursts of sheet-metal sound, none of which bore any kind of harmonic relationship to what had gone before. But the one thing I couldn't deny was that it *worked*. With the backing tape, and the light show, and the fact that this was an actual dinosaur playing a Gibson Flying V guitar, it was possible to make certain allowances.

Hell, I didn't even have to try. I was smitten. And that was before Derek opened his mouth and started singing. Actually it would be best described as a sustained, blood-curdling roar—but that was exactly what it needed to be, and it counterpointed the guitar perfectly. Different parts of his brain were lighting up now; the hunter-killer region was much less bright than it had been before he started playing.

And there was, now that I paid attention to it, more than just migraine-inducing squeals of guitar and monstrous interludes of gutteral roaring. Derek might not be playing specific notes and chords, and his vocalisations were no more structured or musical, but they were timed to fit in around the rest of the music, the bass runs and drum fills and second guitar solos. It wasn't completely random. Derek was playing along, judging his contributions, letting the rest of the band share the limelight.

As a front man, I'd seen a lot worse.

"OK, that'll do," Jake said, killing the music, pressing another button to retract the guitar and mike. "Way to go, Derek. Way to fucking go."

"He's good."

"Does that constitute your seal of approval?"

"He can rock. I'll give him that."

"He doesn't just rock," Jake said. "He is rock." Then he turned around and smiled. "So. Buddy. We back in business, or what?"

Yeah, I thought to myself. I guess we're back in business.

I'M MAKING MY way back down the Antonov, thinking of the long hours of subsonic cruising ahead. I pass Jake's desk again, and this time something on the ancient, battered, desert-sand camouflaged ex-military surplus laptop catches my eye.

The laptop's running some generic movie editing software, and in one of the windows is a freezeframe from tonight's show. Beneath the freezeframe is a timeline and soundtrack. I click the cursor and slide it back along to the left, watching Derek run in reverse on the window, hands whipping around the guitar in manic thrash overdrive. The set list is the same from night to night, so I know exactly when Extinction Event would have kicked in. I don't feel guilty about missing it—someone had to take care of the Budokan accounts—but now that we're airborne and there's time to kill, I'm at least semi-curious about hearing it properly. What exactly was so great about it tonight, compared to the previous show, and the one before that?

Why was it that Jake didn't want to hear that Extinction Event was even more awesome than usual?

I need earphones to hear anything over the six-engine drone of the Antonov. I'm reaching for them when Jake looms behind me.

"Thought you were checking on the big guy."

I look around. He's still got the bottle of JD with him.

"I was. Told him I heard he'd done a good job. Now I'm just checking it out for myself. If I can just find the point where…"

He reaches over and takes my hand off the laptop. "You don't need to. Got it all cued up already."

He hands me the JD, punches a few keys—they're so worn the numbers and letters are barely visible now—and up pops Derek again. From the purple-red tinge of the lighting, and the back-projection footage of crashing asteroids and erupting volcanos, I know we've hit the start of Extinction Event.

"So what's the big deal?" I ask.

"Put the phones on."

I put the phones on. Jake spools through the track until we hit the bridge between the second and third verse. He lets the movie play on at normal speed. Drums pounding like jackhammers, bass so heavy it could shatter bone, and then Derek lets rip on the Flying V, unleashing a squall of demented sound, arching his neck back as he plays, eyes narrowing to venomous slits, and then belching out a humungous, larynx-shredding roar of pure theropod rage.

We go into the third verse. Jake hits pause.

"So you see," he says.

I pull out the phones. "I'm not sure I do."

"Then you need to go back and listen to the previous performance. And the one before that. And every goddamned rendition of that song he's ever done before tonight."

"I do?"

"Yes. Because then you'd understand." And Jake looks at me with an expression of the utmost gravity on his face, as if he's about to disclose one of the darkest, most mystical secrets of the universe. "It was different tonight. He came in early. Jumped his usual cue. And when he did come in it was for longer than usual and he added that vocal flourish."

I nod, but I'm still not seeing the big picture. "OK. He screwed up. Shit happens. Gotta roll with it, remember? It was still a good show. Everyone said so."

But he shakes his head. "You're not getting it, buddy. That wasn't a mistake. That was something much worse. That was an improvement. That was him improvising."

"You can't be sure."

"I can be sure." He punches another key and a slice of Derek's neural activity pops up. "Extracted this from the performance," he says. "Right around the time he started going off-script." His finger traces three bright blotches. "You see these hotspots? They've come on in ones and twos before. But they've never once lit up at the same time."

"And this means something?"

He taps his finger against the blotches in turn. "Dorsal premotor cortex. That's associated with the brain planning a sequence of body movements. You slip on ice, that's the part that gets you flapping your arms so you don't you fall over." Next blotch. "Anterior cingulate. That's your basic complex resolution, decision making module, right. Do I chase after that meal, or go after that one?" He moves his finger again. "Interior frontal gyrus/ventral premotor cortex. We're deep into mammal brain structure here—a normal Rex wouldn't have anything you could even stick a label on here. You know when this area lights up, in you and me?"

"I'm not, strangely enough, a neuroscientist."

"Nor was I until I got involved with Derek. This is the sweet spot, buddy. This is what lights up when you hear language or music. And all three of these areas going off at once? That's a pretty unique signature. It doesn't just mean he's playing music. It means he's making shit up as he goes along."

For a moment I don't know what to say. There's no doubt in my mind that he's right. He knows the show—and Derek's brain—inside out. He knows every cue Derek's meant to hit. Derek missing his mark—or coming in early—just isn't meant to happen. And Derek somehow finding a way to deviate from the program and make the song sound better is, well…not exactly the way Jake likes things to happen.

"I don't like improvisation," he says. "It's a sign of creative restlessness. Before you know it…"

"It's solo recording deals, expensive riders and private tour buses."

"I thought we got away from this shit," Jake says mournfully. "I mean, dead bodies, man. Then robots. Then dinosaurs. And still it's coming back to bite us. Talent always thinks it knows best."

"Maybe it does."

"A T-Rex?"

"You gave him just enough of a mind to rock. Unfortunately, that's already more than enough to not want to take orders." I take a sip from the JD. "But look on the bright side. What's the worst that could happen?"

"He escapes and eats us."

"Apart from that."

"I don't know. If he starts showing signs of... creativity... then we're fucked six ways from Tuesday. We'll have animal rights activists pulling the plug on every show."

"Unless we just... roll with it. Let him decide what he does. I mean, it's not like he doesn't *want* to perform, is it? You've seen him out there. This is what he was born for. Hell, why stop there? This is what he was evolved for."

"I wish I had your optimism."

I look back at the cage. Derek's watching us, following the conversation. I wonder how much of it he's capable of understanding. Maybe more than we realise.

"Maybe we keep control of him, maybe we don't. Either way, we've done something beautiful." I hand him the bottle. "You, mainly. It was your idea, not mine."

"Took the two of us to make it fly," Jake says, before taking a gulp. "And hell, maybe you're right. That's the glorious thing about rock and roll. It's alchemy. Holy fire. The moment you control it, it ain't rock and roll no more. So maybe the thing we should be doing here is celebrating."

"All the way." And I snatch back the JD and take my own swig. Then I raise the bottle and toast Derek, who's still watching us. Hard to tell what's going on behind those eyes, but one thing I'm sure of is that it's not nothing. And for a brief, marvellous instant, I'm glad not only to be alive, but to be alive in a universe that has room in it for beautiful monsters.

And heavy metal, of course.

Sarging Rasmussen:
A Report
(by Organic)

Gord Sellar

IN MOST OF *the* Shine *stories the positive change that happens is implemented through actions of individuals, groups or companies (and eventually, one hopes, the people), who often have to fight—apart from the barrage of real-world problems—the political powers that be. In "Sarging Rasmussen" Gord Sellar proposes—maybe only partly tongue-in-cheek—that it might be better to, well, go with the flow.*

This may be true (I suggest with one cheek bulging) for Gord himself: after venting his frustration that a certain Australian stole his ideas before he had them (see "The Egan Thief" in FLURB #4*), he saw his stories published in* Asimov's, Interzone *and* The Year's Best SF *(and other fine venues). So maybe at the next SF convention we all should be 'Broing Sellar'...*

Were people really so - alone, granpa? /
disbelief in her deep brown eyes /
Yes, dear, said I /
Old friends laughing in the back of my mind

—David Heijl—

"I Don't!" Hunter screamed, tears trailing down his
cheeks, lit by the trendy piezoelectric floor-powered
club lights pulsing to the fashionable heart-attack
thump of Malaybeat techno. "I let Bagheera amog
me and fuck it all up! I don't got shit!"

I managed to fight my urge to start calling him
by his real name—Wilfred Chan—but I made the
mistake of reasoning with him. "What? Listen, you
do. *You got game.* Trust me. I've seen your work,
Hunter, ever since you first came to Den Haag. I
watched you amog Marko Rechschild, and co-bro
Park and Almeira into signing that Pacific RI treaty,
all in three hours! You even banged that hot little
attaché from the IECWP before the committee went
into session! Shit, man, you got so much Game you're
a legend! Game 1.0, Game 2.0: new guys dream of
being like you... what're you crying about?"

A smile almost cracked his face in half as he
remembered bonking that secretary, but then reality
flooded back, slamming his frown back into place. He'd
been amogged—knocked right out of his synthetic alpha
male mindframe, reduced to inaudible mumbling. Once
again a low-status, never-gets-laid, can't-save-the-world
loser. The club noise swallowed his broken little voice.

But his words flashed boldly across my comptact
lenses: What about the Reefs? The IPBR display in

the corner of my right lens showed his body temp running high, though so was everyone's in that place, but his pulse rate and respiration were all in the red. Then Muggle[CC] kicked in, blaring terse, blood-red warnings across my comptacts: HOSTILE. UNBALANCED. TOX?

You can always trust software to tell you the truth you're trying to ignore hardest.

The Muggle[CC] app was one of the finest tools in the Game 2.0 kit. It told you which chicks really just wanted to be left alone, and when a suit had been rubbed the wrong way beyond the point of no broability. For analyzing people you didn't know, possible targets, it was the most kickass app around, like a wingman who was never scared to realityslap you upside the neocortex. But Hunter had been my mentor once; I felt a stab of guilt about what I'd have to do to him. My doubts swirled momentarily, and the comptacts picked that up—my system was monitoring me, too—and flashed me emphatically: TOTALLY FUCKING HOSTILE, DUDE. A moment later came the default addendum, built in to urge restraint: SORRY.

I embraced my guilt for a second—I figured it kept me human—and then I shoved it aside. Compassion for fuckups and flakes is what crippled the green movement so badly that Game 2.0 became necessary. Besides, I've worked too hard to burn off the residuals of my own Average Frustrated Environmentalist Crusader mentality. I didn't have time to be an AFEC anymore. There were protocols for handling backslides like this.

"Listen, man," I said, setting my hand on his shoulder. And then I felt it, right through the fine black Italian arachnosilk: Hunter was shivering, almost shaking. "What the fuck are you on?" I asked, snatching his peacocky mirrorspex from his face, and taking a good look at his surgically-Eurasianised eyes.

Dilated pupils stared back wetly at me, the left one huge and the right still dilating. Hunter cringed from the sudden brightness. He ignored my question and exhaled slowly. Brain haemorrhage, it had to be. The pupils: textbook images flooded back from one of my pre-med bio courses, before I'd fled into a pharmacy program.

Fuck! For what? A couple of fucking *coral reefs* that were doomed anyway, because Diaz and Abral and Rodriguez were playing let's-compare-dicks with ASEAN again? Always with the drama, Hunter was, and now he was probably gonna end up brain-damaged, if not dead on the spot. We had to get that shit out of his system fast. My Winger^{CC} app had already alerted the other guys, thank fuck. He stared at me, grunted my name, and then, with a sudden jolt, he slapped himself in the face and started howling, nothing but vowels and slobber. Nobody had noticed, lucky for us.

By then Homboyostasis and Biosfear had shown up on either side of Hunter and looped their arms through his. They hauled him out of the place with all the efficiency of professional bouncers, with me at their side.

"Get him to a DTC, or he's fucked for sure," I hollered once we in the hallway, away from the pounding beat, wondering if there even *was* a detox centre close enough to save his ass. "Maybe too late already. If not, when he wakes up, tell him he did his best, and buy him some time in a vippy tank, okay? I'm gonna go back in and shake-close this treaty if it takes both of my front teeth and one of my balls."

By then, they'd stuffed him into a cab and piled in after him. "Sure thing, Organic," Biosfear said to me with a nod, while Homeboyostasis shouted into his cell phone and fumbled with the taxi's emergency medikit. Before the cab had even pulled away, I was back in the hallway, making my way back into the noise. Strutting, already: if there was one thing that would get me through the next two hours, it was inner game.

And thank fuck, my inner game was deep as the Mariana Trench, and solid as titanium steel, or the sight of Hunter losing his shit would have done me in.

Fuck s-closing, I thought to myself. *Fuck handshakes. I am gonna t-close*, I told myself. *I'm gonna fuckin' treaty-close this deal*, I repeated, and took a deep breath as I reached the dancefloor.

Finally, I caught sight of Gilberto over by the bar, laughing as he talked to a tall skinny black guy—I didn't quite recognize him but I was pretty sure he was on some human rights land mines homeless children immunization whatever-the-fuck committee we usually didn't have to game—and Sigrid Rasmussen, a slightly chunky middle-aged blonde— HB 6, if I were pressed to rank her sexually, because I don't like big girls and because of her age—who was the Assistant Secretary of the Taskforce for the Deacidification of the World's Oceans. Who was, everyone agreed, playing a little too friendly with the WTO-run oversight council, and needed to be reminded that whatever profit motive mattered now would mean nothing once the reefs were all toast.

The world's reefs. Not the world, just the world's reefs, I told myself. We could always engineer something artificial if we had to, I reassured myself dubiously. *You can do this.*

Then I kicked myself with the 3 Second Rule: never wait more than three seconds to approach a person, or else you'll overthink it. I thought of Mother Earth for a moment, and then waded into the pulsating crowd.

Not for the first time, I wished these WTO/UN dickheads would start acting their age and hang out someplace besides night clubs.

We started out as far from idealists, of course. As my teacher, Praxis, said when he met me: "Environmentalist? Ha, you know who gets laid less than a green radical?"

"Nobody?" I said, wishing I'd mentioned my day job as a lab tech instead of how I spent my weekends.

It was true, though. Women had seen fit to chain themselves to trees beside me, and join me in hijacking oil tankers on highways, and march arm in arm with me in the streets of a dozen countries by my side. But I'd gotten precisely one girl out of a bra in my life, and that had lasted just five weeks. 37 days, to be precise. And that had been four years before.

"'xactly," Praxis said with a sneer. "Nobody. But we're gonna change all that. *You're* gonna," he said, on day one.

That was back in the days when fellas like Praxis were called mPUAs. Guys like him made a living running "boot camps" for AFCs, the Average Frustrated Chumps. Guys who didn't know how to talk to women and were willing to spend a thousand bucks for a weekend of being coached on how talk to women.

Guys like me.

Mostly, they learned by being forced to go sarging—approaching thousands of women in a row, until they stopped pissing themselves with fear and grew a backbone. And Praxis was right: during that weekend, he changed my life... or, well, really, *I* did. He'd taken me and the other AFCs—a hardware engineer who called himself Axiomatic, a lonely high school teacher we dubbed Homework, a recently-divorced cop called Slammer, and some Japanese poet or something—and baptized us by fire. We went out sarging all weekend—chatting up hot women in bars and bookstores and coffeeshops, coming onto them and hassling them, teasing and rubbing shoulders and even scoring some phone numbers.

That weekend was the first time I ever wore leather. *Tight* leather. *Peacocky* leather. Praxis taught us routines, taught us cocky-funny, taught us rules of thumb and dozens of techniques, and by the end of it, every one of us had learned the secret: there wasn't one. Getting a woman's phone number—or anything else, for that matter—didn't require magic, or an eleven-inch cock, or perfect white teeth. All it took was asking for it in the right way, once she was ready to give it... once you'd helped her become ready. Pretty soon, we were having the time of our lives with the kind of babes who'd terrified us just months before. I was no longer Andrew Dalton: I had become Organic, and now I was swimming in women. Tall women, short women, dark and pale, funny and serious, wild and schoolmarmish alike. I tasted every flavour there was. I'd learned techniques for getting them to come home with me in less than thirty minutes of first contact. For engineering a threesome. For getting them to give me a sponge bath dressed in nurse uniforms, while speaking in fake Polish. (Look, everyone has his kinks, and whoever claims otherwise is lying.) For the first time in my life, I was getting laid like a truckload of linoleum. And it was the part of me that was really, really enjoying all that sex that spoke first when Katana had laid out his plan.

That was the part of me that had stopped caring about how many trees got cut down at Clayoquot sound, and didn't give a shit about the coral reefs and strip mining in the Northwest Territories. They say that a sense of impending death makes people have more sex—it's a mammalian instinct. Well, the first year the icecaps melted completely in summer? I made that work for me, and worked out my own mammalian panic all at once. From there, I hadn't looked back, not once, at the dying Earth.

Not till that day. And it hurt to look again at what I'd once cared about—which I think is why I yelped, "That's fucking crazy, Katana! The tools we have... they're for pickup. For getting laid. Not for... saving the world."

"Yeah, man," Biosfear said, nodding his head. "What d'ya wanna do, seduce the sun into shining less brightly? Sarge lumberjacks? Toss a few negs at metacorporations and hope that they go sweet on us?"

Biosfear laughed at the absurdity of it. We all did.

"You're not listening, bros," Katana said, his hands parallel in front of him like some kind of loony Japanese evangelical minister. His eyes shone with some kind of insane, holy-fire light. "You can't seduce the sun, but you don't need to. The environment? The ecology? It's people. I've been rereading Dawkins and Page..."

We all groaned.

"...and there's something to this extended phenotype thing," Katana went on. "The world is what we *make* it. What governments decide. How giant companies decide to behave. But governments and companies, what are they?"

"People," Biosfear said. "They're just people, and so they can be seduced..."

"Wrong," said Katana, flicking at the wall with his keychain remote. The smartwall flickered, and images from satellites flooded it at high speed, corporate logos and national flags flashing superimposed onto creeping desertification, megastorms, and black-smoke flashes of brief, vicious water wars. "They're persons, legally and functionally. They're the ultimate amogs. And they can be amogged too."

Someone who hadn't known us would have taken one look around the room at us in our freaky peacocky clothing—Homeboyostasis' purple fur vest, my depilated scalp, Biosfear's animated Magic Eight Ball T-shirt cycling through its advice—No Way!... Yes Way!... Maybe!... Go Fuck Yourself!—and declared Katana's attempt to sway us a complete, hopeless failure.

Goes to show you what total strangers know about anything.

At first, we figured that swaying the head of a WTO/UN Committee to see things your way might be a *little* bit different from scoring a phone number off the hottest chick in a bar.

But in the end, sarging is sarging. It's all the same game, and all the skills are transferrable. Peacocking, for example. As I walked up to Gilberto—the secretary to the head of the committee for reduction reef fishery—I held my chest out, the way a quarterback stands when he walks past a street fight. I strutted slightly, comfortable in my skin, in this bar, comfortable around Gilberto. Clubs and clubbers didn't scare me anymore, despite all the years of nights that I spent wanking at home, alone, while Gilberto was dancing his ass off as he climbed the ranking ladder of the youngest WTO/UN hierarchy pyramid ever.

None of that mattered. I was confident.

My suit was Libyan, not that you'd ever know: most people can't tell it from the Italian stuff. (The difference, my friend, is price.) The slight untidiness of my hair was as carefully engineered as the piezoelectric bricking system under the floor that powered the lights and audio in that ecoclub. When I spoke, my voice was a half-octave lower than it'd been for most of my adult life. My smile was natural, of course—practice anything in the mirror enough and it becomes natural. And, yeah, I'll admit: there was a gentle cloud of pseudopheromones surrounding me, telegraphing virility by advertising much higher levels of testosterone than any real, healthy human male could possess.

"Gilberto," I said with a serious, professional smile, and then I noticed Bagheera. Fucking Bagheera. She was headed straight for us, a look in her eye that was straight out of a nature documentary. A panther about to sink her teeth into an antelope's neck.

A beginner ePUA would've looked around frantically, breaking the spell I'd begun—even by then—to cast over Gilberto. But my wingmen were well-trained, and I let them do their jobs.

Bagheera was closing fast as I shook Gilberto's hand, ignoring his *Who-the-Fuck-Are-You?* look. My grip was firm, but not much firmer than his, and

I shifted my posture slightly to match his own.

"Good work today," I said. We'd all seen it on the WTO/UN netfeed: Gilberto slapping down a conservation measures offshoring initiative put forward by the G14. The standard crap—have someone else clean up their air, and trade their measures for the right to keep shitting into the sky and ocean. After verbally bitchslapping the American rep for twenty minutes straight, Gilberto had gotten a standing ovation.

And dared to go out in public the same night.

I let my smile drop ever so slightly, and then matched Gilberto's when he responded with a grin. My timing, of course, was perfect: I'd trained this particular skill for weeks. His response was immediate, a glow in his eyes and a sudden display of comfort. Next, I spoke just a little too quietly. When he leaned forward, I knew I had him. AMOGs don't lean forward: they say, "Pardon me?" or "Say what?" The other guy can repeat himself, louder, or reposition himself. But I stepped closer to him, setting my hand on his back in the way that buddies do, turning my back to Bagheera as she approached. That would buy a few seconds.

"I wish we had more guys like you in the trenches," I said. *Yeah, that's right*, my eyes said. *I'm from upstairs*. Suddenly my easy magnanimity held a different meaning for him. It flashed in Gilberto's eyes. Maybe, just *maybe*, I was the *real* Alpha Male of Group.

Gilberto nodded happily, thanked me, and picked up his drink. He glanced into the glass as he sipped it, his body screaming a single message: *Whoa. Upstairs*.

That was when I caught sight of Antigen and his wing-babe Greenfire leading Bagheera across the room and away, cordial and professional as all get out. Not for the first time, I thanked God for Greenfire. She was an insider chick who'd ended up on our boards one night by chance after being seduced by Antigen. She'd decided she liked how we were working the WTO/UN—"The only rational approach to this bloody organization that I've ever heard of!" was how she put it, according to Antigen—and teamed up with us.

I turned to the African, and his name flashed across my spex: *Echewo.*

"Mr. Echewo!" I said, shaking his hand firmly, my smile exuding confidence and *Have we met before?* We hadn't—I've never had any reason to talk to someone in human rights—but there was a faint glimmer of do-I-know-you on his face, one confirmed by my Muggle[CC] software, and I wasn't about to help him out.

The game was on, and I was well on my way to bro'ing these fuckers. Soon I'd be able to start working my real target.

EVERYONE HAD TO start somewhere, and I started with Hunter, in a club called Il Barra Spaziaratta, in Sydney. I'd paid 1500 canuckbucks to fly down there, and another $1500—in Canadian, because Aussie money was crashing then—to do a boot camp with the best, because back then that was what Hunter was: the best of the best of the mPUAs. He was an mPUA 2.0: a master of the older PickUp Arts, and a pioneer in the newer, technology-fuelled 2.0 subscene.

I'll never forget the first time I went sarging for real, post-boot camp—the terminology roiling in my head, tumbling through my mind as I realized that all these words and concepts really referred to real-world things. To *people*.

Sets, which meant groups of women—and mixed groups of women and men together—had to be opened. *DHV*: I had to Display High Value. *AMOG* the competitive males. Try (stupidly) the Jealous Girlfriend Opener. Dodge the inevitable slap—this was 2016, after all, and it was beyond obsolete. *Peacocking. Negs.*

I walked over to a triple set: HB 9.0 in a red cocktail dress; HB 2 punky in a plaid skirt and leather vest over her blouse; HB 7.0 whitetrash with a nose ring and an animated tramp stamp dancing on the small of her back. I followed the 3 second rule, approaching the set immediately and engaging HB 7.0—who was so *not* my target—as I worked the social game a little.

I ignored HB 9.0 persistently.

They smiled at me like a little boy who had picked and bought 'em ditchflowers, and HB 2 punky ruffled my hair with a smirk.

"Are you trying to pick one of us up?" they said, glancing meaningfully at HB 9.0. They knew what I was doing, understood that the girl I ignored was my target.

They *knew*.

I wasn't little. I was almost six feet tall, and if my body was a bit slim, I wasn't exactly skinny. I was dressed in a long black jacket, and fake gem-encrusted shades. Later, I realized that they looked like Elton John's, but that night, I'd thought I was peacocking. And I thought I'd looked cool, and had been on top of things.

But they'd read me like a trashy sex blog.

"Do you want me to?" I tried, with my winning smile. When caught, play it cocky-funny. Okay, I said to myself.

And then it happened. I wondered, *Am I showing too much tooth?* High school yearbook pictures flooded my mind. Happy birthday videos. Teenaged rants on Youtube in 2008 that I made after my mother screwed up my hair, and all the nasty comments about my teeth. Hours of sitting in a chair when I was twenty-six, getting all that dental work done. Lasering 'em white.

I wavered.

It showed. My smile imploded, lips twisting together. Their eyes registered the change. I saw myself reflected in their bedroomy eyes, and between the long lashes and the lovely lids, what stared back at me was Chump, Chump, Chump, Chump, Chump, Chump. (They had six eyes between them, after all.)

HBPunky started laughing first, and then HB 9.0 spun on one stiletto heel, her arm around HB 7.0's shoulder.

Hunter was right there beside me, and he said, "Duuuude. That's, like, nothing, dude. They have *issues*. You connected, at first. Totally. No big deal. Take it in stride. Just takes practice, bro."

But all night long, I saw them glancing at me, grinning among themselves. When we took off for another club, one without them around, I noticed other girls looking at me the same way, before I even talked to them.

Failure. It was just like life before boot camp. A series of failures, of women laughing at me. It sucked. *I* sucked.

"Dude," I said to Hunter, at the front door of the second club. "I don't think there's much point, man... I just..."

And then he slapped me. He just fucking slapped me right across my face, out of nowhere, and I fell on the ground, right there one the sidewalk. I fell down, not because he'd hit me so hard, but because I hadn't had any idea it was coming. I was just so shocked.

"Surprised, huh?" Hunter shouted. "Didn't expect life to bitchslap you right in the face, huh?"

I sat up, hand on my cheek. "Life didn't slap me, Hunter. *You* did." I could still feel the burning handprint on my face.

"Shut up," he commanded me, "and listen." Then he reached down, grabbed my free hand, and helped me to my feet. "Life is like that. Life will smack you at any moment. No warning. No announcement. That's how life works. It bitchslaps you with everything that matters: a chance at pussy, random senseless danger, a job opportunity you never knew you wanted... and finally, it bitchslaps you with death."

I stared at him with widened eyes, in his purple leather Aussie cowboy hat. He was turning unprovoked assault into a life lesson. A parable. And finally I was starting to get it.

"When life bitchslaps you," he said, and I realized the muscles in his arm were tensing again, "You need to be paying fucking attention..."

And then he threw his fist at me.

My hand had come up without my thinking about it, but it was only when I looked that I realized I'd blocked his punch. My fingers were closed around his fist, and he was smiling like a maniac.

"Organic," he said, using the pseudonym I'd written on my "Hello! My name is..." sticker back at Boot Camp orientation, and which had become my handle online at the PUA wikiboards. "Buddy, you learn quick. You're one of us, just... in larval form. You'll be rockin' in no time, bro."

It was a routine, straight outta some boot camp trainer guidebook, the routine that was designed for the most promising recruit when his courage failed. Funny thing was, it turned out to be true. I *was* one of them, and a few months later, I'd become a real PUA. I'd gotten more numbers in three months than I had in all the years before then; I'd slept with five different girls, two of them together. The techniques that the mPUAs had refined were stunningly powerful. They turned me from a Geek Ignominous to a Geek Adonis, or at least that's what I saw reflected in women's eyes.

Now, every PUA loses his powers occasionally. There was a night in Barcelona when every chick in the bar looked straight through me; routines and moves that had worked in a thousand other bars all around the world, failed me inexplicably that night. There was a night at Loco in Amsterdam when I found myself suddenly in my old rut, begging for approval from a trio of HB 9.5-10s. Suddenly I was back to being that gawky, balding geek that everyone else had forgotten, and I got shot down so hard I felt I'd never sarge again.

But mostly, I was like wine or whiskey: I just got better and better with time. As I mastered the Game, I diversified. I picked up chicks at political protests and municipal libraries. I got laid in the bathroom of a Starbucks in Cairo with an HB 9 that I'd just met minutes before in line, with just a few words of xNLP whispered into her ear. Blonde. I still remember the scent of her vegan backpacker shampoo.

It was like I'd woken from a long, deep sleep, into a world absolutely crammed with opportunities. Ice cream shops. Public parks. Blues concerts. Pet stores. Divorce lawyer's office waiting rooms. At a frigging dental clinic, my face still numb from the nerve block.

It changed me. Well, of course it did. Power always changes people. It transformed my awareness of what human beings are—because once you start sarging, you never lose sight of that: we're mammals. No matter how much fancy, clever neocortex you slather onto our brains, we're animals. Sure, we talk, we dance, we sing, and we build rockets and satellites and the internet. But we're still animals, with animal instincts. Man, reading Darwin after you learn pickup is a totally different thing than reading it when you're an Average Frustrated Chump. AFCs see evolution and sexual reproduction as a system they're excluded from, hopelessly. But PUAs, they're hackers, working the system, kludging the code. DHV. Manage expectations. Isolate your target.

It's the dance of evolution. It's not just *a* game; it's *THE* game, the machinery of evolution and life. It's the reason we have these fancy neocortices that let us talk and engineer airplanes and perform brain surgery. It's a minimalistic obstacle race with time, death, and destiny as moving goalposts. Smart people had been using game theory to discuss tons of stuff, including sexual reproduction itself—but they'd never dared to say what those first mPUAs discovered: that we humans, too, were locked in a game that few of us understood... a game that could be learned. That could be mastered and *gamed*. Not that sleeping with all those women ever filled the hole inside most of us, of course.

And we found ourselves wondering *what* in the world *could* fill that hole.

It turned out that Katana's breakdown was the cold front that set in motion the perfect storm. Guys who had learned to social engineer the way we had, who could sell ice to an Eskimo village, who could talk a nun out of *all* her habits—what could we do, when we finally found ourselves an overriding purpose?

We knew we could change the world. That, if we decided to, we could do more than rock on the fiddle and screw ourselves silly as Mother Earth burned to cinders all around us. We could use pickup to save the Earth.

And Bagheera and the other ecofems knew it too. And they weren't about to let it happen without a fight.

BROING (BRO-ING) IS one of those concepts that never existed in Game 1.0, since that was all about picking up women. Things didn't change till it became just as important to be able to finesse relationships with *men*.

There are seven steps to the algorithm that underlies the Broing process, and they spell out a neat little acronym you can use as a mnemonic: BASTARD. As I broed Gilberto and Echewo, I worked through all seven steps.

Be broable. That was easy, since I was already peacocked for the environment in my suit, with killer posture and my now-perfect teeth; and on top of that, my head was temporarily rewired by the dose of Peacock^CC, my favorite PUA-designed deinhibitant wundapharm pulsing through my veins. I was, for the moment, the kind of man that men wanted to have as a bro. I was broable.

Next was *Assess networks, and infiltrate.* This was the thing I'd struggled with hardest, for some reason. I've never figured out if I have some vaguely sub-autism-spectrum disorder, or just an extra-thick skull, but I'd always struggled to figure out group hierarchies. I was raised to consider people as equals, but the truth is, humans aren't. They never are. Someone's always a little bit cooler, or sexier, or funnier than you are. And someone's always less than you, too. There's *always* disparity.

And once I'd realized that, and started looking, there it was, everywhere. Sometimes it wasn't obvious, but you could always figure it out. In the group at the bar, Gilberto was the AMOG, Echewo second, and Rasmussen was the bottom. Even though Rasmussen was, technically speaking, more important than both of them put together. That didn't matter at the bar: back in the jungle, this is the typical way 2M-1F sets shape up.

I'd already sussed out the triangle, and docked with the AMOG—Gilberto—so I moved on to step 3.

Which is: *Status is for sharing*. Turning a fellow human being into an ally is a subtly different process from rendering a woman receptive to sexual advances. When you're sarging women, you have to Display High Value in order to make her see you as worth pursuing, but also to dispel the feeling that you're pursuing them. That's even more the case with MM (or desexualized MF) interactions: in those cases, only *total* losers pursue. If you're DHVing to a pol and he or she starts reacting like a chiquita in a tubeskirt, you're almost always talking to the wrong person.

With my 3-set, DHVing was easy: besides all the status I was exuding—thanks to the dose of Peacock[CC] I'd just taken—I knew Gilberto and Rasmussen's work and track record inside-out.

My "more guys like you in the trenches," line first set off that faint sense among them that I was *someone*. Someone important enough that they had better not ask my name, in case they were supposed to know already. Four out of five times, that hesitation keeps the set guessing till the close, and this time, it worked. Rasmussen was too busy trying to figure out why I was ignoring her, and Echewo wasn't in his element—he took me for some kind of eco-pol—so Gilberto was my only risk factor... and he'd already warmed to me the second I'd touched his shoulder.

"So why d'you think Chen and Silver are so against the Reef Treaty?" I asked, forcing myself not to smile as Gilberto's eyes widened.

"Silver? What do you mean? He promised us a vote..."

I smiled, raised an eyebrow, and said, "Publicly."

Rasmussen leaned forward, about to ask me who the hell I was, but Gilberto was hooked, and it's a rare woman who'll cut off the current AMOG when he has *that* look in his eye. Gilberto leaned closer to me and shouted, above the music, "Is there something I should know?"

The others in the group leaned forward too, but I kept my back straight. Never lean in to be heard: the AMOG *always* speaks louder instead.

"Recent meetings. Chen and Silver, talking. Late at night."

Gilberto's eyes widened, and he pulled me aside as Rasmussen was distracted enough to forget the question of who I was working for, and whip out her MacBerry to mobtext her staffers.

I watched her and Echewo out of the corner of my eye. The African just sipped his drink, watching them respond to the sudden crisis as Gilberto asked me,

"Are you sure they're talking a pullout? We've been working on this reef treaty for over a year now, and..."

"Well, you know Silver," I said, moving from step four—*Talk shop, then stop*—to step five: *Activate instincts*. Gilberto and me, we weren't standing in a club, drowning in lights, shouting to be heard over the music. Not anymore. Suddenly, we were standing on the savannah, stone tools in our hands, and I was pointing over the next hill at the place where the enemy lived.

Pointing at *them*—someone else, whom I was framing as an enemy. Which made us an *us*, in a very caveman sense. Grunt, grunt.

Usually, it wasn't quite that simple, of course, but Gilberto was an idealist. An uncommon disease, in the eco-pol biz, especially among the WTO/UN crowd. (The guys who weren't scared of getting rich while saving the world—those free of the suspicion that wealth quietly corrupted their successes somehow—went into internal corporate reform and green research. And they didn't hang out in places like this. I know, I've bro'ed some of them too. Think cigars, and cognac, and strippers, and conversations about design and alt-fuel so long you can feel your hair turning grey.)

I saw it happening in Gilberto's head: gears turning, teeth locking and unlocking, and clank, suddenly, *I'm* the bearer of bad news. I was the nettle that got under his jockstrap, the messenger he wants to kill. (Though he won't, because what if I *am* from upstairs?) It's only natural, this negative reaction. His mental frame of reference was that he'd been working for a year on this fucking deal when, suddenly, I told him it's got the life expectancy of a beluga whale washed ten miles inland by a tsunami. His expression harshened and he gripped my arm, a little burst of aggression bubbling over.

"What am I supposed to do *now*?" he growled. "It's too late, isn't it? Why are you only telling me this *now*?"

This is why step six (*Reframe the interaction*) follows on the heels of step five: because step five can so easily go wrong. Human instincts are like monkeys that have grown up trapped in little cages. When you wake 'em up, and let them out, they turn highly unpredictable. Sometimes they slip on a tux and do a dance routine, and sometimes they fling their shit in your face.

The cognitive dissonance was clear on Gilberto's face. My comptact lens IPBR confirmed it: pulse 93 bpm, body temp slightly elevated, respiration shallow. Not surprising—Alphas don't like surprises, or being out of the loop. And he was used to being an Alpha. When Gilberto got mad, he flung his shit and bashed heads in with verbal rocks. He was the type to get his pick of mates and sleeping spots. But I was, maybe, from upstairs, so this was potentially dangerous. So he mapped PER (Prior Experiential References) onto me. Distant daddy issues, I guessed.

So many of us ecofreak types—pol and otherwise—have daddy issues.

Now the stage was set for me to steal the frame. I had to make him important, turn his feelings inside-out and let him feel like it was me depending on him, and me being hurt by his failure, instead of the other way around.

Rasmussen came in just in time. She'd finished texting and making her phone calls, and suddenly hurried back over to us at exactly the moment when Gilberto was about to run AMOG on me— of course, her presence was probably part of what drove him to it. She came on tiptoes, straining to hear our voices.

Perfect.

Stealing a frame requires a shock to the system, just like when Hunter slapped me across the face. Nobody lets his or her frame get stolen without a sudden shock that destabilizes all those underlying assumptions. Of course, I couldn't slap Gilberto or Rasmussen: if I did that, I'd be fucked.

"It's okay," I told them, "But you need to know that we're counting on you. We can't recover unless you pull through for us," I added, looking away from Gilberto and toward Rasmussen. She was going to save the day. She was the one we needed. *Sigrid Rasmussen, you're my only hope.*

Gilberto registered, at least on some level, that he'd been amogged, but he was too stunned to process it quickly enough to properly challenge me. His own hesitation tripped him up, and I talked fast so that it would last. As long as he was listening, he'd be off-balance, and if he was off-balance for more than three seconds, he'd start thinking.

And thinking is the bane of the would-be AMOG.

I was ready for step seven, *Deal with the target*, when I noticed them. Two young white women in business attire, one with her hair in a blunt cut, like millionaire soccer mom, and the other looking like a business exec with her hair in classy beads, neo-African-style. They were only a few feet away, and heading for us.

I recognized them, of course: the blunt-cut was Estraven, and her friend was Bamboo Grove. I felt a whiskey shot's worth of adrenaline dump into my bloodstream. Of course Bagheera wasn't alone, but if I'd known there's be a full-on ecofem incursion, I'd have come better-armed.

ESTRAVEN WAS ALMOST my girl, back when her name had been Monica Dietz. Coulda, woulda. Shoulda? Probably not, but I used to wonder how things would have gone if we had hooked up back then.

The scene: a hippie apartment, stinking of patchouli and burnt sandalwood. One wall absolutely covered in books, and the floor was littered with dirty old beanbag chairs stuffed with hay, instead of the usual comfy styro pods. A faint scent of unmasked body odour hung in the air, the unmistakable sign of true believers.

And then there was Monica, radiant before the pack in her birkenstocks and Indian *lahenga* skirt, her hair hanging in narrow dreadlocks and an earnest-sloganed tee stretched across her chest. Despite the nose rings, the sketchy teeth and hair, and all that windy rhetoric she was spouting, she was *hot*. The hottest girl in the place. Sitting on a beanbag chair in the back in my jeans and t-shirt—I'd dressed down for the occasion—I saw her through the eyes of the other guys in the room.

Not that there were many guys there. 80% of the world's environmental activists are women, which was one of those little facts that had led Katana to his genius insight, even though we'd soon realize that sarging activists was a dummy's Game. In this particular room, there were only two other men, both too awkward and uptight to hook up with any serious woman, let alone an ecofem.

Guys like I had once been.

"They don't want us to think about the environment. They'd rather catch a profit for now, and float off into space on the almighty dollar," she growled. Then she read us a poem she'd written, which I guess was supposed to be about what we should be thinking about. I'm pretty sure *she* thought it was a nature poem. About fish, and birds, and elm trees going extinct on the day she got her first period.

But as she read it, I looked around and realised that I was probably the only guy in the room—maybe the only *person* there—who understood the poem was really about. She was dying for a man to come and lay her. To not be some namby-pamby friend, to not woo her with his sensitivity and dedication to Gaia. She wanted a guy who would sniffle at her eco-feminist rhetoric, and instead of mumbling along, would kiss her on the mouth and fuck her up against the wall. She had itches that nobody had ever scratched. It was clear in her voice.

And she kept glancing at me.

Maybe she could smell it on me, the outsiderness? The lingering scent of Starbucks and unfair-trade chocolate? This was only a few months after Katana had catapulted us through that quantum mental leap to Game 2.0—I was still more comfortable in night clubs than ecoMarxist meetings in hippie lofts in North Vancouver. Not that I showed how awkward I felt there. She'd have seen confidence, the carefully rehearsed carefreeness of my gait, my smile. My eyes on her as she spoke.

A few hours later, Monica and I were sitting on her balcony, drinking some—fuck, I don't know what it was, some kind of homemade apple wine or something. Pretty crappy stuff, but she was saying how it was totally sustainable, zero-footprint stuff, and I told her it wasn't bad. I touched her on the shoulder as I said, "really good, actually," working a little old-fashioned NLP magic so she'd associate my touch with boosts in positivity and approval.

Not that the NLP was totally conscious by then: it was more instinct, but she caught it. I saw a flicker in her eyes, vague suspicion that grew a little stronger with my every move. When we were chained to a tree and chanting, a few days later, and I rubbed my shoulder against hers. When I asked her about how she'd become an activist, and read her eye movements. She'd looked down and then away, the clear sign of a kinesthetic mind. Monica was one of those rare people whose inner-world wasn't visual or auditory: she made her way around going on gut feelings and intuitions. Maybe that's how she figured out what I was up to.

A week after our first chat, we were curled up on my couch, pulling back from a kiss to catch our breaths, when I felt her eyes look straight into me. That's not romantic metaphor: she was seeing *into* me. Seeing the *real* me, inside. That's how it felt.

Now, most women love that feeling, but it freaks out us PUAs. She must've seen that, too. She asked me, "How are you doing it?"

Welcome to the PUA's worst nightmare. If she knew already that I was Gaming her, then how long would it be before she figured out everything? I backslid: old, familiar toxic shame and fear of an AFC/AFEC flooded me. All my careful mental hacks—positive self-affirmations, fallback routines, accumulated confidence and freedom to just be with her collapsed into terror and self-loathing.

I took a breath, stared into her eyes, and tried to think of what to say. Nothing. Something to say. *Nothing*.

Mystery, I thought, with the one brain cell that had any Game left in it.

So instead of speaking, I touched her on the chin, and in that instant, her head tilted back, and all my doubts and uncertainties melted away. When my lips touched hers again, I felt my game surge back. In a little while, we'd be in my bed, I knew, candles burning all around us, her hemp skirt draped on the back of my chair, her belly under my palm, her dreadlocks all around her head like an angel's spiky halo. She'd give herself to me that night, I realised, and relief flooded me.

Not anticipation, which was what I *should* have felt. *Relief.* Because I thought I was in control. The outcome was secured. In the back of my mind, a little alarm went off. At the time, I thought it was because I was really falling for her. Like, seriously. And there was a pang of guilt at the fact I'd met her in the process of sarging the ecoMarxist group she led. *Now*, I think differently. The outcome is never, ever sure, and if you want it to be, you're bound to be fucking up your Game somewhere, some AFC shit getting in the way. But that night, I was hazy with endorphins and giddy with fear, and some dark corner of me was eager for a little self-sabotage.

She sensed my hesitation, too. She was entranced, of course, and we did sleep together that night. But she felt that weird twist in my Game. It woke her up when the sun rose, and sent her searching for a reason to doubt me.

She found plenty.

When I woke, she wasn't beside me, but I heard the soft hum of my computer fan, and the faint bleeping sound as she opened page after page.

The ePUA forums...

Fuck.

I rose silently, cringing. I'd left my computer on, logged on to the Game 2.0 discussion board. Where my half-written report on sarging the North Vancouver Eco-Marxist Activism Cooperative was in the drafts text box. Then came terror, and my involuntary gasp, and her turning with eyes so hateful I felt like my balls were about to wither and fall off.

Hell hath no fury like an ecofeminist Gamed.

AND NOW, HERE she came.

"I'm love haokan haokan haokan baby," the sexy voice proclaimed over the thumping beat, and I watched her approach, her stride confident. Challenge was issued by every step. *Bring it on*, growled the sway of her hips. *Let's do this*, her eyes telegraphed.

She fleshed her best *You're dead meat, asshole*, smile, narrowed her eyes, and then turned her gaze on Rasmussen.

Estraven wasn't really Monica right now, just like I wasn't really Andrew Dalton when I was sarging. I was Organic: strong, powerful, the best bro a man could find, the most eligible man in sight. And it wasn't acting anymore: I *was* Organic.

She had become *her* role, too. Estraven had morphed into a thing of primal, visceral beauty, thinly veneered in a pantsuit and a business-casual hairdo. The faintest highlights of blond in the black suggested strands of purest sunlight lost in her hair. Footsteps so confident in those Donata Garibaldi pumps that you could imagine her walking a rope bridge in 'em.

Most sane women give off at least a vague aura of self-containment. They're civilised. Until they're fucked with, they usually don't show their claws. But when I looked at Estraven, those diagrams of the human body mapped off the amount of brain devoted to them flashed through my mind. The ones with a human body that's 90% eyes and thumbs? Well, Estraven was 90% claws and cunt.

And she was entrancing. Despite myself, I found myself momentarily smitten. That moment was all it took. Not only did I falter, but I lost track of Bamboo Grove, who'd hung back and was now gone. Probably somewhere near, ready to swoop in if needed.

"Counselor Rasmussen," I said, "This is..." I said, dropping a half-beat into the introduction. My game was off. She jumped ahead of me and start running an AMOG gambit on me.

"Monica Dietz," she said, extending her hand for a firm shake, first to Rasmussen—sisters first—and then to Echewo and Gilberto. As she shook his hand, she turned her wrist slightly so that her hand ended up on top of his cupped palm. In some dark corner of his mind, she'd begun writing a narrative: herself as the lovely maiden, her dainty knuckles waiting for his princely kiss. But before it became conscious, she withdrew her hand, and shook mine. Plain old handshake.

"Andy," she said, of course using the diminutive. Her tone was more dismissive than familiar. She was casting me as the wannabe knight. As if I was the unfavoured competition, someone she'd dumped once long ago. Gilberto's were eyes on me. She held on, forcing rhe handshake to last just a smidgen too long.

Fuck, I thought loudly as I felt the wave of insecurity tremble through me. *She's really good.*

People love to hear their own names, but they hate to hear their own name while wearing another persona. Especially abbreviated in a way that reminds them of... negative experiences. Let's leave it at that.

"Nica," I said. That's what she'd always been called among the activists, and I hoped it might be a good returning shot. But it didn't work on her. Didn't faze her at all. *She was expecting it.* "How've you been since..." I paused, furrowing my brow ever so slightly, as if with sympathy, and in my comptacts I scanned the whole set's IPBRs. Nothing unusual, beyond Estraven's seething, subliminal hostility. "Since last time?"

"Oh, excellent. Better than you could imagine." She beamed at me, overcompensating slightly. Nobody else was picking up this confrontational undercurrent. The audience was blind and deaf, as we played out our drama.

"Wonderful! Say, I heard you're also pushing hard on the reef deal." *Work with me*, I suggested with my eyes. "Dr. Gilberto here's *the* person to talk to," I said, "if you wanna hear the scoop on China and Argentina." And to him, my smile said, "Don't thank me, bro."

Isolate your target. It's not like she had any reason to focus on Rasmussen, or to *not* talk to Gilberto.

Gilberto caught it, and smiled widely at her. He was married, supposedly faithfully, but who'd mind spending five minutes hashing out second-hand news with a woman who looked even half as hot as Estraven? Nobody, that's who.

When I turned back, Bamboo Grove was shaking Rasmussen's hand. Crestfallen, I took it in with a brief glance, and then looked back at Estraven and Gilberto.

I felt eyes on me.

Echewo. He grinned, and I realized suddenly that he *knew*. Sometimes it happened. You ran into that sometimes, no matter how smooth your Game was. Women who sensed you were a PUA. Guys who were just more sensitive to social interactions than most men, or who had ePUA buddies and knew enough to catch on.

He pointedly held my gaze before glancing over at the other two pairs.

"I think we're alone now," he sang softly, not breaking his smile for an instant. He had, I noticed just then, absolutely perfect teeth.

"Looks like," I said, and furrowed my brow as he put his arm around my shoulder.

"It's cool. Let them play their move. You've already broed Hector, and Rasmussen's already on board."

"She is?" I said.

Echewo nodded, sliding one arm around my back. "Yep. And don't you dare take credit in your sarge report, Organic," he scolded me, eyes half-serious above that perfect-toothed smile. "Now who's *she*?" he nodded at Estraven. "In real life, I mean? To you?"

"An ex, kind of." I shrugged. "She and I..."

"Naw, man, by in real life, I mean online. What's her ecofem name?" He said it like it was an easy mistake, and patted my shoulder. He radiated magnanimity the way a cup of hot cocoa radiates comfort on a winter night. Too much.

Why the fuck was he broing *me*?

"Wait, what's *your* handle?" I asked.

The grin went sly—a bit sympathetic, with just a touch of amog—and he said, "I'm in a slightly different network."

Like rogue fungal software, Game 2.0 had spread round the world, creating subcultures we'd never imagined. What had we created, without even knowing it?

An invite message popped up in my left comptact. Some kind of social network site I'd never heard of before.

"Trust me," he said. "You want in."

I accepted it. Nothing happened.

"You need one more invite from an insider. Once you accept both, we'll be in touch. And the world will never be the same..." he said, and excused himself, leaving me standing there like I'd just met some kind of Greek god. *Deus sex machina*, I thought, as he walked straight up to Greenfire as if he knew *her*. And then he kissed her on the cheek and started talking to her, and I realized from her reaction that he *did* know her.

Greenfire was one of them, too? Whoever *they* were... she must have been watching us.

Watching us for *them*?!?

The reefs were gonna be fine, if Echewo wasn't fucking with me. Estraven was laughing, her hand on Gilberto's arm. Bamboo Grove was nodding earnestly as Rasmussen gestured around, as if complaining about the deafening music.

I stepped up to the bar and ordered a glass of 30 year old Lagavulin, the same thing I always drank to celebrate a successful Hague-sarge. I ordered it in perfect Dutch, even though the bar-tender spoke fine English. That was how many times I'd done it. With my first sip, a sense of immense calm washed over me.

Us Game 2.0ers feel like we're the only ones who've been working the system for good. Bravado has kept us going, believing that only we stood between the biosphere and cash-crazed ruin. We, the brave, intrepid few who gave a shit about the environment, who saved the world by hacking the human mind. But that was a fairy tale, a lie we'd created to give ourselves the balls to try do *something*.

And here was a whole 'nother network we'd never heard of, using *our* hacks and techniques—and fighting for the same thing! I was hit again by something I'd felt that first night home, after my first boot camp. That sense of relief. *I'm not the only one. We're not the only ones.*

Then I felt a hand on my shoulder. A voice whispered into my ear, "Hello, Andrew."

"Monica," I said, not turning. My learned instinct was to let her come to me; after running that amog on me, I wasn't going to offer myself up for emotional clawing, and anyway, I was above this. The sarge had been run long before I'd shown up, and her attack on me had achieved nothing. I was above scrapping with ecofems now. I'd been invited up into a new, higher echelon.

She slid next to me and smiled, a faint patina of glitter makeup twinkling on her cheeks. She was stunning: those stray dark locks on her forehead, her no-way-they're-real lashes, the way one eye closed just a smidgen more than the other when she smiled. The tiny wrinkles on her lower eyelids.

Careful, Organic, I reminded myself.

"We never did say goodbye properly." She set one hand on my shoulder, and taking my drink away with the other, she sipped it. She set it back down on the bar so that her arms ended up almost around my neck. "Ever wonder why?" she asked, eyes twinkling.

"Not really," I said, playing it cool. *I'm beyond this now, chickie*, I told myself. *I probably never have to worry about you ecofems again.*

"Some girls try to change guys," she said in a low, hard voice. "Some girls pine over the guys who break their hearts." She ran her nails along the back of my neck. "And some of them just wait for the guy to grow the hell up." Her smile was wry.

My Game was gone now. I stood there perplexed, her arms basically around me, and watched her watching me. I couldn't figure out exactly what kind of move this was. Some kind of elaborate, deep-structure amog? Maybe a highly-morphed variant of xNLP?

I didn't know what she was doing, but one thing was sure. She was hacking my mind. Hardcore.

I narrowed my gaze briefly and launched a few apps, which immediately burst active. The data slammed into my view in a cascading sequence of factlets. She was wearing comptacts, of course: there was an IPBR output running on one lens, displaying *my* status. Besides the Scotch, there was a biochemical trace on her breath that was a well-known, common marker of having taken Peacock[CC]. Her heartbeat and respiration were slightly elevated, which in most women signalled arousal... or rage.

"Don't those guys usually *outgrow* them by then?" I was as nonchalant as I could be against a slowly rising tide of vestigial AFEC paranoia.

"Think you've outgrown me?" she said, one nail scratching my hairline. It felt good, especially with her eyes on mine, her voice echoing in my mind. I thought of her on my couch, and remembered she'd done this then, too. Scratched one nail along my hairline.

Fuck. She'd seduced *me* that night?

"We'll see," she said. "I haven't given up on you yet," she said with a sharp little grin, and smoothed the back of my neck with one soft hand. Then she leaned into me, touched my chin, and I felt my eyes close reflexively.

Then nothing. When I opened my eyes, she was smiling at me, and Bagheera and Bamboo Grove were there, too, by her side, eyeing me with amused smiles.

"There's hope for you yet, kiddo," Estraven said. "See you around. If you've manned up enough." Then she threw me a look that was pure seduction.

On my left comptact, a window popped open.

It was the second invite, the one that followed up Echewo's. And it was signed: LOVE, ESTRAVEN.

And then she was gone.

I minimised the invite window. I was surrounded by suits drinking and dancing. Once again alone. My wingmen were gone, my overpriced drink—a Scotch older than I was—wasn't doing anything for me, and Estraven, which was what I had to call her, since I couldn't call this glorious woman Monica, still was right there in my head.

Was this some sort of counter-game? Was I being mindfucked? Maybe it was some kind of cognitive virus or something? But that feeling Estraven gave off, that intense attraction... it felt *real*. Were she and I really on the same side?

A red light went off in the upper left corner of my left comptact. It was a call from Biosfear, probably a status update on Hunter. A patch of window opened up automatically, though the call wouldn't be opened till I approved it. Biosfear was looking sidelong, his expression bored, his peacocky shades perched on the top of his authority-evoking brush cut. And as good a wingman as he was, I wondered if he would have done any better than I had if Estraven had scratched the back of his neck.

I thought then—and I know now, though that's another story—that he would've crumbled. She had game... *monster* game. She was my equal. And that pulled some tiny, deep trigger somewhere in my mind. I felt something. I didn't know what, at first, because for me, that feeling was something I'd had to train myself to feel. I'd played so much fake-it-till-you-make-it that I barely recognised the real thing when it swept through me.

It was faith. Faith in myself, faith in her. Faith that in this random world, in this senseless universe, despite my blunders and mistakes and successes and despite all the chaos and cynicism that had soaked into everything and everyone, I'd found my way right where I needed to be: on the doorstep to the underworld where people really were saving the world from itself.

And what I did next is why this will be my last posting on this board, guys. Because, yeah, it's been great, but I have better things to do.

Yeah. I maximised the second invite message, took a deep breath, and accepted.

Scheherazade Cast
in Starlight

Jason Andrew

IN ONE OF *my many attempts to inspire writers, I started a series of 'Crazy Story Ideas' on the* Shine *blog. In part 3, posted on May 23, 2009, I mused about positive developments in Islamic countries, and wrote:*

  'Maybe this could take place in Iran?'
  and
  'A quiet revolution needs power to grow, and free power from the Sun, and subtle power in the form of Facebook and other modern forms of communication might just provide that extra push towards a change, a non-violent one.'

  Then—on June 12, 2009—the elections in Iran, with its well-known protests took place, which took even me by surprise. Yes, I was predicting something of the sort (and wish I had written 'Twitter' instead of 'Facebook' and was certainly wrong on the non-violent part), but did not expect it so soon. I was thinking about at least ten years in the future. Which goes to show that with near-future SF, sometimes you're too fast (working nuclear fusion, anyone?) and sometimes you're too slow.

All part of the game. Anyway, inspired by recent events (I suppose, and maybe a tiny bit by my crazy musings), Jason Andrew conjures up a modern-day Scheherazade, one that might haunt the Iranian-powers-that-be even more than Neda Agha-Soltan...

> **Above the rioters' ruinous flames, a holoPhoenix shone. Hope rose like Holy Fire. The Rocking Raven Brigade beat chaos and despair.**

—Gillian Gray—

THE QUR'AN SAYS that all people are a single nation.

It has always been the will of man to separate us in thought, in clothing, in language. Separate, we can be controlled. Separate, we can be killed in the quiet of the night and disappear into myth. Separate, we forget that in the end we have the power.

I was five when my mother was cast into a cell. Her alleged crime? Selling narcotics. Her real crime? She had been elected to parliament. The Iranian Assembly of Experts declared that all women candidates for parliament were disqualified in the year 2006. In the shadow of night, men with masks took her and none even whispered her name in fear of retribution. I never saw her again. But I kept her in my heart and mind. Remembering her courage to defy a government that wanted to oppress its citizens.

My eldest brother died three years later in the protests over the Presidential election. He wore a regal green jacket and marched in protest over the fraud that kept Mahmoud Ahmadinejad in power. He died from a blow to the head in the middle of the street. He was not forgotten. A girl only a few years older than myself captured his image. Tweets of protests were sent across the world. We protested in the light of the world broadcast to any that wished to see. No man worthy of the name can withstand the suffering of another if it is within his sight. And we showed that day that such deeds can never again be done in secret, can never be hidden in the shadows.

The Qur'an says that all people are a single nation. Though we failed that day, we were shown the way by the will of Allah. Globalization has been a dirty word for oppressive governments. They want to keep their borders clearly defined with walls of stone and barbed wire and land mines. They want their citizens to think only of what happens in their lands, to their familes. They want us to forget that we all are one family.

Technology blurs those borders. It allows information to flow freely. It is the bane of any oppressive government. There were no more barriers to hide us away from the rest of the world. No firewalls that could keep out our stories. The world hungered for reality entertainment. When I was ready, I stepped into the starlight.

My v-casts are circulated around the world. Every action recorded and captured in amber for the world to study. Anyone in the world can watch me. I am Scheherazade cast in starlight, telling a story each night to keep my head. I competed against drunken bears roaming free in Butte, Montana. I told the world of the food shortages, the war, tragedies, and love against the tale of seven strangers trapped in a house forced to live together. I battled against Big Brother by showing stories about all of our brothers and sisters. We showed the world that the greatest stories come not from forced drama, but from life and living despite the darkness.

Each night before I slept, I checked my ranking. I was safe as long I had eyes upon me. Or so I believed. I am shamed to admit that I was drunk with my new celebrity. I had messages from foreign leaders, proud mothers, and little girls seeking a role-model. I thought that I had made a difference.

And then the men with black masks came for me. I was drinking coffee in a café on a unseasonably warm winter day. I heard the screeching of the truck before they slipped the hood over my head. The hard barrel of their guns poked into my back as I desperately tried to gasp for air. They threw me onto the bed on the truck and held me down. I was so terrified that I could not even scream.

I had no voice, but others screamed for me. The Qur'an says that paradise lies at the feet of mothers. I waited, held down, but the truck did not move. I heard a swarm of voices around me. The death squad had come for me, but you stopped them. No man wishes his mother to see his darkness. The women took me from the death squad with violence. My bonds were cut and the hood removed. And then we cried.

That moment our country changed.

My youngest brother was taken one thousand nights ago; almost three years ago. This night he was returned to me. He is thinner than I remember, but tall and strong. I am told that it is a symbol of the new government. A time of hope. A bridge to help unite a desperate people. That is a lie.

My brother's freedom is a symbol of your power. It is your will that brought him to the light. It is your will that won the parliament election. Your will that convinced the Guardian Council to validate the elections.

And tomorrow will be my one thousand and first broadcast, and on that day I will be sworn in to parliament. I will take the office for which my mother died and thus Scheherazade must complete her own tale. To you mothers and daughters of Iran, to you I leave the stories. It is only in silence do we lose the spark that Allah has breathed into each of us.

The Qur'an says that all people are a single nation. I believe that this is a statement of universal truth. The world has grown too small to ignore our neighbors. We are one family.

And I wait. I wait for your stories to change the world.

Russian Roulette
2020

Eva Maria Chapman

EVA IS ANOTHER *writer I met over the internet. She posted regularly on the* Shine *blog, and submitted tweets for @outshine (of which I published a few, one of them right after receiving this story).*

While the main intent of the Shine *anthology presence on social sites like MySpace, Facebook and Twitter is promotion (get the word out), so far it has also been instrumental in bringing me into contact with a number of writers I might never have found in the SF community. Eva has written a memoir about her Russian émigré family in Australia and a historic fantasy involving Kaurna Aborigines.*

Her enthusiasm for Shine *is so great she decided to turn her hand to SF, and if "Russian Roulette 2020" is any indication, I hope that she will write much more of it.*

In these modern days, it seems that maximum cynicism equals great coolness. As this high-spirited and spiritual story shows, it's high time to exorcise those nihilistic spirits...

She spoke for the first time. Roses fell from her lips. Pearls. Her body turned into luminescence and butterflies. It surprised no one.

—Mercedes M. Yardley—

"Take it off?" Wingnut was incredulous. "What do you mean, take it off? Hey, MV, Colleen's telling us to take off our ZiSleeves!"

MV was distracted by the Russian girl in the blue dress. Dazzled. Who did she remind him of? A little Amish looking, perhaps. Hair in a braid. No makeup. And her arm didn't glow with LED lights. His own ZiSleeve bleeped at him. It was Jeezbob from New York. "Come on man, your move." They were in the middle of an exciting game of Robodroids. MV was cornered in a hell-hole by vicious robots, with no way out.

Wingnut poked him sharply. "Hey dude, listen up, this is serious shit!"

MV reluctantly disconnected his earchip and put his attention on his teacher. Was she saying: "Take your ZiSleeves off?"

Colleen knew she had a rebellion on her hands. Like when the school banned earchips during assembly. Trying to tear this lot away from their ZiSleeves was tantamount to gouging out their livers. These kids were truly in the grip of what psychologists called weblock.

"This is dogshit," whined Wingnut. "Let's get back in the Solaritza and skedaddle back to the plane."

"You know we can't do that—we don't have permission to land in LA before schedule." Flights were severely restricted, not only to cut emissions, but to curtail the spread of rapidly mutating viruses.

Wingnut looked horrorstruck. "Then let's go back to the Expo in Moscow." Wingnut had loved Crystal Island—the largest solar powered building in the world, full of avant-garde technology and newly launched Web 4.0 applications. He had purchased 3D glasses and 3D Sims for his ZiSleeve and was dying to immerse himself in juicy porn world. He'd had a peek on the bus and immediately experienced being slammed between bouncing tits and arses. God it was good.

"What kind of backward crap dive have you brought us to?" snapped Rachel. She objected to being wrenched from her avatar, Astrid, who had just purchased a castle (charging it to Daddy's account of course). She was looking forward to buying outfits that befitted being Queen of such a castle. Her IMVU playmate had just bought a black steed and looked fabulous on it! The unfortunate fact that in her first life, Rachel could warm her hands between the fat folds on her stomach, made it even more imperative to buy the gold bikini for her gloriously slim, Second Life self.

"Do we really have to?" whined Enrita, looking like the spoilt Brazilian princess she was, zapping microbes with her nano-wand. Her wealthy family had exchanged the gated suburbia of Rio for Los Angeles when food riots had got out of control. Not that LA didn't have food riots. Plenty of them. It was just that LA cops had more sophisticated weaponry—like ray guns to paralyse the starving mobs. "Mamae will freak out if she can't get hold of me."

Colleen sighed. She knew it would do them all good to extricate themselves from the Controller, as she called it—so like Big Brother it was scary.

"We want a reason!"

Colleen approached Rada, the girl in the blue dress, who had met them off the Solaritza. "Could you explain why they have to take their ZiSleeves off? They're like a third arm. They won't take them off for even a moment."

Rada faced the hostile group.

MV videoed her to Jeezbob, texting, "Whaddya think of this chick? Knockout tits. No bra!"

"We welcome you warmly to our school." Her voice and presence were mesmerising. The sun shone through her dress, emphasising her womanly shape. Even Wingnut stopped fiddling with his 3D glasses and gawked.

In a voice that would tame a horde of starving rioters, she continued in impeccable English. "We will give you an orientation talk in our hall, followed by lunch. This part of the school is techno free, for many reasons. We request that you remove all phones, sleeves and electronic gadgets."

She immediately quelled the low rumbling that swirled in the courtyard by pointing to beehives nestling under the eaves of the building. "One of the reasons is that your equipment interferes with the bees. We believe it may disrupt their dances."

They all looked up at the beehives. Some incredulous. Others curious.

Fortunately this did make sense. Most of them had spent the last two Springs in apple orchards, hand pollinating apple blossom. Tedious and time consuming but necessary, as in 2017 there were no apples in the stores. No one knew for sure why bee colonies were disappearing at such an alarming rate all over the world. A variety of culprits such as pesticides, varroa mites and oscillation frequency from radio towers were implicated. Perhaps this Russian girl was right. And there was something about Rada's voice that was authoritative without sounding bossy.

"Well I'm keeping my nano-wand," muttered Enrita, who zapped all surfaces for germs wherever she went.

Rada continued, "We keep our Web equipment over in the Tech block." She pointed to the other side of the large quadrangle, attractively peppered with trees and flowers. "You can put it over there."

Nobody moved. Colleen looked to MV. Armed with a scholarship to Yale, he was the most popular boy at school, the highest Flashtrix scorer and boasted the greatest number of PipStream followers.

MV tore his eyes away from the delectable Rada and noticed trestle tables outside the Tech block. It made sense to get on the right side of this chick. He wanted her. And MV was renowned for always getting the girl he wanted.

"Come on dudes, let's put our gear on those tables in the sun. At least the batteries can get recharged."

Rada rewarded him with a stunning smile.

"I'm in, dude," he texted Jeezbob.

MV walked slowly across the quadrangle, his forefinger manoeuvring his way out of the trap Jeezbob had set. He finally hit off the sound with a big sigh. The air crackled with the rips of zi-cro pulling apart, as he and his classmates reluctantly disconnected themselves from Mother Web. Glancing reproachfully at the beehives, they laid down their gizmos. Some still owned the bulkier ZiPad-3, but the flexible ZiSleeves were now all the rage. They were lighter and enabled simultaneous screens to operate. MV liked to maintain his supremacy on Flashtrix , joust with Jeezbob, download ZiTunes, upload ZiNaut, keep up with PipStream and watch baseball.

MV felt naked without his ZiSleeve and rubbed his left arm. It looked skinny and pale compared to his other. He was also dismayed to notice his skin fungus had spread. Mysterious skin diseases had become rampant. Well at least he didn't have asthma or diabetes like half of his classmates, or small genitalia, a scourge of boys born after 2012. He shuffled back across the quadrangle with his fellow web orphans, their school logo glowing green from the back of their T-Shirts. They filed in into a spacious hall with polished wooden floors.

The future cannot be predicted but futures can be invented, was inscribed in gold above the entrance. A 3D painting that looked like a Hubble photograph vibrated off one of the walls. Light shone down through a myriad of stained glass panels. It was almost like a Church—a wooden vaulted space which sparkled with refracted light. Another beautiful girl was addressing the group.

"Hello our most revered guests. My name is Tania. We welcome you to Tekos School. May we co-create a positive vision for the future, in this our Space of Love..." Wingnut rolled his eyes and muttered, "I'll give you some positive lovin' baby!"

As she continued her welcome, MV looked around in awe. The room's splendour matched that of the outside. When he first emerged from the Solaritza, the Tekos bus which had brought them to this school in the Krasnodar region in Southern Russia, he had been impressed. Attractive low rise buildings nestled against a blaze of green forest. He had zipped an image into Archipedia, at the very point when Jeezbob forced him into a bunker full of rayzoids, so hadn't yet seen the answer. He automatically tapped his non-existent ZiSleeve to retrieve it. Damn. He would have to ask instead. As the Americans were being shown to their quarters after Tania's welcome, MV found Rada.

"Like your buildings. Who's the architect?"

"We are. We designed it ourselves."

"Yourselves?"

"Yes and built it too. This is the third building we have constructed. The first two were burnt down."

"Burnt down! By who?"

"By 'whom,' surely?"

"Yeah, yeah, whom, whatever." She was really unnerving him.

"Oh, by the Church."

"The Church?"

"Yes, a local branch of the Russian Orthodox Church. They think we are a cult and are dangerous."

Rada and Tania, demure in their braids and cotton dresses, certainly did not look dangerous.

"The Church burnt you down? You must be joking."

"No." Laughed Rada. "When Communism collapsed, the Church vied with the Mafia for control. Alexey II, the first post-Soviet Patriarch, reputedly ex-KGB, was very rich and drove a BMW. A perfect example of a new breed of autocrat, jostling for power."

"What a drag!"

"A drag?"

"Demoralising to have to rebuild," he translated.

"No not at all. Our designs have improved a lot! We have incorporated more sustainability." She pointed up at the walls. "Used more natural products. Our buildings breathe—they are healthier. And we have managed to accommodate the bees better in the new design."

"Why don't you have them in the garden?" (*Like normal people*, he refrained from adding.)

"Oh, they love being near us. They thrive better and they create beautiful honey for us."

MV ignored this as loony and loopy. Reminded him of that sugary, whole-Earth business his grandmother was into.

"The bees are very fragile at this present time— they are a barometer for how much we have wrecked the world, so we take extra-special care of them."

The front of the building was graced by a spectacular, 3-dimensional piece of art. His right hand automatically went for the Digiclick, to send it to Wikiflickr. Again he had the unusual task of having to ask a real person.

"Who's the artist?"

"We are—we students created it together."

MV was stunned. He had heard that this school was exceptional; that kids young as fifteen were completing university degrees, excelling in Maths and Physics. This had been the whole point of Colleen forcing them away from the Crystal Park—to check it out. Most of the Tekos kids had gone home for the summer but three seniors, Rada, Tania and Vassily joined their principal Michael Shchetinin, as hosts for their American visitors.

"Shove over MV! Hogging all the chick action again!" It was Wingnut, barging in as usual. "Hiya Rada. I'm Wingnut." He ogled her.

"Wingg-nut?"

"Yes, let me introduce Wingnut," said MV, ignoring Wingnut's unbelievable social ineptitude, "called so, not because of his political views, or sticky-out ears, but because he resembles the old Ninja character from the affluent times. And his father is still rich as fuck."

"Ri-ich as fuck?" repeated Rada, quizzically

The way the well elocuted 'fuck' burst forth from those rosebud lips was enough to send Wingnut into a paroxysm of hysterical giggling. He didn't know where to put his goofy self. He went automatically to his Zi. He had no idea what to do without it. No wonder his grandparents smoked themselves to death, he thought. Without zyburbia at your fingertips, what else was there to do?

By this time the trio had circled back to the hall where drinks and lunch were laid out. Sumptuous salads, freshly baked breads and pies overspilled the plates.

"Ooh, cherry pie!" Wingnut swooped. "That looks cocklickin' good." He couldn't stand the way that Rada was looking at him. Spooky. He dived into the cherries, drowning himself in their delectable sweetness. He, like his classmates, was embarrassed to eat naked, as it were. They couldn't bear being without their earchips for non-stop music, their screens for the latest podcast or video, or their Ziboards for surfing and texting. Rada, Tania and Vassily were attentive hosts. There was so much TALKING going on. It felt a bit much!

"How can you guys stand it without Live-stream?" Rachel asked, stuffing her mouth with potato and beetroot salad. "Don't you even have laptops?"

"Yes, I have a laptop and a phone," said Vassily, "but they are in the Tech building. I only use them sometimes, and then in the evening."

"God, how boring. What do you do?"

"It is not boring at all. We dance, sing, have fun."

Rachel nearly spat beetroot in disgust.

After lunch there was a massive rush for the ZiSleeves.

Rada reached for MV as he set out to join the surge. Her touch on his pale arm was warm and inviting. "Would you like me to show you the forest, MV?"

He felt his eyeballs burning as she looked into them. He thought of his PipStream, which would be overflowing; and Jeezbob, waiting for his next move. "Yeah sure," he said uncertainly, "after I do a quick pip shuffle."

A flicker of her disappointment flashed between them. He felt like a junkie; starving for his next fix. However he was reminded of another kind of fix altogether; the way her arse curved brought warmth to his groin. He'd heard Russian girls were hot. "Okay," he said impulsively, "I'll come." He couldn't remember the last time he had even gone for a walk, let alone without his ZiSleeve.

Rada led him through a garden that radiated out from behind the Tech building. Flowers spilled onto paths, intricately laid with attractive stones. Rada picked a daisy and threaded it into her braid. The clear skin on her face glowed in the streams of sun that filtered through the trees.

She led him through the solar garden and past the windmills.

"Are you totally off-grid here?"

"Of course," she trilled. "We have very hot summers and in the winter when the wind sweeps down from the Steppes, the windmills take over. Like how you would say...?" She chose her words carefully. "The demented howling of the wind is miraculously converted into the sounds of a flute concerto by Mozart—beautiful to listen to on a wintry evening."

"You are beautiful to listen to all the time." The thought bubbled from him like within a cartoon. The way she spoke fascinated him. Her words held a beauty that stirred a small neglected pebble resting somewhere in the vicinity of his heart. It felt starved of juice. He promptly dismissed the sensation as sentimental hogwash.

They walked towards a forest of cedars that swayed tall and majestic, whispering their distinctive hum in the breeze. MV breathed the sweet pine scent into his lungs.

"Do you have forests near you?" asked Rada.

"We did have but they are disappearing fast." MV tried to push the dreadful fires of 2016 out of his mind. Angeles National Forest had been razed to the ground, taking with it many human lives including those of his favourite uncle, aunt and cousins. "In the north of California some forests do remain, but many are dying." He looked up at the cedars but did not see the tell-tale brown foliage which was causing the demise of many of those trees. "Your trees look pretty healthy."

"In Russia, forests cover 45% of the land mass— the most extensive reserves in the world. Also this area is full of rivers, mountains and rich black earth. In the last ten years there has been a massive cleanup of the industrial pollution that was a legacy of Stalin, and the American factories which poured in during the 1990s. Now our trees are very happy. They love to supply us with fragrant air." She went up to one and spread her arms upwards in worship.

Oh no, not a treehugger too. The thought was rapidly followed by another. *This babe is in perfect position for me to ram her against the tree trunk.*

But before this thought could be brought to fruition, Rada skipped lightly away and led him into a glade with a pond. She ran about frolicking and did several cartwheels, her light summer dress cascading over her womanly body in such mesmerising whirls that MV couldn't tear his eyes away. Her reddish gold hair escaped from its braid and fell in waves down her back.

Wow, this chick is hot—I'm sure she ain't wearing knickers! If only he could vid-port this gorgeous sight to Jeezbob.

"Can you cartwheel MV?"

Cartwheel! MV had never cartwheeled in his life—that was so uncool! He shook his head vigorously.

"Oh please try." With that she did a series of perfect arcs around him ending in a spectacular somersault.

"Well—er—er—" he stuttered.

"Oh, come on. Try!" Her eyes danced, green like the light through the trees. So hard to resist her plea.

So he tried. It wasn't good. His ZiSleeve arm was weak and the other crippled by a wii tennis injury. He crumpled unceremoniously to the ground, cursing violently.

Rada ran up to him with concern and massaged his arm. He felt the pain ease. He smelled the mead of her breath. Now was the time to make his move. Slip his tongue into that honeyed portal. But something stopped him—a strange emotion. Was it shyness? This was bad—he needed Jeezbob to knock some macho sense into him. What was wrong with him? He always found seducing chicks so easy.

"Let's go for a swim. It is so hot!"

With that she peeled off her dress and dived in. He was right. No knickers. Hell! She came up laughing. "Come on."

MV was still reeling with shock at the glimpse of her brown body unencumbered by undergarments.

"Come on," she repeated.

MV was not averse to skinny dipping, but this was something else. She was expecting him to take his clothes off and dive in. Just like that. In such a natural, innocent way. He thought ruefully of the skin fungus that had spread over his back.

"Come on MV—it is wonderful in here." Her pearly teeth shone in the glints of the water. It did look inviting and he was sweltering.

As she disappeared under again, he took his clothes off and dived in, catching his breath as the cold hit. But within a few seconds he was up and paddling. Divine. Very different to the pools in LA. No chemicals—just pure water. Rada was splashing about and laughing with infectious delight, her hair plastered in a thick wodge over his forehead. He thought of all the LA girls who never wet their sleek hairdos, preferring to preen in gaggles on edges of swimming pools, showing off their latest designer swimsuits.

Rada splashed him. He had such an urge to splash her back.

She playfully splashed again. This time he did splash back and they had a glorious orgy of splashing. He felt exhilarated. Like a kid.

She then jumped out and spread-eagled herself on the grass, offering her body to the sun. He climbed out slowly, mesmerised by the bush of gold curling hair, bejewelled with droplets of water, that sprouted over her pubis. It looked unruly, untidy, wild. Every girl he had ever seen naked was either shaved or clipped. He had an immense desire to run his hands through it. Or film it with his Zi-Lens and put it on YouTube. He envisioned the title with a chuckle. *Wild beaver on the loose.*

Now dude, enticed the inner seducer. *Now is the time to tease apart that bushy fuzz and jump her. Look, she's just lying there asking for it.*

Yes, jump her! responded his inner gallery of observers, including Jeezbob with his rakish grin.

But instead he collapsed next to her, enjoying the warmth of the sun on his body.

Rada had picked up his T-Shirt and was examining the school logo glowing from it.

"Groovy, eh?" said MV proudly. "Silica nanoparticles blended into a light-emitting gel, then printed onto the cotton to form pixels. The gel consists of a ruthenium compound that emits a bright light when a voltage is applied to it, along with an electrolyte and..."

Rada looked away and dropped the shirt. He was taken aback, just when he was in full flow. He had been instrumental in getting these logos embedded in schoolwear. The girls back at school had been impressed. And had shown him how much.

"Ruthenium!" said Rada "That is a rare trace element! I thought you Americans had learnt your lesson, plundering the planet for your endless vanity!"

"But this technology's from Japan. You must admit it's amazing? The way the letters sparkle?"

She shrugged. "It is not interesting to me. I prefer the sparkle on the water, the blue-green glow on a blowfly, the glinting of dew in the grass. And it is certainly not as interesting as the sparkle that comes from your eyes." She looked deeply into them. Such a pure look. Again she reminded him of someone. Who the hell was it? Then he felt a strange emotion—like prickles of tears at the back of his eyes. Was he going to cry?

"What do the initials MV stand for?"

"Hey dudika, no-one, but no-one knows that!" He drew back, welcoming the anger that squashed unfamiliar feelings.

"Really? But surely your mother must know."

Was this girl dumb, or just silly?

"Of course she knows. She gave me the stupid name."

"But what name is it?" She was persistent.

"It is such a dumb, embarrassing name—it truly sucks."

Rada screwed up her nose quizzically. "But she must have given it to you for a reason."

"Well yes, it was my great-grandfather's name. He was from Ukraine."

She sat up with alacrity.

"Ukraine? So your family comes from this part of the world?"

"Yeah but a long time ago." He was distracted by the bounce of her breasts as she became more animated. The pink nipples bobbed enticingly.

"So what was your great-grandfather's name?"

"Miroslav." He spat out the word with disgust. "Can you imagine such a name in sophisticated LA? Horrible."

"Miroslav." The name rolled off her tongue like a bubble of poetic syrup. So different to his pronunciation. She jumped up and started cartwheeling in glee. Naked. God he wished he had his Zi-Lens!

"That is such a beautiful name. Do you know what it means?"

"Fuck no. I don't want to know."

"It means 'peace.' Do you mind if I call you Miroslav?"

"Only in private. Not in front of my classmates."

She looked slightly dejected but agreed.

"What about your name, Rada? What does that mean?"

"Happiness."

They dressed and walked back. MV felt strangely refreshed and peaceful. Perhaps there was something in the meaning of a name after all. Rada did radiate happiness like he had never seen before.

Rada skipped ahead, cartwheeling occasionally. She was so wholesome—like a kid but also a woman—he couldn't take his eyes off her. Back in LA he would have fucked this chick by now. But Rada aroused him in a whole different way. He felt warm and his skin tingled all over.

Back at the school, the afternoon sun was settling over the cedars. He saw his mates sitting outside the Tech building absorbed within their Zi worlds. He felt a strange revulsion. His own ZiSleeve sat on the trestle table, lonely and winking furiously. He moved towards it leadenly. He zi-croed it on. It felt like a shackle.

VASSILY WATCHED RACHEL'S ZiScreen over her shoulder, as her avatar, resplendent in a gold bikini, was about to be seduced by Demoloron on his black steed. "Rachel," he interrupted. "Did you know that the futures you keep dreaming up in Second Life, you can dream up in real life."

"And did you know Vassily, you are annoying me intensely," replied Rachel, her cheeks wobbling exasperatedly. "Why don't you go and dance or whatever the fuck you do in this stupid place." Vassily immediately leapt up and did a Cossack dance right there in the courtyard, in front of her. An old man with silver hair took up an accordion and played it in accompaniment. Rachel turned away scornfully.

"Who's that old geezer?" Wingnut asked Colleen.

"That's Mikhail Shchetinin, the guy who started this school over 25 years ago. He's about to give a talk."

"Jeez. Spare me," said Wingnut, getting up to go.

"Wait," commanded Colleen. "I think you should stay and listen." Separating Wingnut from his zyberworld was like dislodging a prehistoric mammoth from permafrost. But she had promised Wingnut's father she would try. It was he who had invented the ZiSleeve, so he felt responsible that his only child had disappeared up it, so to speak. He had arranged the plane for the school trip, as a reward for Wingnut's class finishing school. The only way he could entice Wingnut to visit Tekos, was the promise of the Moscow Expo first. Colleen sighed. How was she going to prise Wingnut away from the Web by even a millimetre? Tania came to her aid by announcing in front of the gathering, that she would be translating. Wingnut decided that Gorko the Viking having his way with Saxon slave girls would have to wait. Instead he feasted his eyes upon Tania as she began to translate for the benevolent-looking old man.

"The present is not something that has just happened to us, we have all participated in its creation..."

Yeah, thought Wingnut, admiring her blonde, blue-eyed beauty, *I could create a perfect sex slave out of you darling.*

NEXT MORNING MV was woken by singing. Cursing, he went to the window. He'd been up half the night catching up with pips and downloads. Just a few hours away from his ZiSleeve was lethal. It mustn't happen again.

Out of the window the garden looked resplendent in the morning sunshine. Tripping through it barefoot was his nemesis, that temptress Rada. It looked like she was singing to the flowers. Bloody hell—what a kook! Colleen had made such a mistake bringing them to this Godforsaken place.

Well it must be near midnight in New York—time for a game before Jeezbob hit the sack. He closed the curtain. Jeezbob had manoeuvred him into a cave full of unexploded mines, and the sound of whizzing, banging and explosions drowned out that wretched singing.

A shaft of sunlight slipped through a crack in the curtain and caught his face. Dammit. It reminded him of the sparkle on Rada's pearly teeth. He went to the window. Oh God she was cartwheeling again. As she came up, she spied him.

"Come, come outside! It is so wonderful out here." He was torn. Then he saw the quote above his door.

If we don't change our direction, we'll wind up where we are headed.

Boy, was this place trying to brainwash him? He decided to take his ZiSleeve with him. As protection.

"Oh okay, but I'm not doing any more cartwheels."

"Of course not—I want to show you the gardens."

"Just for a short while." Out he went, armoured with his ZiSleeve.

The garden was bursting with vegetables and flowers. Cabbages the size of footballs swelled out among a riot of nasturtiums.

"You grow all your own vegetables?"

"Yes, and fruits, and healing herbs. We use permaculture techniques."

"Do you guard your gardens?"

"No."

"Why not?" In LA, gardens had sprouted everywhere—disused lots, sides of roads where guerrilla gardeners had to become more guerrilla-like to protect their produce. MV earned extra money by patrolling gardens at night, entertained by his ZiSleeve of course.

"Well Miroslav." She lowered her voice as she said his name. Despite himself he thrilled at the way she pronounced it. "We have plenty of gardens in Russia. And land. You must remember the Soviet Union collapsed twenty years before the world financial crash of 2009. Fortunately most people, even those in the cities, still had access to a dacha and garden. In the early 1990s while Russia boiled out of control in a soup of intrigue, power and greed, these gardens saved Russia from starvation and possibly another revolution."

"Revolution may have been a good thing."

"No Miroslav—our country was worse than a battered, bloody dog after seventy years of revolution. In 1995 there emerged from the Siberian Taiga my heroine, the eco-mystic Anastasia, who persuaded hundreds of thousands of people to turn away from the transient attraction of luxury consumer goods, and delight in the simple pleasures of planting seeds and creating gardens. By the time Capitalism cracked apart, President Medvedev was passing legislation for people to acquire land cheaply, so they could be self-sufficient. What was great was that these people were well educated and technically literate and brought their new knowledge to the land. My parents were successful city people who became quickly disillusioned with a Western copycat lifestyle; they traded their concrete coop in Moscow for an eco-house in the countryside, at first commuting while they built it."

Her eyes sparkled as she spoke of her parents. "Oh Miroslav I wish I could take you to visit them, so you could eat one of the apples from the tree they planted when I was born. It would help your skin condition."

MV looked at the rosy flush of her skin and longed to touch it—to somehow infuse it into his own.

"So what is so special about this school?" He had avoided going to Shchetinin's talk, pleading Zi overload.

"We learn how to create a positive future."

"How?"

"In many ways, but basically by relating to each other and thinking."

"Thinking?"

"Yes, most people only use a fraction of their thinking capabilities."

"Well I don't. I think all the time."

"Miroslav, you never have time to think—a slave to your ZiSleeve."

"I'm thinking the whole time—responding to hundreds of pieces of info every day, through my live-Stream."

"Just Nowism; downloading data. Reacting. Not retaining it."

"Yes I am."

"I doubt that. When do you contemplate deeply, sharpen your understanding—ponder whether something optimal in the present may not be optimal in the future? Do you observe nature for example? Work out the true laws that govern everything?"

"Well—er..." MV thought of his mother who commented sadly that old-fashioned daydreaming had disappeared?

"Well Miroslav—the deep, quiet thinking process is alien to many today because of the influence of the technocratic world. People spend their entire life marshalling their thoughts towards using and creating better widgets and gadgets. You are seduced by these substitutes for real life."

MV's Wii injury throbbed. His ZiSleeve winked and beeped.

"Substitutes! You're unbelievably arrogant! You should have seen the amazing devices at the Expo. Technology that will save our planet."

"Miroslav, the planet needs greater consciousness, reflective awareness, not just technical fixes."

But MV was back at Moscow's Crystal Island. His eyes glazed over. "You should have seen the robots."

"Just clever inventions, nothing more."

"Inventions? Robots will take over."

"Only the brains behind them will take over. Our brains. Technology is created by us; by our thoughts. It is us humans who are amazing. Robots, at best, are useful servants.

"Look at this ZiSleeve! I can get any piece of information I want at any time. I'm being better educated than anyone in mankind's history." MV's Zi bleeped obligingly in emphasis. "I'm proud to be part of a cross-fertilisation that's driving a generation of new scientific knowledge and technological innovation at an unprecedented rate."

"Yes that is good—it makes you flip from topic to topic easily and you learn a lot quickly, but it also makes you lazy. Your mind is continually searching for input—the latest disaster, the latest news, the latest—what do you call it? Thrill." She pronounced it 'T'rill.'

MV had to acknowledge that point. Each day brought an exciting breaking news story on ZiNet— plenty of them—cyclones, fires, riots, floods, sieges. There was even a special part of YouTube called SiegeTube where people could tune into their own reality siege. It felt dull if a day went by without a disaster to tune into.

"But it's good to be tuned into the world. I'm connected to millions of people in real time. Live-streaming."

"Real time? A delusion. Just an impression of real life. Live-streaming enslaves you to the web. Why are we here? How can we save the planet? How do we relate to each other? They are the real time questions."

"I am relating to others all over the globe. Strangers reach out to each other—open up, express themselves more easily. I respond to so many people."

"Yes but you never have time to deeply ponder. You are mesmerised by the web like a baboon is to a red bottom. Easily led. Never stopping to think."

MV struggled to put aside the image of the baboon following a bottom. "But amazing movements have been achieved by, as you call it, 'red bottoms.' The massive Internet-led cleanup in Estonia in 2008 and the dramatically successful City Food Banks started in Holland in 2009 by Kim Bunt, have spread all over the world. People are clearing rubbish, and starving people in major cities can now eat fresh, locally grown produce."

"Yes, I admire Kim, but for every one of her there have been ten charlatans spreading doom and gloom—creating a negative future and influencing thousands of gullible followers."

MV thought of all the 2012 doomsayers—like Jonas Potter whose followers avidly ingested his tweets on how the planet was destroying itself by greed and would end on Dec 23rd 2012; who sailed with him on a plastic barge to the floating plastic debris in the Pacific, which had grown larger than Texas, to await the end. When it didn't happen, Jonas persuaded the group to immolate themselves; a perfect example, MV had to admit, of what Rada described as 'creating a negative future.' MV shuddered, remembering the images of burning bodies and plastic which flashed on every screen across the world.

And then a few days later another siege dominated the screens. The world quickly forgot the plastic martyrs, whose charred remains had still not sunk to the bottom of the filthy ocean.

They came to a wooden seat and sat down.

"Are you trying to tell me that my online stuff is bad?"

"No, I am online too."

"You are?"

"Yes I am in communication with gardeners all over the world. Kim is one of them."

"Gardeners?"

"Yes I have several hundred thousand followers in Russia alone on TwitRus."

MV's mouth fell open. As a fifth grader he had boasted the most Twitter followers of his age group, but it had peaked at 10,000 before Twitter sank without trace, just like Jonas and his followers.

"What I'm saying, Miroslav, is that you think the Web is the be-all and end-all of life."

"But it's great, being in touch with so many people everywhere."

"I agree. Our gardeners' forum is amazing and a fantastic vehicle for disseminating valuable information and support. But it is not a substitute for direct contact. This is why Colleen has brought you here. Tekos teaches you how to have both. What Shchetinin helps us discover is that we humans have so much more creative potential than we dare imagine. It is not dependent on the Web. We become easily enslaved by technology, fear, greed, envy. He set up this school so students can flower into who we truly are. And when we contact each other—look into each other's hearts, share each other's dreams, the potential for healing the planet explodes a thousand times! And you will see the positive results beginning to manifest in the Krasnodar region."

"But the Orthodox Church obviously doesn't think so?"

"Oh, many priests don't want people to take control of their own destinies."

The way she looked at him made him want to dive away into his music, his videos, his games, anything to escape those orbs of green fire trying to ring him in. Off-grid world was unnerving. Made him feel uncomfortable. At least with his ZiSleeve he was in control. He was king of his castle. He could dictate all.

"I'm hungry. When's breakfast?"

"Stay here in the sun. It's good for your skin. I will bring breakfast."

MV didn't resist. Besides, he could reconnect his earchip and disappear into music.

Rada brought back a tray of watermelon, apricots and muesli.

"This muesli is packed with cedar nuts from our trees. So healing for your body." She touched his cheek.

No escape! he thought, sinking his teeth into succulent watermelon, trying unsuccessfully to listen to the latest track from Blazedinger.

"We grew these watermelons. Full of sunshine and water. We are lucky to have plenty of both."

MV disconnected his earchip resignedly. This chick sure liked to talk a lot.

"Miroslav, who do you have direct contact with? Your family?"

MV thought about his mother complaining that the kids were always absorbed in their ZiSleeves. She had tried to ban Zis at dinner but he and his brothers caused such a fuss she gave in. Now WebMother accompanied them at meals. RealMother began blogging other mothers, all complaining about their mono-syllabic families gripped by weblock.

"You eat together?" Rada interrupted his thoughts.

"Well, sort of."

MV's Zi winked like an alien between them as they crunched their muesli.

"You eat together with your Zis?"

"Well, er-yes."

"So who do you have real contact with? Girl friends?" MV thought of all the girls he'd bonked with his ZiSleeve on. He felt another strange emotion. Was it shame? He feigned a coughing fit.

"Do you ever take your ZiSleeve off?"

"Er-no, yes. I switch it off at baseball matches. Dammit Rada," he spat out a watermelon pip. "I like this technology."

"I'm not saying anything is wrong with the technology—it is how we use it. The technology is there to serve us. For example our solar greenhouses extend the growing season." She pointed to the glass structures glinting in the solar garden. "It's our relationship with technology that is important— either we dominate it or it dominates us."

They finished their breakfast. The group were getting ready to go out in the Solaritza.

"Come see our Tech block." She took his hand and dragged him through the door of the wooden building, inscribed with: *Never doubt the power of a small group of thoughtful, committed people to change the world. It is the only thing that ever has.*

"Wow," said MV, marvelling at the inside. "Cool. You do have some serious bit of kit. Holographic screens. Your own databanks?"

"Yes, two of them—we are able to store valuable information without being held hostage to web pirates and unpredictable crises with bandwidth."

MV thought of Wingnut who used up more bytes than a starving crocodile. Not that it bothered him. Just charged extra bandwidth to his dad's account.

"And here is our server."

MV had done a summer internship for Wingnut's father. Here was a chance to show this smart-arse broad a thing or two. He fired a question at her.

"So what's your PUE for this?"

Rada didn't even bat one of her gorgeously curved eyelashes. "Oh it hovers around 1.05."

MV's's jaw dropped jaw dropped. Even the most energy efficient servers didn't score so low.

"Yes," Rada continued. "We take our Power User Efficiency very seriously. We don't like to waste precious energy on ancillary functions. And because it comes straight from the sun and wind, we are even happier. Oh, there's the Solaritza, ready for boarding."

"Oh by the way, where do you plug the bus in?"

"We don't. Our Solaritza is capable of converting and storing energy when there's no sun, with nano-antennae which absorb infrared rays."

MV texted Jeezbob. *This chick is driving me mad—invading my headspace, man.*

Just fuck her brains out, dude. That will shut her up.

He was too ashamed to tell Jeezbob that he hadn't even made out with her yet.

The Solaritza took the group on several excursions, including Krasnodar city with its abundance of trees, gardens and fountains; crucial as cities all over the world sizzled in higher temperatures. A large industrial complex which once housed Philip Morris was now a myriad of gardens on various levels, swarming with people who resembled industrious ants. Tania informed the visitors that these were once factory workers who decided that feeding the city's inhabitants with fresh produce was better than making cigarettes which were slowly killing them.

They went to the Sea of Azov and brought back a crate of fresh fish.

They soaked in thermal and salt springs which were abundant. MV noticed his skin fungus fading.

On other days, Shchetinin invited the group to tackle an issue that interested them, Tekos style. This was so different from the classroom approach they were used to. Shchetinin did not *teach* anything. He offered himself, Tania, Rada and Vassily as resources if needed, and showed them tools they could use to tackle seemingly insoluble problems. One involved drawing 'rich pictures' with coloured pens. MV scoffed. "Child"s play!" Resented the absence of his ZiSleeve. But was astounded by the new ways of seeing the problem this facilitated. The group was encouraged to deepen contact with each other, to really listen and to bounce ideas off each other. This fostered greater depth and clarity and a sense of collective potential. It was as if a new collective organ of sight was opening up. Often the group would lapse into deep silence. MV found this surprisingly nourishing; just a silent communion where he found he could access a deeper place within himself. Invariably profound insights would bubble up. The group would be energised and ideas would fly around like brilliant fireworks.

Rada told them how the presence of the Tekos School had affected the Krasnodar region; how students had gone out into the community and helped people envision a positive future and begin working towards implementing it. This was often met with great resistance initially—for example when they wanted to close down the Pepsi Cola factory. However, as in the Philip Morris case, the positive vision won, and a new enterprise evolved. The place was now run by local people, making local produce such as berry juices, jams, wines and cedar nut oil.

So the days at sunny Tekos rolled by. For some it was interminably slow; for others it was rushing too fast.

Rachel had been persuaded by Vassily to walk each day, and feast only on morsels of fresh fish and berries. She could feel the fat falling off. Demoloron, on his black steed, was fading fast into zyberspace. She had little desire to follow.

Enrita found that washing dishes in the summer kitchen and sharing a joke with the others was fun. Her nano-wand gathered dust in her room.

Wingnut clung desperately to his porn world, but kept wanting to follow Tania around.

MV felt he was on a roller coaster. The more he found out about Tekos, the more questions he had, and the less he felt attached to his ZiSleeve. His total obsession with Rada continued, unabated.

One morning MV woke with a start and raced out to Rada who was doing her usual routine of singing to the flowers.

"I now know who you remind me of! You have her body and a certain look in your eyes—Guidolon's girlfriend, Trisuron."

"Oh Miroslav!" Rada leapt up and hugged him. It took his breath away. "Trisuron is my heroine—I am a great follower of the weekly adventures of Guidolon, the Giant Space Chicken. This series is so popular in

Russia. I want to be like Trisuron. A ray of love beams from her forehead with which she melts away the latest giant monster. This is what I aspire to."

Rada sprang up and did Trisuron's victory dance. So sexy, funny, delightful.

MV stared enraptured. This girl never ceased to amaze him.

"WHAT DO YOU you dream of, Miroslav?"

It was a hot afternoon after one of Shchetinin's sessions. MV and Rada had just been cycling.

Dreaming of bonking you darling. The thought bubble rose unbidden.

She must have caught his look, or worse, read his mind. "No, I don't mean immediate gratification."

He caught his breath. Was she a witch?

"What do you dream of in the future?"

He thought of the dreams he'd had as a kid— become a baseball star, be captain at school...

"Go to Yale—work on saving the dying oceans." This had been the topic in today's Shchetinin group and they had come up with some brilliant ideas.

"Sounds good. What about family?"

"You must be kidding, I'm only 18."

"I dream of a man who is worthy of me, with whom I can create a space of love. I see it clearly in my mind's eye. Our own piece of land with an orchard, a garden, and where we can live in joy with our children."

She looked at him, her eyes blazing; he imagined sparks flying from them.

He felt naked in her gaze. He found himself feeling decidedly unworthy of her. Rada's laugh, tinkling through the trees, and the quality of her attention, stirred something deep within him. He remembered hiking with his mother, in the beautiful Angeles National Park long before the terrible fire. He saw her dejected face when he refused to accompany her the next year and the next. Great sadness swept over him. So many lost opportunities. He decided then and there that he would go hiking with her when he returned. And he silently vowed never to wear his ZiSleeve at dinner again.

JEEZBOB HELP! THIS girl is driving me wild—I don't know if I'm coming or going!

Well I sure hope it's more coming than going, man. Get a grip—slam her against a garden wall. You know they love it!

You don't know this girl, thought MV.

RADA TOOK MV to a large dark cellar. The shelves were stacked with produce in bottles. Strings of garlic and bunches of dried herbs hung from hooks. Intoxicating odours enveloped him. She took a jar of cherries and opened it. The smell hit him.

"Close your eyes!" She slid something wet, round and squelchy into his mouth.

The taste of the cherry was just divine—he opened his eyes to see her licking sticky red liquid off her fingers.

"Wow, that's amazing." It was even more delicious than anything he tasted when he had the munchies after smoking weed.

"The secret is in the bottling. The fruit must go straight into the jars after it is picked and sealed in immediately with beet sugar or honey." A drop of juice glistened on her lips.

"Rada," dared MV, "Have you ever been kissed?"

"Many times, by my family and friends."

"No I mean, by a boy? A man?"

"Oh no, Miroslav—that would be mixing juices and I intend to do that only with the father of my future children."

The countless girls he had bonked indiscriminately whirred before his eyes; he felt shame.

She picked up some jars of peppers, beetroots and cucumbers and put them in his arms. "For lunch!" She also took some cherries.

"I will make these into cherry dumplings. Especially for you." She licked her lips with such an enticing look, his legs turned to jelly.

A TRIP WAS planned to the Dolmens, ancient spiritual tombs in the nearby hills. Rada was staying behind to work in the garden. MV mumbled an excuse to Colleen—overflowing inbox. Wingnut decided to stay behind too, ensconcing himself behind the Tech block so he could watch his porn 'without being judged by these freaks.' He, or strictly speaking his avatar Gorko, was embarking on another sex slave game in the bowels of Second Life. A secret enclave where huge wads of cash were needed, as the players sank deeper into their lustful orgies. *That stupid Tania*, he thought, *she says money can't buy happiness. Well she's wrong. Gorko with his huge 3D cock can buy as much happiness as he wants.*

MV sat in the quadrangle chuckling at the latest from LaughTube. He watched Rada coming from the garden with radishes in her hands. She smiled warmly at him as usual, but then her face darkened. MV turned to follow her gaze.

He saw shadowy figures creeping around the edge of the main school building, carrying what looked like cans. The unfamiliar smell of petrol hit his nostrils.

"Stop right there!" commanded Rada.

One of the figures jumped up. He approached her carrying a gun.

MV, who was hidden behind an apple tree, quickly pipped Jeezbob.

Hey we're being attacked.

Yeah, pipped back Jeezbob. *I can see it all.*

Really? A picture of the garden flashed onto his screen. MV looked up. He understood. Wingnut, abandoning Gorko, had quietly climbed up a tree behind the Tech block, with his Zi-Lens. He shivered as he recorded the scene below. This was the best reality TV people could watch—but it was dangerous for the recorders. Most of them got shot. Wingnut hoped against hope he wouldn't be noticed. This would be such a scoop for SchoolTube.

MV watched breathlessly as the men moved into the quadrangle. He was now in full view. One ran up to MV shouting at him to take off his ZiSleeve.

MV felt like he was divesting a weapon as he ripped it off. He didn't dare look up at Wingnut, hoping all was being relayed to Jeezbob. Knowing Jeezbob was in the frame, so to speak, comforted him. They both knew how to get out of tight spots.

He was led at gunpoint further into the quadrangle.

Rada was calmly standing in front of the ringleader.

"Hello Dangovich. Before you burn us down again, why don't you let me show you around. Tell you about what we do. You can invite your boss."

Dangovich felt her gaze uncomfortably warm on his face.

"Stop staring you wi-itch or I put bullet between zose green eyes."

MV thought Rada was wasting her Trisuron ray of love on such a dickhead. But what could he do? He so wanted to protect her—to be worthy of her.

"Leave her alone, dude," he dared. The honcho span round.

"Ah, stupi-id Americanyitz." He spat at his feet. MV sprang back in terror, feeling as rattled and useless as Guidolon the giant Space Chicken.

"This proves you are cult," Dangovich spat at Rada. "Mi-ixing wi'zis cheap scum."

Dangovich grabbed MV by the neck, and put the gun to his face.

He had strict orders. To burn the place down. It was assumed it was empty for the summer. But if any cult members were around, they must not be harmed. That would only make martyrs of them. But the boss hadn't said anything about filthy *Americanyitzi*.

God, thought MV, *this is like that game I played with Jeezbob where we were attacked by a Triad gang. How did we get out of that?*

The reality was so different. He was terrified. Dangovich reeked of garlic and sweat. That plus the cold metal against his cheek was vomit inducing. Nausea and terror had never been part of zyber-games.

He caught Rada's gaze—it was so beautiful, reassuring, calming. Trisuron looking at Guidolon. He managed to take a breath.

"Let him go," Rada said. "He is a visitor."

What an inane thing to say, thought MV.

"Vi-isitor hey? Bringing stupi-id ideas to zis country!"

"Hello, Comrade!" said MV, feebly.

Dangovich gave him a look so icy that the Pole caps would not dare melt another centimetre, his breath so pungent that MV's nose nearly dropped off in protest.

In NewYork, Jeezob was staring open-mouthed. His finger throbbed. He wished there was something he could click to wipe this asshole out. "Siege," he pipped.

"Siege! Siege! Siege!" was pipped all over the world. ZiFlickr relayed the images to SiegeTube. Web addicts everywhere glued themselves to their screens.

Wingut trembled as the scene unfolded. It was all he could do to stay up in the tree and not fall out.

Rada calmly thought through her options—just as long as MV and Wingnut didn't do anything unexpected. She sent a look at MV with the intent, *Everything is fine—no heroics.*

MV misread the look and thought. *She looks naively calm—I'll have to save her.*

Rada knew this was a big test for her. Of everything she had learnt. Could she keep love in her heart in the face of adversity? Could she do what many others had done before her? Mandela had lasted 28 years; Aung San Suu Kyi, 26 years; the Dalai Llama, 55 years. She, Rada, was 18 years old. She didn't think she could last 5 minutes. She recalled tears of joy when the Dalai Llama triumphantly re-entered Lhasa. She quelled her trembling knees by remembering what Suu Kyi said. "You must never let your fear take over—if you do they have won."

She must focus on a positive outcome for this situation. She took a deep breath. Like Trisuron she must send out a ray of love.

"Dangovich, put the gun down."

Dangovich, studiously avoiding her green eyes, prodded MV. He hadn't had so much fun in years; not since he'd been bodyguard to Alexey, the Patriarch.

"Americanyitz! You knaow Russian Roulette?" Dangovich pointed the gun to the ground and pulled the trigger. There was an ominous click. "The next cli-ick could put a hoawl in your stupi-id head." He shoved the gun back into MV's face.

"Clusterfuck scumbag!" shouted Jeezbob, scaring his cat.

MV thought he would faint. He could see Rada's eyes. Was that light coming from them?

"Dangovich, please let the American go," she said in her melodious voice.

Dangovich caught the way she looked at MV.

"Ah so you like zis boy hey? Well we make him dance for you before we shoot his brains out."

With that he pointed at MV's feet. This was too much for MV. "Do you know everyone's watching you, asshole?" he yelled, pointing up at Wingnut. "You're on screens all over the world!"

Oh no, thought Rada.

Dangovich swung around, saw Wingnut, and fired. Wingnut came tumbling down. Birds in the trees scattered in fright.

Screens across the world went blank.

Jeezbob froze in horror, frantically pushing different keys; trying to find news channels, anything.

Two of the thugs shoved a trembling Wingnut into the quadrangle. MV was hugely relieved to see him alive.

"You okay, Wingnut?" Rada asked anxiously.

"Everyone knows what you're up to. What a scumbag you are," shouted MV, wishing he didn't sound like a strangled chicken. "Pictures have already gone out all over the world."

Dangovich turned menacingly towards him but was startled mid-turn by a loud ringing from within his jacket. He pulled out an old ZiPhone.

If phones could swear and appear irate, this one did. If it were in a cartoon, angry faces, sparks and bubbles of Slavic expletives would be exploding from it.

Dangovich blanched a sickly parsnip colour. He held the spitting gadget at arm's length and gestured his men towards their car.

"You lu-ucky zis time, you wi-itch. I have orders to gao immediately."

With that Dangovich and his thugs all piled into their vehicle and drove off, tipping over petrol barrels as they went.

Rada ran over to the barrels and righted them. "Don't want the fumes to hurt the bees," she said, looking up at the eaves.

"Hey, how about me? I nearly got shot. You care more about those damn bees than me."

She walked back. "You were never in any danger, Miroslav."

MV felt like he was in a Guidolon episode where the guys were stupid and ineffectual, and the heroines sassy and victorious. He looked around to see if Wingnut was listening, but he was busy tapping on his ZiSleeve and reconnecting to the world.

"What do you mean, I was in no danger? Dangovich was playing Russian Roulette with me." MV fervently wished his voice would come down out of chicken register.

Just then the Solaritza swooped in and Colleen, white as snow, leapt out. "Are you okay? Rachel saw it all on her Zi and we returned as fast as we could."

Shchetinin hurried across the courtyard and hugged Rada.

"You just missed Dangovich. Apparently the boss was not happy about his boys being splattered all over SiegeTube. Ordered him to abort plans and get out. It was wonderful that Wingnut recorded it. He is a hero."

Tania ran over to Wingnut, hugged him, and started searching his body for bruises. Wingnut ripped off his Zi and let himself snuggle into Tania's warm body. This felt so much nicer than anything Gorko got up to.

MV felt terrible.

He followed Rada who had gone back to the garden.

"I so wanted to be a hero, but I was useless," he said. What he really wanted to say was, "Oh Rada, I so want to be worthy of you."

"Not at all," said Rada, looking up from picking sweetcorn. "You saved the day by alerting Dangovich to the fact that the world was watching what a thug he is. He hated that. Not what he had in mind for the image of the Russian Orthodox Church."

That night there was a feast. Enrita helped grill perch and carp in the summer kitchen. MV and Wingnut, the heroes, were feted and toasted with berry wine.

"To MV and Wingnut," toasted Shchetinin, Tania translating. "Thanks to them, the SiegeTube video has already had a million hits on YouTube."

"Yeah!" Wingnut punched the air.

"Yes, and what is excellent news is that the new Russian Orthodox Patriarch saw the video. He was so impressed with how Rada handled the situation and how the place looked, that he wants to come and visit—to start a dialogue with Shchetinin." Whoops of joy filled the quadrangle.

"Another toast!" proffered Rada. "Here's to building up trust and contact, and using the Web to facilitate that. If it wasn't for our American guests the event would not have been recorded. Three cheers for Live-Stream!"

As the cheers died down, Shchetinin took up the accordion and played a lively tune. Vassily leapt up, grabbing Rachel for a dance. She did not resist.

Rada approached MV. "Oh Miroslav," she whispered. "You still look so miserable."

"Just like Guidolon, I was chicken shit."

"But what else could you have done?"

"If I was stronger or knew karate, I could have flattened the bastard." MV felt tears springing from his eyes. "I'm sorry, my Trisuron." The 'my' slipped out unbidden. Rada caught it with a tiny flutter of her eyelashes.

"Well my Guido, I had another plan, but yours was much better."

"What was your plan?"

"Ah for me to tell you that, you will have to get to know me more," she said coquettishly.

"Oh Rada I want to know you so much more." He took a deep breath. "I want so much to be worthy of you." Finally he had said it. "But I will be leaving soon." He looked dejected again.

Rada leaned up to him and ever so gently put the tip of her tongue into his mouth. The scent of berry wine and mead was intoxicating. The delicate lick produced waves of liquid pleasure, far more delicious than anything MV had experienced in his whole life. His loins felt on fire.

She darted away.

"Well Miroslav. You will be back." Her eyes sparkled green fire. "We have now officially mixed juices."

Thoughts like gladiators
in the arena of time,
Fight to create the new paradigm.
Thumbs down it will suck,
Thumbs up it will SHINE.

—Eva Maria Chapman—

Castoff World

Kay Kenyon

WHEN, AT THE *Calgary WFC, I told Kay that I would be doing an anthology of near-future, optimistic SF, she was literally the first one to send me a story. Which is a blessing in disguise: while it's fantastic to already have a great story, your evil editor doesn't want to accept too much too soon in fear of having the turn down great stories that come in under the wire.*

Thankfully Kay was very patient with me.

As the ghosts of Hector Malot's Sans Famille *('Nobody's Boy,' although I prefer the Dutch translation't title 'Alone in the World' better) and Daniel Defoe's* Robinson Crusoe *haunt the interstices, "Castoff World" is 100% Kay Kenyon: highly inventive world-building (even if the particular 'world' is claustrophobically small), topical & contemporary, and inhabited by characters you root for, every inch of the way (even when one of the characters isn't human).*

By its chosen theme, all stories in Shine end on a high note. But it's only with a couple where the finish is really exuberant. That most of those—like "Castoff World"—are in the back of this anthology is no coincidence...

CHILD KNELT AT the edge of the ocean and carefully spread the bird bones on the water, putting them out to sea. She waited for them to burst into feathers and rise from the ocean, flapping in circles, corkscrewing into the wind.

Not this time, though.

Child always hoped to see the leftover bones from meals reform in their proper shapes: seagull, turtle, swordfish. When she was little, she used to think Grappa was saying they had to put meal leftovers *out to sleep*, not out to sea. So even though she knew better now—being almost seven—she still thought of the bones as sleeping. And it was their little fun thing that they said, her and Grappa: *out to sleep*.

She checked the fishing lines on this side of the island for any catches—none—and scanned the horizon for pirates. The blue-green sea stretched in gentle swells to the edge of the world. No pirates today. If you saw pirates you had to crawl to the trap door to meet Grappa who would have a rat for protection. They'd practiced many times, always quiet and serious, but Child would have liked a glimpse of pirates. The book had a picture of one, but Grappa said, no, that was like in the movies, and not a real pirate. Movies was a before word. The book didn't have a picture of movies. But it had other before things, like fire hydrant, bicycle, and nano assembler.

"You dropped a bone, Child."

Grappa stood, his beard fluttering in the wind, and pointed to the tiny bone.

"Can I watch Nora kick it off?"

He nodded, and they crouched beside the bone, watching as the nanobots slowly moved the fragment toward the water's edge. You couldn't see the nanobots because of being too small, but they were there, working hard, passing the bone to the nanobots next to them. It would take all afternoon for Nora to put the bone out to sleep. Child would come back later to check on the progress.

"Nora doesn't like our garbage," Child pronounced.

"Not her kind." Grappa stood and looked out over their floating home. It was made entirely from garbage, an island of toxic trash, collected over years of swirling round the ocean gyre. The more garbage collected, the bigger Nora got. Here and there you could see plastic bottles, sty-ro-foam cups, white and yellow bags, and crunched up cans. Over there, a collection of tiny stirrers and straws, lined up like a miniature forest. (Forest: many trees clumped together. Tree: tall growing thingy.) Nora was going to break all these things down and make them into good stuff so that bad stuff wouldn't leak into the water.

Grappa said Nora wasn't alive. But they called her *her*, because he said you could call ships *her*, and what they were on was like a ship or maybe a raft.

Grappa held up a bulky sack, his eyes sparkling. "A new rat."

They tramped over to the rat collection, carefully hung up on little poles so Nora wouldn't try to eject them. Nora couldn't take any extra weight, or the whole ship might go down. Things like a dead rat could go into the ocean, because it was good stuff that could rot. Nora just collected bad stuff like pee-cee-bee, pee-vee-cee, dee-dee-tee, and nurdles so she could turn them into derm. The trawlers were supposed to pick up the Noras once a year, but there weren't trawlers any more, so their Nora was starting to have a weight problem and threw overboard anything that wouldn't hurt the ocean.

It was Grappa's idea to hang the dead rats up on wooden poles. Sooner or later Nora would take apart the wooden poles and flush them away, but until then they had good stashes of rats in case of pirates. When the oldest rats got too slimy, out to sleep they must go. But neither did you want a nice-looking dead rat. Best was a just-right dead rat, one rotted just so, and that's how come so many rats all lined up.

Using scraps of fishing net twine, Grappa secured the body onto a pole. Then Child followed him, past the privy hole, past the hot spot, to his big net where they finished pulling the catch from the webbing. Her hat slipped off while she worked.

She caught Grappa's eye. Quickly, she stuck the broad brimmed hat back on her head so as not to get skin sores.

But he kept looking at her. "Where's your belt, Child?"

"I don't need it. I've got these." She pointed to the little nuggets that went down her shirt. They slipped into holes on the other side, keeping her shirt closed against the sun.

Grappa came over to her, fingering the nuggets. "Buttons. Where..."

"Nora made them." They'd started as little nubs and then grew in about a week to be the right size for the holes.

He gazed at her in silence.

"Maybe she told her nanobots to help my shirt stay closed."

"Nora's nothing but a Nanobotic Oceanic Refuse Accumulator."

They faced off on the old argument. If she talked back, he'd frown and mutter, *Just like your mother. Magical thinking.* Mom died soon after she was born. Grappa said that when they put her out to sleep, a tern hovered over her, circling like a guardyan angel.

Grappa went back to sorting the catch, looking up at her now and then, and squinting his eyes at the buttons. In the end his catch was—not including the rat—three medium-sized fish, two tiny crabs, and a piece of sty-ro-foam.

HOLDING THE FLAKEY blue piece of garbage, Child asked, "What was it?"

Grappa pulled his hat down tighter, getting his face sore into the shade of his brim. "Oh, it's polystyrene foam."

She rolled her eyes at the big word.

"Well, it was a cooler. People used it to keep food, maybe for a picnic."

"Picnic?"

"The family going some place fun to have a meal."

"We could have a picnic."

He eyed her, scratching his beard. "Might could."

"When mother comes back. Then."

He didn't answer for awhile. "What makes you think she's coming back, Child?"

She shrugged. "Out to sleep."

"That's what we say."

"Yes."

"Maybe we shouldn't say that anymore. Call it out to sea."

"Let's not, though."

He pointed to the hot spot, where they threw the bad stuff. It was a big pile in the middle of their garbage island where most of Nora's nanobots worked.

Child made her way over to it. The closer she got, the more the tiny nurdles clung to her feet and legs. You could brush them off, except then they'd stick to your hands. They leapt up on her like fleas, but that was just stat-ick, Grappa said; they weren't alive. Grappa had strict ideas on what was alive and what wasn't. *Nurdles are pre-production industrial plastic pellets. Everything plastic gets made from nurdles. The ocean is nurdle soup, Child.* He smiled at that, but she didn't know why.

She tossed the sty-ro-foam into the hot spot. Maybe people didn't throw the cooler in the ocean, only lost it, like the ghost nets that still caught fish and turtles. But whether on purpose or on accident, Nora was against it.

Even so, Child liked garbage. It made Nora bigger and stronger, all made from derm, the material left over after Nora changed pollu-tants into good stuff. And sometimes things that came into their nets got a story going, a story of before, the time when Grappa was an ocean-o-grapher, and helped make the Noras. Some of the best stories were from: cath-ode ray tube of teli-vision (check out picture in the book), inflated volley ball (learn to play until it got bumped into ocean), and the doll's head (if lonely in time before, you could have a small friend and talk to it). Child kept the doll's head until Grappa said he couldn't stand to look at just a head. Then they argued about whether hot spot or out to sleep. *People don't go into the hot spot*, she insisted. Grappa turned away.

She doesn't know the difference, she heard him whisper. When she finally put the doll's head in the hot spot, it sank down, becoming island.

The really exciting thing? There were more islands like this out there. Probably every Nora had a child and a grappa. She kept a sharp eye out for other Noras so that she'd have a playmate, but the only time she saw one, it was a lonely, empty place. Except for seagulls nesting and churning around it in the air, a white gyre.

THE OCEAN ROCKED them in their den under the trap door. Lantern light splashed off the smooth sides of the desal-inizer that Grappa said was too heavy for Nora to eject. Child watched his bearded face as he leaned against the desal-inizer and considered a bedtime story.

"Tell about Mom and Dad again."

"Well, your Dad was a good fisherman. Kept us going those first years."

"Until the tuna fish took his fishing pole." In the lantern's glow she imagined the tuna swimming away, laughing, and Dad so mad he threw his hat in the ocean after it.

"Yes. Dragged it away. He made others, but none were as good as that pole we got from Reel Good Sports. It about broke your Dad's heart to see it go."

She glanced up at the ceiling at the big red kayak. It hung by leather cords out of Nora's reach. It had two open places for people to sit in, and together with a second kayak that had got lost, this was how they got to the island: Dad and Mom and Grappa.

Nora wanted in the worst way to get a hold of that plastic kayak, but she let them have a few other things in the den without pulling them apart. For instance, she let them store food for a few days. Also a plastic bag or two to carry stuff around and also a few ghost nets, even though they were poly-propy-lene. Grappa said Nora had to go against her program to allow it. *She wants us to be happy*, Child had said once. Grappa had looked at her funny. *She doesn't know* happy. *She knows garbage detox and sequestering.* She'd objected, *But, Grappa, we're helping her pick up garbage. We dragged in that big drum. We catch sty-ro-foam, don't we?* He scratched around his face sore, not answering.

But the red plastic kayak was too much for Nora. Every now and then, they'd come into the den and find that Nora had chewed through the leather straps and the kayak had fallen.

Grappa was saving the boat for when it was time to go to shore, which would be when it was safe, when there'd be picnics and stores again.

"Reel Good Sports was a *store*," she said, hoping to keep Grappa talking. "You could point at things that you wanted, and trade monies for them."

"Well, the owner was long gone. We just took things. Buying things, that was in the time before."

"On land."

"California," Grappa said. "It used to have stores, a lot of them."

"And toasters and cars and baseball gloves. Except Mom and Dad didn't, just you, Grappa. You had cars and toasters."

"Oh, for awhile, and then I didn't anymore. I raised your Mom in a compound where we didn't have cars or such. When the bad men came we escaped. She was grown by then and we hid in the woods until your Dad came along and helped us—"

"And then we were a family."

"—and then your Mom was pregnant and we needed a safe place for you, so we found the kayaks and scouted around for a portable desalinizer. I knew where Nora was, because I brought my GPS with me, and we came here, to be safe."

"Except for the pirates. They're not safe."

"Lights out, now." He blew out the lantern, and pulled derm mats over them.

"How was Nora born?"

"Lights out."

"Yes, but how did Nora get born? What was her Mom?"

She closed her eyes and thought about how Nora kept growing, and that maybe someday she'd stretch all the way to land.

"A seed," came Grappa's voice. "We put little seeds in the ocean, and programmed them to sweep up garbage."

"Seeds with nanobots."

"And you told the nanobots to get garbage out of the water and to make DERM from pollutants."

Sleep tugged on her, but she wanted to prove she knew what derm was: "De-graded Rewoven Refuse Matters."

"*Materials*. Degraded Rewoven Refuse Materials. And the Noras got big, some of them. This Nora swirls in a big vortex, vacuuming up one of the North Pacific gyres, just a never-ending clockwise rotation. Whole thing's kept in place by a mountain of high pressure."

"Like the Great Pacific Garbage Patch."

"Except that one, that's as big as Texas."

Texas was a place so big you could walk for months and you'd still be there. Whenever they wanted to say how big something was—like the tuna that defeated Dad—she and Grappa would say, "big as Texas."

She fought against sleep, because Grappa was talking even past lights out. But the great ocean gyre had her in its arms. The gyre was a huge ocean creature that danced in a big soft circle, carrying turtles, volley balls, tunas, ghost nets, and their island around and around and around and into dreams.

"GRAPPA, WHY ARE you sleeping out here?"

Sometime during the night Grappa had got up and left the den. This morning she found him top side just waking up in a nest of derm.

He brushed the nurdles off his clothes. "Oh, its nice out here, Child."

But she thought he looked cold. "I don't like it when you sleep out here."

He started to make their breakfast fire in the metal drum that Nora let them keep. Child tried rotating the sticks, but she didn't have the knack of it, yet. Once the fire was going, she fetched crabs they'd saved from yesterday and they roasted them. The ocean had big swells today, rolling softly under Nora, lifting and settling them, the sunlight caught in the tops, going along for the ride.

"I'll be sleeping up here from now on," Grappa said.

"No. Nothing should change."

"Listen to me, Jessie." Oh boy, when he called her her real name, that was the worst.

"I've been collecting garbage a long time. But now I've got the same sore your Dad had. Soon I'll have to... have to be done with it. When the time comes—" He nodded toward the edge of the island, toward the ocean gyre. "You know Nora can't keep me. You help her. Can you do that? Because if I'm down in the den you won't be able to put me out to... out to ..."

"But we'll always be together. You said, Grappa."

"I said." He turned away. "It's just sleep, Child."

As his words sank in, they released a weight from her chest, as though a big rock had lain atop her. It lifted, letting in a good light that fired up her heart like a lantern. So he'd be coming back. They'd all be coming back.

That's what she'd been trying to tell him all along.

She put the crab shells in the ocean and watched as they bobbed away. Then she sat down to watch her nets, pulling them in now and then, expecting good luck today. She hummed a tune and lay down on her stomach trying to see the nanobots. Looking real close, sometimes she saw a seething and sparkling, and she knew the bots were breaking down pee cee bees and other pollu-tants and car-cino... car-cino...

Underneath her she felt the ground heave, and a big wave jolted the island, sending Child rolling down a sudden hill. Then, unthinkably, she fell off the side into the cold water, into the ocean. She sank, popped up, gulped air, sank again. Down, down. Under Nora, her hands and elbows hit plastic bottles, a huge jumble of them. Down here nurdles floated everywhere like fish eggs. Mustn't get trapped under Nora. Need to get to the edge... Overhead, Nora's shadow loomed dark, except the bottles glimmered with a sunken light. She grabbed the nearest plastic bottle that was stuck fast to the others, and pulled herself forward, chest aching, breath gone. She slapped at the bottles, pulling, pulling.

Popped up. And there, Grappa shouting. Grappa throwing a net. She reached for it and he pulled it closer, closer, until he bent down and hauled her over the side. As she sat hunched over, retching and coughing, he slapped her on the back. She spit salt water out, and nurdles, too.

Then he tore the net off her and pulled her into his arms.

After awhile he carried her to Nora's exact middle and told her to stay put. He came back with a water jug and her second set of derm clothes. She shivered hard, but he wanted her to wipe down with fresh water, so she did. That's when he pointed to the jacket she'd been wearing. It was puffy and didn't fold like normally. Then it slowly wilted, like the air got let out.

As Child dressed in dry clothes, Grappa picked up the wet jacket and examined it. "Life vest," he said. "Little air pockets that must've filled up when you hit the water."

"Nora, I guess."

"You ever have... nanobots on your clothes, Child?

"Sometimes."

He looked around at the island, as though expecting to see nanobots gotten big.

They sat together then, his arms around her, and they watched the forever blue sky without their hats on so her hair could dry. The great sky stacked overhead in an ocean of light.

"Grappa, Nora puts the bottles underneath."

"There's bottles down there?"

"It's all bottles. Just a million bottles, all stuck together."

He looked down at the ground. "For floatation."

"Do we float on the bottles?"

Grappa put his head in his hands. After a few moments he said, "We do if she strengthened the bottles and they're full of air."

Child put her arms around him. "The nanobots do it, Grappa. It's all right."

"They're getting smarter," he said, like he was speaking to the gyre, and not to her. "They've had to. All these years on their own, and no trawlers." He seemed confused and not as happy as he had been a few minutes ago when he pulled her from the water.

To lighten the mood, she said, "The nurdle soup tastes terrible." She pointed to the water where the nurdles floated under them, swimming with Nora.

He smiled a little. "I'm going to make you seagull soup, how's that?"

And he did, but it took him a long time, and when they'd eaten, he slept.

THE DAY WAS blue and bright like every day. A high pressure system sits over our heads, Grappa always said. It drives back the rain. Since they didn't get rain, she'd had to learn how to run the desalinization box and how to clean the salts from it. And she finally learned how to make fire from two sticks. Those were the last things, the hardest things, to learn just before Grappa died.

In the full sunlight the kayak's lovely red sides looked more scuffed than when it hung in the den.

The kayak was supposed to be for getting to shore, but Child couldn't just push Grappa into the ocean.

Dragging the kayak to the edge of the island, she pulled it over onto its side. Somehow she managed to get Grappa into the little boat, and turn it right side up again.

She sat for a long time, leaning against the kayak, staring out to sea. "I know you said to keep the kayak, Grappa. But I just can't." She stared as birds lifted their wings, letting the air currents take them higher. She wished Grappa could go up, like a bird, like Mom, instead of out to sleep. But it was only for a while. So she got up her courage, and walked behind the kayak and leaned against it, pushing, pushing. It didn't budge. She tried pulling from the front. No better.

Then from the back again, and this time she thought she saw little sparks along the path where the kayak pressed into the derm. And the boat moved an inch, and then an inch more. The nanobots, she thought. Nora had finally got her hands on the plastic kayak.

At last the kayak slipped over the edge. Child knelt, watching it go.

"Always together, you said."

It's only sleep.

OK, then.

VOICES OVERHEAD. A man laughed, but not a nice sound. Child felt the ground shake from people stomping around. She was still breathing hard from throwing everything into the den: cooking drum, fishing nets, bird traps. Then kick up the derm over the privy holes. Lastly: throw the rats overboard, but save a slimy one.

JUST BEFORE GETTING into the den, pile derm on the trap door and put the rat there. Grappa said that keeps them from looking too close, because the rat stinks and looks bad.

The pirates were looking for stuff, because sometimes the Noras had usable things collected. Also they would take a bunch of derm to make clothes and bedding. She had to hide, because the pirates might also steal her.

She eyed the trap door. It would be her last chance to see a pirate, if she just opened the den cover a little ways.

But the sounds they were making were getting angry and loud. She huddled into herself. As she folded up as small as possible, her heart knocked hard inside her chest. Her pulse came into her wrists, bumping like crazy. *If you ever have to go to sleep, to be with your Mom, there's one way,* Grappa once said. *You cut your wrists, using something very sharp. It hurts a little, but then you put your wrists into the DERM, and let them bleed. Don't look, though. Then sleep comes. You understand? Only if you have to. If things are too sad. All right?*

All right.

Sometimes, like during that big storm once, she calmed herself by thinking about Mom and what she looked like. *What color was her hair?* He'd said, *Black. It was black, Child.* Just like the tern, then, all white with black on the very top. Somewhere out there, a tern rode over the world, looking down on her. Keeping watch.

Smoke curled down from the chinks in the trap door. The pirates were burning something.

She climbed the ladder and tipped the door up, just a little. Blazing, jumping fire. They'd set Nora on fire. Beyond, she saw the boat oaring away. She rushed down into the den to get the big jug, and then up the ladder and, pushing the jug out ahead of her, slithered out onto the derm.

The boat was still too close for her to stand up, so she crawled to Nora's edge, filling the jug with ocean water. Then she poured it over her head, like Grappa told her in case of fire. The jacket puffed up around her. Once more she refilled the jug. By now, the boat was so far, the men looked small. She threw the water on the closest flames, burning hard, making popping noises. Back for more water, but by the time she got a jug-full, the fire stopped, going to embers.

Amid the smoldering derm, she sat down and watched the boat until it disappeared. Maybe the pirates were mad that alls they found was a dead rat, so they set a fire. Nora hadn't liked the fire. Air pollu-tion.

"The rat worked really good, Grappa."

I said.

You did.

IN TIME, THE weather changed. Storms came, and Nora thrashed and rocked on her platform of plastic poly-mers. By this, Child knew that the island had passed from the great ocean gyre. Nora was headed somewhere, and this worried Child because where would they go?

Nora's sides had built up into little walls. Child never fell in the ocean again. It was harder to get the nets in and out, but fishing got better outside of the gyre, and Child was not often hungry.

As she grew, her clothes changed, getting bigger. Now she had only one shirt and pair of pants but they never got dirty.

The desal-inization machine finally broke—that had been two hundred days ago—but she collected rain water now, in a drum. Also Nora caught rainwater into a little pond that was seldom empty.

And the island sailed on.

In rough seas, Nora pitched up and down, but the waves just broke on the walls she'd built. And the island got taller. In time it was too hard to cast nets down, and so Child trapped birds. There were more of them than ever. She got hungry, though, if the wood was too wet to make a drum cooking fire. That was a problem with being outside the gyre: it rained a lot. Nora hadn't yet learned that Child needed dry kindling to cook. She tried telling Nora so, but that wasn't how Nora learned.

Child never saw another Nora. Finding a friend or a grappa on a Nora had been a childish thing to believe, she knew. And she was used now, to being alone. Grappa was back there, still circling the old gyre, his red kayak going round and round. It seemed like a thing she'd dreamed, that Grappa had been with her. She began to doubt that he truly slept, because she'd packed the paddle in the kayak, and he would have come for her by now. But maybe the gyre creature wanted to keep him.

She sat with her back to the cooking drum—still warm from her last meal—and paged through the book, faded, torn, musty. There were land animals: cat, horse, and others whose names she'd forgotten. There were things like clock, chair, space elevator, ship with masts, and skis.

She fell asleep in the warm afternoon. When she jerked awake she saw a whale.

No, something too big for a whale.

The horizon had a black lump that didn't move. It got bigger.

THEY WERE CLOSING in now, people in little boats, staring at her and Nora. Children too, pointing at her. The shore drew near. She saw trees dark against the sky, and farther inland, wooden buildings with windows and smoke drifting from what might be cook fires. It was where Nora had been taking her, following whatever trail the nanobots could sense, whether the taste of soil or smoke borne on the wind.

Dozens of little boats. The people in them kept their distance, chattering and looking past Nora, as a bigger ship came around the headland toward her. Many oars came out, and they beat up and down together. She thought the sailors would come on board Nora, but instead they used spikes to secure ropes to her and began pulling her to shore. Then Nora was caught up in waves rolling onto the beach, and, with people pulling from the land, Nora creased into the sand with a heavy smack.

For the last time Child went down into the den. Looking around at her possessions, she picked up the book and Grappa's hat. Before she left, she pressed her forehead against the soft, rewoven refuse of the wall. "You never needed those trawlers, did you? Got the garbage out of the water all on your own."

Back on top, she saw a growing crowd of people on land.

The people turned to watch two large creatures approaching from down the beach. The creatures stopped some distance away, pointing at Nora. Then Child saw how it was people riding horses.

It was time to go. Child stuck wood staves into the derm and looped a fishing net over it, trying to snarl it so that it wouldn't slip. Then she used the net to climb down.

Her feet landed in shallow water. Surrounded by a crowd that gently urged her forward, she walked closer to the horses with people on them.

One horse rider was a woman. She had yellow hair pulled back into a knot at her neck, and wore clothes with bright colors. She leaned forward, saying, "Your name, child?"

"Yes."

"Where did you come from?"

Child tried to answer truthfully. "A North Pacific ocean gyre."

"Who made your clothes?"

"Nora."

The woman turned to the man next to her, also on a horse. "She is a gift to us."

He nodded. "But what is that?" He looked past Child, down the beach.

Child turned. There was Nora, pulled up on the sand. From here, Child saw how Nora had lovely smooth sides coming to a point in front. In back, a blade jutted out and down into the waves as they crested into the shallows. Strangest of all, the side of Nora that Child could see had a beautiful moving circle on it, traveling round and round, sparking like sometimes the nanobots did. Then she saw how it was a picture of the ocean gyre, because a small red dot rode on the circle, slowly, slowly moving like a kayak on a softly turning wheel.

"What is that thing?" the man repeated.

"It's a ship," Child said. "Her name is Nora."

And it was a ship, more than ever, more than she had ever guessed. Nora had made herself beautiful so people would want to bring her onto the land. So at last her task could be finished, to get the bad things out of the ocean forever.

The woman smiled at her. "Would you like to pet my horse?"

Child came closer, putting her hand on the creature's nose, feeling its soft warmth.

At this, the people began to press closer, putting their hands on Child's clothes and exclaiming, but friendlier now that the woman had let her pet the horse.

A boy about her age pointed at Child's ankles, where her pants had puffed up from being in the water.

"Life vest," Child told the child.

Nearby, where a tree leaned over the beach, a dark-headed tern flew in, settling onto a branch. It flapped white wings, tucking them close, keeping watch.

**They died, each species, one by one. Cats then owls; owls then ants. They died.
But now look.
They rise, each species, one by one. They rise.**

—Penelope Friday—

Paul Kishosha's Children

Ken Edgett

AND ONCE AGAIN *it is through the wonderful internet that I found—probably because Ken found out about Shine—an exciting new writer.*

The email exchange Ken and I had over several of his @outshine submissions is quite typical of how the Shine anthology progressed at large: initially, Ken sent tweets that were quite nice, but fell outside of @ outshine's remit (which is basically the same as for Shine: optimistic, near-future SF). As with a lot of initial Shine submissions, they were mostly about humanity getting into space. Now while I certainly don't mind us getting into space, I had to insist that we—humanity— need to solve the problems we have on Earth, as well.

So, as his tweets became ever better aimed, I finally accepted one (which is printed after the story). I hope and suspect it also helped him write the story below, a fantastic tale of hope, which—among other things—seems to say: why can't we do both? Solve our current problems on Earth and go to space?

I guess it's what we can expect from an optimistic Mars geologist...

ONE DAY, JOE *the Martian was making the <u>engine</u> for his flying space ship. The year was 2074. He and his family were getting ready for a trip. All of a sudden, Joe's son had blown a <u>circuit</u> in the space ship! His son was injured. He had broken a leg. A big <u>bubble</u> formed on his leg.*

15 February 2006

I WAS DOODLING on the little Marriott-provided notepad when my cell phone vibrated. Oh good, I thought, I can step out for a cigarette. The speaker, a fortyish female JPLer that I didn't know, droned on about the development schedule for a Titan mission that would never leave the ground. As I left the conference room, I flipped open the phone and pressed the 'send' button.

"Kishosha," I said as I headed through the hallway toward a double glass door and Pasadena sunshine.

"Paul—"

Happiness? I switched from English to Kisukuma. "Happy? Why are you—" I stepped outside and tried to hold the phone between shoulder and chin while I fumbled for my cigarettes and lighter.

"It's mother. She is asking for you."

I had the cigarettes in one hand, lighter in the other. But I stopped short of taking one from the pack. "How long does she have?"

"I—I don't know. How soon can you be here? If I tell her, perhaps she will hang on..."

I was supposed to be explaining NASA's planetary protection policies after lunch. "If I can get a flight this evening, I can be there on Friday—wait, is she in the hospital?"

"No, no, we are home. The doctors can't do anything at this point."

"Tell mother I love her. And I am coming." I hit the 'end' button and stuffed the phone, cigarettes, and lighter into a single pocket inside my jacket.

I returned to the conference room and my laptop and used it—and the hotel's wireless—to arrange a flight. LAX to Mwanza by way of Amsterdam and Kilimanjaro. It was going to cost me, but I'd saved for just this sort of thing.

After packing up the laptop and its cord, I pulled Harold Franz out into the hall, explained what was going on, and handed him a thumb drive with my viewgraphs on it. Harold would give my talk. As my counterpart at JPL, he pretty much knew the spiel, anyway.

THE MARTIAN FAMILY could not go on their trip. Joe tried an experiment to cure his son faster. Now he tried it on his son. It worked and now the space ship was fixed and the family left. Soon they landed on planet Jupiter. They decided to stay there for the night. Joe's little girl always goes off on her own at night. That night she found a fun activity. She called it Drop-the-Rock-in-the-Canyon.

24 February 1980

THE WHOLE FAMILY had gone to bed. It had been an exhausting Sunday of worship, song, and fellowship at the church. My favorite part of Sunday Mass came afterward—the potluck dinner. My uncle Azimio, one of my mother's brothers, was visiting for a few days. He didn't come to Mass, but he did show up after Father Mtambalike gave the blessing so he could share in the feast of chicken, fish, rice, ugali, cassava, beans, mangoes, and so forth. The fish were very fresh, caught early in the morning on Lake Victoria.

While everyone was sleeping that night, uncle Azi and I hiked out away from the home, into the cotton fields. The sky was brilliant with stars and a high, gibbous moon illuminated from the west.

He lit a cigarette. He offered me one but I was only nine years old. I said no.

"Do you see that bright red star over there?" He pointed into the eastern sky as a mosquito buzzed near my ear. "That is Mars."

"Mars?" I wondered.

"It is another world." In the moonlight, I could see his face as he blew smoke from his nostrils. "A world like we live on, only smaller and farther from the Sun."

"How do you know? What is it like, there?"

"It is a cold, desert world."

"A *cold* desert?" I doubted that a desert could be cold. "Does anybody live there?"

He put his arm around my shoulder and we continued gazing at the red star. He said, "The Americans landed two machines there—they found no one."

"Well, maybe they were looking in the wrong place," I suggested.

Uncle Azi laughed a deep, happy laugh. "Perhaps. But I'll tell you this: The first human beings on Earth were Africans. The first human beings on Mars, too, could be Africans."

AFTER THE NEXT 99 *years they landed on Pluto. It was cold there. Quickly, they saw a <u>leopard</u> frozen* *solid! It had a tag, it read: African leopard put here in the year 2080. The Martians put him in the space ship. Soon he came back to life. They trained him. They named him <u>Beauty</u>.*

5 March 2006

THE SKY WAS overcast and the temperature and humidity were fairly comfortable for late summer in Tanzania. I was having a cigarette out by mother's old truck. I heard from behind me, in Kiswahili, a boy saying, "Uncle Paul, are you alright?"

I turned around and there was my sister's eldest son, Enos. He was thirteen or fourteen. He was carrying a football under his left arm and a battered folder in his right hand. One of mother's dogs—I didn't know his name—trailed him.

I pulled the cigarette from my mouth. "Sure, uh, Enos," I looked at him, then down at the dog, then at my cigarette. "I am fine. I was just thinking about how I need to go into town and get some more of these," I held out the cigarette.

"Mother says they're bad for you."

"She's right," I winked.

At first, Enos didn't seem to know what to say. Then he looked like he remembered why he had come to find me. He set the ball down on the ground and then waved the folder at me and said, "Mother found this in the house, while she was going through Grandmother's things."

"And?"

"In here are some stories you wrote." He handed the folder to me.

I opened it and looked inside.

I'd forgotten about these! "Did you read them?"

"I did, yes," Enos looked uncertain, perhaps worried that he shouldn't have.

"And what did you think?"

"Well, not bad, for a kid," his eyes sparkled. "And I liked your drawings. How old were you?"

It was shortly after Uncle Azimio's 1980 visit. "Nine. Maybe ten, something like that," I replied. "I did them for my spelling homework."

"So, that explains the underlined words."

"Indeed."

I flipped through the folder while the cigarette hung from my lips. There were five stories in all, each one illustrated with pencil and crayon. They detailed the adventures of Joe the Martian as he visited the many worlds of our solar system. As I looked at these forgotten treasures, I realized how much this effort—this spelling homework activity— must have influenced my career choices. All the way to NASA Headquarters.

Something slipped from the folder and fell to the ground.

Enos picked it up and dusted it off.

The book!

Enos opened it and began to read a random page out loud, in Kiswahili, "There were faint marks on one wall. 'What's this?' Jim asked. 'It's a Martian painting. Most of the paint has flaked off this one, but in some of the others they're still in good shape. The dry climate preserves everything.'" He stopped, flipped through the pages, pausing at some of the illustrations, and said, "I was looking at this, earlier, too. Someone translated the whole book."

Hand-written in the language of the Waswahili, the translation was crammed into the narrow spaces between the English sentences. I told him, "Yes, yes, I remember this very well. *The Lost Race of Mars*, written—oh, I think almost fifty years ago—by a man in the U.S., Robert Silverberg. Uncle Azi—your grandmother's brother—he found this book among donated goods at a church in Arusha."

Enos continued flipping through the yellowed, paperbound kid's book while the dog sniffed around my ankles. I dropped my spent cigarette and stamped it out.

"Who translated—"

"Uncle Azi. He knew I couldn't read the English. I'll tell you though, later on, it helped me learn English to see the words right there, with Kiswahili on the same page."

Enos handed the book to me and I put it back in the folder while he said, "Do you want to kick this ball around?" Then, more eagerly, "Are you going in to town today? To get those cigarettes?"

"Would you like to come along?"

We sent the dog home and made our way down to the road, passing the ball back and forth. At the road, we continued playing with the ball for about twenty minutes before we were able to flag a dala dala for a ride into town.

ONE DAY JOE went for a walk. He was <u>anxious</u> to see the rocks that grow. Joe said, "This is a cold day." Sure enough, it was cold outside. When Joe came to the growing rocks, some were in a type of <u>triangle</u> shape. Over Beauty they kept a hot light so he could keep warm.

16 March 2006

"WHEN ARE YOU going back?" the schoolteacher, a young Asian from Canada, asked me. Her name was Kelli Pak. I think she was hoping I could take some things to her family.

"I'm actually not going back," I explained, "I'm going to close out my work, remotely, and then I'll be staying here."

Mother, on her deathbed, had made me promise. "Paul, my beautiful son," she'd said, "Don't go back to the States. Tanzania needs people like you. Stay here and find a wife. Have some children. Tend to your siblings and their children and their grandchildren, when they come. Take that wonderful education of yours and use it here."

How can you refuse your mother's dying wish?

And so, here I was, in a school just outside of Mwanza. It was run by missionaries from a megachurch in Alabama. The headmaster had a brother at NASA Marshall, and people around here talk. And so I was invited to come speak to the children at the school. "Tell them what you do. Tell them about the planets," the headmaster said in English. "They've never seen a Sukuma scientist who works in the States. They will enjoy hearing about what you do."

Kelli Pak's children were six, seven, and eight years old. They looked nice and clean in their little uniforms.

"Welcome and good morning, Doctor Kishosha!" they said in unison, in Kiswahili, as I was introduced.

"Good morning, children!" I smiled.

I looked at the teacher again. She was cute, but a bit young—maybe twenty-three—and a bit too small and thin for my taste. She nodded a bit as if to say, "Go ahead, the class is yours."

"Uh—As Miss Pak explained, I, uh, work for NASA. The U.S. space agency."

A boy shouted, "Are you an astronaut?"

Another added, "Have you been in space?"

"Miss Pak said you went to *space*," a girl said.

I looked at the teacher. She nodded again, indicating, "Continue."

"Well, no, I'm not an astronaut."

Everyone sighed with disappointment.

"But I am here to tell you about the planets. Other worlds."

They seemed to lose interest after that. I began rattling off the names of the planets, but the kids were looking out the window, or at Miss Pak, or at their notebooks.

What did I know about talking to little kids?

Miss Pak came over to me and put her right hand up on my left shoulder. I turned toward her and she motioned that I should lean down to match her height. She whispered in English, "Try another approach."

Flustered, I didn't know what to do.

Then it hit me. Worth a shot, I figured.

I went over to the chalkboard. Yes, chalk.

I drew a character on the board. I made a narrow parabola—with the vertex at the top—and gave it two legs, two arms, two antennae, a huge smile and big, dark eyes. The kids were watching me, now. I looked at Miss Pak and she was smiling but she also had look of "what is he *doing*?" on her face.

"This is Joe the Martian," I began, "He is from Mars."

I drew a circle and shadings to represent the polar caps, dark Syrtis Major, and the light Hellas basin. Inspiration struck: I moved to the left and drew the sun, Mercury, Venus, and Earth.

"This is Earth. Where we live," I pointed, and then drew in a moon, "and the moon. And this is Mars, fourth from the sun," I pointed again, "where Joe the Martian lives."

I proceeded to draw more planets. "These are Jupiter, Saturn, Uranus, and Neptune. They have rings around them," I drew the rings, with Uranus' tilted near ninety-eight degrees.

Past Neptune, on the far right side of the chalkboard, I drew a bunch of small circles, none much bigger than the moon I'd drawn. "These are what we call the KBOs. This one," I pointed, "Is Pluto. People argue about whether it is a planet. I think so. It has three moons: Charon and two so recently discovered that they don't even have names yet."

The kids seemed to be getting bored again. So, I drew a cat. With whiskers. And spots. Above Pluto.

"And this is Beauty the Leopard. He is a male leopard."

The kids began to buzz.

"Joe the Martian found Beauty on Pluto. He was frozen solid."

"Miss Pak! Miss Pak!" I turned around and one girl was waving her right hand in the air.

"Yes, Husna-Beth?"

"Why is the leopard *frozen*? Why is he on *Pluto*?"

"Doctor?"

"Uh—people—Basukuma—brought him there but left him behind. By accident."

"Why?" A boy asked.

"The Basukuma were on their way to the stars."

THE GROWING ROCKS *break easy. When Joe got back to his space ship he and his family went to sleep. The next day they were ready to go home. When they tried to leave, an electrical invisible fence <u>surrounded</u> them. They could not leave! They were stranded! That day they saw life on the planet! Out of the growing rocks came strange creatures! They were <u>MIGHTIER</u> than the Martians. The creatures had special rocks that blow up! Soon the creatures started to bomb the Martians! A feud started. The CREATURES against the MARTIANS.*

18 July 2011

PIZZA AND BEER. Wooden tables and white plastic chairs under a roofed patio setting. I sat in the smoking section.

Very shortly after my return to Tanzania, I managed to convince the faculty at St. Augustine's—SAUT— to give me an office. I finished what NASA work I could, there, managing as best as possible with the intermittent electricity and Internet access. Eventually, they got me to teach some classes and were even able to pay me, although for a couple of years I had to live mainly off my closed-out NASA retirement account. Lucky for me, I'd withdrawn that money before the economy turned down in 2008.

Five years later, I was doing well. No wife, no kids, but I had students and I had an apartment out near SAUT. About two or three times a month, I would come into the city in the evening to have pizza and beer at Kuleana's. It is a good place—they help the poor street kids and it's a magnet for foreign visitors.

I sat alone with my laptop, taking advantage of the neighboring hotel's wireless capability to skim the day's news and respond to e-mails. In another year or so, the plan was to have wireless for the whole city—the Internet café owners were banding together to set it up and charge modest fees for its use.

Then I heard a voice. A woman's voice, with a hint of a Russian accent. "Paul? Paul Kishosha?"

I turned my head around. Four Chinese men were engaged in vigorous conversation and cigarette smoking over a table covered with empty fish and chips baskets and beer bottles. Beyond them I saw a blond-haired, brown-eyed white woman at a table of six—there were two white women, a black woman, two black men, and an Indian man wearing wire-rimmed glasses.

They were all looking at me.

It had been some years, but I recognized the eyes. And the smile. Smiling, brown eyes that instantly made me feel somehow comforted, content, and beloved.

"Elena Ivanova! *Karibu*! Welcome to Mwanza!" I got up and started toward her, leaving the laptop and half-eaten pizza, but carrying my cold, sweating bottle of Serengeti.

She stood and we embraced, then we both stepped back as her hands slid down to my waist. "Wow," she said, smiling. "Wow!"

"How have you—"

In Russian, she said, "Go get your pizza before the flies get to it—join us! Join us!" She pushed me back toward my table, while her five companions moved their chairs to make room for one more.

Their pizzas and beer were arriving as I set down my closed laptop with my pizza plate on top of it. I ordered a couple more bottles of beer—they only let you order beer if you have food.

In Kiswahili, Elena explained to the others, "This is Paul Kishosha. We went to school together at Moscow State University." She turned to me and said in Russian, "My God, that was, what? Sixteen, seventeen years ago?" And then, in Kiswahili, she said, "We graduated together." She turned toward me, "And then you went on to..."

"Florida. For my Ph.D."

"That is right, Florida. And now you are with NASA?"

"I was. I'm living here, now. At St. Augustine's."

She introduced me to her companions. They, like her, were science journalists. The other white woman was from Canada; the black woman came from Kenya. One of the black men was from Uganda, the other from Rwanda. The Indian was a fellow Tanzanian, born and raised in Dar es Salaam.

"What brings you all to Mwanza?" I wondered.

Elena responded, "A conference of east African science journalists and researchers." She looked proud. "We have over a hundred and thirty others joining us tomorrow when meeting gets underway."

The lights suddenly went out and I heard a collective, "Awwwww."

Flaky electrical grid. I was used to it. I began pulling out a cigarette as I asked, "So, what happens at these meetings?"

The servers came around with lit candles. They placed one on our table as the Canadian woman—I don't recall her name—said, "We look at ways to improve how we're explaining the latest science to our readers, viewers, and listeners."

"We're looking at ways to grow our audiences, interact with more scientists, and fund international travel to cover scientific meetings," Elena added.

I picked up the candle and used it to light my cigarette.

SOON THE FEUD *ended. The creatures died off. Two days later, a space craft came from Earth. The Martians told the people that they could not get off the planet. The people were <u>panic</u> stricken. The men gave a hundred <u>shilingi</u> to Joe and a small, metal <u>whistle</u> to his child, Abyon. The men sent for more men, women, children, and supplies by a <u>secret</u> radio. They were happy.*

19 July 2011

WE SPOKE IN a mix of Russian, English, and Kiswahili.

"I have to get to meeting," Elena kissed me again.

"It is still dark. And raining. What time is it?"

"I don't—" she leaned over the bed, fumbled around, and came up with her cell phone. "Six seventeen."

"And the meeting starts when?"

"Eight."

"No problem. I can get you on a taxi at seven-thirty."

"Can I use shower?" she placed an arm across my chest and rested her head on my shoulder.

I laughed, "You can, but you won't like it. It is a bit cold."

She kissed me again, and then she started to get out of the bed.

"Where is light switch?"

"The power's still out. There's a flashlight on the floor, right bel—"

"Found it!"

She got up and headed toward the bathroom. I sat up, found my cigarettes, and lit up.

"Paul? What are those?"

She was shining the light across my one-room apartment, toward the corner opposite the front door.

"Oh those," I smiled, "A little hobby of mine. You didn't see those when we came in?"

"Was dark. And I was preoccupied, as you may recall."

I smiled.

"So, what are these?" She walked over to my one table in the whole place. She was admiring my puppets. They were made of modeling clay. Joe the Martian was hot pink, and Beauty the Leopard was yellow with black spots. They were standing in one of my three Mars sets—the one with layered rocks. My camera and tripod were nearby, but not pointing toward the characters.

She noticed the camera. "You take pictures of these?"

"Stop-motion animation. My nephew, Enos, and I, we've been learning it from the Internet. Something we're doing for the kids."

She had a look of surprise as she turned her head and scanned around the room, presumably looking for evidence. "What kids?"

"Other people's kids. In the *schools*. Around Mwanza. I make short videos that explain various science concepts. I visit the schools and show them to the children. Or, some kids play them, themselves, on cheap laptops provided by one of the NGOs. I also do shows for the street kids—the ones who aren't in school."

"Do these guys talk? Have voices? You do voices?"

I laughed, "My nephews and one of my students—well, former student—they do the voices."

"And these videos, they are on Internet? How many videos? Can you show me some?"

"Don't you need to get that shower?"

"Uh—yes. Can you show me videos later, after the meeting? You can join our group for dinner..." She was excited.

"I can do that, sure."

I kissed her quickly, and then she started for the bathroom. Half way there, she turned back toward me and twirled the flashlight beam just below my waist. "Care to join me?"

I smiled and said, "That'll make it a little warmer."

THE DAY THE other men came to Pluto they had a <u>parade</u>. The people would <u>allow</u> the Martians to stay. Now it was 25 April 4075. Abyon couldn't wait for the <u>ninth</u> of May, for it would be her birthday. Soon Martians moved to the people city. This made Joe remember the time when he was only 8 years old. He had gone on a school trip to Earth.

18 April 2013

"TO SUMMARIZE, WE'RE expecting a little light rain in the morning and partly cloudy conditions this afternoon with a high of twenty-eight. Tonight, overcast with a low around sixteen. Up next on StarTV MorningStar News, we'll meet Doctor Paul Kishosha, creator of *Joe the Martian's Adventures*, a new show airing each Saturday morning at nine, here on StarTV," the beautiful young anchorwoman, Teresia Bilame, teased.

During the commercial break for Coca-Cola, HIV prevention, and wireless smartphone services, I was directed to put out my cigarette and join Miss Bilame on a set that resembled a western-style living room—a couch, a couple of comfortable chairs, a coffee table, bookshelves behind the couch, and a television.

Miss Bilame faced one of the cameras and read from the teleprompter, "Welcome back to StarTV MorningStar news." She smiled and said, "Joining me this morning is Doctor Paul Kishosha, the creative force behind *Joe the Martian's Adventures*, a new program running each Saturday morning here on StarTV at nine."

She turned toward me, "Dr. Kishosha, how are you this morning?"

"Paul, please. And I am well. Very well on this fine Thursday morning, Miss Bilame," I smiled.

"So, tell me about *Joe the Martian*. The show has been airing for three weeks, now. How is it going?"

"Uh—so far, very well. Excellent indeed."

"And your subject is science?"

"Our subject," I winked, "is entertainment. For children. And their parents and grandparents. Everyone," I smiled again. "It is an entertaining show with a little sense of humor so that the whole family can enjoy. But, you are right, it is also about science."

"And, so, what is a typical show like?"

"Each show has a variety of things. There is always an animated piece featuring Joe the Martian and Beauty the Leopard and a visit with a real, east African scientist, doctor, or engineer. We also like to show children doing a science project—like planting trees and flowers in their schoolyard, or setting up a weather station. And there is *always* an update on what is happening in the sky with the stars, planets, and the moon. We offer tips on disease prevention and protecting the environment, and we like to show something going on in nature—wild gorillas, flamingos on Lake Natron, an erupting volcano, the silence of snowfall on Kilimanjaro, things like that."

"Let's see a clip."

They showed a couple of minutes of the five-minute claymation piece about Joe and Beauty exploring the dunes of Titan. These were compared with the linear dunes on the coast of Namibia, and other dunes in the Sahara. It was from our second episode.

"The Martian," Miss Bilame smiled, "is really cute. Titan, that is a moon of," she looked at an actual note card that she picked up from the coffee table, "Saturn, right?"

"Indeed it is, Miss Bilame. A wonderful world orbiting our sixth planet from the Sun."

"Why, Doctor Kishosha, are the characters rendered in clay? Why not use computers? Is it too expensive?"

"We use clay because it is fun. Kids respond to it. Yes, computer graphics would cost more, but, honestly, clay is more fun. And clay is something a child can work with at home."

"Speaking of cost, how did you fund your project, *Joe the Martian's Adventures*, which runs each Saturday morning here on StarTV at nine?"

I thought about Elena. I'd not have done anything like this if it hadn't been for her. After seeing my novice attempts to use these characters to convey simple science concepts to children—that the Earth goes around the sun, the moon goes around the Earth, for example—she said, "You need to distribute these more widely. Put them on Internet.

Television. Something." Then she got really excited. "I think you can get funding for this! A science program on Internet—or TV—or both! I can help you! And—Oh, God, this is great! The east African science journalists—they know *everyone*. They can put you in touch with many African scientists..."

I replied to Miss Bilame, "We've gotten started using a mix of sources. The government, of course, is a major sponsor, through COSTECH—"

"That's the Tanzania Commission for Science and Technology," Miss Bilame interjected.

"—and the EAC—the East African Council— they're helping with distribution of the show to Kenya, Uganda, Rwanda, and Burundi. We're also working on getting some support from my friends at the space agencies in the US, Europe, and Russia to dub the show in other languages—English, French, Spanish, Arabic, Russian. We haven't started with that yet, but we will. We'll put these out by satellite and over the Internet for our international fans," I smiled.

"Fans?"

"Oh, yes," I chuckled. "Right now, you can download the shows we've already aired. And Joe and Beauty have their own social network sites. They already have hundreds of young fans. And we've been receiving e-mails from children all over Tanzania— some in Uganda and Kenya—just from the first three episodes. And the parents—they enjoy the wholesome programming and wonderful health and environment tips. Some of the kids make their own Joe and Beauty drawings on their computers, and e-mail them to us," I held up a printout of one of the pictures and a camera operator zoomed in on it.

Miss Bilame turned toward the camera to her left

and said, "The web addresses for Joe the Martian and Beauty the Leopard are on the bottom of your screen. You can also go to Star-T-V-T-Z-dot-com for all the latest on the show. That's *Joe the Martian's Adventures*, each Saturday morning here on StarTV."

She turned back toward me and asked, "Any plans to make some *Joe the Martian* t-shirts?"

I laughed, "When we do, would you like one?"

JOE SOON BECAME *very rich. He had a human <u>guard</u> to watch his house. The guard's name was Magembe Juma the <u>Seventh</u>. He had a <u>graceful</u> wife named Magdelena Fumbuka. The next day was ccccold. The whole planet was under half a meter of snow and ice! Everyone stayed in their homes. The next day a red hot meteor struck the planet! All of the ice had melted. No one was hurt for the meteor hit <u>somewhere</u> else. The water was quickly drained into a crater.*

25 February 2019

IT WAS A sunny day and all of Mwanza was beautiful and clean for Joe the Martian Day. Children and their families had spent the last week cleaning up their city. The solar panels on the homes on the hillslopes above the city were glistening. Some of these homes had been freshly repainted, as well. Visitors from all over east Africa—and beyond—began arriving on Saturday. The hotels were full. The restaurants were doing a brisk business. My staff gave tours of the Joe the Martian studios out near SAUT throughout the weekend.

I wasn't sure what to make of this day. It wasn't my idea. The city council voted to declare 'Joe the Martian Day' to be the last Monday of February, now and into the future. It would bring in tourism dollars, they said. It would showcase the city for investors from all over the world, some hoped. Me? I was feeling shy about the whole thing. I was surprised, although pleased, by the impact that these characters and their approach to science education was having in east Africa—and beyond. But I was feeling uncomfortable about having to head downtown to preside over the First Annual Joe the Martian Day Parade. I wasn't in this for the public attention.

"Paul?" My notebook, sitting on the kitchen table, queried as I sipped a cup of hot tea. I was looking out over Lake Victoria through the back window of my hillside home of three years.

"Yes?"

"You have an incoming call from Elena Ivanova."

"Oh, wonderful! Put her through."

Elena's beautiful face, with its smiling eyes, appeared on the notebook screen. "Elena! So wonderful to see you."

"Guess where I am?"

I couldn't tell. The sky behind her was blue; that was all I could see. No clouds. It looked as sunny where she was as my heart was feeling at that same moment.

"Does this help?" She swung her phone around.

"That's my house!"

"Can I come in?"

"It's unlocked. Wow! You're really here?"

Her voice echoed through the house and from my notebook as she said, "Right here, Paul, my friend!"

I headed to the front door. We embraced.

"What—what are you *doing* here?"

"It's Joe the Martian Day. Where else would I want to be?" She smiled.

"Come in, come in—let me show you my back patio. I have a wonderful view of the lake," I shut the front door and led her through the kitchen and to the back door.

"Can I get you anything? Tea? Water? Wine?"

As we went out through the back door, she said, "Wine? It's only nine in the morning. You trying to get me drunk?" She winked.

"Wine it is." I went back into the house and I heard her exclaim, "Oh, Paul, it is beautiful here! What a wonderful view you have!"

I returned to the patio with two glasses and an opened bottle of a South African cabernet.

"Sit, sit," I suggested as I poured wine into each glass.

She sat at my little outdoor table. I moved the other chair next to and closer to her so that our knees touched under the table. We toasted, "To old friends!"

"And Joe the Martian!" she exclaimed. Our glasses clinked and we each took a sip.

Then she said, "Paul, no ash tray? No cigarettes?"

"I quit!" I said proudly, "The doctor said 'you smoke too much, and you work too hard.' Well, so I quit smoking."

"And did you cut back on work?"

"No, not really. I love what I am doing," I smiled. Then I asked, "So, really, why are you here?"

She sipped her wine. Swallowed. And said, "I've been transferred to Nairobi."

"That's wonderful!" She'd been working in Mumbai, reporting on developments in south Asian science and technology for the BBC and journals like *Nature*. "When do you move there?"

"I just arrived. Last week. And I couldn't wait to come down here and see how you are doing." She smiled again.

It had been a few years. She'd been married for part of that time. It hadn't gone well. We kept in touch, but we'd not seen each other while she was in India.

"But, Paul, here is the thing—"

Maybe it was the early morning wine, maybe it was the way the sun glinted off the lake. Or her smiling eyes. It was her. Here. At my home. In Mwanza. I suddenly felt *alive*.

"—I don't have to *stay* in Nairobi. I think the real action in east African science and technology development is *here*."

I took a deep drink from my wineglass.

She continued, "What you have done—what Joe the Martian and Beauty the Leopard have done—for science and education here—it is just astounding. Children all across east Africa are growing up with those lessons they learned from Joe and Beauty in mind. They're choosing technological careers. And their parents and grandparents are embracing this, as well. Do you realize that Tanzania leads the world in off-the-grid production of electricity? That its new products for water purification are selling better—because of their quality workmanship—than anything China or India is producing?"

"But Joe the Martian didn't *do* all of that—we've only been on the air for six years—wait a minute—what are you saying, Elena?"

"I'm coming to Mwanza. And I'd like—"

"Paul?" It was my notebook. I could hear it through the window. It was still on the kitchen table.

"Paul, this is a reminder. You have thirty minutes before you must be downtown for the parade."

ONE DAY JOE *was trying to make a new machine to get through the* <u>*electric*</u> *fence. Then Joe tested his machine. "It works!" said Joe. When Joe landed back on Pluto he told the people. They were overjoyed with* <u>*excitement*</u>*. So they built more. They collected rocks and things. Soon there was a big party and everyone took off.*

7 June 2047

THE LATE AUTUMN air was cool and dry. The sky was overcast but there was no threat of rain. Precision Air's 17:30 dirigible to Bukoba was passing overhead and toward the lake. Carolnine, Elena, and I were walking home from the market. Carolnine carried a basket of fresh vegetables and bread on her head, just as the women of Mwanza used to do. She also carried some fresh tilapia and a liter of nonfat milk inside her refrigerated torso. There was a festive mood in the marketplace we'd just left. Street musicians were playing, and children— fresh out of school for the day—were buying treats from Kisukuma-speaking robovendors.

When we arrived at our hillside home overlooking the lake, there was a woman of perhaps forty or forty-five years sitting on the bench on our front porch.

As we approached, she looked uncertain as to whether to get up. Whether we were who she was looking for.

"Carolnine?" I said.

"The house is reporting that the woman is Sandra Nakabuye."

Elena said, "Sandra Nakabuye. That sounds familiar. Why does it sound familiar?"

Carolnine responded quickly, "She was one of the crew members of the Second International Mars Expedition. They returned to Earth four months ago."

As we reached the porch, Nakabuye stood up and offered her hand, saying, "Doctor Kishosha?"

I received and shook her hand and said, "That's me."

"Oh, it is so wonderful to meet you!" she gushed, "And you must be Elena Ivanova!" She hugged my wife.

"And you are Sandra Nakabuye. Of Second International Mars Expedition," Elena said.

"Second *International*, yes. Third crew on Mars."

I opened the door. "Come, come inside! Welcome to Mwanza!"

"Thank you!" She entered and we followed her in. Carolnine closed the door and headed toward the kitchen. Before leaving the front room, she turned and asked, "Can I fix you three something to drink?"

I looked at Nakabuye and asked, "Water? Juice? Tea? Iced tea?"

"Oh, no thank you. I actually can't stay long." She reached into her shoulder bag and pulled out a gift-wrapped cube of about eight centimeters on a side. "I came to give you this."

She handed the small package to me. It was heavier than I expected, and cool to the touch. I said, "What is it?"

"Open it."

Elena's eyes met those of Nakabuye. Then they met mine. She nodded.

I tore off the gift-wrapping. It was a glass cube. Embedded at its center was a rounded, reddish-gray granule of about 3 millimeters in diameter.

Elena beamed. She asked, "Is it?"

"Yes, it is," Nakabuye began, "I was given permission by the U.N. to give this to you. I brought it all the way from Mars, just for you, Doctor Kishosha."

I didn't know what to say. I looked at Elena, and she was wiping a tear from her cheek.

"I don't know if you realize what an impact Joe the Martian and Beauty the Leopard have had on Africa. The world, for that matter! I grew up with those characters. I had all the dolls: Joe, Beauty, Mandy the Elephant... all of them."

I'd sold *Joe the Martian's Adventures* in 2026. The videos, the lesson plans, e-books, toys, t-shirts, everything. The buyers formed JoeCorp, still headquartered here in Mwanza. Really, the children of my nephew, Enos, mostly ran it.

JoeCorps did well. They are still doing well, with plans for a theme park in the works. Children today more readily recognize Joe the Martian than they do Mickey Mouse, Big Bird, and Samuel Snapturtle. Well, maybe not Samuel Snapturtle.

"Anyway, Doctor Kishosha, I just wanted to thank you for what you'd created. For the inspiration. When my mother was a little girl—four years old—she was living on the streets of Kampala. A church group found her, took care of her, and plopped her in front of a television every Saturday morning for *Joe the Martian's Adventures*. She became a lab technician at a hospital. It paid well. She met my father, an engineer. They had my brother and me. They raised us on a steady diet of Joe the Martian. I really think the characters and the exposure to African scientists and engineers helped my mother—and, later, me—

to dream big. Bigger than our circumstances and ourselves. Honestly, I am humbled to be here."

Elena and I both hugged her, simultaneously.

She thanked us again, and then she had to go. She had to be out at the airfield to catch a flight to Mogadishu. She said she had to participate in a peer review inspection of the still-to-be-named Space Elevator—the world's first—under construction there.

Elena put the cube—with its little piece of wind-rounded basalt from a dune field in Melas Chasma—on a shelf amid photos and holos of my mother, siblings, nephews, nieces, and their children. She put it next to the photo of Uncle Azi.

Feeling amazed and satisfied, we headed out to the back patio. The sky was clearing toward the west. Several sailboats were out on the lake, and a beautiful sunset was beginning to take shape.

Carolnine brought us each a cool glass of chardonnay as an AfriquExpress dirigible was passing by. Elena and I watched in silence as the sun went down over the lake.

Mother asked me to stay in Tanzania. I stayed. She asked me to marry. I did—a little later, perhaps, than she had in mind—but I did. Mother also asked me to have children. Although I never fathered any, I gave birth to Joe the Martian and Beauty the Leopard. And *they* had children. First, all over Tanzania and the EAC, then eventually, the world.

And now, two worlds.

A HUNDRED YEARS *later Joe came back to Mars. The Martians had a big party to welcome them back. All of a sudden a big meteor came crashing down to*

Mars. Then the BIG BALL OF FIRE blew up! Then it was <u>silent</u>. Two days later everyone burst into <u>laughter</u>. Joe started to tell this story about Pluto. Joe started to grow some growing rocks he found on Pluto.

THE END.

—*The Martians' Adventures: Book 3, Trip to Pluto*, by Paul Kishosha, age 9, April 1980.

Surgeon airships, new angels, visit lonely
clearings and conjure health from chaos,
creating smiles from pain—the alchemy of
medicine.

—Ben White—

Ishin

Madeline Ashby

WHEN RUDY RUCKER *published one of my stories in* FLURB #6, *I reckoned my claim-to-fame for that one would be that I shared a table of contents with* Bruce Sterling. *Now, I'm not so sure. Appearing in the same issue was a young woman whose story* "Fitting a New Suit" *made a hell of an impression, and whose Shine submission* "Ishin" *completely swept me off my feet.*

A woman who is a regular contributor to Frames Per Second Magazine *and* WorldChanging Canada. *Who had stories published in* Nature *and* Tesseracts. *Whose piece about optimism in manga she sent me for 'Optimism in Literature around the World, and SF in Particular' still averages over a hundred hits a day, six months after it's been published.*

Seeing how quickly she's developing into a major writer, I suspect that my future claim-to-fame might be that I shared a ToC with (and later published) Madeline Ashby. Just check this very finely-wrought story of two men—one hardened and one idealistic, or is it the other way around?—who try to turn a total political, social and cultural quagmire into fertile land, who fight the good fight in a situation that makes 'hopeless' look like a tea time distraction, who face the most harrowing and complex of odds. And still.

Eppur si muove...

"HEISER," THE OLD man says in Brandon's ear. "Wake up."

"Sir, yes sir," Brandon mutters, but doesn't leave the bed.

"I know you haven't moved, Heiser." From across Jalalabad, the old man punches Brandon in the ribs. He feels it reverberating through his clothes, hears the soft shudder of it like a mobile phone buzzing in an independent film theatre.

"Don't go hurting yourself, old man," Brandon says. Now his eyes are opening. His room is bare, blank, tinged blue by dawn through broken shutters.

"Come on. First prayer's already finished."

The old man, Singer, wakes approximately five minutes prior to the dawn call to prayer. Sometimes Brandon feels this through his clothes, which have been defaulted to the mirror relay setting for longer than he can remember, when Singer rises and a slight pressure vanishes from Brandon's back or side. Most of the time, though, Singer remains perfectly still until the prayer has finished. This is one of the silent, unacknowledged realities of their partnership that Brandon is grateful for.

"There's a present outside your window," Singer says.

Now Brandon does get up. He pads to the window and opens it. The shutters squeak dryly. Outside, hovering, is their drone: four wings, all black, her hindparts heavy with twelve hours of surveillance.

"Hello, Tink," Brandon says, extending his hand. The UAS does a brief identity check and flits over to his open palm. He carries her gently into his room, opens his laptop, watches her crawl delicately to an open USB port and insert herself there. Data streams from her body: shipment logs for aid packages, border sentry comments regarding volunteers and their orgs, patterns of food voucher distribution, search-and-record audio keyed to specific phrases associated with the black market. The afterglow of a war long waged, codified and made sensible through transfer from one machine to the next, ultimately destined for some years-from-now report doubtless coloured by self-congratulation on the part of those least responsible for its success.

"Put your shoes on," Singer says. "It's time to go."

He FIRST MET Singer in a Kabul hotel conference room, while they listened to a presentation on the Ishin program. He looked like the kind of man who watched films whose titles Brandon could never pronounce. He was half-human, half-owl: gold spectacles over colourless eyes hidden in a craggy face under close-cropped hair. He seemed to not be paying very much attention to the presentation. He wore no uniform. Private contractor, Brandon guessed.

"If you're here," the presenter up front said, his face made ghostly by the light of a humming projector, "it's because you're uniquely qualified for this project."

Oh God, Brandon thought. *Here we go.*

Ishin, they learned, was a surveillance co-op involving tiny unmanned aerial systems. It was also the Edo Period word for renewal and restoration. Ishin-enabled systems could communicate with other systems, from swooping, missile-equipped predators in the air to lumbering camel-bots on the ground. This would further cut out human interference, they were told, by reducing the semantic drift between orders from up top and orders to machines. Once all the bots used Ishin, you could speak to a drone or a packbot and soon all the available systems would know the orders and start cooperating.

"It'll be like a counter-insurgency," the presenter said, his eyebrows wiggling with obvious delight. "A *robot* counter-insurgency."

"Doesn't that mean they'll just ask us to leave?" someone asked.

Everyone but Brandon and Singer laughed. But Brandon immediately saw the problem. Ishin-eqipped bots did not need to *ask* anyone for anything—unlike their colonized counterparts, they had no need to perform politeness. They reacted, behaved, and made decisions utterly unburdened by the crushing constraints of self-awareness.

When Brandon looked at the silent man sitting across from him, and saw the blank glare of projected light reflected in his spectacles and the flat, disinterested line of his cracked lips, he knew this man saw the same problem.

OUTSIDE THE HOTEL lobby, in the haze of afternoon sunlight, Brandon found the owlish man wiping off his spectacles and examining them. He peered up into the sky. Something up there was circling.

"Falcon," he said, pointing. "They're coming into vogue, again. Good hunters."

"Falconry?" Brandon asked. "What's next, jousting?"

The other man continued squinting up into the sky. "I know you." He put on the spectacles. "You figured out that schoolbus deception. How that town fooled the satellites into relaying false bombing recommendations."

Brandon shrugged. Lately he'd gotten a lot of attention for having figured out this particular puzzle. It was part of why he'd wound up in the hotel listening to the Ishin presentation in the first place. "Anybody could have figured it out, eventually," he said. "No town that size has that many schools."

"Especially after prolonged exposure to depleted uranium."

Brandon winced. "I guess."

"Bill Singer," the man said, in the same vaguely apologetic tone other men sometimes used to explain their diabetes or their flat feet. "What do you think of Ishin?"

Again, Brandon shrugged. "It's a good idea, if it works. I think if you expand the applications, it could be more interesting."

"Such as?"

"Like, if you included more bots in the network. Farm-bots, for example. You could get moisture readings from a few acres and forecast the need for new fertilizer and seed shipments a year from now, then relay the data to re-purposed predators. Teach them to act like crop-dusters."

A new dimple formed on one side of Singer's wrinkled face. He nodded to himself slightly, as though making a decision. "If you were offered the project, you'd take it?"

"Sure," Brandon said. "The bombing stuff—it's mostly over, now. And it's already ruined gaming for me."

"A well-documented side effect among soldiers of your generation."

Brandon wondered if this was true. He only knew that he couldn't pick up the controller like he used to, anymore. The same games just weren't as fun. The shooter comms, which had once sounded like cheerful pubs in his headset, now sounded like louder, monosyllabic versions of the room where he worked. Even RPG's had gone sour for him: all that inventorying and fetch-questing looked too much like a camel-bot's work order. Now he played games intended for sheltered, gifted children, the kind only purchased by well-meaning but tragically un-cool parents.

"I'd take the job," Brandon heard himself say.

"Even if it meant your re-locating here for a prolonged period?" Singer's head tilted. "I heard they flew you in for a consult. Are you missing Provo?"

Brandon snorted. "There's no love lost between me and Provo." He shrugged. "It's safer than it used to be around here, right?"

The dimple appeared again in Singer's face. He nodded once more, shoved his hands in his pockets, and descended the broad, white steps of the hotel's entrance. He crossed past a dry fountain filled with desiccated palm fronds.

"Uh, sir," Brandon said, instantly wondering why he had felt so compelled to address him as such, "you're headed outside the green zone."

"I want to smoke, and the hookah here tastes like candy." Singer made a half turn, khaki overcoat swirling with his abrupt motion. "Well? Are you coming?"

DURING THEIR RUN, they speak very little. Brandon hears only Singer's breathing and the occasional Pashto phrase pushing past his lips when he encounters children or women on their way to market. Singer is out in the suburbs where things are quiet. Here in the city, Brandon runs into more and more Westerners, often joggers, huffing to each other in German or French or English. There are more Western women, too, the kind that have collected too many rape kits, their shoulders cut like gems. They move in packs for safety. Brandon always makes room for them on the street.

His earbud only comes out in the shower. As with the run, Brandon's body and Singer's move in perfect concert. He imagines that they perform the same rituals in the same order, foot to scalp. It is this way immediately after the run, too, when they throw themselves into Singer's callisthenics routine. Singer says it's the same one he learned in a burn ward on a base in Okinawa, when all he had was early morning television and a cheerful woman in a leotard. Brandon once asked about the burn, but a moment later Singer re-set the comm line and pretended like he hadn't heard the previous message.

Most days Singer moves locations, living in the charred husks of bombed-out buildings under the shadows of mountains blunt as molars. They have met in the flesh only a handful of times. But already Brandon knows him as though the tunic and its secret golden threads and its broadcast pulses were really Singer's skin, and not an approximation necessitated by distance.

IN BRANDON'S ROOM, Tink patiently awaits her dismissal. Her batteries have drawn fresh charge from his laptop.

She feels faintly warm when Brandon invites her onto his shoulder. As he reviews the night's data, another feed pops open on his screen and Brandon sees himself in miniature, face blue with mechanical light. Tink moves and the camera follows: Singer, having fun.

"Stop hacking our drone," Brandon says.

"I'm patching her security as I go. Don't worry; she'll look intact when the next fellow comes along." Onscreen, the camera focuses sharply. "And don't roll your eyes when I'm watching you."

Brandon covers Tink's eye with the flat of his palm; the screen shows a blur of skin and creases. In his ear, Singer smothers a snort and Brandon feels the softest squeeze across his ribs, the vibration of suppressed laughter across miles and miles of broken city. When he looks, the camera's gaze has shifted to his mouth, the focus just as tight as before, so that out of context his smile looks like it belongs on a different person—someone who isn't paid to tag coordinates with information about pot grow-ops where community gardens are supposed to be, or regularly index the facial recognition criteria of men who linger too long outside new playgrounds built with charity money. Through Singer and Tink's shared eye he looks younger, newer, normal.

He watches himself speak: "I'll take the south quadrant's tags, okay?"

"Sure," Singer says. "Meet you in the middle."

Tink buzzes off, accidentally clipping Brandon's ear in a warm and humming kiss before zipping out the window and into the bright day that lies waiting below.

THE SECOND TIME Brandon met Singer was when they got Tink. She came in an armoured briefcase, nestled

in layers of heat-dispersing foam. Brandon had re-
located by now, his belongings confined to a duffel
at his feet and a half-shell on his back that carried
his more precious tools. Singer carried even less. The
man lived out of his pockets: an Art Deco tie clip re-
purposed to hold cash, a fab-ceramic multi-tool that
could survive most checkpoints, and his mobile, a
combination reader/phone/wallet/ camera that did all
his heavy lifting. He had perhaps two outfits in his
entire wardrobe, each thin enough to be rolled and
stuffed down cargo pockets once intended for rifles.

The technician opened the case in yet another hotel
room, this one in Jalalabad, on an afternoon when
the smog had settled evenly over the well of the city.
Brandon could already taste the rain in the air; he
imagined it coming down black and toxic enough to
pit the paint on all the tiny little cars below.

"I leave tomorrow morning," the tech said. "So if
you discover any issues between now and then—"

"We won't," Singer said.

"Well, thanks for the vote of confidence, but—"

"It's well-warranted. Why do you think you got
the contract?" Singer bent and lifted Tink free of
her foam. Standing across from him, Brandon could
almost feel the technician's blood pressure rising.
Singer apparently had, too: "Don't worry. We'll take
good care of her."

"It's very delicate," the technician said, his voice
ragged with jet-lag and worry and mild exasperation,
the sort of things that Brandon now recognized as love.

"I know." Singer brought out his reader with his
other hand and thumbed open an app; Brandon
recognized the corporate logo from the technician's
soaked polo shirt. Singer tapped something, and the

UAS hummed to life. LEDs lit up along the ridges of her body, and her wings prepped themselves for flight. Something on Singer's reader chirped, and he smiled. "She just texted me," he said. "We're good to go."

He keyed in a command, and the UAS rose straight upward—and into a ceiling fan. Her pieces sheared away from one another, scattering across the room.

"Sorry, sorry," Brandon said, inserting himself between them. "He didn't mean to, he—"

"Heiser." Singer's hand pulled at Brandon's shoulder. "Look."

From the bed, the UAS' wing-parts blinked rapid-fire. The other pieces blinked back. The wings buzzed over. They alit on each piece in turn, wiggling until the pieces locked together before rising once again.

"You see," Singer said, "she can re-build herself."

The technician sighed and slumped, his shoulders sinking low as his head rolled forward. "Jesus Christ. I heard you were crazy, but *damn*. Don't ever do that again, okay? At least, not where I can see it."

"I'll be sure to erase all the pertinent records." Singer keyed more commands into the reader. The UAS dipped and swerved around Brandon's head. "Heiser. Walk around. Let her accumulate some data for recognition."

The UAS droned over Brandon's head as he made a show of perusing the technician's other luggage, picking things up and putting them down. Then one item genuinely attracted his attention, and he unzipped it fully to the sound of the tech's protests. The UAS dove into the bag. She skittered over Brandon's fingers. When Brandon pulled the fabric free, she had attached herself to it, a glowing insect on laundry. It was a black viscose undershirt. Gold wire spread across its surface, radiating from the heart outward across the stomach.

"What's this?"

"It's nothing." The tech took it from Brandon's hands with light, careful fingers. "And it doesn't work."

It was funny, how those last three words made Brandon almost physically hungry, how they crowded his brain with questions about how and why and what for. He looked at the shirt anew. He had never taken apart clothes before. Just the prospect made his fingers itch. As though having read his mind, the UAS crawled over the cloth, her lights blinking and blipping as she followed the paths made by each golden thread.

Brandon felt Singer moving to stand a little bit behind him. "Relay armour?"

"Well, yes," the technician said. "I was trying to make something a little less bulky than what's already on the market. But for a full set of features, you really put on a lot of extra weight."

Again, Singer pulled out his reader. "Do you have a patent?"

"Pending, yes."

"Ah." Singer thumbed through various apps, selected one, opened a document, performed a Turing, and decisively punched a single button. "Done and done. You'll be receiving an invoice."

"Excuse me?"

"I just bought you out," Singer said. "Heiser. We're going."

"But… But it's *my* design!"

"Consider us beta-testers." Singer snapped his fingers at the UAS. She darted over to him and danced up his arm as he moved for the door. "You can buy it back after we de-bug it."

In the stairwell, their words were punctuated by the blink of lights that had attracted too many flies. "Do you have, like, a *fuck-ton* of money?" Brandon asked.

"I have *access* to a fuck-ton of money."

"Won't you have to explain the expense? I mean, he said it himself. There are already better models out there."

Singer pulled open the door. Through it, an air-conditioned breeze wafted in from the lobby. Brandon smelled chlorinated water and heard smooth-jazz re-mixes of Sufi chants. He was getting so sick of hotels.

"You wanted it, didn't you?" Singer asked. "It was all over your face."

"Well, yeah, I was curious, I wanted—"

"Then that's the explanation," he said, and handed Brandon the shirt. "Have at it. Rip it apart. Get your hands dirty."

They stepped out into the lobby with their drone in close pursuit. And as they walked past a gaggle of girls wearing lanyards and badges emblazoned with the logo of the latest NGO to visit the city, Singer said casually: "You know, they trained me in a hotel just like this one. A long time ago. It was abandoned, but the satellite still relayed this same terrible music. When they left us each night, it kept playing. I could hear it through the floor."

Brandon frowned. "What were you doing on the floor?"

Singer's hand came up, twitched in the air near Brandon's head, then darted back to his own scalp and scratched there. "Not much," he said. "Let's go get something to eat."

"OH, DEAR."

Brandon pauses, his fingers suspended over the keys. "What?"

"Stoning in progress. Well, a pebbling. Some girls going home for lunch. Their route passes some labour pick-ups."

Brandon accesses Tink's feed. Onscreen, the girls have formed a defensive cluster, heads ducking slightly as they walk onward. As Brandon watches, one of them brandishes her mobile and starts snapping pictures. Tink's view is exceptional; he can see the defiant press of the girl's thumb and her quick, almost unfazed dodge when a rock whips past her ear. Another girl dashes backward and grabs her elbow, tugs her back into the group as it re-assembles itself.

"Can we get her phone number?" Brandon asks.

"Probably. If we break some laws." Through the earbud, Brandon hears Singer typing. "The mobile's old; she probably got it as a donation. Could take a while. Better if you just hijack Tink."

Brandon accesses Tink's command line and inputs his own hack: ↑ ↑ ↓ ↓ ←→←→573. Now she belongs to him entirely, priorities momentarily forgotten, processes un-logged, movements off the grid. He directs her with his finger. She swerves, hovers, waits as Brandon plots safe Euler paths between the school and the nearest teashop. She pounces on the girl's mobile, planting herself inside the phone, streaming the maps there. The girl nods as the first image pops up. Brandon watches through Tink's eye, sees the slightly worried faces of the other girls as they look back at the labour pool on the corner, watches their lips move with a mixture of frustration and fear. When Tink withdraws they escape.

The people here are already so used to the bots, Brandon realizes, that they barely recognize them as surveillance. They are part of the landscape. As in a fairy tale, they have come alive through prolonged use: real dragonflies, real camels, real birds of prey.

For the first time, he thinks that this might have been the plan all along.

When he releases her from the hack, Tink zings upward and into the sky. She homes in on the beacon from a predator above, first aligning herself with its wide, arcing flightpath, and then pinning herself to its white steel flank. It blinks at her rapidly, and she dives off and streaks away back into the city.

"What was that?" Brandon asks.

"A work order," Singer says.

BRANDON COMPLETED HIS hack of the clothing just before his birthday. He remembered the date only when the automated portions of his various profiles alerted fellow users to the fact that they should send him cards and in-game money and heartfelt wishes for his safety. He answered the last with assurances of his protected status: *I'm being looked after.*

He only realized how literal this truth was on the night of his birthday, long after his host had fed him elephant ear pastry and a custard of rosewater and pistachios, long after he had answered the video chats from his parents and friends and their repeat questions (*what time is it there, are you all right, do all the women wear veils, do you miss bacon*), when he had finally drifted asleep and heard in his ear: "Come up here."

He thought he might be dreaming. That happened, sometimes, the way his television or his sound dock or his other devices used to weave their sounds into the narrative of his sleeping mind, back when he lived in places with stable electricity, before Singer. Now Singer's voice wove in and out, skipping from character to character in his dreams until Brandon became conscious of the coincidence and opened his eyes.

"I'm asleep," he said now.

"I'm on the roof," Singer said.

And he was. When Brandon leaned out of his window, clinging with one hand to the eaves, he saw gargoyle shape staring down at him. "You sleep too deeply," Singer said.

"What are you, the fucking Batman?"

"I'm not sure. Have you ever considered a career in the circus?"

"Huh?"

"Come up here."

"No." Brandon leaned back into his room and waited. Nothing happened. Finally he leaned out again. "I have something to show you."

It should not have surprised him when Singer unfolded himself into the room, feet first and then the rest of him, but it did. Now Singer stood surveying his room—lit solely by laptop glare the shadows were sharper, and the hour felt later.

"It's good," Singer said. "Plain."

"Why are you here? Is Tink okay?" At night their only worry was the occasional owl that might mistake her for food.

The laptop glare rendered Singer's spectacles momentarily opaque. "You have an hour left of your birthday."

Singer had let him off the earbud that day, so he could call his family and friends without a third party listening in. Now Brandon wondered if those calls had really been all that private. How long had Singer been on the roof? Brandon had heard nothing—no thumps or bumps or scrapes, not even stray dogs below barking at a strange man crawling the skyline. Tink had told him Singer was across town like always. But Tink could be hacked.

He grimaced. "With all due respect, sir, this is why you have no friends."

Singer peered over the top of his spectacles. "You think I have no friends?"

"I kinda doubt it, yeah."

"I have friends, Heiser." He pivoted lazily toward the window, gently pulling the shutters closed. "Just not the kind I enjoy spending any time with."

Brandon frowned. "Then those aren't real friends."

"Oh, they're real friends." Singer smiled thinly, still staring at the shutters as though he expected them to blow open. He turned back and the smile changed, became real. "You said you had something to show me."

Brandon took down two tunics from his makeshift closet—a wire strung between two walls that served as a rail. He held them up for Singer to see. "Finished."

Singer's gaze played over the fabric: the copy was almost exact. Brandon had found a tailor who knew about these kinds of things, a man used to repairing body armour. He had made it comfortable, distributed the weight of the wires so the sensors stopped dragging and pouching.

"They're maps," Brandon said. "Like that game, 'Warmer, Colder.' There are buzzers inside, and you plug in the coordinates and use the wires like a compass, so even if you don't have a map, even if your phone dies or—"

"Let's try them."

"Oh. Okay." He held one out. Singer plucked it free of his hands and laid it on the bed before shrugging out of his coat and folding it in equal lengths—each fold precise, practised, ritual. He removed his glasses and placed them atop it, then tugged off his shirt—a single layer of what Brandon suspected was recycled bamboo or PET bottles or maybe both. Under the shirt Singer was thin, the kind of thin that hurt to look at, like carvings of Christ in a Mexican church.

Singer must have understood, because he paused and said: "Your eyes sting like an interrogator's cigarette, Heiser."

"Sir, are you, uh…healthy?"

"Of course I'm healthy."

"Because you don't look healthy."

"And you're getting to be quite the nag." He gestured. "Well, let's test them out."

Brandon struggled out of his shirt. He felt flabby and indulgent next to Singer, who stared with folded arms. He tried to get into the tunic as quickly as possible. He heard a seam pop in protest. When he had finished, he avoided Singer's eyes and reached over to the laptop, commanded the clothes to wake up. Instantly they buzzed, hard, like wasp's nest humming around his ribs. He bent double, at once tickled and discomfited, and dialled down the pressure.

"You keyed them to each other," Singer said. He was clutching the nearest wall.

"I thought… I mean, if we had to find each other… If there was a bombing…"

"Oh, the intent is noble. But the result..." Singer took two strides across the room. Their clothes thrummed. It was hard for Brandon not to writhe, not to laugh, not to scream, with the wires dancing over his spine. But Singer was standing there straight as ever, like this weird half-tickle half-shock was just something he dealt with, like they'd covered it in some manual or some secret training camp or some other situation Brandon shuddered to imagine. Only Singer's fists told the truth: stiff but shaky, thumbs held down like they were itching for an eject button.

"You see, this is just untenable," he said. "The closer we get, the more it hurts."

Brandon reached over and shut the clothes off. "Sorry, sir—"

"Call me that again, Heiser, and I'll put you in a fucking chokehold."

"Brandon," he said. "My name is Brandon."

"Well, *Brandon*, you can lie down now. Let the big boys have a turn." He grabbed the laptop. Brandon settled for watching, and crawled up onto his bed to look over Singer's shoulder.

"Your eyes. I still feel them. Shut them now."

"Yes, s—"

With unerring accuracy, Singer's hand snapped backward and reached for Brandon's throat. Brandon dodged at the last second and Singer got his eyes, instead, and he pressed them closed, palm smooth as Bible paper, until Brandon quit trying to open them.

"I'm really sorry," Brandon said, when his hand withdrew. "I didn't know it—the shirt, I mean— would feel like that. I just wanted to try something new." *Something difficult,* he wanted to say. *Something impressive.*

He heard the sound of fingers on keys. "Just because it didn't work this time doesn't mean it was a bad idea, Heiser," Singer said. "Good ideas are poorly executed on a regular basis. The point is to keep trying. If that were not true, we would be out of a job."

When Brandon woke up, Singer had re-set the clothes back to their default mirror relay position.

"It won't help with proximity," Singer said the next morning, "but once we figure out how to load things like heartbeat and pressure detection, it'll have its own uses. I can know exactly how much rubble you're buried under, should the occasion arise."

"Why am I wearing your coat?"

"Oh, that," Singer said. He lit a cigarette. "You looked cold."

"Tink's been gone awhile," Brandon says, when they had finished tagging her most recent sweep of the city. Singer had put in an odd image search request: he wanted to know how many food stalls also sold cigarettes on the side. Offhand, he said, he knew most of them, but he wanted to test Tink's ability to sort two images together in order to create a meaningful answer.

"She's fine," Singer says. "You know, these people are breaking about five different laws regarding resale. I think there might even be copyright infringement on this sign." He forwards Brandon the picture.

"Definitely," Brandon says. "Where is she?"

"A hammam," Singer says. Brandon knows the word from somewhere, but doesn't bother looking it up. "Some men are meeting there. Don't worry, I'll delete the footage. Look at that! They also sell condoms!"

"Halal condoms?"

"No such thing. Condoms aren't haram. They're like birth control for elderly Catholics."

"Elderly Catholics still need birth control?"

Real laughter buzzes down into his ear, sharp and unexpected, and Brandon thinks he can hear the length of Singer's neck in the depth of that single sound.

BY THE DATE of Tink's first review, the clothes were perfect. The tweaking had been the most fun—across town, Brandon felt Singer rip himself apart and sew himself together, felt each clumsy stitch and heard the other man's almost-laugh when his fingers slipped.

"Next time we'll get arms," Singer had said. "Then you can guide me."

But now Brandon was alone. Really alone. Alone in a way that he hadn't been in a long time—no phone, no bud, no lifestyle prosthetics of any sort. He had even shut the shirt off. The higher-ups liked you to be bereft when you were talking to them. No cheat-sheets, no devices, the review was an intellectual all-meat special. The guard had ticked off every device and piece of equipment as he surrendered it. He watched them take everything—his phone, the bud, his wallet, his documentation, his whole life—and pour it into a plastic dish.

Right now they were probably ransacking his inbox. He'd done nothing wrong—hadn't gone too far off-mission, hadn't even circumvented the company firewalls that siphoned his communications home through tapped lines. They wouldn't find anything. But they liked to be sure.

Scary, how well he could rationalize it.

Now he sat in a room in yet another hotel—this one more like a hacienda, perhaps once the home of someone from the former ruling party—in a wooden chair with one short leg. It rattled gently as his right knee jigged up and down. He watched the superiors peer over their glasses as they looked at sheaves of paper.

Paper, he thought. *No wonder we're losing.*

"What is your opinion of the Ishin program, so far?"

The woman was obviously tired. She sat hunched like a turtle over the table. Her face had that odd blankness that too much authority gives after a while, like she really didn't care about the content of the answer so much as the way he delivered it.

"Well, it's all in the written portion of my report," he said. "Ishin's a great idea. It could be better deployed, though."

She blinked. "Oh?"

"I'd like to see it hooked up to more stuff. Like farm-bots. And the pipelines. So we could find out about shortages."

"Shortages?"

"In water. Or oil. There are pressure monitors in each pipeline; we could tell when one went low and investigate."

"There are already whole teams devoted to that very purpose."

"No, I mean—" And here he knew that the whole thing was getting away from him, because the whole panel had frozen, cat-like, while he bleated on. But he was nervous—more nervous that he'd thought he'd be—and when he was nervous he speculated, wildly. "I mean we could use it to *predict* things."

They blinked, like predator drones signalling each other high above their target.

"I mean surveillance is this great tool. It really is. But watching what's *happening* only goes so far. We should be looking at what's *going to happen*, instead. We could be taking *measurements*. We could be *predicting* the problems *before* they happen."

He leaned forward in the chair. It pitched forward and he had to correct, quickly grabbing the chair before it toppled over and slamming himself back in it. The others on the panel continued watching him. "It's just that there's a whole other level to this conflict," he said. "And it has to do with things like people starving. It has to do with lack. I mean, stability's hard to fight for when it's just a pipedream, you know? But we could turn this place into something functional. Self-sustaining. That's what Ishin should be for, not just watching which tanks go where, or who's growing poppies or whatever."

His inquisitor's bristling eyebrows rose. "You think our concern with drug trafficking is misplaced?"

"*No!* I mean, no. Of course it's serious. But we should look at *why* the drugs sell in the first place. I mean, it's our guys who are taking them, you know? Not just our guys globally, but our people on the ground. Why do you think we started busting more grow-ops after we arrived? It wasn't just sharper eyes; it was a *market* that sprang up the moment we got here. *We* brought that market. *We* brought that problem."

Throats were cleared. Papers were shuffled. He'd blown it.

And then, like a ghost, a hand stole across his stomach and up over his heart to his shoulder and squeezed. And he knew instantly why he was nervous, why he was babbling. He was filling a silence. They had cut him off from more than his technology. They had cut him off from Singer.

But Singer had fixed that.

"What about your partner?" a man asked, as he made the papers fit into neat right angles before tucking them between pristine folds of cardstock.

"Singer?" He hated his voice for cracking.

"Yes. Your partner."

Through their clothes his partner was insistent. Anyone watching Singer now might think he was mid-heart attack, the way he must have been gripping his left shoulder. "My partner…"

Brandon let his own hand trail up to his left shoulder, to where he felt Singer's hand translated into tiny wires and servos. He kneaded, tried to make it look normal, like a sore joint and not communication, not *I'm here, I'm listening, I'm with you.*

Singer squeezed back.

"My partner's a smart guy," Brandon heard himself say. "He's probably the smartest guy I've ever worked with."

Singer's hand wasn't leaving.

"And he's, uh, pretty hands-on," he added, unable to resist the joke, "even though he lets me do my own thing most of the time."

"Has he been asking you to do more than your share of the work?"

Brandon rubbed his shoulder so Singer could feel it. "No. Why?"

"He applied for a patent recently."

The clothes. Of course. "Well, whatever that's about, he handles it on his own time."

"Good."

After that the questions were clarifying ones, about odd phrasing in his report or figures they didn't quite understand, math he'd let go unexplained. But it was easier—the whole thing, the conversation, the answers—with that slight pressure on his shoulder. By the end he was joking, he was laughing, he was making sense. And none of them mentioned the clothes. None of them noticed. None of them knew.

When he left the room, Singer was sitting outside.

"Why, Heiser," he said. "What a surprise."

"Uh, yeah," Brandon managed to say.

"You look flushed. Are you not feeling well?"

He swallowed. "Thirsty."

Singer's eyes slid over to the guard manning the door. "You'll let me help my subordinate find a drinks machine, won't you?"

"Down that hall, to your right."

"Thank you."

Then Singer was steering him under mosaic ceilings and filigreed windows, toward a humming monolith of light and brand names. He produced a card from one pocket, flashed it at the machine, and held up a bottle of aloe juice a moment later. "Drink up."

Brandon drank. Watching him, Singer momentarily peeked over his shoulder and said in a low voice: "We should get your heart checked, Heiser. I thought it was going to pound right through your chest."

Brandon only sputtered a little. "I got nervous." He drank again, quickly. "They took all my stuff. I felt naked."

Singer's head tilted. "But not quite."

Brandon shook his head. "No, not quite." He checked for people watching, but there were none. He kept his voice down anyway. "How did you do it? Mine wasn't even turned on."

Singer leaned against the machine. "If I told you it was an accident, would you believe me?"

"I… I guess…" Now he felt stupid. "I guess it was just good timing that it happened during—"

"I thought you were shut off for some other reason, at first." Singer shifted weight. "I thought something might have happened. I thought the system might be in need of repair."

Brandon nodded. "Oh."

"So, you see, I had to invent a little workaround. You know, while I was on my way. Because you weren't answering your phone. And because Tink couldn't find you."

Now he felt worse than stupid, he felt ashamed. He hadn't even thought to tell Singer where he was going or how much tech he'd have to surrender. He just figured the other man knew.

"I'm sorry—"

"Don't be sorry. I was overzealous. I forget that there are things I shouldn't be allowed to see."

"I know, but, you got there right in time, I was freaking out—"

"They tried intimidating you?" His voice had taken on a strange, sharp new edge.

"No, nothing like that." Brandon straightened. "I just didn't know how nervous I was until I got in there, you know? I don't want to lose the project. It's, uh…" Singer's glasses made his eyes that much bigger. "It's special. To me. The project."

"The project." Singer blinked. "It's important to you."

"Very." Brandon's head jolted up and down of its own accord. "I want to stay with it. It's um… fulfilling, I guess." He bit his lip. "It's not really something I've ever done before. If you know what I mean."

The dimple appeared at the side of Singer's mouth. "I think I do." He clapped Brandon on the shoulder and made for the hallway. His real hand was a great deal warmer than the wire-and-servo version. One of Singer's fingernails grazed him right under the collar as it moved.

"It'll be late when you get out," Brandon said. "You won't make it back to your camp in time. You should come stay with me. For tonight."

Silence. Brandon heard the squeak of Singer's shoes pivoting on the marble floor. He turned. Singer had his hands jammed in his pockets.

"I don't think that's a good idea just now," he said. "They'll think we're... plotting something."

It occurred to Brandon, as he watched Singer leave, that the distance between them stretched not only over years or miles or skill, but attitude. He saw the weight of years not in the lines around his eyes but in the way they never quite looked at him directly. Like they couldn't. Like he needed Tink for that kind of watching, too.

THEIR DAY IS over, now. Tink is free again, and is with Singer receiving new orders and fresh charge.

"Are you shivering?" Brandon asks. There's a trembling in his clothes that he can't identify.

"There's a stiff breeze," Singer says. "Winter's coming."

Brandon hacks Tink's eye and focuses now on the place where Singer has been sleeping for the past few days: a rooftop, half-crumbled on one side, accessible only via the adjacent roof and equipped with a pup tent, a roller jug of water, and a lantern-sized solar oven which can heat maybe one can of tea at a time.

"You'll have to come inside," he says.

"I don't do well in small spaces."

Singer could be referring to anything, but Brandon guesses prison, or maybe the kind of training you get for prison, and he feels an almost palpable indignation at the thought. He translates this into nagging: "You'll freeze!"

"Nonsense. I know how to keep warm."

"Stay here," Brandon says, before he can stop himself. But then the offer is on the table and he has to back it up: "Stay the winter."

Silence. "...You know, that wasn't quite part of my plan."

"Think of all the stuff we could get done!"

"Oh, I can well imagine." There's the oddest hint of a laugh in his voice. "But I would feel badly about sponging off your host's good graces."

"We wouldn't need a host." Brandon likes this idea the more he talks about it. "I've learned more Pashto by now. And what I don't know, you do."

More silence. When Brandon peers through Tink's eye, he can't read Singer's face. It's as flat and blank as ever. Even the set of the shoulders is perfectly still.

"I mean, you can think about it," he hears himself say. "You might not want—"

Singer looks up and directs his gaze right at Tink, and Brandon could swear the old man knows he's there behind her eyes because he reaches out a hand. He looks tired, thin and cold and a little sad for some reason. Brandon catches himself leaning forward as Tink swerves through the air to land on Singer's open palm.

"I know you think it's a good idea..." Singer can't even look at the machine in his hand. And

Brandon realizes that what he thought was reticence or disappointment is actually shyness—improbable, inexplicable, but nonetheless evident. "I know you think it's what you want—"

"Yes." There, he's said it.

Singer snorts. "It's a good thing they put you in robotics," he says. "You're too impulsive to serve anywhere else."

"I'm not impulsive, I just like getting what I want."

"Don't we all." Singer grins and lets Tink go. Brandon guides her upward, releases the hack. She shoots upward—

—and into darkness.

Through Singer's bud, he hears a sharp cry, dry and shrill. Onscreen, an error message pops up. It says that the drone has encountered outside interference. It suggests a raptor is responsible: a hawk or falcon or owl. It shows him a list of native species, complete with colour photos and Latin names.

But then something slams straight into his spine, right between the shoulders, the clothes humming with impact. Tink's eye portion wriggles free of the bird's maw. The feed is damaged. It pixels randomly. He catches a glimpse of the scene as she climbs: men with pipes.

Across the city, through the threads and wires, Brandon feels the beating.

"Run," Brandon is saying. Onscreen he watches Singer struggle to his knees. The screen seems too small, not big enough to contain the enormity of what he's seeing. He watches Singer retrieve something from one pocket. It's white and sharp and curved like pliers. The multi-tool. He leans forward a little, shifting weight, lurching, and blood spreads over one man's trousers.

The clothes work overtime rolling Singer's beating over Brandon's back.

"*Run!* Why aren't you *running?*"

"They want the *footage*, Brandon, get her *out of here*," Singer says.

Too late, Brandon remembers the meaning of the word *hammam*. It means "bath house." He remembers, too, that this is where Tink had been sent on orders from the predator drone. *Don't worry*, Singer had said, *I'll delete the footage*.

Because it would be sensitive.

Because it was one of the last private places in the city. One of the last places their eyes, mechanical or organic, could not yet see. One of the last places to conduct business, illicit or otherwise, one of the last places to escape constant observation.

Brandon realizes this in the instant between one blow and another. They followed her. She flew straight to Singer. And Brandon kept her there. Dawdled. Gave them time to arm themselves. Time, even, to get a falcon. The one creature to whom a UAV was all too vulnerable.

"Heiser, requesting immediate evac for Singer, coordinates…" The phone is in his hand before he remembers grabbing it. But here time seems to slow down. He can't get the words out fast enough. He hears each second of dead air as the dispatch office relays him, tries calming him down, tells him to breathe, and his clothes are one big hive of activity, one long vibration, because for Singer the blows are coming that fast, that widespread.

"Get out, get out, *get out*," he hisses.

In his ear, Singer answers by groaning.

"Ten minutes," the dispatch says.

In his ear, Singer catches his breath but Brandon feels no punch or kick. They've gone off-map. The groin. Maybe the head.

"That's not fast enough," he says, and then a little lower: "I've got people coming, Singer, there are people coming—"

"Hack Tink, damn it," Singer says. Brandon hears blood in his voice. He feels a kick in the gut. The clothes ring hollowly in the empty room. In the city it is evening; he smells meat grilling and hears children laughing. In the suburbs, in the long shadow of the mountains, he hears Singer cough. He hears his breathing slow.

He hacks. But not Tink. Months later, he still remembers his old systems, his old job, his old skills.

"Singer, I'll be there, two minutes, I *promise*, I'll be right there—"

"You're already here," Singer says. Brandon hears the dry scratch of dirt underfoot. He hears the grunt of effort when Singer shuffles forward, a rip in fabric, and an angry, almost annoyed shout. Cursing.

"Stop *fighting* them, and *get out*—"

"—already there."

The ear bud is failing. Too many strikes. Too much damage. Head trauma.

"I can't hear you—"

"—in two places," Singer says. "—our own map, you know?"

Onscreen, the nearest predator, now fully under Brandon's control, shows him a display of Singer's coordinates. He sees the shapes darting in and out for extra strikes. Sees Singer's coat spreading around his body like blood.

Luckily, his new predator is armed.

Onscreen, he watches the building next to Singer's rooftop transform itself into a pillar of smoke and dust. He hears shouting. He watches them flee. Some of them are hobbling.

The bombing stuff, he had told Singer, *it's mostly over now.*

Really, he had just been getting too good at his job. Too practised. A little too cavalier, perhaps, about human life. A little bit unburdened, possibly, from the crushing constraints of self-awareness.

"—eally don't mess around, do you?"

"Are you okay?"

"...Bleeding."

"There are people coming. And the predator." He circles it, dives low, so Singer will see.

"Should find Tink."

"Fuck the drone. Stay awake."

"Tall order."

Across his stomach, Brandon feels a slight pressure. A hand. Singer's. Slowly, Brandon places his in the same spot.

"—brig you for this, you know."

"It's okay." His hand clenches the clothes.

"This is actually a lot better than I was expecting." Singer's voice is remarkably clear. "You know, this was my lifetime achievement award. For services rendered. I could pick any project. Any person."

The pressure on Brandon's belly increases just a little.

"I'm looking at the moon," Singer says. "It's come out very early, tonight."

Unable to stop himself, Brandon peers out his window. The moon is there, etched on the sky, a shiny coin. "I'm looking at it, too," he says. "I'm right there with you."

"I know you are."

"Singer." He blinks. "Shit, this is hard—"

"No, it's easy." Through the clothes, Singer rubs Brandon's shoulder. "You've made it very easy. If you only knew... how scared I used to be..."

"Of what?"

No answer.

"Of what?" he asks again, staring hard into the sky and keeping his voice, somehow, just above a whisper. "What were you so scared of?"

But the pressure fades, slides away, and his clothes are lighter now with only one man wearing them. Soon, the shadows of his room fill with the chirps of error messages. A missing heartbeat. Lost input. He hears the team arrive on the scene. He hears sirens for the building he has just destroyed.

He realizes, belatedly, that the predator remains under his control.

Then he's going over feeds, inputting street names, finding faces. Tink has logged all the falconers in the area and after that it's just a process of elimination. He checks the faces. This one. That one. He swears he recognizes one of them. Even if it was just a half-second glimpse of bad video. He knows that face. He'll know it forever.

He knows where it lives. And how to destroy it.

"Heiser, what are you doing?"

A stranger's voice. He rips out the earbud. How dare they? Always watching except for when it matters most. His phone rings. He throws it to the other side of the room.

They had warned him about becoming too much of a machine. About identifying too strongly, adopting a mechanistic attitude. As though machines were somehow to blame, and not this thing inside him, this force that roared and spun like a sandstorm. This utterly human thing.

He is already pressing buttons. Already drafting excuses. *They had important footage,* he would say. *They stole it. And then they killed my—*

At his window, something buzzes. He turns and sees a single glowing eye, like a firefly, blinking unsteadily in the darkness. Damaged. Broken.

"Tink," he says. He crawls over and scoops her into his palm. She's ripped open and raw—delicate wires now twisted in odd shapes, wings battered. "How did you get here? Did you fight the falcon?"

In his hand, Tink wiggles worm-like, then begins blinking. A moment later her second pair of wings arrives. They fly unevenly, one wing all crushed so the segment moves in circles. Slowly, carefully, they attempt to re-join each other. The pieces don't quite fit, but they keep trying. They blink ceaselessly at each other, bleeding light, struggling to understand what's missing.

HE'S AT NARITA, at the duty-free bar, where they serve sample-sized sakes from bottles he still can't quite justify buying. Has his own firm, now. Prefers working for himself. Lives out of his mobile. Currently he's using it to interview a new recruit. She's in Korea. That's where things happen, these days. He's flying there later today.

"I've been told I have kind of an attitude problem," she says.

"How's that?"

"I'm not really good at holding back."

"In what way?"

"I once suggested we would be safer billeted in a fort made out of PET bottles, like those garbage-picker kids make."

He pauses, examines his glass. "Seriously, or were you just mouthing off?"

"...I'm sorry?"

"Were you suggesting it seriously, or were you being passive-aggressive?"

A long pause. "Now that you ask, I'm not so sure."

"Fair enough."

"That's not really why I was let go, though."

"What do you think the reason was?" This answer is never quite the truth, but he likes hearing the recruits' version when they give it.

"They found out I was gay, and then they kicked me out," she says, with a barely-suppressed yawn. "Good riddance."

"You're gay?"

"That a problem?"

"Well... no. Was it a problem for your old team?"

"Only this one girl. Because I was our team's field medic. I tried telling her that it meant I'd know the terrain better than some bullshit ROTC rat fresh out of high school, but that didn't go over too well."

"Shocking."

"I know, huh?" She's laughing. "Anyway. I figured you should know. If you think it's going to be a problem for anybody, I'd rather hear about it now than later."

Over the phone, he hears something rumble. She curses in Korean. Her details say trilingual, medic, once delivered a baby behind enemy lines after rescuing the mother and others from a labour camp. Has no problem with bloodbots or minilabs. Knows how to read their findings. Feels comfortable with placing them in the right people at the right time. Willing to do undercover work to make it happen. Useful, when his latest project involves mapping the wartime spread of sexually-transmitted disease from within the body in order to locate secret rape camps.

"Sorry, but I have to go," she says. "I know it probably sounds bad, me cutting my own interview short, but I think something just exploded a couple blocks away. I'd better get there before the collectors do. Seriously, you would not believe how old some of the shit being fired is. Real relics. It's crazy. People are *selling* it."

"Have fun," Brandon says, and lets her go. She is clearly more at home in her work than in selling herself, anyway, and he likes that. She's younger than he was when he entered the business, and already twice the hero he can imagine ever being. It's a little scary. He hopes she doesn't burn out. It would be a loss. It has been his good fortune to meet exceptional people in his line of work, and his regret to lose some of them. He doesn't do much with these people, just winds them up and lets them go, sometimes nesting them together like hard, bright jewels. Perhaps that's a mistake on his part, his detachment, the way he deals with people remotely.

But he can tell her this later, after he's arrived. She might like to know. All his people might like to know, actually. He should tell them. He should remind them that he knows they work hard and that he appreciates it. He fishes in his pocket for his flashpass and his fingers brush old robot pieces, impossibly chunky and sharp, he reflects that the world has really only made it this far by being composed of people who insist on re-building things stronger than they were before, more lasting and useful, with room for everyone. When he gets there, to where all the hard work is, he'll tell his people he knows how difficult it is. He'll tell them he knows the sacrifice they're making, the strength required to go slow and make steady progress instead of grand gestures. And they'll stare at him and wonder what's wrong and why he gets like this, sometimes, and he'll tell them to be safe and do their best.

I emancipated my robot when she told an elaborate lie. I realized then, that she'd developed a mind's eye.

—Ken Edgett—

About the Authors

Jason Andrew lives in Seattle, Washington with his wife Lisa. By day, he works as a mild-mannered technical writer. By night, he writes stories of the fantastic and occasionally fights crime. As a child, Jason spent his Saturdays watching the Creature Feature classics and furiously scribbling down stories; his first short story, written at age six, titled 'The Wolfman Eats Perry Mason,' was rejected and caused his Grandmother to watch him very closely for a few years.

Madeline Ashby can be found at her blog, escapingthetrunk.net, and @madelineashby on Twitter. She immigrated to Canada in 2006, where she joined Toronto's Cecil Street Irregulars genre writing workshop. Since then, she has been published in *Flurb*, *Nature*, and *Escape Pod*. When not working on her novel, she's a student of the Strategic Foresight and Innovation program at the Ontario College of Art and Design, a blogger for *WorldChanging Canada* and *Frames Per Second Magazine*, and a fan of anime and manga.

Jacques Barcia is a speculative fiction writer and information technology reporter from Recife, Brazil. His short fiction has appeared in Brazilian, American and Romanian online markets. He's one of the authors actively supporting Greenpunk.net and the Outer Alliance initiative. When he's not writing, Jacques acts as the lead singer of Brazilian grindcore band Rabujos. He's married and has the smartest, loveliest, bookishiest daughter in the world. Jacques is currently working on his first novel. He can be reached at www.jacquesbarcia.wordpress.com.

Aliette de Bodard is a French computer engineer who moonlights as a writer, with short fiction forthcoming or published in markets such as *Asimov's*, *Interzone* and *Realms of Fantasy*. She's a Campbell Award finalist and a Writers of the Future winner. Watch out for her debut novel, the Aztec fantasy *Servant of the Underworld*, published by Angry Robot.

Eva Maria Chapman has successfully pursued a variety of careers; teacher, academic, psychotherapist and director of an energy efficiency company. In her career as author, she is a genre hopper. Her first book *Sasha & Olga*, a memoir, charts the adversities of her Russian refugee family, before and after emigrating to Australia; her second, *Butterflies & Demons*, unveils the extraordinary past of the Kaurna Adelaide Aborigines, combining historic fiction with fantasy. 'Russian Roulette 2020' is her first foray into Science Fiction and has inspired her to embark further into this genre. She is now writing an optimistic novel set in the future. She lives in happy seclusion in a wildlife sanctuary on the edge of Exmoor, England, with her husband Jake. When not writing, or growing vegetables, she likes to make (and wear) hats, party with friends, and frolic with her grandchildren.

Ken Edgett is a geologist whose research has largely focused on the planet Mars. Working at Malin Space Science Systems of San Diego, California, USA, he targeted tens of thousands of images acquired by the Mars Global Surveyor and Mars Reconnaissance Orbiter spacecraft. In 1997-2002, Edgett was a regular on-air contributor of 1-2 minute science education pieces for a children's television program, *Brainstorm*, produced by KTVK-TV in Phoenix, Arizona, USA. He is the co-author of a children's book, *Touchdown Mars!*, published in 2000, and his first published short fiction was in the 2008 anthology, *Return to Luna*, from Hadley Rille Books. In addition to writing, Edgett's present effort includes that of being the Principal Investigator for a camera aboard the Mars Science Laboratory rover, Curiosity, launching in 2011.

Eric Gregory's stories have appeared in *Strange Horizons*, *Interzone*, *Black Static*, *Sybil's Garage*, and more. He has also written non-fiction for *Fantasy Magazine* and *The Internet Review of Science Fiction*. Visit him online at ericmg.com.

Kay Kenyon's latest work, published by Pyr, is a sci-fantasy quartet beginning with *Bright of the Sky*, a story that introduced readers to the Entire, a tunnel universe next door. Publishers Weekly listed this novel among the top 150 books of 2007. The series has twice been shortlisted for the American Library Association Reading List awards. The final volume, *Prince of Storms* will appear in January 2010. Her work has been nominated for major awards in the field and translated into French, Russian, Spanish, Czech and audio versions. Recent short stories appeared in *Fast Forward 2* and *The Solaris Book of New Science Fiction, Volume Two*. She lives in eastern Washington state with her husband. She is the chair of a writing conference, Write on the River, and is currently working on a fantasy novel. All of her work has happy endings, except for those with characters who, alas, must die.

Silvia Moreno-Garcia was born in the north of Mexico and moved to Canada several years ago. She lives in beautiful, rainy British Columbia with her husband, children and two cats. She writes fantasy, magic realism and Science Fiction. Her short stories have appeared in *Fantasy Magazine*, *Futurismic*, *Shimmer* and *Tesseracts Thirteen*. With the help of editor Paula R. Stiles and a band of eldritch writers she publishes the online zine *Innsmouth Free Press*. Silvia is also working on her first novel and be found online at www.silviamoreno-garcia.com.

Mari Ness lives in central Florida, and likes to watch space shuttles and rockets leap into the sky. Her work has previously appeared in numerous print and online venues, including *Fantasy Magazine*, *Hub Fiction* and *Farrago's Wainscot*. She's still hoping to spend time in a space station some day.

Holly Phillips is the award-winning author of *In the Palace of Repose* and *The Engine's Child*. She lives on a large island off the west coast of Canada, and is hard at work on her next novel.

Gareth L. Powell is a regular contributor to *Interzone*. His stories have appeared all over the world and been translated into seven languages. His first collection, *The Last Reef*, was published by Elastic Press in 2008 and Pendragon will publish his first novel, *Silversands*, in 2010. He lives in the English West Country with his wife and daughters and can be found online at: www.garethlpowell. com.

Alastair Reynolds was born in 1966. His first short fiction sale appeared in 1990, and he began publishing novels ten years later. *Chasm City*, his second novel, won the British Science Fiction award in 2002. His ninth novel, *Terminal World*, is due imminently. He is about to embark on an ambitious and broadly optimistic trilogy documenting the expansion of the human species into solar and then galactic space over the next 11,000 years. A former scientist, Reynolds worked for the European Space Agency until 2004, when he turned full-time writer. He is married and lives in Wales, not too far from his place of birth.

Gord Sellar (gordsellar.com) was born in Malawi, grew up in Saskatchewan, and currently lives and works as a professor of English Language & Culture in South Korea. Since attending Clarion West in 2006, his work has appeared in *Asimov's SF*, *Interzone*, *Clarkesworld*, *Subterranean*, and *The Year's Best SF Vol. 26*, among other venues, and in 2009 he was a nominee for the John W. Campbell Award for Best New Writer. This story is dedicated to his buddies named Mike—in Jeonju, Utah, and Toronto alike, for being very different kinds of men, each excellent in his own way.

Possessing a quixotic fondness for difficult careers, **Paula R. Stiles** has driven ambulances, taught fish farming for the Peace Corps in West Africa and earned a Scottish PhD in medieval history, studying Templars and non-Christians in Spain. She has also sold fiction to *Strange Horizons*, *Writers of the Future*, *Jim Baen's Universe*, *Futures*, *@outshine* and other markets. She is Editor in Chief of the Lovecraft/Mythos 'zine *Innsmouth Free Press* (www.innsmouthfreepress.com). You can find her on Twitter (@thesnowleopard) or on her website at: www.geocities.com/rpcv.geo/other.html.

Jason Stoddard is trying to answer the question, 'Can business and writing coexist?' with varying degrees of success. Writing-wise, he has two books coming out in 2010 from Prime Books: *Winning Mars* and *Eternal Franchise*. He's also been seen in *Sci Fiction*, *Interzone*, *Strange Horizons*, *Futurismic*, *Talebones*, and many other publications. He's a finalist for the Theodore Sturgeon Memorial Award and the Sidewise Award. On the other side, Jason leads Centric/Agency of Change, a marketing agency he founded in 1994. In this role, he's a popular speaker on social media and virtual worlds at venues like Harvard University, The Directors Guild of America, Internet Strategy Forum, Loyola Marymount University, and Inverge. Jason lives in Los Angeles with his wife, who writes romance as Ashleigh Raine.

Lavie Tidhar is the author of linked-story collection *HebrewPunk* (2007), novellas *Cloud Permutations* (2009), *An Occupation of Angels* (2010), and *Gorel & The Pot-Bellied God* (2010) and, with Nir Yaniv, of *The Tel Aviv Dossier* (2009). He also edited the anthology *The Apex Book of World SF* (2009. He's lived on three continents and one island-nation, and currently lives in Israel. His first novel, *The Bookman*, is published by HarperCollins' new Angry Robot imprint, and will be followed by two more.

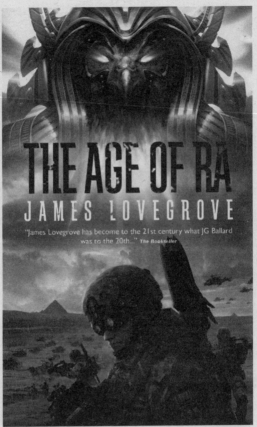

UK ISBN: 978 1 844167 46 3 • US ISBN: 978 1 844167 47 0 • £7.99/$7.99

The Ancient Egyptian gods have defeated all the other pantheons and divided the Earth
into warring factions. Lt. David Westwynter, a British soldier, stumbles into Freegypt, the
only place to have remained independent of the gods, and encounters the followers of
a humanist freedom-fighter known as the Lightbringer. As the world heads towards an
apocalyptic battle, there is far more to this leader than it seems...

 WWW.SOLARISBOOKS.COM

Follow us on Twitter! www.twitter.com/solarisbooks

THE AGE OF ZEUS

JAMES LOVEGROVE

"James Lovegrove has become to the 21st century what JG Ballard was to the 20th..."
The Bookseller

UK ISBN: 978 1 906735 68 5 • US ISBN: 978 1 906735 69 2 • £7.99/$7.99

The Olympians appeared a decade ago, living incarnations of the Ancient Greek gods on a mission to bring order and stability to the world. Resistance has proved futile, and now humankind is under the jackboot of divine oppression. Until former London police officer Sam Akehurst receives an invitation too tempting to turn down: the chance to join a small band of guerrilla rebels - the Titans - armed with high-tech weapons and battlesuits, and take the battle to the Olympians themselves...

 WWW.SOLARISBOOKS.COM

Follow us on Twitter! www.twitter.com/solarisbooks

XENOPATH
A BENGAL STATION NOVEL

ERIC BROWN

UK ISBN: 978 1 844167 42 5 • US ISBN: 978 1 844167 43 2 • £7.99/$7.99

Telepath Jeff Vaughan is working for a detective agency on Bengal Station, an exotic spaceport that dominates the ocean between India and Burma, when he is called out to the colony world of Mallory to investigate recent discoveries of alien corpses.

But Vaughan is shaken to his core when he begins to uncover the heart of darkness at the centre of the Scheering-Lassiter colonial organisation...

 WWW.SOLARISBOOKS.COM

Follow us on Twitter! www.twitter.com/solarisbooks

COSMOPATH

A BENGAL STATION NOVEL

ERIC BROWN

UK ISBN: 978 1 844168 32 3 • US ISBN: 978 1 844168 33 0 • £7.99/$7.99

Telepath Jeff Vaughan is approached by billionaire tycoon Rabindranath Chandrasakar, who wants him to read the mind of a dead spacer on an unexplored world on the edge of known space. On Delta Cephei VII, Vaughan finds himself drawn into a web of treachery and deceit in a bid to discover what an alien race is concealing from humanity - a secret that could change forever the course of human expansion through the galaxy.

 WWW.SOLARISBOOKS.COM

Follow us on Twitter! www.twitter.com/solarisbooks

A COMBAT-K NOVEL

ANDY REMIC

The new master of rock-hard military science fiction

BIOHELL

UK ISBN: 978-1-84416-650-3 US ISBN: 978-1-84416-590-2

www.solarisbooks.com

The City: a planet filled with corruption, guns, sex, and designer drugs. Zombies roam the streets and are out for blood. The Combat-K squad are dropped into this warzone to uncover what's turned this planet into a wasteland of murder and mutations. Soon their focus is on the Nano-Tek corporation itself...

SOLARIS SCIENCE FICTION

A COMBAT-K NOVEL

ANDY REMIC

HARDCORE

UK ISBN: 978 1 844167 93 7 • US ISBN: 978 1 844167 92 0 • £7.99/$7.99

Charged with finding the evil Junk's homeland and annihilating them, Combat-K head to Sick World, a long-abandoned hospital planet once dedicated to curing the deformed, the insane, the dying and the dead. The Medical Staff of Sick World - the doctors, nurses, patients and deviants, abandoned with extreme prejudice, a thousand-year gestation of hardcore medical mutation - and their hibernation, and they can smell fresh meat...

 WWW.SOLARISBOOKS.COM

Follow us on Twitter! www.twitter.com/solarisbooks